Praise for
The One True Thing

"*The One True Thing* weaves together a beautifully complex tapestry of lives and relationships. As the point of view shifts from one character to another, across time and space, new vistas unfold and hidden motives are revealed. And running through the whole novel is the thread of Bridget's garden, a deeply nourishing place with its own fertile role in the story. Newbery's descriptions of nature are second to none; this is a novel to immerse yourself in."

— Jane Rogers, author of *Mr Wroe's Virgins*

Also by Linda Newbery:

Set in Stone

Quarter Past Two on a Wednesday Afternoon

The Shell House

Sisterland

Lob

The Key to Flambards

This Book is Cruelty Free: Animals and Us

the
one
true
thing

linda
newbery

WR
Writers Review Publishing

First published in Great Britain in 2025
by Writers Review Publishing
www.writersreviewpublishing.co.uk

Copyright © Linda Newbery 2025

The moral right of Linda Newbery to be identified as the author of this work has been asserted in accordance with the Copyright, Designs and Patents Act of 1988.

All rights reserved. No part of this publication may be reproduced, stored in a retrieval system, or transmitted in any form and by any means, electronic, mechanical, photocopying, recording or otherwise without the prior permission of the copyright owner.

This is a work of fiction. Names, characters, businesses, organisations, places and events are either the product of the author's imagination or used fictitiously. Any resemblance to actual persons, living or dead, events or locales is entirely coincidental.

Print ISBN: 9781068526404
Ebook ISBN: 9781068526411

A CIP catalogue of this book is available
from the British Library.

Cover design by Owen Gent.
Interior design by InsideStudio26.com.

*For Bernard Johnson, stonemason,
with grateful thanks for all you've taught me
and for many happy days at the Pig Sty.*

Bridget

MAY 2012

Drawn outside by the first pale light, she stood on the terrace gazing down at the garden. The air was moist, carrying scents of mown grass and honeysuckle. Mist traced the stream's course along the valley and a hazy stillness promised warmth later; she pulled her wrap more closely around her, considered going in to get dressed but stayed where she was, looking down the slope of lawn with the sense that this hour was hers alone. Birdsong swelled from the woods beyond - croon of woodpigeons, silvery trickle of willow warbler and, closer, the throatier song of a blackbird. Soon swifts would shriek overhead and the day would be in full flight.

So many times she'd stood like this, caught in the spell of dawn chorus and early sunlight. Today it was both familiar and strange: too bright, too loud. Against the wall the clematis and climbing rose were fully out, the deep purple of *Étoile Violette* against the pink-flushed clusters like hedgerow dog roses. Next year she wouldn't see them. Next May the oaks would come into leaf, lambs would bleat in the fields, the blackbird would sing from the ash tree; all without her. In three weeks it would be midsummer, and from that turning point her life would wind down as the days shortened. Each seasonal shift, each subtle change of light, each flowering and fruiting, would be the last she would know.

Through all her planning and tending, digging and planting, this garden had made her. Now, slowly, inexorably, she would be unmade. Her mind jibbed, incapable of taking in the prospect of its own absence. *I won't be here* – why should that simple thought strike with such force? Didn't everyone face that, from the first shocked realisation, far back in childhood? It was an inescapable fact, the essence of being alive.

Time would run out: *was* running out, as she stood puzzling. Time had been a trickster, persuading her that there'd always be plenty to use or waste, spend or spare. Now it was slithering away. The time left to her, the only time that had meaning, would be gone before she could decide what to do with it.

Anthony, driving home from the consultation, had seemed more shaken than she was. Last night he'd wanted to share her bed, breaking the habit of years; gently but firmly she refused. Physical closeness, so unaccustomed, would be at odds with the severance she already felt. She found herself assuming an air of stoicism that was almost melodramatic, needing his unspoken respect as a buttress.

The pang of loss she felt was not for herself, not for Anthony or Meg nor even the girls, but for this. The orchard saplings she'd planted last year would mature and bear apples; the cuttings in the cold frame would grow roots. Other hands, she supposed, would prune and weed. The dazzle of growth flaunted itself. The garden wouldn't notice when she was gone.

Meg

NOVEMBER 2018

WHAT THE POINT OF THIS was, she had no idea: driving miles to see a man she'd never liked and who disapproved of her. It would cost her a day's work; all she'd managed before leaving was a few emails and invoices. But it would be churlish to refuse a request from someone who lay dying.

On the phone, Suzanne had said, "He really wants to see you. I couldn't make out why, but he was definite. I know it's a long way, but if you could possibly..."

Meg left a long pause, then found herself saying, "All right. Is Jane there?"

"No, she's on her way back from India. Kerala. She was on a yoga course there. I only hope she'll make it in ... in time."

Meg almost asked, "Are you sure it's me he wants to see?" before wondering whether, in extremis, Anthony had had a change of heart. They'd barely communicated in the nearly six years since Bridget died – a mutual loss that could have turned into some kind of belated rapport, but led instead to a terse correspondence about Bridget's headstone. His eventual choice, bland, machine-cut lettering in polished granite, still rankled, as he'd surely intended. Jane, conveying his decision, had tried to be tactful, but there was no way of hiding the deliberate slight. Meg had taken for granted that she'd make the headstone, as she knew Bridget wanted. But with Anthony the only thing to take for granted was that he'd be obstructive. Always had been.

She still felt the loss of Bridget as an ache. The moment when she came into the workshop with the awful news, so casually mentioned, struck again with the rawness of shock. Making the headstone would have been an act of faith. Meg had no religious belief, but choosing and carving the stone would have been her final gift. All she could do. And everything.

The design was pinned up in her workshop; she was unable to part with it. The wording was from a Thomas Hardy poem Bridget liked: *The thrushes sing as the sun is going ... as if all Time were theirs,* and, underneath, *Bridget Harper, gardener and maker, 1943 - 2013.* In the graveyard at Lower Stortford, in graceless juxtaposition to the lichen-encrusted local stone of older generations, was the headstone Anthony had chosen instead. Visiting alone in early spring, Meg had no argument with the place itself: a country churchyard with paths through primroses and violets in rough grass, a robin singing from the ancient yew. It overlooked the valley where the stream traced its course, and beyond to Wildings and the mature trees that seemed to guard it, huddling close. But oh, the contrast of the polished granite with the stone she'd have chosen: a local limestone, iron-rich, with subtleties of colour revealed in the cutting, blue-shaded grey against ochre and rust. A stone to suit the place, to suit Bridget.

The inscription, in lettering that affronted Meg's eye, read *Bridget Harper, beloved wife of Anthony*, and the dates.

Bland. Meaningless. Not even true.

There was a space underneath Bridget's name and dates which Meg supposed was intended for Anthony, when his time came. She preferred to think of Bridget alone and separate, but now it seemed that the time was approaching for more artless letters to be added. Spelling out another lie, most likely.

Leaving the church after the funeral, Anthony had been steadied by Suzanne holding his arm, as if he'd aged twenty years. Meg had meant to go back to Wildings with the other mourners but had been side-tracked to the pub instead. In the fortnight that followed she cleared out her possessions from workshop and cottage, without reference to Anthony other than to give notice and hand over her keys. Grief – she supposed it must be grief he felt - had turned him ashen and somehow smaller. It was Jane, then twenty-one, who appeared to be holding things together.

She felt a spike of sympathy for Jane, faced with this new crisis only a few years after losing her mother. For Suzanne, too, but Jane was sixteen years younger and the one who – as far as Meg knew - still lived at Wildings. I should have kept in touch, Meg thought; she'd promised Bridget and had fully intended to, until things became complicated. But did that justify breaking a promise?

If there was another burial soon, she'd feel no obligation to attend.

Weary from the long drive, she reached the hospital car park and reached for coins to pay. She'd stay for an hour at most - and that would include getting coffee and a sandwich – before leaving, ideally in time to call at the Great Tew quarry on her way home to collect a piece of stone she'd ordered.

She hesitated at the entrance to the High Dependency Unit. Not easily daunted, she was daunted now by thoughts of what she would see, and what Anthony might have to say that he couldn't have told her back then.

Only one way to find out. At Reception she said, "I'm here to see Anthony Harper."

The nurse consulted a list. "I'm afraid he's very poorly. Are you family?"

"No. He asked for me though. Meg Graham."

"Maybe just a few minutes, then. I'll check. His son's with him."

Son? Expecting Suzanne, she was thrown for a moment before realising that of course it was Rob, the son from Anthony's first marriage, who was here. She knew him only as Bridget's stepson, who'd visited Wildings occasionally during her own years there. She remembered that he'd come to Chelsea, accompanied by a wife of glacial sleekness.

The nurse slipped through curtains enclosing a bed. A murmured conversation, then Rob emerged, his glance showing that he hadn't expected her and wasn't pleased.

Her first thought was how old he looked; she hadn't seen him since Bridget's funeral. Well into middle-age, he had dark hair receding at the temples, and dark-rimmed glasses. He was less handsome than Anthony, though with recognisably similar features; the face of the father could be traced in this son as his less personable ghost, toned down and shaded by petulance.

But Anthony wasn't a ghost, not yet.

"I'm afraid my father's too ill for visitors," Rob told her.

A lot less charming, too, Meg thought. At least, less charming than Anthony could be – used to be – when he chose. He'd never troubled himself to use his charm on her.

"Suzanne asked me to come." She matched his abrupt tone. "Your father wants to see me, she said. You didn't know?"

"Really? I can't imagine why. One moment."

More murmuring behind the curtains, a pause, then the nurse beckoned her inside, putting a finger to her lips as if Meg needed such a warning.

"Mr Harper's very weak, and rather confused. It had better be only a few moments."

Jane

NOVEMBER 2018

SHE WAS CALLED FROM morning practice by one of the reception staff, who came up to the shala and whispered to the teacher. Catching Jane's eye, Rashmika signalled that she was wanted.

Startled, Jane left her mat, following the sari-clad young woman who stopped on the stairs to say quietly, "We have an urgent phone call for you in the office. Your sister." Dark eyes, under arching brows, expressed concern.

"Oh! Thank you." Jane found her sandals among many others and fumbled her feet into them. Rashmika continued to lead sun salutations: "Step through to *virabhadrasana* ... gaze up ... *deep* bend in your front knee ... hands to your mat, step back and down all on one breath -"

The shala was an open-sided, wooden-roofed space, at tree-canopy height for coolness. At the foot of the steps the receptionist stood aside for Jane to hurry ahead on the narrow path. Heat struck her, even in the deep shade of banana palms.

Jolted out of the rhythm of yoga practice, she was intensely aware of her surroundings. Bird calls throbbed and boomed, intoxicatingly close; the air was moist, smelling of watered earth and foliage. This had been her dream for so long that she told herself each day, *India. This is India. I'm here, really here.* But home and ordinary life waited on the phone to snatch her thoughts away. Her mind raced with possible reasons for Suzanne to call – not to leave a message, but to have her summoned from class. An accident, fire, car crash?

In the fan-cooled office a young man in shirtsleeves handed her the phone.

"Janey, sorry. I couldn't get you on your mobile," said Suzanne's voice.

"What's wrong?"

"It's Dad. He's in hospital, seriously ill. Is there any chance you can get back?"

. . .

The coast of Kerala fell away: groves of trees, stretches of inland water, glistening sea. From her window seat Jane gazed down, taking in the last glimpses of India as it receded to the dimensions of a map, or of Google Earth. Already the retreat had been shoved into the past, curtailed in a flurry of apologies, phone calls and emails, and a taxi ride along dusty roads to Trivandrum. Then the anonymity of the airport, the waiting punctuated by messages to Suzanne: **Tell Dad I'm on my way. Give him my love. How is he?**

Her hands fiddled with the cap of a water-bottle. Nearly three hours to Dubai, then another wait for the connecting flight. So much sitting, after the three-times-daily yoga practice of the last ten days, the breathing exercises and meditation; her shoulders were tense, her thoughts racing.

She focused on the fading coastline and concentrated on *pranayama*. Deep, full breaths: long, slow exhalations.

"Get here as soon as you can," Suzanne had said, her voice wavering, "if you want to see him."

"But what's – "

"Pneumonia. Severe. Oh, Jane - being Dad, he thought it'd go away if he ignored it. It was his cleaner who called the paramedics. By then he was really ill."

"But they're treating him? How can it be so bad?"

Suzanne explained about complications, sepsis, critical care; she was at the hospital now, with Ed. It felt impossible to Jane, a trick played while she hadn't been watching. The rush of the journey and now enforced stillness, strapped into her seat, made her half expect to wake up under the ceiling fan, with striped sunlight falling through the blind and nothing more urgent to do than eat a banana and get ready for practice. This must be a dream, laden with self-reproach. But how could she have foreseen? Dad had been fine, right up to the day she left; she kept thinking that, as if obstinacy would make things different. He'd tracked down and bought her an adaptor plug for Indian sockets and had driven her to Birmingham for her night flight. Starting a cold, he'd been anxious in case she caught it. Her last words to him, an afterthought at Departures, were "Buy yourself some Lemsip."

A cold. How could something so commonplace have landed him in hospital?

If I'd been there...

A whirl of panic overcame the steady deliberation of breathing. *I can't lose both parents. It can't happen again.* Although it was five and a half years since her mother died, everything came back in sharp detail: squeak of shoes on shiny floors, smell of hand-sanitiser and trolleyed meals, the dread of hearing bad and worse news; finally the hospice, light filtering through thin curtains, and days of waiting that felt interminable. Then, when the end did come, it seemed to have rushed up too fast. Her mother died a few months short of her seventieth birthday. Most of Jane's friends had considerably younger mothers, but still it felt wrong, premature.

Her dad was seventy-nine, a big, strong man, if not exactly active.

"He's given up," Suzanne had said. "He's never been the same without Mum."

Jane's mind blurred in protest, repeating *he mustn't die* like a mantra. There had been no prognosis, as with Mum; no trying to come to terms with the inevitable. The phrase made her think of bargaining, negotiation, whereas in reality it was all one way. Here's how it is. How it will be. Tough: get used to it.

She shouldn't have gone to India. If she'd been at home, she'd have noticed; would have got her father to a doctor before pneumonia took hold. But how could anyone have predicted that he'd succumb to illness so quickly?

At Dubai, simmering in frustration for her delayed flight to be announced, she began texting Tom, against her better judgement: **Heading back. Dad in hospital. Outlook not good. Cd u poss pick me up from Birmingham, 9?** She wondered what he'd be doing, and checked the time: two pm in England. At his computer, perhaps, searching for images, PhotoShopping – he could spend hours lost in that. Or he'd be emailing clients, or meeting someone, or maybe just dossing. Whatever, she knew he'd drop it and come for her if he could. In spite of everything. Tom was obliging like that.

Another message pinged in before she'd finished. Suzanne: **What time at Birmingham? Ed will meet you + bring you to hospital. Sx**

Great. Thanks, Jane sent back, and deleted her text to Tom. Best not to involve him.

. . .

Her brother-in-law was in Arrivals, waving, coming towards her.

"You OK?" He gave her a hug.

"I'm fine, thanks. You? Have you come straight from the hospital? How is Dad? And Suze?"

Ed shook his head slowly. "It's not looking good, Jane. Sorry. Your Dad's peaceful though. They've got him sedated. Suzy's pretty exhausted. She's spent most of the last two days at the hospital."

Outside, Jane shivered in November air that held the premonition of winter. Reaching the car she pulled a sweater from her rucksack.

"Have a sleep, if you can," Ed urged her. "You must be whacked. It'll take around an hour, and who knows what time you'll get home?"

"Oh, but tell me everything, first."

Ed filled out what Suzanne had said: the cold that turned to pneumonia, the cleaner's insistence on seeking help, the urgent admission. "They put him on oxygen, and on a saline drip, and high-impact antibiotics, and there was a drain to get fluid out of his lungs."

"Sounds horrible."

"He was confused for a while, then sleepy. Suzanne told him you're coming - she thinks he understood."

They were on the M6, passing signs to Coventry, Warwick, Nuneaton. Ed asked about Kerala and the weather, but her mind was dulling; she'd slept only fitfully on the longer flight from Dubai. Her head drooped, then jolted upright.

"Go on - have a doze," Ed told her. "Put your seat back."

At the hospital he nudged her awake and dropped her by the entrance before going on to park. She hurried in, jolted into renewed dread. The hospital was familiar from her mother's stays here: signs to Fracture Clinic, Radiology, Outpatients; soft-shoed nurses and brisk medics. To enter as a patient would seem like surrendering identity, putting yourself on a conveyor belt to healing or dying or slow deterioration. Now her main thought was for Dad to know she was here. She broke into a jog, her eyes scanning the signboards.

The nurse at the desk in the High Dependency Unit summoned another, who took Jane into a side room and sat her down. Seeing her expression Jane knew in an instant what she would say.

"I'm so sorry. Your father passed away less than half an hour ago."

Jane's hands flew to her mouth. "No. No," she blurted, in a voice that sounded thick, unrecognisable.

"I'm so sorry," the nurse said again, a hand on Jane's shoulder.

But it can't be true! I'm here now. He should have waited -

The nurse was talking, explaining: Jane saw her mouth moving but was unable to take in the words. There must be some mistake. Dad was here somewhere, expecting her, if only she could find him. She stood, looking around wildly.

"Your sister's with him," the nurse said. "Do you want to -"

At that moment Suzanne appeared, gave Jane a distraught look and stood biting her lip, head bowed. They embraced, and Jane felt her sister's body shuddering.

"Oh, Janey! He's – he's gone."

Gone. Jane was numbed by the speed of things, but here was Suzanne, weeping uncontrollably now, snatching at tissues.

The nurse withdrew and they sank into chairs, Jane still dry-eyed, trying to take in the enormity of what had happened.

"I can't believe it," Suzanne kept saying, between sobs. "It was only yesterday he ..."

"Were you with him?"

"Yes – but oh, you so nearly made it ... Do you want to see him? I - asked them to wait before they ..."

Jane hesitated. "Yes. No." She had seen her mother die; had seen the lifeless form on the bed and felt for a fleeting moment that she understood the cliché *passed away*, before disbelief argued that Mum had only nipped out for a minute and would be back soon. "Yes."

"Come on." Suzanne took her hand as they went into the corridor, and explained to one of the nurses, who nodded and came with them. Jane was trembling, reluctant, wondering if it wouldn't be better to remember her father as she'd last seen him. The energy of her dash from the car had been punched out of her. Like an invalid herself, groggy and faint, she let Suzanne guide her past several bays, each containing its own quiet drama, and round a corner to a screened bed. The nurse parted the curtains and there he was, Dad but not Dad, in the waxwork stillness of death.

"Oh, Dad," Jane whispered, while Suzanne wept silently.

It was the shell of what he'd been. Jane looked at his face, at the closed eyes that would never look at her again; she resisted an urge to grab his arm and shout *Dad, come back! I'm here now, I've come specially!* The nurse beside her made soothing sounds, a professional sympathiser doing a routine job; death was commonplace. Mum, waiting to be transferred to the hospice, hadn't wanted histrionics or even tears. "It's what happens, Jane. It's just an end, an ordinary end. Not a tragedy." Being calm, even blasé, had been Mum's way.

But this was more baffling, because unexpected. A mistake, an oversight, and now no going back. Death was so mysterious, so decisive. But Dad's expression, Jane thought, made him look peeved at finding himself in such a state, eyebrows raised as if there might yet be time to object.

. . .

It was past midnight when they reached home. Ed drove Jane and Suzanne there before heading on to Buckingham; Suzanne was to stay at Wildings so that she and Jane could register the death next day and make a start on the innumerable tasks that would follow.

The house was in darkness, the car headlights reflecting in windows; Jane was thankful not to have returned alone. When she saw her father's Audi in its usual place by the hedge, she couldn't help exclaiming: "Oh! His car's here!" thinking for a befuddled moment that he'd somehow driven himself home.

"I'll come in with you," Ed offered, fetching Jane's case from the boot, but Suzanne told him, "No, don't, darling. You go on home. It's been a long day and you've got work tomorrow. We'll be fine."

Jane found her key, wheeled her case into the hallway, turned on lights. How different the house felt already: too big, too empty, her father's absence thrumming into her ears. Ed waited until they were inside before driving away; Suzanne closed the door and she and Jane looked at each other, unwilling to go farther in. Then Suzanne took off her coat and moved towards the kitchen.

"I'll make us a hot drink. I'm too wound up to sleep, but if you want to go straight to bed that's fine. You must be exhausted."

"No - my body-clock thinks it's waking-up time. Tea would be good. I'll just take my case up."

On the first floor Jane caught herself tiptoeing past the open door of her father's room before realisation struck; she stopped, wanting and not wanting to look in. It couldn't be real, this wrong turn that could surely be put right. She went on up to her own room, left her case and returned to the kitchen, where Suzanne was making toast.

"You must be hungry, and it's a while since I've eaten."

"Thanks." Jane had only picked at the airline meal, and now she did feel hungry, or at least hollow, but food had no appeal. She opened the fridge to find it tidy, with a fresh container of milk in the door next to a carton of Oatly she'd left there. "Sheila must have come again to clean up. That's good of her."

The kitchen felt like the centre of the house, with its big pine table where meals were eaten, homework done and plans made. In Mum's day there had been flowers or sprays of leaves and berries in jugs on the windowsill, garden magazines and seed catalogues on the table, postcards and lists on the noticeboard. Now the room was tidier but there were traces of their father everywhere - half a meat pie in the fridge and the farm shop sausages he liked, an open packet of Lemsip on the worktop. So, Jane thought, wrung with remorse, he did what I said. If only I'd been here ...

Thursday's *Guardian* was on the table, folded to show the cryptic crossword, half-completed. She resisted an urge to sit down and try to solve the remaining clues for him.

The house was warm, the central heating on automatic settings. Wasting precious oil, Dad would have said – the house's dependence on oil had been a point of contention between them, Jane urging him to switch to a heat pump, he resistant. She heard his arguments so clearly that he might have been speaking into her ear. How soon did you forget what a person sounded like? How they laughed? It felt wrong, peculiar, to be doing normal things while her mind turned in an uncomprehending loop.

"We're orphans now." It sounded flippant. "Does Rob know?"

Suzanne had made tea. "Yes. He visited earlier, then I texted him the news, and he phoned back. If he can get time off he'll come over tomorrow. Today, I mean."

"Was Dad - did he know what was happening?"

Suzanne nodded. "I think so. But he was wandering, towards the end. Once he called me Bridget."

"Did he know I was on my way?"

"Yes. Tell Jane, he said, and I said you were coming. He was heavily sedated by then, lapsing in and out of sleep. And – a funny thing - he asked to see Meg Graham. He was insistent."

"Meg? Why?"

"He didn't say. I had to look up her website, then I phoned. I don't know if she made it – Rob didn't say and I forgot to ask."

"Perhaps she didn't. She's in Stroud now. It's quite a way."

Dad and Meg? They hadn't even liked each other, Jane was certain; she couldn't imagine why Dad would ask for her. Unless - a change of mind about the headstone? She went to the cupboard for butter for Suzanne and found a smeary remnant, coated with breadcrumbs from – presumably - Dad's last breakfast. She no longer ate dairy products but his habit of leaving toast-crumbs in the butter had always exasperated her; now clinging to that annoyance was a small, meaningless tribute. She put the dish in the sink and took a new pack from the fridge.

They sat with their father's *Guardian* and unopened letters. Neither had chosen his carver chair, but both looked at it, as if his ghost might materialise to join them for tea and toast. Jane thought of her grandmother's death, years ago, and people saying at the funeral that she was with Grandpa now. No doubt acquaintances would say that about Mum and Dad, meaning it kindly, though Jane knew for certain that both would dismiss the idea as superstitious nonsense. As for the assumption that they'd *want* to spend eternity together – she had no illusion about that.

"Finding vegan food must have been easy in India." Suzanne said.

Jane nodded. "*Delicious* food, fresh, spicy – everywhere."

But Suzanne had spoken flatly, her attention elsewhere; her eyes filmed with tears as she gazed around the kitchen. "Oh, Janey. It feels so different, already – doesn't it?"

They had both grown up here, Suzanne from the age of eleven, Jane since birth, and to Jane it was still home. She'd returned during the various offs of her on-off relationship with Tom, and more recently when she and Suzanne thought Anthony couldn't manage alone, a problem they'd planned to solve with regular care arrangements if only he could be persuaded. Jane still slept in the bedroom that had been hers since infancy.

Now what? The absurd thought flashed into her mind that she'd stay on as caretaker, keeping everything ready for when her parents came back.

Unable to finish her toast, she pushed the plate away. "What'll we do? It's all too much!"

She wasn't sure what she meant: what to do about their father being gone, about the house, the funeral, all the other things that would jostle for attention. She thought of her father's study, where he worked in a muddle of papers, files and books. Someone – she, they? – would have to confront it all. But not now.

"I know." Suzanne was yawning. "I can't think straight, and I'm sure you can't, with jetlag on top of everything. Let's go to bed. We'll have loads to do tomorrow."

"I'll help you make up the spare room bed."

In her own bed at last, her head reeling with shock and fatigue, she had the sensation of being far out at sea, in a large and comfortable liner heading into the night with no one steering.

...

She dreamed that her father had died, and woke before four to the sick realisation that it was true. When she next surfaced it was full daylight. She felt groggy, eyes burning.

She showered and dressed, finding socks and a sweater, nostalgic for Kerala, where sandals and thin fabrics were the invariable choice. In dungarees, T-shirt and sweatshirt she felt bundled up, yet still not warm.

In the kitchen Suzanne was red-eyed and sniffy. "Rob's coming. He's taken the day off."

Jane took the coffee Suzanne poured for her. "How long can you stay?"

"I'll have to go home tonight, for work tomorrow," said Suzanne. "We can do the registering today and start thinking about the funeral. I'll go back early evening. Why don't you come too, stay a few nights? You shouldn't be here on your own."

"Thanks, but I'll be OK here." Jane thought of how strange it would be, the house empty of Dad. But she felt strongly that it shouldn't be abandoned.

"Sure?" Suzanne gave her a sideways look.

"Course," Jane said. "I've often been here on my own when Dad was away." But that had been different, knowing he'd be back.

"Well, the offer's there. I'll see about taking more time off next week." A pause, then: "Would Tom come over?"

"I'm not that desperate. Honestly, I'll be fine, Suze. Thanks."

She went to the back lobby, put on her mother's waxed coat and clogs, and took her coffee outside.

Her habit of slipping on this coat had blunted the memories of sorting through Mum's belongings after the funeral, deciding what to donate to charity shops. Her mother had given brisk instructions: "I don't care what happens to my things when I'm gone. Do what you like with them."

Neither Jane nor Suzanne had wanted to take their mother's clothes, beyond a favourite scarf Suzanne had chosen and a necklace Jane had kept but never worn, but for some reason they kept the old coat that hung by the back door. It was as much décor as garment, and the first time Jane slipped it on was absent-mindedly, on a sortie to the recycling bins. In the pockets she found an old tissue and an empty seed packet, and tears welled in her eyes. Putting on the coat felt like receiving a gruff hug from her mother, even though Mum hadn't been a huggy person.

Now they must face it all again: the sorting, clearing, deciding. Only not yet: Dad's going was too stark, too new. *He was alive this time yesterday. Now he isn't.* Her brain fogged with denial. She knew from last time how death imposed its own urgent timetable: so much to do, before its starkness had fully registered. She wished she could sit down and ponder, but there were lists and phone calls to make, people to notify.

Everything was hushed and stilled in grey November light. Her clogs brushed wet grass as she walked slowly down the lawn towards the liquidambar, the tree planted by her mother. From the terrace that ran along the whole back of the house, the lawn sloped gently to a woodland edge on one side, and a bog garden by the stream. On the right, an arch in the wall led through to the vegetable plot, neglected now; beyond that was Stables Cottage and the empty workshops. Jane still thought of the cottage as Meg's, though Meg had left soon after Mum died and several other tenants had lived there since.

Both parents had loved this place in their different ways, even if they hadn't discernibly loved each other. Growing up, she sometimes wondered what kept them together; slowly she realised that Wildings itself was what held them. Dad saw it as his birthright, while her mother's career and identity were based here.

What now?

She'd always thought of Wildings as home, assuming that her parents would be here for a good while longer, though that complacent notion was shattered six years ago by her mother's cancer. The house had always been the centre of her life, despite intermittent attempts to break away. After university she'd returned home, lived briefly in Reading while working in marketing, then resigned in favour of yoga training and part-time work at a fitness club. Until recently she'd spent weekends at Tom's, most of the week back here. Often Tom had stayed here too, though doubtful about her arrangement. "You'll end up being full-time carer." She'd rubbished that, arguing that Dad needed company and support and that she couldn't fail him.

And then it was Tom who'd failed *her*. The India trip had been an escape, an experience to engage her fully, to stop dwelling on his shortcomings and her own.

Quietness struck her whenever she returned. The only sounds were birdsong, sheep baaing, an occasional car or tractor. Wildings stood at the end of its lane, with no passing traffic. She found Oxford noisy, to Tom's disbelief; his rented flat was in a quiet (he said) side-street in Jericho, where she was kept awake by late sounds from a nearby pub, people slamming car doors and calling to each other. Here, silence settled around her like a blessing. But today the peace felt redolent of loss, everything in suspension. The thin, wintry song of a robin evoked the past: cutting holly with Mum at Christmas, or Dad pointing out star constellations in winter dark. All her childhood was here.

The garden was dying down for winter. It had suffered badly during the July heatwave, the grass brown and crisp, the stream dried to a trickle. Despairing through weeks of drought, Jane had feared seeing the slow death of her mother's enterprise. But rain came at last and the trees and shrubs found new vigour, the borders dense with seed-heads and berries. A garden should be beautiful throughout the year, her mum used to say, and that midwinter was the time to assess the garden's barest bones, its skeleton. Since her death Jane and her father had been no more than caretakers. Soon Dad would have asked Maurice, who came twice weekly, to sweep up leaves and cut back dead stuff. But two days a week weren't enough to maintain the garden as it had been, open to the public several times during the spring and summer. No one could care for it as Mum had, knowing every plant, every tree; the hollows where frost settled, the waterlogged places by the stream where only bog plants would thrive.

"But what can we do?" Dad said, when she voiced concern. "We can't lavish the time on it that she did. I can't afford a full-time gardener. So, unless you feel like taking over yourself ..."

Jane didn't – how could she? She was no gardener, and had to earn her living. Eke it out, rather, since her change of tack. Her job-share at the fitness centre was her main salary now – far lower than she'd earned as a new graduate - and she'd set up yoga classes in village halls, diffident about her ability to teach. Living here, she'd been protected from economic realities. At twenty-seven she thought she really ought to be independent, not living at home with parents.

Parent. And not any more.

A path curved through the border to an arbour that was almost smothered by a mass of clematis montana. Wherever she looked, something needed attention; she must ask Maurice to prune it hard, or the arbour would collapse. Maurice didn't know yet that Anthony was dead. Who would be his employer now?

She stopped walking, struck by the enormity of change. So far she'd thought vaguely of the house in mourning for itself; herself alone, in far too large a space. But of course the house wouldn't stay empty: her father would have left it to Rob. She recalled her surprise when Suzanne once said, "This will all be Rob's, one day" - as if it couldn't be otherwise. That *one day* was too far off to concern them, but Jane objected, "Why? When he's the only one of us who's never lived here?" Suzanne explained that Rob was their father's son, and the eldest; that was how things worked. Their grandmother, she said, had talked of Rob as future owner, and how Wildings would pass to a new generation.

So Rob, Ingrid and their daughters would move in and she'd move out, like the dispossessed heroine of a Jane Austen novel. Where would she go?

Suzanne had always liked Tom and had mentioned him just now, obviously hoping he and Jane would make up. But

- run to Tom because she found herself homeless? It'd be pathetic. Dishonest.

Don't think about it. Not yet. It seemed indecently premature, with the death not yet registered. Rob was hardly likely to kick her out before she'd made arrangements. She stood looking up at the house she'd taken so much for granted, reluctant to see it as Rob's property. Built of local ironstone, it faced the garden squarely. It had been built in 1903 for her Harper great-grandparents, with the solidity and generous proportions of an Edwardian country house. "And upkeep bills to match," Dad used to grumble. He'd lived here as a boy, returning to take over when his own father died. As a child Jane thought it normal to live in a big house that had belonged to her grandparents, not realising until her teens how very privileged she was.

Far less lucky, though, to have lost both parents while still in her twenties. The parents of Tom, her yoga friend Chitra and others her own age were in their fifties and sixties, approaching retirement or already enjoying the new freedoms it offered. Back in primary school, on occasions when Dad had collected her at the gate he was often taken for her grandfather. And Rob's presence at Wildings, quite frequent in those days, caused confusion when friends came for tea. "He's your *brother*? But he must be as old as my dad!"

Rob never did seem much like a brother; she'd only ever seen him as an independent adult. She was nine when he married Ingrid; when their daughter Sophie was born, she thought it a great novelty to be an aunt at the age of ten. Now Rob was a partner in his father-in-law's property business, with a newly built house in Berkhamsted. To Jane he exuded confidence, prosperity and smugness, and unlike Suzanne and herself he even had parents: his mother and stepfather, both in their eighties. It didn't seem fair - though Jane rebuked herself for that. Her trip to India had begun in Mumbai, where she'd seen extreme poverty – families subsisting in spaces under flyovers and between buildings, children begging on the streets or sheltering beneath sagging cardboard. How did they survive? No concept of fairness or injustice in her own life could have meaning, thrown into such jarring contrast. Her parents had died in their late sixties and seventies respectively, after lives of comfort, fulfilment and material success. How could they – she - not be seen as fortunate?

Her watch was upstairs in the bathroom, her sense of time awry; it could have been eight o'clock, or eleven. She felt cold, a light wind tousling her hair, and Rob would soon be here. At the back door she kicked off her clogs, next to Dad's boots crusted with mud. Maybe she'd clean them, put them ready for when he came back.

For a moment she was hollow with loss, air punched out of her. It would be like last time: reminders everywhere, her mind too willing to be tricked.

"OK?" Suzanne was at the sink. "The milkman's been, so we're OK for coffee when Rob gets here, and I've found biscuits." She was ready to go out, in make-up and smart shoes.

"I'd better change." Jane glanced down at her old dungarees and the sweatshirt she only now realised was one Tom had left behind.

When she came downstairs Rob had arrived, dressed in jacket and tie as if for a business meeting. He was always formally turned out, the sort of man who looked self-conscious in casual clothes, like a politician snapped in a holiday photo. He sat in their father's carver chair, as if confirming that he was to be the house owner.

"Ingrid sends her love," he said, "and condolences, of course. She couldn't get away today - but we're all devastated. How was India?"

"It was -" Jane's head swam with the intensity of colour and sound and smells and experiences that had surrounded her so recently. "Great, thanks. But I wish I hadn't gone. I feel awful about not getting back in time."

"Oh, Janey, don't blame yourself," Suzanne said.

"Can't be helped," Rob said. "No one could have known. It's a shock to us all."

It was like last time: there'd be cards, flowers, the sense that no one really knew what to say, so drew from a stock of safe, bland phrases: *Thinking of you at this sad time. Such a very sad loss.* Reality was less orderly, less assimilable. When her mother died Jane felt it as a shock that wracked her body as well as her mind, though they'd known months ahead that the cancer was terminal. It was as if a clawed hand like the ones on old fairground machines had swooped down, leaving an absence that was almost visible. It was the same now. Perhaps death was something you never did get used to, and even your own death would come as a final surprise.

Suzanne poured coffee. For a while they talked about the last time each of them had seen their father: how he'd looked, what he said; whether they'd missed clues to what was to come.

"We'd better make a list." Suzanne had notepad and pen ready. "Someone'll have to go back to the hospital for the – the certificate."

"I'll do that," said Rob. "Registering the death is top priority. I'll get several copies – we'll need them for the solicitor, bank and building societies and so forth. You two could fix a date for the funeral, so that we can start letting people know."

"It seems so horribly *soon*," Jane said. "Dad was alive this time yesterday and now we're talking about his funeral."

"You can use the same undertaker as for your mum. Then we'll get on to caterers and a florist. Is it the same vicar? Could you phone and arrange to see him today?"

"Her," Jane said. "But can't we have a humanist service? Dad wasn't any kind of believer. He never set foot in a church unless he had to."

Rob gave a small but audible *hfff*, and Suzanne said, "But, Jane, Mum's there. It's not just any church. It's the one we see from here, the one we look at from the garden. I don't think we ever talked about it with Dad, but surely he'd want the same."

"Obviously the church," Rob said. "There's no point discussing alternatives. So – registry, undertaker, vicar. Jane, we'll need names and addresses of people to contact. Do you know where to look? Address book, or more likely a spreadsheet on his computer?"

"The Christmas card list would be a good place to start. Oh, God – his study." Jane leaned her forehead into cupped hands. "How will we find anything in there?"

"He's got shelves full of files and folders. We'll have to work through them," said Suzanne. "You might even find his Will. Or is it at the solicitor's?"

"Bell and Arnold, in Northampton," Rob said. "They've got the Will."

"How d'you know that?"

"From Dad, of course. He's always used them. I'm named as executor, so I'll take care of that if you two sort out the funeral."

"Did Dad talk to you about his Will?" Jane asked.

"About being executor, yes. That was after Gran died – the house wasn't officially his till then. And I know he changed it again when Bridget died. He told me, but didn't go into detail."

On the point of asking whether Wildings would definitely be his, Jane caught Suzanne's eye, and decided it would be indelicate.

"Any more coffee?" Rob asked, and Suzanne got up to refill the kettle.

"I'll phone Bell and Arnold today," he went on, "but we won't get moving on probate till after the funeral. By the way, Suzanne, whatever made you involve what's-her-name, the stone-carver?"

"Oh, Meg - Meg Graham. Dad asked to see her. She came to the hospital, then?"

"Yes," Rob said. "It was completely pointless. He was heavily sedated by then, drifting in and out of consciousness. I'm surprised you didn't realise, and save her the trouble."

"So you'd have ignored him, then?" Suzanne straightened her back, waiting for the kettle.

"I think I'd have assessed the situation, yes."

"*Sorry, Dad,*" Jane said. "*I know you're dying, but tough, I'm not going to do the one thing you want.* Come on, Rob. You'd have done exactly the same as Suze."

"OK, let's not argue," Rob said.

Jane glanced at Suzanne, who gave a slight upward roll of her eyes.

"All I know," Suzanne said, "is he was very definite about wanting her to come. It *is* weird. They weren't exactly friends, were they? I'd be surprised if they'd been in touch since Mum died."

Meg. Her quiet strength had been a constant throughout Jane's childhood.

"Could it have been about the cottage?" she said.

"How d'you mean?"

"Mum wanted Meg to have it. She said so, in the hospice, the day before she died."

Suzanne turned to her in surprise.

"Said so to who?" Rob looked sceptical.

"To me. I was there on my own."

"She must have meant Meg could stay on as a tenant," Suzanne said. "Only Meg didn't want to, did she? She cleared out as soon as Mum was gone."

"If you think Bridget meant to *leave* her the cottage," Rob said, "remember she was on morphine then, and confused. Besides, it wasn't her property to leave. It belongs to Dad, to the estate."

"That's what Dad said, when I told him."

"So." Rob reached for a biscuit. "Whatever he wanted Meg for, it can't have been that. I don't suppose we'll find out, and I can't imagine it matters much."

Bridget

NOVEMBER 1973

By the time she met Anthony, Bridget had decided that she'd never marry. She found boys her own age too immature, while interesting older men were invariably married or attached. That's it, she thought, on her thirtieth birthday; I'm on my own. Liking her independence, she wasn't dismayed - but curious, still, about how it would feel to find someone and recognise him as *the one*. How had so many friends done that? How did it happen so often?

On a wet November evening after a conference when her car refused to start and Anthony offered help, she was struck by his good looks and his authoritative manner as he confirmed that the battery was flat and went in search of someone to lend jump leads. Another car drew alongside and leads were attached; with him at the wheel, the engine started at once.

"I'll follow you till I'm sure you're OK," he told her as she slid back into her seat. She berated herself for not knowing how to solve the problem herself, yet heard herself telling Pat in the office *I was rescued by a tall dark stranger.* It wasn't the sort of thing that happened. Even more improbable was his apparent interest in her, damp and windswept as she was, hair frizzed in fine rain.

"Bridget, you said." He held the door open, looking at her intently. "Bridget what?"

"Williams." She knew that he was Anthony Harper from the London School of Economics, having sneaked glances at the lanyard he wore. "Thank you again – I'm so grateful!"

Next day she was astonished when he phoned the office to say that he'd left his umbrella in her car, and invited her out to dinner. She accepted, thinking he must want to discuss the conference for some reason, or make plans for another. She was wrong. Apparently it was a date, a proper date. She'd found no umbrella; when she mentioned this in the restaurant he smiled and said that it had been an excuse. She felt ridiculously flattered.

He was divorced, he told her, with a seven-year-old son.

"Oh – I'm sorry." She was unsure how to react. "I mean, it must be awful for you, your son so young."

"Mm. But we both agreed that it'd be far worse to bring him up in an atmosphere of warring and scrapping. I see Robbie often. Eliza and I were far too young when we married, that was our mistake. When you're that age you're too keen to rush headlong into things. You don't realise how much time you'll have."

Bridget was silent, not having done a great deal of headlong rushing herself. He must think her so dull.

To her bemusement, he didn't appear to. She was struck by his attentiveness, and by his air of introspection; he feels things deeply, she thought.

Dropping her outside her front door, he said, "I'll call you."

He won't, she thought.

"Tomorrow," he added. He leaned across to give her a formal kiss on the cheek. Then he sprang out of the car and round to her side to open the door.

"He doesn't sound ideal to me," her mother said, on the phone. After two more dinners, a theatre trip and a weekend in Dorset, Bridget had decided that it was time to mention her new - well, lover, as she could now think of him. She hadn't thought of any of her previous boyfriends that way; it was too grandiose a term. The fumbled and often furtive sex in student bedsits and halls of residence had been so different from the two memorable nights with Anthony in a discreetly luxurious hotel.

"Oh, Mum, wait till you meet him, though. He's - charming."

"Yes, I've no doubt he must be, to have won you over so completely. But divorced, with a young child? He doesn't sound *reliable*."

Bridget's mother had been widowed at twenty-three. Bridget had barely seen and couldn't remember her father, but his photograph was on her mother's bedside table: a mild-looking man in RAF uniform who appeared younger and more boyish as she overtook him in age and the years passed. His only grave was the North Sea. Although it sometimes occurred to Bridget that her mother might remarry, no one suitable appeared until she was fifty, when she married Jeff, a man she met on a walking holiday, and went to live with him in Yorkshire. The Bedford house was sold, and Bridget was renting nearby while she considered what to do next.

Soon she and Anthony were spending every weekend

together at his spacious flat in Hitchin, where Robbie sometimes stayed for a night or two. Collecting or returning him, Bridget met Eliza, already remarried and unperturbed by Anthony's acquisition of a new girlfriend. Eliza was blonde, sleek, willowy as a model, making Bridget feel plain and dumpy, wondering again what had sparked Anthony's interest in her. She could only assume that she understood him as no one else did.

He was a conscientious dad: planning outings, reading stories, play-acting. Engaging though Robbie was, Bridget preferred the times when they had the flat to themselves, without constant demands to play games or watch television.

She wondered about going on the pill, but when she mentioned it Anthony said, "Why? Don't. Let's have babies."

"I'm not sure," Bridget said; it seemed too soon to commit herself to another life. But her body thought otherwise. Before she'd properly considered the matter, she was pregnant, and Anthony delighted.

"We'll get married then. Shall we? *Will* you? And I'd better take you to Wildings, introduce you to the folks."

Until then, he'd seemed reluctant to introduce her to his parents. As they headed there a few weeks before their wedding, she sat in the passenger seat, silent and awed, as the car left the village on a narrow lane up to the house he'd pointed out across the valley. "There. That's Wildings," he said, while she thought *that's a mansion, not a house.* His upbringing had been so different from hers. What would he have thought of the brick terrace, two-up, two-down, where she'd spent her childhood, only recently vacated when her mother remarried?

Anthony had told her that the Wildings estate had once included a farm and a hundred acres. His great-grandfather had invested in railways, accumulating wealth used for acquiring land and building the house. Anthony's father had sold the farm and most of the land, investing the proceeds. "That brought in a good income, more than enough to live on."

"Wildings?" Bridget asked. "Named by your great-grandfather?"

He nodded. "Because it was just fields and woodland before the house was built, I suppose."

Introduced to his parents in the formal drawing-room, she read disapproval in their glances, as if the baby in her womb was a ploy to entrap their son and heir. But she was relieved, later, to realise that Anthony's misgivings sprang from embarrassment at his mother's high-handedness. "Sorry to put you through such an ordeal," he told her as they drove away. "I knew she'd give you the thorough once-over."

"She thinks I'm plain and dull." *Compared to Eliza,* but she left that unsaid.

"Well, *I* don't." He flashed her a grin. "And you're not. She disapproves of us, not having what she'd call a proper wedding. She thinks it's underhand, the way we're doing it."

And so, at a registry office with a few friends in attendance, she became Bridget Harper, carried on an irresistible tide, exhilarated by the direction her life had taken but sometimes pausing to wonder how it had happened.

1985, JULY

SHE HAD KNOWN, OF course, that one day Wildings would be Anthony's, but it was such a far-off prospect that she barely considered it.

That time came sooner than she expected, when Suzanne was eleven. Anthony's father died suddenly, felled by a stroke, and plans had to be made. Although the house officially belonged to Anthony's mother, she was too frail to live there alone, so at her suggestion Anthony installed her in Oak Lodge, a luxurious care home in Leamington, and organised the family move to Wildings.

Bridget was horrified to learn how much Oak Lodge would cost, exclusive of extras, but Anthony assured her that funds were available. "My father provided for that. The estate will take care of it."

"Where does it come from? All that money?"

For Bridget's own mother, widowed in the last year of the war, money had been closely guarded, counted, apportioned. Any extras – new shoes, train fares, outings – had to be saved for. Scrimped, as her mother said. Scrimping didn't seem to be a concept the Harpers were aware of, though there was much talk of oil bills, replacing roof tiles and replumbing. "A place like this eats up money," Bridget had heard, many times.

On the day of the move, she felt dismayed. *I don't know how to live in a place like this.* Having always lived in towns, she couldn't imagine this ever feeling normal: the solidity of stone, the garden sloping down to a stream, sheep fields rising beyond. The trees that bordered the garden were heavy with foliage, the unmown lawn full of clover and vetches. A cow bellowed somewhere and swifts screamed high.

Feeling like an interloper she acquainted herself with the high-ceilinged rooms, the generous spread of entrance hall. There were four bedrooms on the first floor, two smaller ones plus a large playroom on the second. One of those bedrooms, Anthony said, had originally been for a live-in nanny. Bridget imagined children in sailor-suits or puffed-sleeve dresses; she pictured rocking-horses, wooden jigsaw puzzles and alphabet friezes in the nursery. Children's voices in the garden, a nanny calling them for tea; maybe a tubby pony for them to ride on the lawn, steadied by the nanny's hand or that of a groom. There were certainly stables, derelict now.

Anthony's father had been the eldest of four children born to the second generation of Harpers at Wildings, but there had been no more large families; Anthony was an only child.

Now it's up to us, Bridget thought. She'd vaguely assumed that another baby, a boy, perhaps, would follow Suzanne, but it hadn't yet happened. Was Anthony thinking that way now, with this house so obviously meant for a family, the home destined for him since birth? She was in her early forties, he six years older. Although forty-two wasn't too old for another baby, the ideal time would have been when Suzanne was three or four, and those years had slipped by.

Well, they *were* a family, even if this house was too large for the three of them. And Anthony already had Rob, his son and heir; he'd be a frequent visitor, with his own allocated bedroom. Perhaps Rob, when his turn came, would be the one to fill the place with children.

During the move Suzanne was staying with a friend, in order not to miss the end-of-term treats arranged for year 6. "It's the perfect time," Anthony had said, "when she's about to change schools. She can go to Northampton Girls."

"There are alternatives. What about the local comprehensives? Wouldn't a mixed school be better?"

"I don't know. You hear such things. And the girls' school has an excellent reputation."

Anthony talked of OFSTED reports, exam results, opportunities. Bridget had allowed herself to be swayed, not only by his conviction but by surveys showing that girls achieved more in single-sex classes. Suzanne passed the selection exam for Northampton Girls and was excited about starting. Bridget kept in mind the possibility of transferring her to a comprehensive for the sixth form if she chose, though Anthony would never encourage that.

But, Bridget wondered, what about me? What will *I* do? She'd never lived so far from busy streets and public transport. Wildings was half a mile from the village, five miles from the larger settlement of Haverton, twenty miles from Northampton. From the terrace she looked across the valley to the small village of Lower Stortford – pub, farm, cottages clustered round a Norman church. There was no question of walking to nearby shops for milk or a newspaper, or to a bus stop.

Wildings was reasonably handy for Anthony's occasional meetings at the Open University, and much of his work was done from home. He'd appropriated the downstairs study and was instructing the removal men to stack his many boxes of books and files in there. Bridget had resigned from her job in educational administration, intending to look for a similar post in Northamptonshire. "No rush," Anthony said. "Even if something comes up, why not take time to settle in? Get your bearings?"

"I can't not work! That wouldn't feel right."

But her scannings of the *Chronicle and Echo* and *Times Educational Supplement* produced nothing suitable. Why was she being so snippy? Why not enjoy this, appreciate how lucky she was?

"It's only a job." Anthony was impatient. "It's not as if LEA work is your life's mission, is it?"

Acknowledging the truth of this, she was stung, although he'd stated it as fact, not criticism. But she felt it a failure not to have found a vocation. She recalled the headiness of her student days in the sixties, when everything seemed open and waiting. The first in her family to attend university, she joined the student Labour party at a time when the world was full of promise: in her final year the Civil Rights Act was passed in America, followed by Labour victory, the first time she voted, that ended thirteen years of Conservative rule. Since, she'd taken acceptable but not particularly challenging work and had let its routines claim her, then settled for marriage and the absorbing, exhausting trivia of motherhood.

A new life here, perhaps another baby - could they make up for whatever was lacking?

In the kitchen she located the box that held the kettle, mugs, coffee and teabags. This kitchen was huge, lined with deep cupboards; there would have been more than enough space for the items she and Anthony owned, if not for the crockery, utensils and equipment that had belonged to his parents. That was the problem, of course. This was *his* house, not theirs; not like moving into an empty place they owned jointly. She should have insisted on a big sort-out before they moved in. Half this stuff needed ditching, taking to a charity shop or auction.

Unwrapping china she saw stark photographs of the Ethiopian famine – starved cattle, the pleading face of a woman with an emaciated baby - and a headline about Bob Geldof and Live Aid. She grimaced: mustn't let this house trap her in its comfortable cocoon, taking away perspective. She had no entitlement to live here.

The men were still carrying boxes in. Perhaps Anthony was right; there was more than enough to occupy her. To be happy, she must make the house her own in some way, which could take weeks of sorting, painting, considering, adjusting. She'd find a job later, especially as Anthony was adamant that they didn't need her financial contribution.

And the garden. However would they manage such a large garden? In the evening, with everything unloaded at last and the removal lorry gone, she went outside. The house was daunting enough, but the lawn resembled a hayfield and the borders were thick with bindweed and brambles. Beyond a wall there were outbuildings, stables, a small cottage – it went on and on. How could she and Anthony look after all this? Anthony wasn't practical; he spent hours at his computer and afterwards liked to relax in front of the TV with a glass of whisky, occasionally going to a gym for exercise. He wasn't likely to start pruning roses or growing onions. Why hadn't he kept on his parent's gardener? It was making work, letting a plot this size get out of hand.

"You OK?" He had come out through the kitchen lobby; he put his arms around her, resting his chin on the top of her head. "Don't overdo it. This is only the first day."

"I was thinking we must be mad." She leaned into him. "This place! It's enough to keep a team of staff busy."

"I was thinking I'm starving. Long time since those sandwiches. Shall I go out for fish and chips?"

"Really? Where?" She'd had been about to suggest a quick omelette, but now her mouth watered at the thought of flaky fish and hot salty chips.

"There's a chippy in Haverton – I phoned, and they're open. It's only five miles." Anthony kissed her hair. "We're not quite in the back of beyond. I'll go, and you get some plates warmed ready. Oh, and I've put champagne in the fridge."

It was their first meal at Wildings on their own, as occupiers. They ate at the ironwork table on the terrace, watching dusk fall over the valley; Bridget put a cardigan round her shoulders and lit a candle, and Anthony fetched champagne flutes from his parents' sideboard. The beauty of the evening - grass and honeysuckle-scented, sky tinged pink and flecked with cirrus cloud - made her doubts seem foolish, her spirits lifting with the celebratory mood. Suddenly everything seemed possible. I can be truly *alive* here, she thought. There's space, growth, freedom. Lovely for Suzanne. And, maybe ... for another child. Her thoughts kept circling back to that, rather to her surprise.

Antony raised his glass to clink hers. "To us. Our new lives."

"To us. And to Wildings."

He gestured upwards. "Look, the swallows are flying late."

She gazed at the dart and flicker, the dark shapes almost too quick for the eye. "Not swallows. Bats!"

"Ah yes, you're right. I've seen them before on warm nights."

"Wings like bits of umbrella," Bridget said. When she saw him smiling at her fancy, she added, "That's not me - it's D H Lawrence. Bats. A good omen! His poem says they are, in China. A symbol of happiness."

They sat finishing their champagne until the last streaks of red in the western sky faded to grey, and lights came on in the hamlet across the stream, beyond the church.

"I could unpack another few boxes." Bridget stretched out her arms. "While I've still got some energy."

"I've got a better idea." Anthony stood, pushing back his chair. "Didn't I see you making up our bed?"

Jane

DECEMBER

I'll get through this, Jane thought. *I can cope with anything except sympathy.*

Hard to avoid, at a funeral.

After the service and burial most of the mourners came back to Wildings, where Ed had lit a log fire in the sitting-room. Drinks and a buffet were set out on the dining table, and Jane circulated with a tray of canapés, relieved to have survived the ordeal without collapsing into tears, and making the transition from graveside starkness to the duty of being politely interested in people she'd never met. Many of the guests were colleagues from her father's days as university lecturer and supervisor: economists, academics, administrators. Very few locals; Anthony had never taken part in village life.

She'd been thrown by Tom turning up at the church. She hadn't expected that, nor for him to hug her as if nothing was wrong between them. Impossible, under the circumstances, to shove him away, but indignation helped her through the service. It was too familiar: dark clothes, scent of flowers and wood polish, the handkerchieves (actual handkerchieves - did people keep them specially for funerals, washed and ironed in readiness?) and above all the sense of moving through a scripted ritual. When she stood to read *The Darkling Thrush*, she almost gave way, remembering last time. Her voice wobbled as she announced the poem; then she saw Chitra in a pew near the back, caught her eye, and deliberately slowed her breathing. The small moment of yogic calm helped her to focus on the words and on her own voice as it rose clearly over the congregation.

Although she hadn't invited Tom to come back to the house, here he was, talking to Ed, who was tending the fire. He must have borrowed a suit; she was certain he didn't own one. He glanced at her and smiled as she moved around the room with her tray.

"Would you like one? Goat's cheese and olive."

"Thank you, my dear," said an elderly man. "You're one of the grandchildren, I take it?"

Had he dozed through the service? The vicar had introduced her when she stood up to read.

"Daughter. I'm Jane, Anthony's daughter," she said, and repeated it when he cupped a hand to his ear.

"Oh, beg pardon. You look so young."

"Well done for your reading," another man said kindly. "Can't have been easy." This was Keith Wootton, an ex-colleague of her father's, who'd known Anthony since their student days in London and worked with him at the Open University. Suzanne had pounced on his name on the Christmas card list: "He'll be useful, if he's still around. He'll be able to contact lots of other people." So it proved. Keith Wootton had emailed names and addresses and volunteered for himself and someone called Ray to speak. After Rob's bland formal tribute and Jane's reading, their speeches had lightened the tone, with anecdotes of skinny dipping in the Thames, short-cuts to exam revision and drunken attempts at putting up tents. References were made to Anthony's happy marriage to Bridget, his beautiful home, his three successful children.

In the words of these strangers, so kindly meant, Jane heard her family portrayed as one she barely recognised. This *Tony* they spoke of wasn't her dad. She was struck anew by the realisation that her parents had had decades of life before she was born, years of which she knew only sketchy detail.

Ray, who'd told the skinny-dipping anecdote, was talking to a group by the window. "Of course, Tony held one record that's yet to be broken. Never did anyone take so long to write an unwritten book." A ripple of laughter; they all knew about it. "He always used to say -" Noticing Jane, he broke off.

The only woman in the group – kind face, arty metallic earrings, grey hair swept up - glanced at her and said quickly, "He did write an enormous number of articles, though. They'd amount to book length if they were all published together." This was Marie, one of the few friends of Anthony's Jane could remember coming to Wildings.

"Ah yes," said Ray, recovering. "*The Economist* and so forth, as well as academic journals. We all had to publish, you know, to justify our positions," he explained to Jane, as if she might not know that.

"What was it he used to say?" she asked.

"Oh – that it couldn't be rushed. That sort of thing. He could always be side-tracked. Did you know," said Ray, taking one of the tartlets, "that I was there the day he met the lovely Bridget?"

"No! Where was that?" asked Marie.

Ray told them at length about a day conference, Bridget present as one of the organisers, 'Tony' as a speaker; Bridget finding her car battery flat afterwards. "We both helped her jump-start it. Knights in shining armour, we were. Might have made a play for her myself. But once the two of them clapped eyes on each other I stood no chance."

"And there was a first wife, wasn't there?" someone asked.

"Eliza. She's over there, with Ingrid," Jane said, in case they hadn't realised.

"Good God, is that Eliza?" said Keith Wootton, staring. "I should have realised. Excuse me. I must say hello."

Ray turned to look. "Keith's the only one of us who goes back that far. I'll get him to introduce us all when they've had a moment. Who was the beautiful girl in white?" he asked Jane. "I don't see her here."

"Chitra. She's my yoga friend."

Earlier, in the church, Jane had fielded a remark from Ingrid: *"White?* At a funeral? What a very peculiar choice!" Her stage-whisper was loud enough to carry several rows, if not as far back as Chitra herself.

Jane explained that Chitra was Hindu, and that white was the traditional colour of mourning, but Ingrid seemed determined to disapprove. "Hmm. If I went to a Hindu funeral I'd be wrong, I suppose, to insist on wearing black, because that's *our* tradition?" she went on, while her daughter Sophie cringed into the pew.

With classes to teach, Chitra hadn't come back to Wildings. In the dining-room, replenishing her tray, Jane found the three teenage girls – Rob and Ingrid's two and Suzanne's Rhiannon - taking refuge there, seated on the floor, not speaking, attention on their iPhones. As she returned to the sitting-room she heard Keith saying, "My God, Eliza, all these years and you've hardly changed a bit – "

During the service Jane had noticed Eliza dabbing delicately at her eyes. Well, it must be weird when a former partner died – someone you'd known intimately, the father of your child – even if the marriage had been brief. Eliza was in her late seventies, though it was true she didn't look it: she was tall, with white-blonde hair sleek and bobbed, silver jewellery setting off a steel-grey dress. Jane had only ever seen her dressed elegantly for formal church occasions: Rob's long-ago wedding to Ingrid, her cousins' christenings and now this.

Eliza and Ingrid had been seated on the sofa talking to each other; she suspected them of eyeing the room with a view to new paint colours and furnishings. They were both elegant, fine-boned women of the sort that made Jane feel she belonged to another species. It struck her that her dad's second choice of wife had been very different from his first: Bridget had never been much concerned with her appearance, most at home in jeans and sweatshirts, her fingernails short and chipped from garden work. Still, the second marriage had been the longer by far.

For a moment Jane imagined her mother kicking off clogs and coming through the French windows, surprised to see so many people, wondering why Anthony's friends were here but not Anthony himself. If there were such things as ghosts, this was one – a fleeting apparition that brought both pain and pleasure.

Tom was moving towards the door, pocketing his phone. When he saw her he looked furtive, and she guessed he'd been texting someone – Andrea, most likely. Though why should she care? Surprised he was still here, she caught herself thinking that he looked rather appealing, the formal suit and black tie offset by tousled hair. Perhaps it was the contrast with so much age and solemnity.

"Thanks for coming, Tom," she said, as he seemed to be on his way out. "It was nice of you."

"Well – thought I should. After all the times your dad put up with me hanging round the place." He gave a small, intimate smile, his gaze holding hers. To smile back would acknowledge the reference to all the nights he'd spent here in her bed; she looked away, put the tray on a side table and stood aside for someone moving slowly into the hallway.

Guests were leaving; Suzanne helped people on with coats, retrieved hats.

"You've given him a lovely send-off," one of them was saying. "A beautiful service."

"Thank you so much for coming."

"Do let us know if there's anything we can do. Anything at all."

As Jane moved to help, Tom followed. "Will you be OK?" His glance swept past her, up the staircase, as if indicating how huge and empty the house would feel when everyone was gone.

Of course I won't be OK. But she nodded in reply, and attempted a smile.

"I'll call you tomorrow," Tom said. "Shall I?"

"Thanks. That'd be good."

He gave her a quick hug and kissed the side of her head. "Love you, Janey."

She made a sound that was half-gasp, half laugh: the cheek of him! She found words. "No you don't, stupid!"

At the door he turned to say something else, but people were in the way now, making protracted farewells. He waved instead, and was gone.

. . .

In the kitchen, when all the voices and chatter had gone and the house settled into quietness, Jane and Suzanne hugged each other and wept a little.

"It's over," Suzanne said. "It went well, didn't it? Everyone said so."

It was as if the guests' feelings were more important than their own. The day had the feeling of theatre, experienced at one remove; Jane had returned to a role first played nearly six years ago, under-rehearsed both then and now. Aftershock quavered through her. *We've put Dad in the ground. Done this terrible thing. He was here, doing ordinary, everyday things - now he's over there, for ever.*

Funeral practicalities had imposed their own urgency: so much to organise and decide. Now what? The future stretched into an uncertain void.

Suzanne started putting away cutlery. "Why don't you come and stay with us? You're not officially back at work till next week - surely you don't want to stay on here by yourself?"

"There's Simon in the cottage."

Suzanne looked momentarily puzzled. Simon was the current tenant of Stables Cottage, using it only midweek, for work in Northampton.

"You know what I mean. Alone in the house. Why not, for a few nights at least? That'd be OK, wouldn't it, Ed?"

Ed brought in a tray of glasses. "Course! Good idea." He'd been a great support in his unobtrusive way: handing out drinks, putting logs on the fire, organising taxis or lifts for those who needed them. "Come with us tomorrow."

"Thanks. That's really kind. But ... I don't want the house left empty."

"You might feel different in the morning when things are more normal." The word dropped into a silence; Suzanne looked disconcerted, hearing what she'd said. "Well. Not normal." She looked at Jane closely. "Tom was hovering. Is there a chance you might -"

"No. None. I didn't even know he was coming. And – about staying with you – problem is, I've promised to cover at the gym, and there's my own village hall classes. It'd mean such a lot of driving to and fro, from yours."

Only later, getting ready for bed, did she recall that Meg hadn't come. A card had arrived, a photograph of a stone angel, with the message *Sorry to hear the news. I'll be in touch.* But she hadn't mentioned coming, and – Jane considered it from Meg's perspective – why would she? Being at the church would have meant seeing the headstone: that ugly, artless lettering so unsightly to Meg's eyes, a renewed insult from the dead man.

. . .

Early next morning, closing the front door and already not relishing the prospect of returning alone later, Jane wished for a moment she'd accepted Suzanne's invitation. They were all leaving, Suzanne and her family heading home, Jane to teach yoga in a village ten miles away.

Having qualified eight months ago she was still self-conscious about hearing her own voice in gym studios and community halls, not sure why anyone would be convinced. She knew that the proper study of yoga could take a lifetime, and that in spite of her certificate she'd barely started. This group, though, was a friendly and undemanding one. All female, most were newcomers to yoga since September, ranging from young mums in leggings to several older women newly retired from work, and eighty-something Beryl who was surprisingly bendy.

The hall's heaters didn't quite overcome the chill; warm layers stayed on. Jane's attention was engaged in demonstrating and watching; she suggested easier versions of even the most basic poses, helped and adjusted, introduced a couple of variations she'd learned in India. For that hour she felt focused and purposeful. Then Beryl said, at the end, "I heard about your father, dear. I'm so sorry. It's good of you to come and teach us, so soon."

More condolences followed, echoing and widening as the second group entered. Jane would have preferred them not to know; kindness was too hard.

"Thank you, thank you all. But let's make a start or we won't have the full hour."

Mats on the floor, socks and sweaters cast off, the room warmer now. This group was more experienced. Sun salutations, *surya namaskar;* her voice and the creak of floorboards as weight shifted; audible breathing, bodies moving as if in a choreographed dance, some fluid, others slower to keep up; a quiet focus, settling into the rhythms of the practice. Put everything else aside for this hour, she always said at the beginning, and tried to do the same herself.

Afterwards, when she'd stowed mats, belts and blocks in her car and discussed a dodgy knee at some length, she found a text message from Tom. **Coming over. Are you around?**

Heading home now, she returned. She sat at the wheel for a moment, unsure what she thought about this. Relief, resentment, curiosity ... Why hadn't she replied **Sorry, I'm busy?** She could change her mind, put him off. But she dropped her phone into her bag and turned the ignition key.

. . .

He wanted to pretend nothing had happened; that was his way. He kissed and hugged her with an eagerness she didn't return.

"I'm treating you to a pub lunch. You need a break."

In spite of her coolness she was relieved not to be alone today, to have someone intent on looking after her. He's my ex, she told herself. *Ex.* We can still be friends.

"Thanks! But I'd rather go halves," she said. "Shall we go to the Chequers? The Plough's nearer but there'll be people who know about Dad."

In the pub a log fire threw out warmth. Tom went to the bar for drinks while Jane bagged a table and watched him as he waited. He had a way of falling into conversation with anyone he met, engaging them with his easy charm. He wore the striped rugby sweater she'd given him for his birthday and as usual his hair was dishevelled from his habit of shoving his hands through it. She thought of the Trump protest they'd attended in July, a carnival of resistance as the press had called it: happiness and purpose alongside the outrage, laughing at the slogans and banners and being photographed in front of the cartoonish placard Tom had made. On a day like that she'd wanted no one else but him.

"Menu, and specials on the board." He put down two glasses and a folder. "Two vegan things plus the soup."

"Thanks. So how come you're free today? After yesterday? I thought you were up to your eyes."

"I worked for a couple of hours last night when I got back. Wanted to see you on your own."

"Why?"

"Because."

Their eyes met; Jane looked away first, remembering his bizarre declaration yesterday. "Well, it's nice of you," she said lightly.

"You did well, in church," Tom said. "Reading that poem. Not sentimental, not a tear-jerker. Just right."

An aged thrush, frail, battered, gaunt, in blast-beruffled plume / Had chosen thus to fling his song / Upon the gath'ring gloom ... Jane heard her own voice reading, resonant in the stone church; the tremor as she tried to keep control. *I might have thought there trembled through / His happy good-night air / Some blessed hope, of which he knew / And I was unaware.*

"It was Mum, really, who liked Thomas Hardy. That was one of her favourites. We had it at her service too."

"Good choice. What'll you have?"

She looked at him sidelong, thinking for a moment that he meant poetry for her own funeral, but he was studying the menu.

"Cod and chips for me." He passed it over.

"How's Andrea?" Jane asked, when their orders were placed.

"Oh, come on." Tom gave her an exasperated look. "I've told you, that's history. I don't even know where she is."

"So whose idea, for her to move out? Yours or hers?"

"It was ... mutual. I wish you'd believe me, Janey. It was a mistake. She was never like you."

He took her hand across the table, lacing his fingers through hers; she looked down for a moment, pulled away, and said, "You could say that."

She knew Andrea from one of Chitra's classes at the gym; they'd had coffee together a few times, and Jane had in fact introduced her to Tom, when Andrea needed a web designer for a marketing project. Blonde and groomed, Andrea had the kind of body perfectly suited to yoga: long-limbed, supple. "If he goes for leggy blondes, why even bother with me?" she raged at Suzanne when she found out; then berated herself for reducing both Andrea and herself to types.

"D'you still see her at the gym?" Tom asked.

"Couple of times, when I'm on Reception. Haven't spoken since that night she walked in."

"Let's not talk about that. She's gone now. It's over. Trust me."

"Trust? Hmm."

Bitchy, when he was offering support, but she couldn't help it. Tom looked rueful. When their food arrived he salted his chips and offered the biggest to Jane, who'd chosen stuffed pepper and salad. It was their usual ritual.

"How about you?" he asked. "You won't stay on in that huge house on your own, will you?"

"No. Won't have the choice. It'll be Rob's, once everything's sorted."

Already she disliked the idea, irrationally preferring to see herself as housekeeper, looking after things for her parents. Rob and Ingrid ... she imagined their confident voices saying *Of course we had to get rid of all that ... knock down this wall, refit the bathrooms, redecorate throughout ...* They wouldn't respect the house and its past. But that was ridiculous. Should they be expected to maintain it as a museum?

"Do you know that for sure?" Tom asked. "Have you seen the Will?"

"No. But Rob's meeting the solicitors today."

"Not you and Suzanne?" He held out a second chip, but she shook her head; too easy to slide back into comfortable habits.

"There was no need. Rob's the executor."

"Can't imagine he'll turn you out on the street," Tom said. "Anyway, you needn't *be* on the street. You can come back with me. Why not?" His foot nudged hers. "Today, if you like. We can go back to Wildings when we're done here, get a few things. Move you in properly over the weekend."

His presumptuousness needled her. "No! I can't leave the house empty. Besides, there's so much to do – sorting Dad's things, his papers, his clothes. I'm starting later on."

"I don't see why you should do that on your own. Won't the others help?"

"Yes, course they will. Look, Tom, we're not picking up where we left off. What makes you think I'm so keen, all of a sudden? I ... need to be on my own. Get used to Dad not being there. Thanks for this, and for yesterday, too. I'm glad you came, but - let's leave things as they are."

He gazed at her with hurt puzzlement. His eyes were greenish blue with dark rims to the irises, beneath expressive eyebrows he could use to comic effect; she felt a tug of exasperated affection. But she saw, too, the bafflement of someone used to having his way, getting out of difficulties with a winning smile and a show of regret. He trusted that he could make mistakes, recover and move on, like a dancer momentarily wrong-footed.

"If that's what you want." He shrugged, and after a moment carried on forking up chips. Jane's phone played its silvery tune and with relief she rummaged in her bag.

"Rob?"

"Hi, Jane. How are you fixed for tomorrow? Could you come to Suzanne's? We all need to meet."

"Yes, fine. Why?"

"I've just left the solicitors. There are – some surprises in Dad's Will."

"Oh? What?"

"I can't tell you over the phone. It can wait till we meet. See you there, eleven-thirty?"

She agreed, and rang off, wondering what Rob could have meant. Debts, perhaps? Less money than he'd expected? But their father was an economist. Money was his area of expertise, from an academic perspective at least. He knew how to manage his affairs.

"Only Rob," she said, in response to Tom's quizzical look. "He says there's something in the Will we need to talk about."

"Yeah? Perhaps he's not getting the house after all! Your Dad's left everything to a cat sanctuary?" he guessed. "Or to a long-lost cousin? No, wait. He's left it all to *you*. That's what it is."

"Don't be daft. It's only some minor thing, I expect."

"Then why the big mystery? No, it's what I said. You were his favourite."

"Oh, Tom - don't be daft!"

"You were the one who went home to be with him. And more than that. The way he looked at you, spoke to you."

Jane poked at her salad, no longer hungry. "You're imagining it. Anyway, there's no point making wild guesses. I'll find out tomorrow."

. . .

She'd lost the knack of sleeping. Her mind, in overdrive, played a random slideshow: her father frozen into a waxwork, the hospital corridors, Suzanne sobbing, the coffin lowered into the grave. Over and over and over.

Yogic breathing didn't help; nor did listening to the radio. When at last she drifted briefly into sleep she was jolted awake by some small sound – the gurgle of a pipe, a creak. The house seemed alarmingly huge, full of empty air.

Tom could be here if she wanted him.

Her bed was single, too narrow to share in comfort, but they'd slept so closely entwined that it hadn't mattered. Then, being awake in the early hours had meant making love, flinging back the duvet, Jane trying not to think of her father's room below. "Shhh! He'll hear!"

"So what? I don't think he'd be too shocked, would he? Mmm ..."

Trying to settle, she thought of lying in Tom's arms, his body curled behind hers, his breath on the back of her neck; of turning to him in the morning, drowsy and warm.

Oh, this was hopeless. Sitting up, she turned on her lamp and reached for a sweater. She thought of making tea and toast but baulked at the prospect of going down two flights of stairs, switching on lights. What if someone was outside, watching? But to close the blinds would be to acknowledge her fear.

How old are you? Scared of creakings in the dark?

If Simon had been at Stables Cottage at least there'd be someone nearby, but he was away on business this week. It was half a mile to Lower Stortford, twice that along a single-track lane in the other direction, to the nearest farm. What if someone broke in? Plenty of people knew that her father had died, and might surmise that she was alone here.

On her feet now, she pushed back the curtain. As her eyes adjusted she gazed at the church tower across the valley, squatly square against clouds backlit by a waning moon.

Dad had been here so recently and now he was over there in the ground. Unthinkable. Impossible to take in.

When the coffin was lowered she stood between Suzanne and Rob, arms linked as if to stop each other from toppling in; then, after the awful solemnity of final prayers and the sprinkling of earth and roses, she'd looked at Suzanne and thought *She's my only close relative now. The only one left. If anything happened to her I'd have no one.* She never thought of Rob that way.

The new grave was there above her mother's, mounded with fresh earth and heaped with flowers. So cold, so alone, in November darkness. Perhaps the Hindu way was better – strewing the body with flower garlands, burning it on an open pyre while mourners wept and wailed. More theatrical, more complete.

Mum had been brisk, matter of fact, about burial. Eventually we'll be gone, she said; long gone, dissolved into the nitrogen cycle. But actually not gone at all - born again in atoms that assemble themselves into new plants, new creatures. That way we live for ever. The earth is the only thing that matters.

Jane looked at the last text message her father had sent, in reply to one of hers from Kerala: **All sounds great. Take care. x**

His final words to her.

She scrolled through all the texts they'd exchanged since she got her new phone: mundane messages about picking up a loaf on her way home, a reminder to get her tyres checked, a delay at the dentist's. Right up to that final one, with no hint that he was ill.

Through a blur of tears she read the silly, precious messages back to the beginning, recalling the whens and the whys. The trivia of everyday life, so precious, so unregarded.

Bridget

1988, MAY

GRADUALLY BRIDGET ASSERTED HERSELF at Wildings. Enlisting Anthony's sometimes reluctant help, she moved some of the heavier furniture to a spare room on the second floor, replacing it with pieces they'd bought together; she swapped velvet curtains in the sitting-room for lightweight cream ones, and removed all the nets. Their double bed had been put into the former guest room, which had an adjoining bathroom. Even Anthony hadn't wanted to sleep in the larger bedroom that had been his parents'; it was designated the guest room, with Suzanne occupying the one at the rear. Bridget regretted that their own bedroom didn't overlook the main part of the garden, instead giving a view of the cedar tree to the side of the house and the quiet lane.

With Anthony installed in his ground-floor study, she claimed the small back bedroom as her workroom. She filled shelves and folders with brochures, fabric samples and her own notes. From the desk that had been Anthony's as a schoolboy, she gazed down the lawn and imagined how the garden might look if she had time and money to spend on it. Idly she drew sketches, diagrams; she borrowed books from the library. She bought a new box file and labelled it *Garden Ideas*.

. . .

"I've got an idea," she told Anthony, in the kitchen. "A way to put our cottage and outbuildings to good use, and bring in some money."

"Oh?" He was sorting through the post, preoccupied.

"Doesn't matter if you're busy. I'll tell you later."

It was a school day for Suzanne, a working-at-home day for Anthony. At such times he closeted himself in his study with the door closed, emerging only for coffee and lunch, grumpy if interrupted.

Bridget had plenty to do indoors but went outside into fitful sunshine, her spirits lifting. There was so much to occupy her here. She'd finished a maternity cover for the local authority education department and was looking for work elsewhere; but now she thought: well, why? Her feminist instincts rebelled against being a stay-at-home wife, but that wasn't what she was planning; she wanted a project of her own. And here it was: this place, this garden. Her new idea was more than self-indulgence.

The previous week, the mother of one of Suzanne's school friends with whom Bridget occasionally had coffee had invited her to visit artists' studios in neighbouring Oxfordshire. "Artweeks. It happens every May. Open studios, workshops, little galleries – all free. You see the loveliest tucked-away places, and pretty gardens and villages, not to mention the work itself. You'll love it."

Bridget did. They visited three villages and saw pottery,

screen-prints, paintings, photography and jewellery; they chatted to the makers and admired, or sometimes pretended to admire, the work displayed. Bridget bought a small screen-print for her study, her friend a pair of earrings. She returned home, her mind buzzing. Some of the artists and craftspeople exhibited in their homes or in purpose-built studios, others in barns and haylofts, sheds and summerhouses and old forges; any suitable space was pressed into use.

She thought of the neglected outbuildings at Wildings, and the semi-derelict Stables Cottage. With such demand for housing it was criminal that the cottage sat empty; how could anyone be so carelessly wealthy as to own a house but not bother to make it habitable? Time to put that right. How rewarding it would be to clear these buildings of cobwebs and clutter and make them fit for use!

She and Anthony had talked about the cottage – modernising it, making it available to let - but he'd shown no inclination to begin. Well, *she* could do it.

Her in-laws' old gardener, Frank, came twice weekly now to do mowing and maintenance, and the lawn and beds were gradually looking more orderly. But Bridget wanted more than a well-kept garden with neat borders. She wanted one that was rampant, exuberant; she wanted to know that she had grown this plant from seed, nurtured another from a cutting, planted that tree for its autumn berries. So far she'd done little more than tend pots on the terrace or plant a new perennial in a gap.

Through an arch in the wall, in what had once been a vegetable garden, nature asserted itself in a foam of Queen Anne's lace, buttercups and tangled goose grass, the hedges so thick with may blossom as to seem weighed down. It had rained heavily during the last week, and the lushness of new growth was heady, almost overwhelming. A blackbird shrilled its alarm and ran ahead of her on the overgrown path, low and furtive, leading her away from its nest in the hedge. Here she would make her parterre. She'd drawn diagrams, considered materials, made a planting plan. Now she was ready to start. By next summer ... she saw her new beds lush and productive, with hazel wigwams supporting beans and sweet peas, surrounded with rainbow chard, frilled lettuce and purple-blue cabbages. There was space here to provide for the family through the year; she'd learn how to grow potatoes and onions, swedes and carrots and salads.

But now she was diverted by her new scheme. She lifted aside a rickety gate and went through to the stableyard.

Nettles and brambles had forced themselves through cracks in the paving, taking hold. She would ask if Frank could put in extra hours, make a start on clearing. She stood on the concrete, looking, considering, imagining.

Flanked on three sides by brick buildings, the yard was approached by a separate track from the lane. The cottage, presumably meant for a groom or gardener, had its own small plot adjoining – a thicket of elder, thistles and brambles. She gazed at it speculatively. The door was unlocked, opening at one firm shove into a sitting-room with a fireplace and grate. Rolls of lino, a mattress with springs protruding and some pieces of dusty furniture were stacked against the wall. Behind, the kitchen had been stripped out, leaving dangling wires and flexes where a cooker had been, and plumbing for a sink. The stairs of bare wood creaked as she went up. There were two bedrooms upstairs, both with browned and tattered floral wallpaper, one with a fireplace. The bathroom had a toilet, basin and a curved-top bath, stained brown from iron in the water.

There was no sign of damp, that was something, though the place smelled musty and mousy. From outside the garden fence she looked at it with satisfaction. This would be a rewarding project, alongside the more leisurely work on the garden. Anthony would be glad for her to take it on, saving him the trouble.

Next the outbuildings. There were two large stables, still with their half-doors, mangers and hayracks: one full of rusty machinery, the other empty. Suzanne, seeing them for the first time three years ago, had exclaimed, "I could have a pony, my own pony! Oh, Mummy, please say I can?" To Bridget's relief, this yearning was short-lived. Soon after starting at Northampton Girls, Suzanne reported that the girls in her class who had ponies were snooty and went hunting, and claimed that foxes were vermin and deserved to be killed. For a brief period Suzanne took riding lessons, but none of her new friends rode, and Bridget pointed out that looking after a pony would mean getting up early in winter, in darkness and cold, to muck out the stable. Ponies were forgotten when Suzanne's interest shifted to pop groups; posters of Tears for Fears, Duran Duran and Wham! now adorned her bedroom walls.

Alongside the stables was a harness-room, with pegs and racks, and next to that a large room with galvanised bins which must have been a feed-store. Stretching along the third side of the yard was a long, low building divided into partitions: stalls for pigs or cattle.

The stables and feed-store could be converted into workshops, leaving the partitioned barn for her own storage space. She imagined the cottage bright and clean, windows open and washing on the line, and the workshops busy and productive.

"Good idea," Anthony said, when she finally had his attention. "The cottage seems to be structurally sound. There's no harm working out some costings."

Jane

DECEMBER

"Come on, then," said Suzanne. "Tell us."

The five of them had assembled round Suzanne and Ed's dining-table, as if for a board meeting: Suzanne and Ed, Rob and Ingrid, Jane. Ingrid wore a silk shirt, tailored trousers and jet earrings; casual weekend clothes weren't her style. While Jane thought of Ed as immediate family, she never could see Ingrid that way, and wished Rob had come without her. Though of course Ingrid had as much right as Ed, as any of them.

Rob, at the head of the table, had manila folders labelled *Probate* and *Accounts* in his own handwriting, and *Wildings* in Anthony's. At the sight of the slanting capitals Jane felt a tremor of anticipation, as if Dad might appear in person to address them.

"I had a long meeting with Malcolm at Bell and Arnold about the Will. It's not what we expected." Rob cleared his throat. "I'll start with one of the minor surprises - Dad's left ten thousand pounds to Meg Graham."

Ed looked nonplussed at this, while Jane and Suzanne exchanged glances. Jane was first to speak.

"It's odd, this – about Dad and Meg. We still don't know why he asked her to go to the hospital."

"Anyway, it wasn't about the cottage." Rob looked at her. "More about that in a minute."

"Meg's not on his address list," Suzanne said. "When Dad asked me to contact her, I did it through her website. She was as surprised as I was that he wanted to see her."

"She wasn't at the funeral, was she?" Ed asked.

"No," said Jane. "She sent a card, though."

"This is Meg who did the Chelsea garden with Bridget?" said Ingrid.

"That's right," Suzanne said. "We assumed Dad wanted to see her about the headstone, didn't we, Jane?"

Jane nodded. "I could ask. She said she'd be in touch."

"Anyway, that's not the biggest surprise." Rob's glance swept round them all. "I have to say, I'd assumed the house would come to me." He gestured towards Ingrid. "To us. Dad never made me think otherwise. I naturally thought he'd want to keep it in the family."

"Yes, of course. We all thought that," said Suzanne. "So – what are you saying?"

"There's a trust fund for each of the grandchildren, and a few bequests and charity donations. The income from house and estate is to be split three ways. And that means the house will have to be sold."

"No!" Jane was first to respond. "Sell Wildings? On top of losing Mum and now Dad? You can't mean that!"

Suzanne looked puzzled rather than shocked. "Can't we find a way round it, Rob, if you want to live there?"

"Split three ways," Rob repeated. "But wait. One part

comes to me. One to you, Suzanne." He paused. "The third part goes to someone called Sean McBride."

"Who –?"

"Who, it appears, is a son of Dad's he never saw fit to tell us about."

A brief, stunned pause; then a flurry of questions.

"Dad's *son?* But -"

"No! How can that -"

"What about *Jane?*" Suzanne asked.

This silenced them all. Everyone looked at Jane, whose mind blurred in the further shock that Dad hadn't included her with the others. She was left out; someone they'd never heard of was more important. She saw astonishment in Suzanne's face, concern in Ed's, curiosity in Ingrid's.

"Indeed. No, Jane, you're not forgotten," Rob told her. "Dad's left you Stables Cottage, and ten thousand pounds."

"Meg's cottage?" Jane couldn't take this in; her thoughts looped back to the first revelation. "But this, this son – who is he? How old? I don't understand."

"None of us does, Jane. It's a complete surprise."

"Dad had another son – I mean *has*? How? You mean - while he was married to Mum? Who's the mother, then?"

"It rather looks as if Meg Graham's the mother, don't you think?" said Ingrid.

"That's what I assume," said Rob.

Suzanne made a sound between snort and laugh, while Jane shook her head vigorously.

"Meg and Dad? No! They didn't even like each other. Did they, Suze? Besides, Meg *lived* at Wildings. For *years.* How could she have had a child with no one knowing? She and Mum were best friends – it's impossible."

"No. Jane's right," said Suzanne. "It can't be Meg. But – I

don't understand! How can it be true? Why would Dad keep a secret like that? And if it *was* so secret, why this, now?"

Rob gave a *search me* gesture. "It's in the Will, in black and white. That's all I know."

Jane gazed helplessly at Suzanne, dizzied by what she could see only as her father's betrayal – of Mum, of her, of them all.

"What does this mean?" Ed asked. "What'll we do?"

Rob picked up a folder. "As I said. We've got no choice but to sell the house, pay the inheritance tax and divide the proceeds by three."

"We can't," Suzanne said flatly. "Wildings belongs to the family. Always has. I can't believe that's what Dad wanted!"

"There's no alternative. Think about it," said Rob. "Even if Dad had left it to the three of *us,* there'd be hard decisions to make. That's why I assumed he'd leave the house to me, the other assets to the two of you, to avoid complications. As it is - well. I'm getting the house valued, as the first step."

"Already? But do we have to go along with this? There must be something we can do – some way round it!"

"Look, Jane, you can do the maths when we get the figures, but the simple fact is this. We can only keep the house if we somehow find the capital to buy off Sean McBride."

The name *Sean McBride* was beginning to sound like a sneer, an insult to all of them.

"Where is he? Can you contact him?" Ed asked.

"Through the solicitor, yes."

"If Dad's left me the cottage ..." Jane said. "What if we sold it, instead of me having it? Would that help?"

"Hardly." Rob sat back. "The cottage is worth a fraction of the value of the house and grounds. We're talking well over a million. You'd do well to keep it, I'd have thought. There's a tenant, isn't there?"

"Yes. Simon. He stays Monday to Thursday."

"That bit's straightforward. Tell the letting agent to give him notice, then you can move in."

"Is there any point appealing?" Ingrid asked. "Did you ask Malcolm?"

"No chance. Dad changed his Will when Gran died, and ownership of the house passed to him. But he didn't bring Sean McBride into it until these latest amendments, after Bridget died. Malcolm says they discussed it at some length. Dad was well aware that Wildings would have to be sold."

"But he wasn't expecting to die yet, was he?" Jane said. "He was thinking ahead. What *was* he thinking? What did he mean us to do?" Her thoughts butted against the inescapable fact that Dad was not available to ask; there could be no explanation. Ever.

"He could have told *me*." Rob sounded peevish. "I'm his executor. Why spring it on me like this?"

Because, Jane thought, this must have been what Dad wanted. He must have imagined us all sitting round a table, absorbing this shock. Why? From motives of shame? Humour? Wanting to spring a surprise, play a final trick?

"All this about the house is one thing. But what does it mean about Dad and Mum?" Suzanne was on the verge of tears. "If ... if this is true, and Dad had another child ... Mum can't have known. How could he do that? And *when?*"

Ed clasped her hand. "How old is the other son? Do we know?" he asked Rob, who shook his head.

"He must be an adult – can't imagine Dad would leave such a big share to a child, or a teenager. And Dad was seventy-nine – unlikely to have been siring children in his late sixties or seventies. So I assume the guy's at least in his twenties, but it's anyone's guess."

Around my age, Jane thought. A half-brother, growing up alongside her, invisible. How much deception would that take, how many lies? And this sort-of brother had barged her aside, taken her place. Didn't she matter?

But of course she'd mattered. She knew that. She remembered Tom saying *You were your dad's favourite.* Though not believing it, she had no doubt that he'd loved her. Her mother had always been busy with site visits, shows and commissions; it was mostly Dad who read her stories when she was little and helped with homework when she started secondary school. She'd sat with him in the kitchen with her algebra, the *x*s and *y*s that danced around the page, a secret code. "It's like a puzzle, but we'll solve it," he explained. "See, we've got x minus 5 on this side. If we *add* the five to both sides, what do we get?" And obediently the puzzle sorted itself out. Answering a question correctly in class, she realised that Dad actually did know, and what he knew was the same thing the teacher wanted.

"You'll contact this McBride person, presumably," Ingrid was saying to Rob.

"Malcolm's on to that. The Will says his last known address is in Brighton."

The conversation went on, wondering, speculating, blaming. Suzanne, red-eyed, said, "I must see to the lunch," and went into the kitchen.

"Yes, let's have a break while all this sinks in." Rob picked up his folders. "We'll start to make plans later."

Although she no longer felt like eating, Jane went to help Suzanne, who stood by the sink looking out at the garden. They hugged silently. The kitchen was full of warm cooking smells, meaty and herby. Jane hated meat fumes getting into her hair and clothes, but this wasn't the time to recoil.

"I've made pork casserole. And an aubergine one for you." Suzanne blew her nose vigorously. "This is all so – I mean, losing Dad's bad enough, but the house as well, I never thought – and now this. Mum *couldn't* have known." She gave Jane a doubtful look. "Could she?"

"I can't get my head round it! I mean, we know they had their differences, but even so, another son -"

"Their marriage was a bit unconventional. Even if it seemed normal to us. I'm not sure if you know this, but Marie, you know, who was at the funeral - she was once Dad's, well, mistress, to use an old-fashioned word."

"Marie and Dad? Really? So *she's* the mother? Why didn't you tell the others just now?"

"Because it's very unlikely. Barely possible."

Jane recalled Marie in the sitting-room at Wildings, her kind, sharp face, and how she'd spoken up for Dad when his ex-colleague Ray seemed to criticise. As a child, Jane had registered her as one of her parents' friends, too old to be interesting.

"But she used to come to dinner when they had people round," she said, "and she was at *Mum's* funeral."

"We-ell, that's how it was." Suzanne gave a grimacey smile. "This happened when you were quite small, and they stayed friends ever since. I knew, but sort of pretended not to. Marie and Mum were quite friendly after a while. Mum seemed quite OK with Dad having an affair. You know how her career took off. She was out and about, always in demand, and Dad had Marie. You'd have thought it was nothing unusual. It's odd that Dad didn't see so much of Marie after Mum died, when you'd think he'd have wanted her around."

"Why do you think she can't be the mother? But then, why McBride?" Jane recalled the Christmas card list, the funeral invitations. "She's Marie Frederick, isn't she? Maybe she married again, after?"

Suzanne shook her head. "No. I can't believe it's her. She and Dad were both quite old when it started, in their fifties at least. And even if there was a child, I don't see why they'd have kept him secret, the way things were. How, even."

"But who else *is* there?"

"Someone we don't know about." Suzanne took serving spoons from a drawer. "I used to wonder why Mum and Dad stayed together - I mean, Dad could have gone off with Marie, and Mum didn't seem to need anyone. But they did - for our sake, I always thought."

"It's a wonder I appeared on the scene, with all this going on," Jane said.

"But you made all the difference. You saved their marriage."

Jane weighed this in silence, remembering what Tom had said. It made no sense, especially now, in the light of the Will.

"As for the idea of Dad and *Meg* -" Suzanne made a wry face. "That's ludicrous."

"Yes! Rob and Ingrid don't know Meg, or they'd never suggest it. Does *Meg* know, though? She and Mum were so close, all those years. She might be able to tell us. I must go and see her - I've been meaning to, for ages. I've never even seen her new workshop."

"Good idea. She must know why Dad asked for her." Suzanne hesitated, looking at Jane. "That thing you said - about Mum wanting Meg to have the cottage. Why didn't you tell me at the time?"

"Because -"

Jane thought of the hospice, those final morphine-hazed days when she'd watched and waited, almost willing her mother to die, for it to be over. In a brief waking moment her mother whispered, "The cottage - I'd like Meg to have it," as if they'd been in mid-conversation on the subject, but had drifted into silence before Jane could respond. Afterwards, in the strange numbness that felt removed from time, Jane relayed this to her father, wanting the continuity of Meg staying on.

"Because Dad ruled it out," she said now. "It was only a random thought, he said, because of the morphine. I suppose he was right. And the cottage wasn't Mum's to give away."

"Now it'll be yours!"

"I know - that doesn't feel right."

Suzanne gave her a sympathetic look. "Nothing feels right at the moment, does it?"

"No. So -" Jane collected her thoughts. "Where are we? Dad had a secret son – we've got a new *brother*."

"Yes. And however it happened, and wherever it leaves us now, none of it's his fault – Sean McBride's, I mean." Suzanne opened the oven door, releasing a hot meaty waft. "I think we should meet him, don't you? He's as closely related to us as Rob is – he's *family*."

"Yes," Jane said, on a rising note of doubt; the notion was still too raw.

Ed came in and rummaged in a drawer for a bottle-opener, then caressed Suzanne's arm. "Are you OK?"

"I think so, darling. Could you lay the table, Jane, while Ed sorts out drinks?"

Years ago, asked by Jane how she knew that Ed was the right person to marry, Suzanne said that she not only loved him but trusted him completely. Jane found this dreamily romantic in a distant, grown-up sort of way, but understood later that Suzanne wanted a marriage very different from their parents'. From the age of ten or so she'd been aware that their relationship wasn't a close or loving one. Taking this as normal, she was surprised and even a little disapproving when friends' parents were openly affectionate. Suzanne and Ed's devotion to each other was shown in kisses and hugs, *darlings* and mutual concern, while she couldn't remember her parents ever calling each other *darling*, not once. Yet, with her, Dad was always free with endearments and praise.

Had he been like that with this other child, his secret son?

...

Dusk was falling as she returned to Wildings. Seeing Dad's Audi she suppressed an idiotic leap of hope, quickly replaced by doubt, even fear. So much had changed. Her father had become a stranger, with relationships, *relations,* he'd kept hidden – a son who was clearly important to him. It was a torment to know nothing but the name. Where is Sean McBride, she wondered: what does he look like, and does he know about the Will? About *us?* She had the uneasy feeling that perhaps she'd been watched, envied, even begrudged, all her life.

Wildings as it would appear on RightMove would already be distanced from her life here: a desirable country home, attracting moneyed strangers.

Even before this, she'd known that things had to change. *We can't go on living like this. Can't take it as our right to own a big, poorly insulated house that runs on oil, Dad and me in a house big enough for eight or ten. The planet can't afford it.* When she saw reports of climate breakdown, ocean warming and mass extinctions she could scarcely believe that humanity had a future. Such thoughts had become a background sorrow. In October, people calling themselves Extinction Rebellion had blocked bridges in London, deliberately courting arrest, to draw attention to the climate emergency. Impressed, she thought *That's what we need, yes – outrage, headlines every day, politicians taking notice. I should join them.*

Selling the house was insignificant, set against this frightening outlook where permanence and stability would have no place. Wildings was an island of privilege, imagining itself bolstered against the coming catastrophe.

She should have set lamps on timers. Instead of going indoors she went round the side of the house to the vegetable garden and through to the stableyard. A sensor lamp came on as she approached, flooding the yard with light. The fence surrounding the small cottage garden gleamed white in the dusk. On the wall was the *STABLES COTTAGE* sign, carved in slate. She'd taken Meg's skill for granted, only later appreciating the depth of knowledge and practice behind it.

This could be home, she thought: mine. Dad wants me to have it, wants me to stay. She imagined sleeping in the small front bedroom with its dormer window, having breakfast in her own garden in summer. It felt like a child playing at being grown up. And the cottage felt rightfully Meg's, even though Meg was far away. She toyed with the muddled idea that Dad had left her the cottage with the idea that it should go to Meg after all.

As a child she'd loved watching Meg cut letters in stone with sure movements of chisel and dummy, her radio playing jazz or Radio 4. Sometimes she shared a sandwich lunch with Meg and Mum in the cottage, drawing on scraps of paper while they talked. She liked the cottage's self-containment, and the way Meg had made it her own. It seemed that she had everything she needed: home, work, purpose.

When Meg moved out so soon after the funeral, it was another loss. Parting, Meg had promised to keep in touch, but with a shading of doubt that suggested she might not – and hadn't, apart from Christmas cards. Examining that, Jane felt let down, though she too had let things lapse.

She looked back towards the house, its mass dark against a sky that still held waning light. If Wildings were sold, she'd have no right to the garden, the house, to anything except the track from the lane and the cottage itself. She would be barred from her own home, her childhood.

If Wildings were sold ...

The conversation had gone round and round, alternatives put forward, argued over, rejected.

"We'll be clobbered by inheritance tax," Rob had said, "whether we sell or not. And the problem is that anything we decide must be agreed with Sean McBride. He's an equal party."

"But *I'm* not. Am I?"

"Well, no, Jane. Not where the house is concerned."

"You can still help us decide," Suzanne said quickly.

"Why do you think Dad's treated me differently from you two?"

"I assume," Rob said, "it's because you're the only one without your own home. He wanted to provide for you."

"Lots of people would be grateful for that," Ingrid pointed out.

"I'm not *ungrateful*. Given a house of my own – and it's lovely, the cottage! Just *wondering*."

"If you don't want to live there you could sell," Rob told her. "Buy a small place somewhere else."

And then the last link with Wildings would be gone, Jane thought now. Her mind stalled at the thought of strangers in the house and garden. They wouldn't appreciate her mother's work, her passion; they might dig up the plants she'd nurtured or neglect the garden altogether, though she felt a pang at this, knowing that she and her father could have done more. Maybe she *should* move away; buy herself a flat. It felt unreal to think of buying and selling property. She'd never seriously imagined owning a home, earning as little as she did now.

Worse than the thought of Wildings in other hands was a suggestion Rob had thrown in. "We could sell the orchard as building land. With provisional planning permission it'd fetch a high price."

"No!" Jane had protested. "Mum's orchard? She planted most of those trees."

"Come on, Jane. The place can't be preserved in aspic. There's space for maybe six good-sized detached houses if planning was granted."

"So then -?" Suzanne prompted.

"Just a thought. I'd have to look further into it. It would help with the inheritance tax, for sure. If we sell, it won't make much difference to any of us, will it? Even you, Jane, in Stables Cottage. The orchard's on the far side."

Jane retraced her steps. They were arguing over a mansion and its acres, far more space than any of them needed. Her experiences in India made this wealth and privilege seem almost obscene. On TV news and in the paper she saw desperate refugees from Syria taking to the roads and the sea with only what they could carry. So many people had nothing but their lives and their determination to survive.

Simon, the current tenant, wouldn't be here till tomorrow night. With no particular reason to come to the yard, she was barely aware of his comings and goings. An agent handled the letting, as Dad hadn't wanted the bother of rent-collecting or inspections. She wasn't sure when Simon's current six-month period would be up; she must find out, warn him he'd need to find an alternative.

Shivering, she turned back to the house. The nights were closing in, Christmas not far off. "It'll be an odd one, this year," Suzanne had said as they parted. "You're welcome to come here, Janey – isn't she, Ed?"

In their mother's time, Christmas had meant a houseful of family, games, excitement, a big tree in the hall; Mum used to make a ceremony of decorating the tree on the winter solstice, never before. Jane felt the need of a proper farewell to all the Christmases of her childhood.

Only when she was inside, turning on lamps, did she remember agreeing to go to a party this evening with Chitra and Karen. The effort of getting changed and setting off again would be too much, let alone being sociable, when she needed to absorb the day's revelations. And going out would mean another return, very late, to the dark and empty house.

If Tom were here … they'd light the fire, cuddle up on the sofa and watch a film …

Well he's not here, is he? And not going to be. Get used to it.

Bridget

1989, FEBRUARY

Two of the workshops were ready, the cottage renovations under way. The yard had been re-concreted, and Bridget placed half-barrels at intervals, planted with bulbs, their shoots already showing. The stables, harness-room and feed store had been re-plastered and re-wired; partition walls had been demolished to make three good-sized working areas, and the harness-room now had plumbing, a toilet and a washbasin.

The long barn was to be her store, the herring-bone floor looking rather beautiful, swept clean. It gave ample space for sacks of compost, pots, tools, wheelbarrows – everything she needed, handy for work in the vegetable garden. She pictured herself potting up plants, chatting with her resident painters or potters, admiring their work. Wildings sat so close to the Oxfordshire-Northamptonshire border that she could apply to be an Artweeks venue; her artists could run workshops; she could set up a stall of garden produce and flowers. Her imagination soared. Wildings could become a little arts and crafts community, a name that might come to mean something in future, like the Newlyn school or the Ditchling group.

Now she needed artists.

She advertised in the Northampton *Chronicle and Echo* and the *Oxford Times;* she put up postcards in libraries and local art shops; she contacted the Artweeks organisers.

Days passed. What if no one came? What if her scheme came to nothing?

At last, a phone call. "I saw your advert about a workshop to rent."

"Yes, yes?"

"My name's Meg Graham. I'm a stonemason."

A stonemason! Of all the arts and crafts Bridget had thought of, stone-carving hadn't crossed her mind. And a woman! Unusual, surely.

Meg Graham explained that she was apprentice to a memorial mason but now planned to set up on her own. "I need a place where customers can come and visit. Would that be OK?"

"Yes, of course. There's plenty of parking space."

They discussed rent, bills, heating, and arranged for Meg to visit. Bridget was intrigued by the idea of a woman engaged in such solitary, exacting work, and by Meg's voice: calm, measured, sure of herself. Expecting someone her own age, she was surprised when Meg got out of her small red Fiat and strode across the yard; she was in her twenties, Bridget guessed.

Meg's handshake was firm, her gaze direct. She was taller than Bridget (who, at five foot three, was used to being shorter than most people), with hazel eyes and skin lightly tanned even at this raw end of winter. Thick brown hair was fastened in a pony tail that sprang out in corkscrew waves. She wore walking boots, work trousers with reinforced knees, scarlet sweater with a quilted gilet over it and a scarlet and grey striped scarf.

Looking at the stables, she was clear about what she wanted and what she would bring. A plan-desk, with an Anglepoise lamp, for working on designs. Cork board on the wall to display drawings. Space inside or out for storing large pieces of stone. Workbench. Chest of drawers. Easels. Trolleys, for lifting and moving chunks of stone. Meg explained that she did all kinds of stone-carving that included headstones for graves. She needed to manoeuvre them into a van to transport them for installation.

"You do that yourself?" Bridget was surprised. "Put the headstones in the ground?"

Meg's look implied that this was a silly question. "Part of the job. But I can't manage on my own. My uncle usually helps."

What strange work for a young woman to choose, Bridget thought. She would have liked to ask more, but Meg was brisk and businesslike; questions could wait.

"There's a loo? Somewhere to wash? I get covered in dust."

Bridget showed her.

"This'll suit me fine," Meg told her. "Will it be a six-monthly lease? Payment in advance?"

・・・

"We've got a tenant," Bridget told Anthony. "A stone-carver."

She was cooking dinner, Suzanne doing algebra at the kitchen table. Anthony had finished work and was pouring himself a whisky. He was distracted, not answering; it was

Suzanne who said, looking up from her exercise book, "What's he like?"

"She. Her name's Meg. She seems very -" She pondered, unsure how to sum up Meg. "Purposeful. Organised."

"What does she do? Make sculptures?" asked Suzanne.

"From what she says, most of her work is letter cutting. House-names, gravestones and suchlike."

"Sounds boring."

"Oh no, it isn't! She showed me some photos. Beautiful work, really skilled."

Anthony sat at the table with his whisky and picked up the newspaper. Suzanne looked from him to Bridget, rolling her eyes in acknowledgement that he was in what she called *one of his slumps*. "Had a good day, Dad?" she asked, falsely chirpy.

"Hmn."

"I'm ready to serve," Bridget said. "Move your stuff off the table, Suzy, please?"

Suzanne cleared books and pencil-case into her schoolbag, then put out mats and cutlery, moving around Anthony who sat immobile with the *Guardian* as if in silent protest at Bridget cooking and serving him a meal.

"Did you do much today?" she ventured.

She should have known better. Anthony threw her a cold glance, said, "A little," and carried on reading. Only when the food was on the table did he lower the paper with a faint sigh and attend to the plate in front of him.

It was baffling to Bridget that he was often so moody while or after working. For herself, she relished the total immersion, forgetting time. When she broke off, returning to the preparation of meals and the family's needs, she felt weary but fulfilled. But of course his was academic work, quite different from her labour in the garden or decision-making about the workshops and cottage. Clearly the concentration took a lot out of him. It was years since she'd done academic writing – she recalled late nights in her study-bedroom at York, books spread over the desk, her fountain pen moving across the page or laid down while she found a reference – but she'd found satisfaction in that, however taxing the subject. Why couldn't he?

After years of lecturing, supervising undergraduates, marking exams and publishing articles, Anthony was writing a book: *Economics for the Modern World*. A publisher had commissioned it on the basis of an outline and sample chapters, and he was due to complete the first draft by December. He'd been pleased to sign the contract; he and Bridget celebrated with champagne, and he talked of the opportunities likely to follow - lecturing, conference appearances, broadsheet articles.

"It'll be good to devote myself to a single project," he told her, "instead of being pulled in all directions."

Now, though ...

Things had gone as he wanted, but it gave him no pleasure. He spent hours at his desk, but whether he was working, trying to work, or simply gazing into space, she had no idea. His door was kept closed; sometimes, bringing tea or coffee, she suspected he'd been dozing.

It couldn't be that difficult, writing this book. It was his own subject; he had years of lecturing experience; he'd written student guides and articles for academic journals. Perhaps the problem was the solitude, though he'd said he wanted that. If you were used to working with colleagues, to daily interactions and the demands of a timetable, sitting alone hour upon hour could seem aimless, interminable.

She hoped the book would be worth the effort. He was still on the early chapters, but surely it would gather momentum. Eventually he'd deliver his typescript and be free of it. Afterwards he could go back to lecturing, if he wished. He wasn't yet fifty; retirement was some way off.

Over dinner, thawed a little by food and whisky, he asked about Meg, and Bridget explained about the kind of work Meg did and the commissions she took on.

His mellowing was only temporary.

"It's all very well setting herself up in the stables. But do we really want customers coming in and out? Strangers hanging around, cars parked all over the place?"

"We discussed this before we started renovating. Why look for snags now?" Bridget said, not entirely fairly, since she hadn't thought about clients coming, either. "I don't see why you're worrying. The yard's got a separate entrance and plenty of space. It's not as if people would park in front of the house."

"We'll have to put up PRIVATE notices. And we'll be forever disturbed by people coming to the door and having to be redirected to the yard."

"Oh, for goodness' sake, Anthony. How likely is that?" Bridget brought a dish of apple crumble to the table. "I can't imagine Meg will have throngs of people seeking her out. And she seems more than capable of giving clear directions."

"There are security implications. People poking around in the yard, seeing how to get access to the house from the back."

"It's a bit late to raise that now!"

Anthony refilled his glass. "I don't know why you couldn't leave things as they were."

"Haven't you had enough to drink?"

"Please don't start nagging."

"For God's *sake!*" Suzanne shoved back her chair, making it screech on the floor tiles. "I'm sick of this. Why must you argue all the time? No crumble, thanks. I'm going to phone Helen. *Her* parents don't behave like this."

Jane

DECEMBER

"I WAS CRAP," JANE told Chitra in the fitness centre café. "Cringeworthy."

At the manager's request, she'd covered a yoga class whose teacher had left and not yet been replaced; Chitra, who taught elsewhere on Sunday mornings, had come in afterwards to give moral support.

"Don't believe you."

"No, I was. Problem is, I'm just too *handy,* now that I'm qualified. On the front desk, right next to Dean's office."

"He shouldn't have asked you. So soon."

It had felt so different from her village hall sessions, where the participants looked on her as an expert – which she knew she wasn't. She hadn't taught here before and members usually saw her at Reception or in Chitra's classes; there were puzzled glances as she unrolled her mat at the front of the studio. The mix was awkward in terms of experience, ranging from two newcomers who gasped and giggled at everything and a man who was muscular but not flexible, to a woman at the front who looked faintly bored, anticipating every pose and showily going for advanced variations whenever possible.

"Don't beat yourself up. There wouldn't have *been* a class if you hadn't stepped in. There," Chitra added, as a pony-tailed woman waved to them on her way to the exit. "She's happy."

"It's you she's smiling at. She's relieved to see a proper teacher."

"Oh, stop it! It's enough for you to be back at work, without taking on extras. You need to look after yourself. Learn to say no!"

Chitra's calmness was soothing, holding her in a beam of kindly attention. Nevertheless, as she drove home Jane's inner critic wouldn't shut up. She replayed the class, hearing her voice thin and reedy - daunted by silence she'd talked too much, imagining criticism in every glance, every hesitation.

Why was she presuming to teach yoga? It should be taught by wise practitioners with years of experience, familiar with the spiritual teachings – not by twenty-somethings who'd swapped office clothes for Lycra. Although her studies had led her to texts from Buddhism and Hinduism, she knew that her approach was pick-and-mix, pouncing on a phrase that chimed with her world view, skimming over the rest, borrowing an undefined sense of peace and acceptance like a garment tried on in a shop.

She was trying and failing to emulate Chitra's grace and assurance. Chitra had trained in Tamil Nadu, and yoga had been part of her life since childhood. Jane had come to it only recently, starting at university, then experimenting with teachers and styles before meeting Chitra and finding a keener interest. Daily practice gave her a new physical awareness; never having been sporty she was surprised at her body's suppleness and strength and the straighter and taller way she carried herself. There were mental benefits, too, through meditation; when panic and emptiness overwhelmed her she could usually direct her thoughts inward and find calmness.

Not now.

For a second she looked wildly at the lane ahead, a signpost, a gateway to a rutted track, with no idea where she was heading or why.

If I fail at this ... then what?

• • •

Wanting to salvage the unpromising day, she spent the afternoon searching for Sean McBride.

Her father's bedroom was much as he'd left it. She and Suzanne had stripped the bedlinen after steeling themselves to disturb the poignant tableau: flung-back duvet, strewn slippers, hardback biography with a bookmark half-way through. But it felt too indecently soon to open the wardrobe and cupboards to sort things for charity shops.

Instead she confronted the study. Rob had given her a list of documents to find, but her own search was more pressing. There must be *something*.

One wall was lined with shelves, most stacked with economics books. Files, folder and box-files were at floor level. The desk was topped by a tray of papers, envelopes and leaflets whose contents overflowed. Dad's laptop was there, its lid open. What to do with that, with everything stored on it, Jane had no idea. She switched on, but could get no farther without a password.

Her father's Christmas card list, two printed sheets, lay on the desk; she and Suzanne had used it for the funeral invitations. Although fairly sure that no Sean McBride was listed, she checked again – after all, they hadn't so much as heard the name then. Nothing under McBride, but her gaze landed on Marie Frederick. Although Suzanne had said that both Marie and their father were too old to conceive a child by the time of their affair – could it even be *called* an affair, since Mum apparently hadn't objected? - it was possible that Marie knew something.

Marie was easy to find through the online phone directory. She answered promptly and sounded approachable, expressing concern when Jane identified herself.

"Thank you. Yes, we're all fine. But we did have a shock from the Will," Jane said, and explained about the unknown son. "We wondered if perhaps Dad had mentioned him?"

Marie made no sound of surprise. She *does* know, Jane registered. There was a silence long enough for her to think the line was dead; then Marie said quietly, "I'm sorry, Jane. I never met Anthony's other son. I knew he existed, that's all. And that they'd had some brief contact. Sean was born long before I knew your father."

"So who was his mother? Do you know that?"

Another pause; then: "Presumably the solicitor's involved, if Sean's to inherit part of Anthony's property? I can't say any more, Jane. It has to be up to Sean, what he decides to tell you."

"But why can't we know? With both Mum and Dad gone -"

"I'd like to help, but I really can't," Marie said, kindly but firmly. "I wish you well, Jane. It's hard for you to have lost them both. You coped marvellously at the funeral but I know these things take time to make their impact. I'm missing Anthony too. We didn't see so much of each other since your mother died, but still it was a horrible shock. Far, far worse for you."

Jane sat on the floor to think this through. So Sean was at least her own age, possibly older, and Marie knew about him when her mother – surely? - did not. And there had been contact between him and her father; *brief* contact, Marie said. So why had Dad given him such a privileged position in the Will?

No real answers; only more questions. She was impatient for more.

On her phone she searched for Sean McBride on Google, Facebook, LinkedIn and Twitter, finding dozens of matches – a musician, a judge, a politician, a number of entries from Ireland, too many to be of use. Maybe she should set off for Brighton to find him? But how, with nothing but the name? And he might not even be there now. Was there no way of bypassing the solicitor?

Kneeling on the floor she began pulling out files and folders, looking for anything pertaining to the house - deeds, insurance policies and the like - and the financial documents Rob needed. Several box-files held academic journals; leafing though she found articles written by her father. She couldn't throw those away; there should be an archive of his work. Putting them aside, she picked up a box labelled *Economics for the Modern World,* empty, to judge by its lightness. This was the title of the book he'd been writing, years ago, and never finished. Hadn't he kept his first drafts, his notes and references? Maybe it was all on his laptop.

She began to stack the papers she thought could be discarded: exam syllabuses, prospectuses, conference programmes. The financial stuff, with the house documents, was in the filing cabinet; she knew that Rob had already taken some files. She put aside the National Insurance wallet and another about pension contributions, then pulled out a folder marked FUNERAL.

Jolted for a moment into thinking that her father had planned his own, she saw that of course the contents were about her mother's: a funeral director's brochure, caterers' invoice, the Order of Service, with the photograph Jane had helped choose. She remembered sorting through images with her father and Suzanne before settling on one from *Gardeners' World* magazine: Bridget seated in the arbour with the clematis montana scrambling over it. Looking at it Jane felt battered by a new wave of loss. The clematis was still there, winter-bare but ready to spring back in unrestrained tangles when spring came, while Mum and Dad were both gone.

Her eyes filled with tears. She'd never felt so alone, so abandoned.

The folder also contained, separately, the undertakers' receipt for the headstone. *Polished black granite with inscription.*

That had been a most peculiar choice of Dad's. She'd assumed, as had Suzanne, that Meg would make the headstone when the time came, a few months after the burial when the earth had settled. Meg would have made something beautiful, unique. But she left, and a while later their father announced that he'd ordered a headstone without consulting them. When both she and Suzanne objected, he said, "Well, it's done now, and paid for," as if it hardly mattered.

It did matter. Of course it did. But they let it pass.

Now they'd have to think about adding his own name and dates; Rob had already mentioned it.

"No -"

The word reverberated, startling her; she glanced round as if someone might have heard. Dusk had fallen, the room dimly lit by the desk lamp. She went into the kitchen to make tea, turned on lights and switched on the radio. The house was freighted with loss and absence.

It was only five o'clock: the hours of the evening stretched ahead. She thought of doing an hour's yoga practice then finding something to eat, if she could be bothered. With Dad not here, there was little point. The catering they managed between them had been regular but basic; taking turns to provide, they'd eaten ready meals and takeaways or, when Jane felt like cooking, vegetable bakes or casseroles which her father would sometimes augment with a pork chop or bacon rashers for his own plate.

"*Must* you spoil it by adding dead animals?" she would complain.

Now she closed her eyes, longing for the smell of bacon, for Dad to be busy with a frying-pan.

She felt bereft, lost in the vastness of her own home. On an impulse she picked up her phone and texted Tom.

What are you doing?

Before she'd even sipped her tea, the ringtone sounded.

"Nothing much," Tom said. "You?"

His voice was warm, reassuring as it vibrated into her ear.

"I've been sorting through Dad's stuff." She found herself telling him about her day, the yoga class, her loss of confidence, her indecision about the files and papers.

"Sounds dismal. Leave it. Come over here."

Her hesitation was only momentary. "Yes. Thanks. I'll be with you about six-thirty."

Purposeful now, she went up to her room, packed a few things and put on her coat and scarf before turning off all the lights except for the hallway lamp. Outside, the air was crisp and still; there might even be a frost later. She thought of Mum wheelbarrowing tender plants into the long barn, shrouding pots in horticultural fleece.

As she put her bag on the passenger seat she heard footsteps crunch on gravel. Her heart gave a fearful leap.

"Hello?" called a male voice.

She saw a tall figure against the light, a flash of glasses.

"Jane?"

Simon, from the cottage. She breathed again as he came closer and handed her an envelope.

"Sorry to make you jump. I was going to put this through the door. I wasn't around for the funeral – sorry – but here it is."

"Oh – thanks. That's kind. You're not usually here at weekends?"

"I've been at a conference. No point going home. Are you coming, or going?"

"Going. I'll be back tomorrow. See you in the week, I expect."

"You on your own in the house? Must feel weird. Come over for a drink some time?"

"That'd be nice. Thanks."

Simon raised a hand and turned away as she got into the car. The encounter reminded her how alone she was here, how vulnerable – anyone could come to the door, on any pretext, and force an entry. How much did she know about Simon, living so close yet with little interaction? She reassured herself that he was a responsible tenant and had been thoughtful enough to offer condolences and write a card. Taken aback, she'd replied to his suggestion before thinking; but why not go over for a chat, if he mentioned it again?

What? She'd just been picturing him as potential axe-murderer, for God's sake.

It would feel awkward to mention the end of his tenancy, but she'd have to do it. If she moved into the cottage she could get a dog for company. She pictured a Border terrier or a Jack Russell: a cheerful, busy little dog to chase away the fears and glooms. To keep her sane.

. . .

"So. What was the big surprise? Has your dad given the house to a cats' home?" Tom asked. "Or been declared bankrupt?"

"Oh – nothing very much. Just a few bits and pieces. Rob being melodramatic."

To say more would mean revealing everything, when her mind had exhausted itself with the simple fact that there was a Sean McBride in their father's life, and now in hers. Mentally she rolled the idea back and forth like a beetle with a pellet of dung. How would Tom receive the news? He and Dad had got on well, in a blokey, easily accepting, not too inquisitive fashion.

She *would* tell him. Only not now.

It was so easy to be with him in the comfortably cluttered flat, as if she'd never been away. He made no comment on her sudden change of mind, instead making toast and offering a choice of films to watch. They chose *Withnail and I,* a favourite.

Afterwards they went to bed.

"I've missed you," Tom said, nuzzling into her neck. "I've missed *this.*"

Yes: she had, too. Now she relished being wanted, feeling safe, not having to think of anything except the touch and smell of his skin and his hair as their bodies moved together and their breath quickened.

Tom had put fresh linen on the bed, and clean towels in the bathroom, and had done some perfunctory cleaning. Jane tried not to imagine Andrea here, taking off her clothes for him, teasing, inviting. If Tom was thinking of that too, he gave nothing away. It was as if he'd known all along that Jane would return, and now here she was, and they could continue as before.

But, while he slept, she fretted over the impulse that had brought her here, and what she'd meant by it. If anything.

"*Must* you go back?" he said in the morning, still in bed when she'd showered and dressed.

"I've got a class to teach. And more sorting. What about you?"

"Meeting a new client at the Jericho Café. Free after that. I could come up to yours?"

"Not today, Tom. Maybe later in the week."

"But I thought -"

She was brushing her hair by a mirror propped against the wall; he reached over, caught her wrist and pulled her to him.

"What?"

"I don't like being on my own," he said plaintively. "And we're back together, aren't we? I thought - after last night."

She hadn't meant to imply that. What had she meant? Simply – if she were honest, what she'd wanted was warmth, and closeness, and sex. Was that unfair? He'd been eager enough to offer. And her mind produced the thought *he deserves to be hurt. To know how it feels.*

"Aren't we?" he said, and turned her round to look at him.

"I don't know. It's not that simple."

"Of course it's simple. I want you here. It's only not simple if you complicate things."

She kissed him, wanting to make light of her mistake. "I'll text later, or call you."

Meg

1989, MARCH

MEG MOVED INTO HER workshop on a blowy spring day, helped by her Uncle Terry with his van. Together they carried in her heavy equipment: blocks of stone, easels, trolleys, workbench, chest. Finally her desk, which she positioned in a corner near the wall light. The space nearest the window she kept clear for her easels and bench, so that she could use daylight whenever possible. On fine days she would work outside.

Some of this was new: the workbench and easels. As when she'd bought her first set of tungsten carbide chisels and diamond pads for sharpening, she relished her independence, her self-containment. Her fingers and eyes had learned – *were* learning, would never stop learning - the age-old skills of stone-cutting; now she had space of her own. Of time, she had plenty: time to chip away at a piece of stone for hours, days, weeks – as long as the task needed.

When everything was in place she produced a cardboard box containing a kettle, teabags, mugs, spoons and milk.

"Tea! Let's celebrate with my first brew-up. First of many."

"Be a bit lonely here, won't you?" Uncle Terry stood in the doorway looking out at the yard. "Out in the sticks." It was a cheerless day, the sky grey, bare twigs tossed by the wind; bleak March weather, emphasising that winter hadn't yet given up its hold.

"I like sticks. I like being on my own," Meg said. "Anyway there are two other workshops. There'll be people in those, soon."

"You got work on already, then?"

"Enough to keep me going. A headstone and some house names. I'll start advertising."

"Beats me why you didn't stay with old whatsisname." Uncle Terry had come inside and was examining her chisels, picking one up to test its sharpness. "Then you wouldn't have to bother with none of that. Advertising? – cost you, that will."

Meg fished a teabag from a mug, realised there was no bin, and placed it on the floor. "Mmm. I'll miss George."

He had taught her so much; but she wanted more. Wanted to do everything, independently.

"Two sugars in mine, remember. Well, love, here's to you and your little business. Ought to have champers, didn't we?"

...

She set about making the place her own. With Bridget's permission she put up cork tiles to display drawings for work in progress, alongside photographs of her finished pieces and of lettering and sculptures by Eric Gill, Jacob Epstein, David Kindersley and others who inspired her. On another wall she put up shelves to hold smaller objects such as plaques and bookends. It would be useful to have such pieces to show, as well as her portfolio.

It was a novelty to be her own boss. Although she could easily work on plans and drawings in her Towcester bedsit, she arrived promptly by nine each morning and stayed till after five, bringing sandwiches and fruit to keep her going, with frequent brew-ups. She had a headstone in Cumbrian green slate to complete, and in the intervals when her back ached or she had a fancy for something different she carved small relief plaques that might sell as garden ornaments. Returning to her bedsit each evening she was covered in fine dust that got into her hair, her clothes, her eyelashes. She stripped off on the doormat and bundled her clothes into the washing machine before showering. On four nights each week she tidied herself and went down the street to the Saracen's Head, where she pulled pints, washed glasses and fended off the occasional drunken lurch; on free evenings she was usually too weary to do more than make something to eat and retire early with a book or the radio.

At their first meeting, she'd dismissed Bridget as too middle-class and middle-aged to be of interest, not expecting to have much to do with her. But Bridget was often in the barn, wheeling barrows in and out or potting plants at the bench. Usually she came over to say hello, and to ask about the work in progress. What were the qualities of the various kinds of stone? What if you made a mistake? How had Meg learned to do this? Where had she trained?

Meg explained that she'd taken a fine art degree and that stone-carving had been one of the disciplines she had experimented with; captivated, she'd trained with a stonemason for a year before specialising in lettering. "I was lucky. I got a grant to study at the Kindersley workshop in Cambridge, and my aunt and uncle are in Fulbourne, nearby, so I stayed with them. Here -" She selected a book from the row on her shelf and flicked through its pages, pausing here and there to show Bridget. "See this? Exquisite work, really beautiful. That's when I really fell in love with cutting letters."

"Why?" Bridget seemed genuinely curious.

"The sureness. The simplicity. The way the light catches them. And letters in stone are practically for ever. Cutting letters, it's what the Romans did, or medieval stonemasons. We do it the traditional way – same tools, same techniques. You can't rush or take short cuts. And it's kind of humbling. Working with sedimentary limestone – it's made of things that were crawling or swimming around a hundred and fifty million years ago and more. At the time of the dinosaurs." She rummaged around in a box of offcuts and took out a chunk small enough to hold in her hand. "Look, this is Portland stone, from Dorset. It's got fossils in it - see that bit, and this? If you cut into it, you get an oily, fishy smell – imagine! It's been trapped in the limestone for a longer time than we can get our heads round. But still there, waiting to be released."

"So when you're working it -" Bridget smoothed a finger over the shell-shaped fossil – "you're breathing in the remains of prehistoric life? Bits of bone and shell from creatures that were alive at the time of the dinosaurs."

"Yes."

Their eyes met; she saw Bridget's brown ones widen in wonder.

"It's astonishing."

Meg put the chunk back with the others: limestone knocking against granite, slate, Bath stone. "Well, we're all made of the same stuff. Everything in our bodies has been here since the Earth formed."

She saw this make an impression on Bridget. But when she thought about it later, Meg heard too much of her own voice. She might have been delivering a lecture.

"You're a most unusual young woman," Bridget said lightly, and Meg shrugged.

"I'm lucky to have found my one true thing, the thing I love doing. Not everyone does."

Bridget nodded slowly. "Yes. You *are* lucky in that."

Meg revised her view, seeing animation, fleeting changes of expression, quick understanding and interest. But sensing that Bridget wanted friendship to develop, she kept her distance. It wasn't something she needed.

Jane

DECEMBER

Yoga practice was the best start to any day: pranayama, her CD of Indian music, then the physical postures, stretching and opening into the familiar, beautiful moves of the asanas.

With the more experienced of her village hall groups she rehearsed her plan for Sunday's class, every pose, every transition and variation. She resolved not to be intimidated. She was as well-prepared as she could possibly be; what people took from the session was up to them.

One whole evening she spent crying, defiantly asking herself *Why shouldn't I?* It would be dishonest not to. She felt oddly detached, as if her mind had exhausted itself with grief, the weeping a purely physical release. Many sodden tissues later she showered and went to bed with a mug of cocoa. She slept soundly, used now to the house's night-time creaks and pipe-gurgles. In the morning she looked in the mirror at her puffy eyes and reddened nose, and thought: well, there's no one to see. What does it matter?

She had no class that day, and with food in the fridge there was no need to go out. She planned to continue the sorting before Suzanne joined her on Saturday.

The temperature had fallen sharply overnight. After breakfast she put on a coat and scarf and went outside, boots crunching on frosted grass. The borders were beautiful in low sunlight, bare twigs glowing red, dried seed-heads in shades of rust and sepia among silvered grasses. The liquidambar, on the east side of the lawn with a bench underneath its branches, was almost bare, only a few leaves clinging. As a child she'd helped plant it, or rather made gestures of help; she remembered ineffectually wielding a small spade while her mother stooped to dig, prising out obstinate roots and stones.

Mum had found something; Jane went to look. An unearthed bone lay on the grass. A jawbone, browned with soil and age; a row of teeth, a grimace.

She gave a little scream. "Is it a body?"

"Only a sheep, or more likely a pig."

"Why's it there?"

"Perhaps it died here. Before there was a garden. Or perhaps someone buried it."

A pig's grave. Jane thought perhaps it had been a special pig; a pet, perhaps, that lived here long ago and had snorted and snuffled as if life would go on for ever. Mum dug and dug until the hole was big enough for the sapling, then filled it with water that drained away slowly.

She remembered her disappointment that the tree was so small and slender, but Mum explained that she was planting for the future. "In years to come there'll be a magnificent tree here. People can walk under its branches and sit in its shade. Most likely they'll never wonder how it got here. Who planted it."

"*What* people?"

"Whoever lives here when we're gone," her mother said.

"Where are we going?" she asked, at an age for asking one question after another, and Mum said, "Nowhere. But we won't live for ever" – a concept Jane found curious, but of no immediate relevance. She liked the tree's name – liquid amber, suggestive of molten gold, pouring in a slow trickle, like honey. In autumn the maple-like leaves turned to other colours besides amber – deepest reds, and rusts, and shades of gold, while some stayed green. Fascinated that a single tree could produce such rich, varied colours, she made a collage, gathering leaves as they lay rain-shiny on the grass, arranging them on paper.

The liquidambar was twenty feet high now. Each autumn, when its leaves blazed and glowed, Jane thought of it as her mother's memorial, a better and more fitting one than the polished granite in the churchyard. The pig's jaw was still on a windowsill in the barn, where her mother had set out all the bits and pieces found in the garden: shards of pottery, shells, green glass, fragments of floral-patterned china, a tarnished teaspoon.

. . .

When a wildly impractical idea came to her, she couldn't help sharing it with Chitra in the gym café next day.

"I've been thinking ... wouldn't it be lovely to turn Wildings into a refugee centre, a place for homeless people, or people with nothing? There's so much space - plenty of bedrooms, and the cottage as well, and the workshops could be converted."

"In your dreams?"

"Well, yes."

"A yoga centre would be more practical."

"Refugee centre *with* yoga, then," Jane said. "Couldn't we involve a charity? Get a grant?"

"It'd have to be an enormous one. And your relatives would never agree."

It was Chitra's dream to set up her own studio, away from gym equipment and shouty instructors; she and Jane often talked airily about an incense-scented vision neither expected to become reality.

"What we need," Jane said, "is a billionaire sponsor."

Chitra raised an eyebrow. "Is that all? Easy. There are so many of those around, desperate to give us their money."

Nevertheless Jane's thoughts ran on as she drove home. She imagined families in the garden, sitting on the lawn; there could be children's play equipment in the orchard. Her mother's garden would be properly appreciated by the small community, who'd grow fruit and vegetables for the kitchen. In the evenings people would come together in the sitting-room to listen to each other, sharing their stories, their hopes ...

Seeing it in such detail, she jolted back to reality as she turned into the driveway. Today's post stuck out of the letterbox, dried leaves had collected in the porch and the gravel badly needed weeding.

In the silent house she sorted through the post, which included Christmas cards addressed to her father among business letters about the closing of accounts and policies, then checked for phone messages. Only one: Rob, asking her to phone back.

"I'd like the estate agent to come in the next few days to do measurements and take photos," he told her. "Will you be there?"

"Already? I thought nothing was happening till after Christmas."

"It won't, and all this Brexit uncertainty is putting a brake on the property market. Besides, the house can't go on sale till probate comes through, but we want to be ready when it does."

"What about Sean McBride?"

"Yes, Malcolm's contacted him. He agrees to the sale."

"So that's it? Didn't you find out more? Won't we meet him?"

"I don't see any reason to. If he wants to contact us he can do it through Malcolm."

"But aren't you -" *Curious,* she almost said, but as he obviously wasn't she asked instead, "Is Suzanne OK with this, then – getting started on the sale? I was expecting another meeting first."

"She's leaving it to me," Rob said. "We can talk more over the holidays – we'll all meet as usual on New Year's Day, I suppose? So, about the estate agent. They'll ring you to arrange a time. It's Bridges and Wade, and the person I spoke to is Sam Wade."

"Fine."

"Make sure everything's tidy, won't you? How are you, OK?" Rob added.

Deflated, Jane rang off. In the face of Rob's practicality and purpose, her refugee centre dream evaporated like mist. Things were moving on, and it was beyond her power to stop them. Besides, she had no stake in the house.

Sean McBride did, though.

Even if Rob had no interest beyond transactional matters, Jane wanted more – after all, Sean was her half-brother, as closely related as Rob was, and possibly closer in age. Why shouldn't they meet? Surely he'd be interested in his previously unknown family?

Having done the early shift on reception she was home in time to catch office people still at work. Rob had the Arnold and Bell folder, but she remembered that the solicitor was Malcolm Frost, found the website and phoned.

Malcolm Frost was out of the office; she left a message asking him to call back. Frustrating! Her half-brother might be a mere phone call away if only she could get his number. When the phone rang she snatched it up eagerly, but it was the estate agency wanting to make an appointment. Jane agreed to Monday afternoon, which gave her the weekend, including Suzanne's visit on Saturday, to tidy up.

In her father's study she turned on the heater and radio and spent more than two hours going through box files and folders, putting out-of-date documents through the shredder. Malcolm Frost phoned at six, after she'd given up on him for the day, and she explained her mission. There was a pause while he checked; then he said, "I'm sorry. Your father left instructions that Sean McBride's details weren't to be passed on to the family without his – Mr McBride's - permission."

"So there's no way I can contact him? You must have an address?"

"You can write to him care of us, and we'll redirect. There's social media, of course, or the telephone directory, but it's not an unusual name. If Sean McBride wants to make contact himself, that's easily possible – of course he knows where you live. Meanwhile he'll be kept informed of progress."

Disappointed, Jane rang off. She'd already searched the online Brighton telephone directory as well as social media. Now she looked again at the many Facebook matches, closely examining photographs to see if one of them jumped out at her. A smiling family with young children; a rugby player; some of the men were too old, others in unlikely parts of the world. In this gallery of McBrides she could be looking at her half-brother without knowing.

But she could do as Malcolm Frost had suggested. She went back to the solicitors' website for the email address, and wrote a message to Sean explaining who she was, asking him to get in touch.

Send.

He could ignore it if he chose; at least she'd tried.

In her father's study she returned to the FUNERAL file she'd found on Sunday, and flicked through it again to the receipt for the granite headstone. There'd be no more machine-cut lettering if she had anything to do with it. Not when she'd so often seen the real thing: the beauty and individuality of letters cut in stone, by hand, in the traditional way.

Meg. With so much to do she'd forgotten her intention to visit. She had the address and phone number somewhere, but went first to Meg's website.

MEG GRAHAM:
STONE CARVING AND LETTER-CUTTING.
Lettering in stone and slate:
headstones – memorials - house names
garden sculptures - relief carving

The home page gave the address of Fernhill Barn, Meg's workshop near Stroud, and an email link.

Gallery pages showed completed pieces: a range of house names, headstones, sundials and small sculptures; sandstone, Portland, Welsh slate, Cumbrian green slate, Hornton stone. Admiring the skill and precision of the work, Jane searched in vain for a photograph of Meg. A final page all in black-and-white photography, rather beautiful, had close-ups of Meg's hands at work with chisel and dummy, grainy and backlit to show dust flying and the light and shade of valley cutting. Her face did not appear.

Since her mother's death, Jane had missed not only Meg but the creative hub of the stableyard, especially when open for Artweeks. She assumed that Dad would find new workshop tenants, but he hadn't, using an agency to let and manage the cottage. All three workshops had stood empty since the last occupant left.

Now she and Meg had all but lost touch, the lapse at least partly because of the awkwardness over the headstone. She felt encouraged by the idea of Meg still busy and working. And, she hoped, available.

She began an email:

Dear Meg,

Thank you for your card. Can I come and see you? I'd like to talk about ideas for a headstone.

No. Not yet. She deleted the last sentence, continuing instead **at your studio? There are things I'd like to talk about. I could come next Wednesday, any time, or on Thursday.**

It'd be good to catch up. Thanks!

Jane

She put an x after her name, then deleted it: Meg wasn't an x-y sort of person. There. Done. She could raise the subject of the headstone: whether it was too late to commission a proper one and whether Meg would do it; though it would be rash to ask before putting the idea to Rob and Suzanne. She resolved to talk to Suzanne on Saturday.

It was late evening when Meg replied. **Wednesday fine. Afternoon, about 2? Map on website. Look for sign on lane before sharp bend.**

Meg

1989, APRIL

ON WARM DAYS SHE took her work out to the yard. The headstone was almost finished, and she was pleased with her progress. She had cut the design of oak-leaves and was completing the lettering; it would soon be ready to install.

When Bridget came over to look, she broke off to make coffee.

"Someone's coming to see the spare workshop," Bridget told her. "A painter."

The second stable was now occupied by Leonard, a signmaker past retirement age, who came only infrequently. Used to having the place to herself for much of the time, Meg felt unreasonably irked by the idea of a third person in the yard.

Later that afternoon Bridget came through the gate, followed by a tall young man with a stubbled jaw and fair hair that fell in a sweep across his forehead.

"So this is the stableyard," Bridget was saying, "and here's Meg. Meg - Adam Mullen."

"Hi, Meg." He came closer to look at the headstone on her easel. "Wow."

She was ready to dislike him, for no better reason than that he was young, male and personable. From his quick glance she saw brows and stubble darker than his hair, and eyes with clear whites; his leanness was swamped by an outsized sweater over shabby jeans. He was probably a complete tosser. Anyone could call themselves a painter.

"I know, beautiful, isn't it?" Bridget was saying, about the headstone. "So this is Meg's workshop and that's Leonard's. Here's the vacant one."

They went into the middle stable, and she continued cutting her letter with barely a pause. *T-tink t-tink* went her chisel on the slate, working round the curve of a *D*.

She didn't see Bridget again until the following morning. Bridget was busy now with her vegetable garden; the plot had been cleared and a builder was laying weathered brick paths. As the cottage roof was being re-tiled at the same time, she regularly came to the yard bringing drinks for the workers.

"So," she told Meg, "you'll have a neighbour. Adam's moving in next week."

Meg only raised an eyebrow in response, and Bridget laughed. "I know. He's rather easy on the eye, isn't he?"

"What does he paint?" Meg felt a prickle of resentment towards her for the silly cliché, and for the assumption that tried to pair them like giggling schoolgirls. She continued sorting through her toolbox.

"Large canvases, he said. Abstract."

"Sloshing paint about, I expect. We'll soon see. Don't tell me he makes a living from that?"

"I thought you'd like the company," Bridget said. "Talking of which – would you like to come to the house for lunch?"

"Thanks, but I must get on." She found the fine chisel she needed. "I'm working at the pub tonight."

"Just soup and cake. It needn't take long."

"With you and Anthony?"

"No, only me. Anthony's lecturing today."

Reluctantly, Meg agreed. She'd seen Anthony a few times, checking progress on the cottage or talking to the builders. Introduced by Bridget, he'd acknowledged her with only cursory interest. She'd heard him exchange brisk remarks with the tiler before striding back to the house.

Meg recognised her own tendency to be wary and even resentful of strangers, warming to people only on closer acquaintance. Mildly interested in Anthony because he was Bridget's husband, she saw no reason to like him. He was fiftyish, older than Bridget, quite handsome for his age; she noticed the shape of his head, his dark hair, the way he held himself. He had the air of a man who expected things done to his satisfaction. The daughter, Suzanne, wasn't much like either of them, being fair and slender, already taller than Bridget. She was a mixture of shyness and confidence, a little in awe of Meg. A couple of times she'd hung around the workshop, asking questions. Where did Meg get the stone? How long did it take to carve letters? Was it hard?

She reminded Meg of Gillian; tall blonde girls and women always did. But Suzanne was more languid than Gillian, with the air teenagers often had of being tired by rapid growth. Meg thought of Gillian's febrile energy and quick changes of mood; her sudden enthusiasms for baking or wallpapering or running that as quickly degenerated into despair and disgust. She couldn't see long blonde hair without picturing Gillian on the sofa, hair veiling her face, the silky hair Meg envied, despising her own messy curls.

This was one of the few drawbacks of working alone; there was nothing to dam the flow of thoughts, the connections her brain insisted on making.

At one o'clock, as agreed, she went through the garden to the back door. "Hello!" she called, from a lobby with boots lined up beneath a row of coats on hooks, and Bridget answered, "Come on in!" from the kitchen beyond.

She took off her own dusty boots before entering. God, it was enormous. This kitchen was bigger than her whole bedsit, all done out in cream units, with a table and six chairs. There was even a Welsh dresser, plates displayed on shelves. She might have stepped into *Country Life* magazine. Still, what had she expected?

Bridget served lentil soup, granary bread and crumbly cheese, and poured apple juice.

"Have you got family, Meg? Parents?"

"Only my uncle and aunt, now. Uncle Terry helped me move in. My Mum cleared off when I was two."

"You're not in touch with her?"

She shook her head. "Good soup. Did you make it?"

"Thanks – yes. So your aunt and uncle brought you up?"

"From when I was nine. I stayed with my stepdad at first after Mum went. I lived with him and his girlfriend for a while, but then he was left on his own and couldn't cope. And I wasn't really his responsibility. My real Dad was out of the picture before I was even born." She looked at Bridget to see if she were shocked. "Uncle Terry's my only blood relation. Can't count my Mum. She's in Spain - we don't even know where."

"Complicated."

"You could say that." Meg glanced around the well-fitted kitchen, meaning and not meaning to imply that her background was very different from the comfort and conventionality she saw here.

Possibly Bridget picked that up. Cutting bread and proffering it, she said, "Anthony was married before. He's got a son, Rob – twenty-three now."

"He couldn't have stayed around for long, then - Anthony, I mean. Your Suzanne's fifteen, isn't she?"

"Yes, just. And you, Meg? Is there someone in your life?"

Tempted to retort, "How is that your business?" Meg answered instead, "No. I'm on my own. It's what I'm used to. What I like."

A door banged at the front of the house, making Bridget jump visibly, and Anthony strode in, his face set in a scowl.

"Fucking waste of -"

He stopped, seeing Meg.

"Anthony!" Bridget pushed back her chair and stood up. "I wasn't expecting you – didn't you have a meeting?"

"Cancelled. At the last minute. Peter called to say he couldn't make it. Waste of bloody time."

"Oh, what a shame. Meg and I are having lunch," Bridget said, as if that wasn't obvious. "Do join us."

"In a minute. I need to make some calls first."

"Shall I make coffee?"

"No, don't bother. You carry on."

Anthony went out again, closing the door with firmness just short of a slam.

Meg raised her eyebrows at Bridget, who said, with a little laugh, "Sorry about that. He's under a lot of pressure at work."

The atmosphere had changed; Anthony's arrival had made Bridget anxious, fluttery. Meg saw something false in her manner.

Marriage. Who'd want it?
She finished her soup and stood up.
"OK, I'm going now. Thanks for the lunch."

Bridget

1989, APRIL

"What's the matter?" she confronted Anthony in his study as soon as Meg left. "Why were you so rude?"

"I wasn't. Didn't know you were planning to entertain your tenants for meals, that's all." He was searching in a drawer of his desk, pulling out papers.

"I didn't plan! I asked Meg on an impulse. And she's *our* tenant. Anyway, what does it matter if your meeting was cancelled? You were complaining at breakfast about having to go. You can work on your book this afternoon instead."

"Could you let me get on, please?" Anthony said coldly, his back to her.

"With pleasure. There's soup if you want it. I'm going back to the garden."

She spent the next few hours weeding and digging the wide border, and did not speak to Meg again that day. Her senses filled with the smell of the earth, its rich crumbliness beneath her spade, the occasional chink against stone; the promise of summer to come, sun warm on her back, the sky soft as silk. The trees were still bare but the hedgerows were greening with the first hawthorn leaves, and shoots speared out of the ground in a heady rush of growth. When she straightened to ease her back, she saw, across the valley, ridge and furrow in the pasture behind the church thrown into relief by low sunlight. It awed her to see the land indelibly marked from a time when the village was no more than church, manor, a few cottages and the river crossing. The local map showed green lanes and bridleways that would have been ancient drovers' routes. The past was mapped into the land, in the place names: Coldharbour Farm, Goose Lane, Bull Tether.

Now, digging and turning the soil, she was rooting herself.

What would the medieval labourer with his hand-plough think of her, living in more affluence than anyone deserved? But working the soil was her connection to that simpler life. Tomorrow she'd finish digging the vegetable garden and plant the seed potatoes. She thought of new potatoes in June, smooth and pale as eggs, scattered by a turn of her fork; food for the family dug out of the ground, reward for her effort.

Anthony's moods were short-lived; he'd more than likely appear later and ask about her day, as if nothing was amiss. When Suzanne came home from school he tended to be exaggeratedly cheerful, making an effort for her, not for Bridget. He never apologised; she knew better than to expect it.

Refusing to let his surliness infect her, she was filled with contentment. There was comfort in the knowledge that whatever happened in her own life, the seasons would turn as they always had, everything in its proper time, unchanging: leaf-burst, bud, flower and fruit. The first swallows of the year were already skimming the field beyond; the swifts would arrive soon, and then it would really be summer.

Jane

DECEMBER

Tom swept up leaves while Suzanne and Jane confronted their father's bedroom.

"It's horrible, clearing out a life." With a gesture of defeat, Suzanne went to the window and looked out. "*Two* lives. And our own. Once we've chucked it all out, what's left?"

"Come on, Suze. It's only stuff. Apart from the photos." Jane picked up a framed photograph of their mother from the chest-of-drawers: Bridget, about twenty years ago, tousle-haired in the garden, squinting into the sun. "One of us should keep this."

"You have it," Suzanne said. "There are others."

They worked briskly. When they'd finished, the room looked sadly vacant. With a view to the estate agent's Monday visit, Jane hoovered, remade the bed and fetched cushions from the spare room. Clothes were sorted and bagged, books taken downstairs for shelving, CDs and gadgets boxed.

"Tea!" Tom yelled from the bottom of the stairs.

"Coming!"

"I'm glad Tom's here." Suzanne shouldered two bin-bags to carry down. "I worry about you, here on your own."

Jane didn't reply. Suzanne was fond of Tom, making her doubt her own misgivings. He was solicitous at the moment, so keen to reinstate himself that she'd given in, pushing away the doubt that she wanted more from a relationship. More *what*, she wasn't sure.

Later, though, she was glad Tom was with her. He made up a log fire in the sitting-room, something she rarely bothered with on her own, and they sprawled on the sofa to watch TV, sharing a bottle of wine.

He filled her glass. "What was that thing Suzanne said as she was leaving? About Sean someone having to agree about the sale?"

"Oh -" Jane was guiltily aware that Suzanne had assumed that Tom knew about the Will. She should have told him; she'd intended to, but the moment had never seemed right, or maybe she couldn't confront her own muddled thoughts on the subject. Now, as she explained, Tom listened with growing incredulity. "I'm sorry," she faltered. "I should have told you before now."

"Christ Almighty!" Tom thumped a clenched fist to his forehead. "Families – who can make sense of them? So this was the point of your big meeting, and you didn't even mention it?"

"I was going to tell you, of course I was. And the cottage – I'm really lucky to be left that, aren't I?"

"It's not the same as including you with the others." Tom took a swig of wine, not looking at her. "What the fuck was your dad up to? Why's this other bloke suddenly so important?"

"I don't know." She was wearied by speculating, and now Tom was huffy, their evening spoiled. She wasn't being fair to him – but how could she be, when her thoughts refused to be corralled into any kind of sense?

• • •

Sam Wade was in her thirties, groomed and trouser-suited, accompanied by a male photographer with a tripod and lighting equipment. She took measurements with a light-beam, made copious notes and talked about gatefold brochures, prominence on property pages, targeting of likely buyers. "Often we get a London client looking for a weekend house in the country."

Weekend house! Jane baulked at that, the obscenity of wealthy people in Hampstead or Kensington or wherever keeping a house of this size for weekends and holidays.

"And there's equestrian potential, with the stableyard and orchard." Sam Wade spoke with professional enthusiasm. "The garden and grounds will be a huge selling-point. Maybe you could email me some shots of the garden in summer?"

"Yes, I can do that. My mother's photographs are all on a hard drive."

"She was a gardener and designer of some note, I gather? A Chelsea medal-winner? That's really impressive."

"Yes." Jane resented the thought of this being used to entice status-conscious buyers. Which would be worse – new owners not appreciating the garden, or going for its one-upmanship potential?

"Would you show me outside? I've got wellies in the car."

"When you do the valuation, could you do it with and without the cottage included?" Jane said, on an impulse. "We haven't decided yet whether to sell it."

"Fine, yes. Your brother said it would be excluded, but I'll certainly do that – it would be useful as a staff cottage. There's separate access?"

Jane put her mother's coat on; the photographer, evidently a hardier breed, stayed as he was, in shirtsleeves. Sam Wade reappeared from her car in tartan wellingtons and a Barbour jacket and they walked around briskly as Jane pointed out the long border, the woodland edge, the bog garden. Jotting down notes, Sam assessed everything with her cool gaze that said yes, this is a good opportunity, but I've seen plenty like it and in better nick.

"What did you say this tree was? – liquid - oh, liquid amber. And there's a vegetable garden – a potager?"

"Yes, through here."

Jane led the way and stood looking at tangled bean stems and clodded earth where potatoes had been dug, a few frosted shoots, withered and brown, showing above ground. "It doesn't look much now, but when Mum looked after it – well, it was just wonderful. It can easily be restored."

"There was a magazine article about it, your brother said?"

"Yes. I'll email it to you if you like. It was making this garden that really started things off for her."

"Good, thanks. And the cottage is this way?"

The tour was soon over, photographic equipment stowed in the car. "Well, thanks for your time, Jane – may I call you Jane? We'll be in touch with your brother."

It's too soon, Jane thought. *Too quickly out of control.* In the business world only money mattered: procedures were initiated, things happened. She hated to think of sharp-eyed buyers pinpointing inadequacies: not enough bathrooms, the kitchen not sleek enough.

Indoors, slowly going upstairs, she smoothed her hand

along the banister rail, apologising to the house. She fancied that Dad might arrive home, his key turning in the lock; he'd stand on the mat, looking around. *What's going on? Who are these strangers? What have you done with all my stuff?* She could hear his voice, aggrieved, affronted.

Bridget

1989: APRIL - JULY

ADAM MOVED INTO HIS workshop the following week. With less equipment than Meg had brought, this didn't take long. He installed a number of large canvases and boards, propping them against the long wall: some blank, others covered by sheets. Then he went away and didn't return for several days.

"He's got a part-time job," Meg told Bridget. "Works with a tree surgeon, he said, helping out. Lots on just now."

"A tree surgeon! That could be useful. We sometimes need work done. Roy's done our work for years, but he's more or less retired."

Bridget felt full of optimism. The structural work on the parterre was almost completed, the raised beds ready, the lean-to greenhouse well under way. She'd wait until autumn to plant box and bay and the fruit trees to fan-train along the west-facing wall, but the beds would be productive this year; she'd grown beans, courgettes and leeks under cover in the barn and would plant them out when the nights were frost-free, with salads to be grown in succession. Later she'd move on to the rest of the garden; there was so much space and light, so much good soil. Deciding to plant a tree, she browsed through books. Maidenhair? Liquidambar? A tulip tree, or a narrow-leaved ash, *fraxinus angustifolia,* so glorious in autumn? She delayed choosing, exhilarated by the possibilities.

"Mum, you're obsessed," Suzanne teased, as Bridget sat with notebooks and catalogues.

Obsession, yes. I've fallen in love, she thought, enticed outside in the early mornings; with this land, these trees, this light. Early birdsong – thrush, pigeons, the silvery descending notes from what she now recognised as a willow-warbler – was both soothing and arousing. The green haze before sunrise gave an almost underwater light, seeming to enter her pores and calm her soul.

She remembered what Meg said about her true thing, the passion and purpose everyone needed in life. This must be hers; aside from having a child she'd never known such involvement, such insatiable energy. As she drifted into sleep at night she saw rows of sturdy beets and swedes, the spears of spring onions, the contrast of marigolds against ruby chard. Her notebook bulged with observations, plans, notes for the herb bed that would be the centrepiece.

At first she'd told Anthony about her project, but he was quickly bored. He spent so many afternoons closeted in his study that she assumed he was making good progress with his book, but whenever she asked he was evasive: "So-so," was all he would say. Or "It's plodding along."

"Aren't you enjoying it?" she asked him in the kitchen, late one evening when Suzanne had gone to bed.

"Enjoying? No." He seemed to find the suggestion ludicrous. "It's work, that's all."

"But it's what you wanted! You were pleased to get the contract."

"Yes, and now it's a flipping albatross round my neck. I'll be glad when it's over."

"And when will that be? Are you on target?"

"Since you ask, no."

Bridget ventured, after a pause, "But surely, if you're putting in the hours it'll happen? Now that you're not doing so much lecturing."

"It's not that simple. You don't understand."

"Well, no, I don't understand economics, but I do understand about -"

About commitment, she was going to say, but he interrupted, "Yes, about cabbages and leeks. Very nice for you. Don't interfere, Bridget, and I won't interfere with your planting plans."

"Why are you so angry?" she burst out.

"I'm not angry. It's you who's shouting."

She gave up. He returned to the sitting-room and *News at Ten,* and she went upstairs.

An early riser, she was also early to bed most nights, sleeping soundly and rarely hearing Anthony get in beside her much later. The double bed was so wide that they slept without touching. Anthony had started to complain that she disturbed him when she rose in the mornings, though she took care not to wake him. During the night of one of their frequent arguments she woke soon after two to find him not there, and wondered if he'd fallen asleep in front of the television. As she crossed the landing she heard steady breathing from the guest bedroom; she looked in and saw that he'd made up the bed and was sprawled there, peacefully asleep.

He said nothing when he came down for breakfast.

"Why the change of room?" she asked indifferently, making coffee.

"A good idea, I thought. We won't disturb each other."

"It's a permanent arrangement, then? Not just for last night?"

"Yes, I don't see why not. We can use the spare second-floor room for guests."

Anyone would think they were in the habit of hosting house-parties. Bridget couldn't recall the last time anyone other than Rob had come to stay.

"Fine," she said.

Only later did she acknowledge that it was relief she felt, instead of regret that the intimate phase of their marriage was apparently over. But in fact it had ended some while ago. When had they last had sex? She found that she couldn't remember. Nowadays they hardly touched. Occasionally, on a good day, one of them might give the other a brief peck on the cheek on leaving or entering the house; that was the limit of their physical contact. Recalling times when they'd burned with desire to be alone together, she might have been thinking of two other people.

She did miss that. But it was not specifically Anthony she missed.

Now she relished having the room to herself, being able to sit up and read at three in the morning if she chose, or get up at first light without creeping around. She moved Anthony's clothes out of the wardrobe, his underwear out of the drawers, his spare watch and glasses from the bedside table.

"Have you two had a row? Or what?" Suzanne asked when she registered the change.

"No, it's just that we get up and go to bed at such different times. This suits us better."

The thought crossed her mind that Anthony could be seeing someone. His comings and goings – meetings, conferences, hotel stays - were so irregular that he could easily cover up. Was he having an affair with a colleague? But the strain, surely, if he were, would show itself in edginess or exhaustion rather than in the gloomy slumps that were ever more frequent. If he was involved with someone, it certainly wasn't making him happy.

His changes of mood were unpredictable. Suddenly, animated and cheerful one Friday evening, he announced: "I thought we'd have an outing tomorrow, the three of us. How about Warwick Castle?" He waved a leaflet. "Look."

"That'd be lovely!" said Bridget, concealing surprise. "There's so much to see, and we've never been."

Anthony busied himself with studying a map and checking opening times. "Suzy, why don't you phone Heather and see if she'd like to come?"

"Helen, you mean. *Can* I?"

"Yes, why not?"

The day out was a great success, in fine spring weather, with the Castle offering more than enough grandeur, precipitous heights, dungeons and waxworks to keep the two girls enthralled.

"We should do this more often," Anthony said, driving home. Bridget thought that perhaps his depression was only a phase, caused by work frustrations. Today was a turning-point; they could still be happy together.

"We should!" she agreed. "It was a lovely idea."

That night she lay awake for a while wondering if he might return to their bed. When he did not, she tiptoed across the landing to the door opposite, which was closed as usual.

She let herself in, pulled back the duvet and climbed into bed, snuggling against his back.

"Anthony?"

Abruptly awake, he twisted to look at her. "What? What d'you want?"

"To be together." She stroked his shoulder, its hunched rigidity matched by her own awkwardness. "I -"

He gave a grunt of protest, shifted himself apart and tugged the duvet tightly around his ears.

"What's the matter with you?" she hissed.

He made no sound. She lay rigid with fury at exposing herself to rejection; she curbed the urge to shout at him, demand an explanation, but Suzanne might hear and anyway he never responded to emotional outbursts.

After gazing into darkness for a few moments she got up and went back to her own bed.

・・・

"I'm not going," Anthony said. "You can go without me."

"But they're expecting us!"

In his chair in front of the TV, feet on a stool, Anthony merely shrugged, eyes on the screen. Suzanne was sprawled on the sofa with a fashion magazine.

"What's wrong?" Bridget tried to sound concerned rather than exasperated. "Aren't you well?"

"I just don't feel like going out. Anyway they're your friends, not mine."

"But you've agreed! You can't back out twenty minutes before we're due to arrive!"

She grabbed the remote control from the arm of his chair, and clicked the Off switch. Suzanne turned a page with an air of martyrdom; Anthony looked at Bridget with cold contempt.

"Don't get hysterical."

"Hysterical -"

"You can go on your own, can't you? What's the problem?"

"*You're* the problem - I don't want to go on my own! It's unfair to Mike and Hilary. They'll have cooked for you, set a place."

"Tell them I was taken ill at the last minute." Anthony tilted his head back and closed his eyes. "A stomach upset."

"You expect me to lie for you?"

"Oh, for Christ's sake," Suzanne muttered from the sofa. "Give it a rest, you two."

Bridget knew it was hopeless trying to persuade him. If she succeeded, he'd sit at their hosts' table silent and morose, which would embarrass her more than lying about his absence. She should have guessed. Half an hour earlier, going upstairs to get ready, she'd called to him, "We'll leave at seven, OK?" and received a grunt in reply. He hadn't moved since. Earlier in the day she'd ignored his grumbles: "Blast, we're going out tonight, aren't we? Who *are* these people? Why rope me in? I suppose you'll want to invite them back."

Pausing now in the hallway, she heard laughter from the TV, louder than before. She glowered at herself in the mirror. Even before the altercation she'd felt self-conscious in a flowered dress she rarely wore and sandals with heels. Her hair was misbehaving, kinking into a silly wave at the front. She tweaked at it without result, then took a perfume spray from her bag and squirted it crossly at her neck, the light fragrance only emphasising what a charade this was.

She picked up her car keys, the bottle of wine and garden flowers she'd put ready, and left.

We shouldn't argue in front of Suzanne, she berated herself. Or was it worse to quarrel in private, presenting a front of harmony when Suzanne was present? She was bright enough to see through that, for sure.

Mike and Hilary Morgan were acquaintances rather than friends; she'd met them at a talk by a celebrity gardener at the local library, and fallen into conversation. Hearing of her plans they'd invited her to see their cottage garden near Haverton, and now for dinner. Driving, she rehearsed what to say. The evening was still and warm; a combine moved slowly through a barley field, raising a cloud of dust. The roadside ditches were lush with meadowsweet and willowherb, the ash and poplar trees heavy with leaf. Normally she'd relish the beauty of the evening, but now it emphasised her discontent.

Our marriage is a sham, she thought. When Anthony behaved like this, being in the same room made her skin prickle and harsh words form in her throat, sometimes swallowed whole, sometimes spat out. In more self-reproachful moods she told herself to try harder, humour and cajole him instead of being so quickly impatient. She imagined a different version of herself who could put on the necessary acting performance to win him round, but knew that she couldn't do it. Maybe she just didn't care enough.

I may have loved him once, she thought, but I don't now. And he doesn't love me. She looked back with a blend of pity and scorn on the younger self who'd been so in thrall to him, so easily charmed.

I must leave. I can't go on like this.

She resolved to find a way of telling him. It would be terribly upsetting for Suzanne, and her mind churned at all the practicalities, but it was the only honest thing to do.

Her solo arrival at the Morgans' house was greeted with surprise, then kindly concern as she explained. "I'm so sorry.

Anthony won't be joining us. A nasty stomach bug – really sudden – he just doesn't feel up to leaving the house."

Her words rang falsely; she was no actress.

"Oh, what a shame! We were so looking forward to meeting him." If her hosts suspected she was bluffing, they didn't show it. "I do hope it's nothing more."

Once that awkwardness was over she enjoyed the evening more than she'd expected. If Anthony *had* come, would he have cheered up? Or infected everyone with his sulk? She imagined the Morgans enquiring about his work, Anthony answering monosyllabically, withdrawing into himself. On the increasingly rare occasions when they were seen as a couple, she'd come to resent it. She disliked even the word *couple*, with its overtone of identity surrendered to complacent cosiness.

Driving home, quite late, she hoped not to see Anthony until morning.

Jane

DECEMBER

THE DRIVE TO MEG'S took her into the Cotswolds: high, open landscape patched by cloud shadows, through Stow-on-the-Wold and on to the wooded hills and valleys north of Stroud. Almost there, early, she stopped at a roadside café, using the time to prepare notes for next day's classes. Christmas music jangled, a grinning reindeer stood beside the menu holder on her table and the counter was strung with lights. *Finish buying presents*, she wrote. She'd bought a few things in India but had barely thought about Christmas since arriving home.

She felt nervous of meeting Meg, of what she might know.

At Mum's funeral Meg had looked unfamiliar in a formal coat and black hat, sitting alone at the end of a pew. Daunted by the task of keeping control of herself and being civil to everyone, Jane meant to speak to her afterwards, but Meg didn't return to the house with the other mourners. They met a few times in the following weeks, when Meg was clearing the cottage and workshop, Jane fully occupied with her new job in Oxford as well as supporting her father. There had been only intermittent contact since. Although she'd thought of coming over, she never had.

With SatNav and Meg's directions she found her destination. Behind stone walls, a barn conversion overlooked a tree-lined valley where a threading stream caught the light. A chill breeze tugged at her hair and scarf as she got out of the car. She turned up her collar and looked at the house, timber-clad, with a high window revealing a wooden staircase. She saw a huge copper vase of bulrushes and a dark-red painting on an inner wall. Was this where Meg lived? Surely not, unless her business had taken off spectacularly.

A stony track led towards sheep pasture below. There were stone outbuildings, a lighted window in the nearest one, and a slate plaque: *FERNHILL BARN*.

The door opened to her push. There inside was Meg, washing mugs at a sink.

"Jane! Come on in."

"Hello! Is my car in anyone's way, in the yard?"

"No, fine. How are you?"

"OK, thanks. Well – it's been a bit awful lately. Thanks for your card. And for visiting Dad in hospital. It was a long way to go."

Meg shook her head, opening a cupboard. "Coffee, tea? I've got Earl Grey, Assam or mint."

"Mint, please."

The workshop was long and low, with a stone floor and plastered walls. Meg was well-equipped here, more amply than at Wildings: as well as the sink, she had a fridge, well-stocked cupboard and two-ring cooker. There was a table with three chairs, and a wood-burning stove threw out warmth. Taking off her coat and scarf, Jane thought that Meg had hardly changed.

She wore her habitual winter clothes - jeans, polo sweater, fleece gilet - and her hair, shorter than before and iron-grey now, sprang out in thick curls. She must be well into her fifties, but was the sort of person for whom age seemed irrelevant.

"It's a lovely place," Jane remarked, looking at Meg's work in progress, a headstone with pencilled design and letters she had begun to cut. A finished one stood on a second easel nearby. The workbench held smaller pieces and a row of books supported by carved bookends.

"Yes. I was lucky to find it." Meg poured steaming water. "I've got an apprentice now, a lad of twenty. He works here two days a week and goes to Bath College the rest of the time."

"Do you live here?"

Meg laughed. "In my dreams! I couldn't begin to afford that barn. I moved in before the conversion, and the new owners were happy for me to stay on. I live in Stroud, sharing a house. I've got a partner now."

"Oh?" Taking it that Meg didn't mean a business partner, Jane couldn't hide her surprise.

"Yes. Robin. We've been together nearly two years."

The androgynous name didn't answer the question in Jane's mind.

"How did you meet?"

"Robin's a photographer. Freelance. Saw my website and wanted to come to the workshop to take photos, black and white. Lots of them are on my website."

No help there. Jane nodded encouragingly. "I saw them. Lovely."

Meg went on, "Few days later I was installing a gravestone and needed a hand. So I asked her to come along. After that we kept seeing each other, more and more, till it made sense to move in together."

Meg held her gaze as if gauging her reaction; Jane looked steadily back, surprised more by Meg having a partner at all than by Robin's gender.

"Sorry. Could have helped you out there." Meg gave her an amused look. "Saw you waiting for a personal pronoun."

This seemed to require an answer. Jane said, "That's great, Meg. I suppose – I thought you just didn't need anyone."

Meg shrugged. "That's what I thought, too. I was OK on my own, so was she, and that was part of the attraction. Never expected it. Certainly wasn't looking."

"I'm really glad for you."

Meg reached into the cupboard for biscuits, signalling that she'd talked enough about her personal life. "Tell me about your trip to India. I know you had to cut it short – must have been awful. But before that. Was it your first time there?"

While she answered, Jane glanced at the drawings and photographs pinned to a long noticeboard. Several of the photographs were also on the website, but – she couldn't help exclaiming – here was one of Meg and her mother in their artisan's garden at the 2011 Chelsea Flower Show, Mum holding the silver-gilt certificate, both grinning in a slightly dazed way.

She moved to the board for a closer look. *It's a piece of ephemera,* she remembered her mother saying. *There for a week, then we take it all apart and it might never have existed.* When the stone and the soil, the plants and the mulch, the pump and stream lining were taken away, there was only a ravaged square of mud and grass to show where their creation had been, the high point of their partnership.

"That's not on the website, is it?" Jane asked, thinking that most people would put a Chelsea medal prominently on their Home page, even if the award was for garden design.

Meg came over with the mug of tea. "That? No, I don't think it is."

Something else caught Jane's eye as she turned towards Meg - her mother's name, in pencilled letters on A3 paper:

Bridget Harper, gardener and maker, 1943-2013

Above the name and dates was a design of a thrush on an ash twig, and the words *The thrushes sing as the sun is going ... as if all Time were theirs.* A design for a headstone, pinned up alongside others.

She let out an exclamation; Meg, bringing her own mug to the table, said, "That's the one that never got made."

"Oh, Meg, I wish you had! It'd be a million times better than the one she's got."

Meg was silent. Jane sat too, clasping her tea, all her questions supplanted by the one she now asked. "Why didn't you? We always wondered – Suzanne and I – why Dad went for something so ordinary. Why he didn't ask you. Did something happen?"

Meg gave her a straight look. "Anthony did ask me."

"So, why -?" Jane glanced at the drawing. "That would have been perfect!"

"I did that one for myself. His was different. He wanted it to say *Bridget, beloved wife of Anthony Harper* – which is what he went and had done. As you know. *Wife* – as if she'd been nothing in her own right. I suggested some changes, did some sketches and sent them. He never replied. Must have taken offence with me for interfering, but it was hard not to, when -" Meg stopped, shaking her head.

"When what?"

"When I was only trying to help. But I was too involved to keep quiet."

"So you didn't meet him, to discuss this?" Jane asked.

If Meg had returned to Wildings, her father had never mentioned it.

"No, it was by email and post. Next I knew, he'd commissioned something else, left me out altogether. Well, it was you who told me that."

"He could have found another stone-carver," Jane said, aware that her father's choice could only have been meant as a slight to Meg.

"Yes, he could."

Jane hesitated. "You didn't like him, did you?"

"I – well." Meg's expression suggested that she could say a lot more than she was going to. "They had an odd marriage, your parents. Unconventional. You must have realised that. I don't usually edit what people put on headstones. They can have what they want."

"You thought he didn't love her?"

"Maybe he did, in his peculiar way. Who knows? But it's all wrong, that other headstone."

"You've seen it, been to the graveyard?"

"More than once."

"You could have come to see us," Jane said, with reproach.

"Us? You and Anthony?" Meg raised an eyebrow. "I thought about it – coming to see *you,* I mean - but didn't. I've never thought it's a good idea, going back. Best leave things in the past."

"Perhaps it's not too late for the headstone, though?" Jane looked at her hopefully. "I'd rather get rid of the whole thing and start again, properly. Would you? I wanted to talk to you first. I haven't mentioned it to Rob yet."

"And he'll jump at the chance, you think?" Meg said drily.

"Suzanne and I can persuade him. Or go ahead without him."

"I'll do it." Meg nodded towards the noticeboard. "Course I will. It's been waiting there all this time. But you might want something different."

"We won't!"

"I should have come to see you," Meg said. "I often wonder how you're getting on. I'm useless at keeping in touch, but I was there all the time you were growing up, then nothing. My fault."

"Mine too. Anyway, here I am. What I don't get, though, is why you went all the way to Northampton when Dad asked? After you'd parted like that?"

Meg gave a tight-lipped smile. "Needn't have, but Suzanne wanted me to go. Anyway, I was curious. It's hard to ignore a dying person, whether you like them or not."

"So what did he say?"

"He was beyond talking - it must have been near the end. But I think he knew I was there. It took a huge effort to speak. *Sorry,* was all he said. Whispered, rather. *Sorry.* That's all."

Jane felt a twist of regret at her own failure to arrive in time. She saw the bright hospital corridors stretching ahead, herself hurrying, hurrying, as she had in dreams several times since. Always too late.

"What did you say?"

"I said, *That's all right.* I only stayed a few minutes. Rob was with him and he obviously didn't want me there."

"*Sorry,* though? What d'you think he meant?"

"I can think of lots of things for him to be sorry about. Maybe the headstone. Not doing what Bridget wanted."

Jane considered what more her father would have said if he'd been able to. Not sure whether she should mention this, she did anyway: "I don't know if the solicitor's been in touch, but he will be. Dad's left you ten thousand pounds in his Will."

"You're joking." Meg's eyes opened wide. "Ten thousand? To me? What for?"

"We don't know."

"For the headstone? But wouldn't he have specified, if that's what he meant?" Meg shook her head. "It wouldn't cost that much, anyway. I'd soon be out of business if it did."

"I haven't seen the Will. It was Rob who went to the solicitor – he's Dad's executor. But it can't have said what the money was for. Rob would have told us."

Meg sat back, frowning. After a few moments she got up to refill the kettle. "So what happens to the house, now? It goes to Rob, I suppose? Will he live there? It's a big old place to run."

"Well – that's what we all thought. And yes. I don't know if it can be made more energy-efficient – I did talk to Dad about solar panels and ground source heating, but he wasn't keen. The heating's oil - I dread to think what its carbon footprint is. But tell me more about Mum and Dad being unconventional. When people say that, they usually mean there were affairs, don't they?"

The guarded expression on Meg's face was answer enough.

"So you knew about them? And did you know," Jane went on, "about Sean McBride?"

"Who's he?"

"Dad's son."

There could be no doubting Meg's astonishment. "Son? He had another son?"

"We only found out from the Will. Dad's left a share of the house to this Sean McBride, yes, another son we had no idea of. So you didn't, either?"

Meg said decisively, "Never heard of him."

"Do you have any idea who the mother might be?"

"How old is he?"

"We don't know," Jane said. "From something Marie said, I think he's around my age, or older. Did you know Marie?"

Meg nodded, and Jane told her what Marie had said, and about the proceeds of the estate being split three ways. "So Rob doesn't get the house. None of us had a clue about this. But I wondered if you did? I mean, you were around then, before I was born. Did Mum tell you, even hint?"

Meg shook her head. "I'm sure she didn't know. Anthony had plenty of chances for affairs, and I did know about Marie – that was no secret. I'm sure Bridget would've told me if she'd known."

"She talked to you about Dad?"

"Sometimes." Meg's guarded expression returned. "Well. Quite often. She – found him difficult to live with. He was moody, unpredictable. Saw that for myself often enough. Once I asked why she didn't leave. I know I would have."

"What did she say?"

"She said they needed each other. Said she knew it sounded odd, but they did."

...

Driving home, Jane thought about this. In darkness her headlights picked out dried grass and thistles by the roadside, and once a fox, brush streaming as it ran across the lane, long and low.

They needed each other. She'd seen how her father crumpled after Mum's death, all purpose seeming to leave him. He was interested in nothing, sitting for hours alone in his study. Once, when he was out, Jane saw that he'd left *The Collected Poems of Thomas Hardy* - the copy from which they'd chosen the poem for the funeral service, with her mother's former name *Bridget Williams* inscribed on the fly-leaf – face-down on the desk. It was open at *Poems 1920-21,* the verses Hardy wrote after the death of his wife Emma. Simple, poignant poems of loss and grief, of love not acknowledged until its object was gone.

Her mind replayed the conversation, fastening on Meg's response to the question about affairs. And something else: Meg had a female partner now.

Meg was so direct in some ways, so secretive in others. Jane had suspected she was lesbian, concluding that work was everything to Meg and that she either didn't want a partner or hadn't found one.

Could the relationship between Meg and her mother have been more than friendship? Didn't everything point to that? The headstone, the dispute with Dad, Meg's departure from Wildings because there was no point staying on without Bridget ... and did Meg's hesitation about affairs mean that it wasn't only Anthony who'd had one?

She'd found out nothing new about Sean McBride. Instead she was seeing her parents as strangers, with unfathomable lives and motives.

Meg

1990, FEBRUARY

MEG HADN'T GOT OVER her initial wariness of Adam. Dazzled by his maleness and proximity she could barely look him in the eye, though she cast many a glance, careful not to let him see. He seemed oblivious, to her annoyance – as if female admiration was his due. Analysing this, she had to question its logic. How could she blame him for not noticing the attention she took such pains to conceal?

At first begrudging his intrusion into her work space, she was mellowed by his easy friendliness and generous praise. On warmer days her door was open, and he often came in to see what she was doing.

"That's beautiful. The way you've spaced the letters. The way the light catches them."

"Yes, well. That's the whole thing."

Sunlight glinted on the hairs of his wrist and forearm as he touched the curved ascender of an italic d. His hand was eloquent, long-fingered, the thumbnail smeared with green paint.

"Don't you find it morbid, always thinking about death?"

She shrugged. "No. The way I look at it, my work will last for ever."

"When mine's long gone, you mean. Chucked in a skip."

"I wasn't implying anything about you or your paintings," she said, laughing at his solipsism. "These letters I'm cutting, they'll be around long after I've gone. Isn't that what any artist would want?"

Whenever she came straight back at him he looked drily amused, as if he enjoyed provoking her.

She didn't reciprocate by praising his work. His huge canvases were splashed with paint, randomly she thought, with runs and dribbles and smudges. If there was skill in that, she couldn't see it. Carefully non-committal, she asked about his influences.

He named John Hoyland, Patrick Heron, Cy Twombly, Don Inchbold. "Especially Hoyland. The way he uses textures, what he makes the paint do. Or lets it do."

Meg had seen a documentary about John Hoyland, but the other names meant nothing.

"All men?"

"Gillian Ayres, maybe. I like Bridget Riley but I couldn't say she's an influence."

Previously, he told her, he'd used a friend's garage as his workshop, storing canvases in the rafters. He'd had minor success with local exhibitions and galleries, selling two or three paintings a year. Then the friend moved away, and as Adam's flat was too small for his work and materials he'd looked for a space to rent, and happened to see Bridget's advert. He said little about family, but one weekend mentioned visiting his parents in Derbyshire.

"Do they encourage you with the painting?" she asked.

"Not really. Mum liked the stuff I did in the sixth form, but this – she doesn't exactly say, but she thinks it's crap." A pause, then: "Like you do."

Meg tried to cover the truth of this with a laugh. "I don't really get abstract painting."

"That's OK," he said easily. "I don't mind."

• • •

Next time they met, she told him, "I looked up those painters you talked about. I like Don Inchbold, those moony ones from the sixties. The others do nothing for me."

"He's probably the easiest to like," Adam agreed.

"Patronising!"

"*Not* what I meant. I like his moon ones too."

She was by the window, beginning to cut letters on a piece of Portland. On this mild morning her door was open to the spill of sunlight and the purposeful call of birds. Adam had seen the open door as an invitation to come in, and watched as she cut the serif of a T. There was silence apart from the *tink, tink* of her chisel. At first when he watched her work she'd felt self-conscious, irritated by his way of casually wandering in, but had come to accept and even like it, relishing her own skill in a way that rarely occurred to her.

He said, "You're serious about your work, aren't you?"

"Well, course." She spared him a scathing glance. "People don't want frivolity when I'm making them a gravestone."

"I meant generally. Stone. This is you. This is what you do."

"Yes. It's my one true thing. The thing that makes sense of my life."

"You've been let down in other ways?"

She chose not to answer, angling her chisel for the left-hand side of the stem. "I know it looks deadly dull to anyone who doesn't get it. You must be serious too? About your painting?"

Adam was leaning against the bench, arms folded, one leg crossed over the other, in no hurry to leave. "I like messing about with paint and sometimes selling a piece. I don't feel *driven,* the way you do."

"The drive to live and eat and have a roof over my head is quite strong."

"Well, yeah. You do better than me, but then you work much harder. I'll never support myself by painting, that's for sure."

"But you rent a studio. That makes it more than a hobby."

"It is more than a hobby. I couldn't not do it."

"Then you *are* driven." She wondered why their conversations so often turned to sparring.

He shrugged. "If you insist. Driven but lazy."

"Anyway, why are you standing around? Haven't you got anything to do?"

"I have. I'm doing some tree-pruning for Bridget." He looked at his watch. "I'll go up to the house, as you're not offering coffee. She will, I expect. See you later."

Through the doorway Meg saw him fetch his kit from the van – tool-bag, chainsaw, helmet. He slammed the doors, then glanced over and smiled as he headed for the archway. Irked that he'd seen her watching, she went back to her T.

She felt uneasy at the thought of Bridget making plans with Adam, involving him in her projects. But why should she mind? Bridget wanted her trees pruned; Adam was handy with skills and equipment, and needed the money.

Her chisel hit a resilient piece of fossil in the valley of the letter-stem, flying off without making an impression. She leaned close to examine it. Spoiling the clean line of the letter would ruin the whole headstone.

. . .

So much alone, she was nostalgic for the days of her apprenticeship at the Kindersley workshop in Cambridge. She'd trained for three years, at first a novice, later mentoring a newcomer. It seemed that the focus of her life was held and preserved in the slanting light of the converted schoolroom, where photographs and examples covered every available wall-space and there was always someone chipping at a headstone or plaque, while someone else sat drawing at the table. David Kindersley was a kindly, reassuring presence; his young wife Lida was full of calm energy, making the work fresh and vital. Meg felt privileged to be taught by someone trained by Eric Gill himself – it put her in a direct line, which meant that she in turn ought eventually to pass on her skills to the next generation.

Time passed quickly there, and slowly.

"Blimey, don't you get sick of tap-tapping away all day long?" Uncle Terry used to say. "Do my head in, that would."

"But it's not boring. It takes your whole attention."

It was hard to convey the deep satisfaction of spending hours at a time with her gaze fixed on a piece of stone a foot from her nose. She was absorbed in marking the valley-cuts of each curve and straight, each tail and ascender, at precisely the same angle, spacing her letters perfectly; aware of rhythmic tapping all around her from others, and the work they were slowly creating. The fall of light on a newly cut letter was timeless: beauty, grace and meaning created through simple technique from a chunk of prehistoric stone prised out of the ground. It pleased and humbled her that she and the others could be transported back two hundred years, or five hundred, or eight, with little difference to their working practices. They were continuing the tradition established over centuries through the skill and dedication of anonymous stonemasons, developed by master-craftsmen like Eric Gill and David Kindersley.

Mid-morning, everyone gathered round the central table for coffee, chat and the daily crossword. They shared an easy companionship, this group of disparate people drawn to the workshop for various reasons: some from a background in fine art, others who'd learned calligraphy or experimented with woodcarving. They were disciples, willingly submitting to years of work and study for the reward of handling the tools and making marks in stone. She was proud to be one of them.

Bridget

1990, FEBRUARY

TAKING COFFEE TO ANTHONY she found him slumped in his chair. He quickly sat forward, feigning interest in his screen; as she placed the mug beside him he gave a barely audible grunt.

"Thank you," she prompted.

Silence. Anthony picked up a pen; then said, "Thank you. Very good of you."

She almost turned to go, then made up her mind.

For days she'd rehearsed this. The time was never right: his mood unreceptive, or Suzanne around, or it was just too easy to put off.

Now.

"What's wrong?" she asked. "If something's worrying you, can't you tell me?"

The set of his shoulders told her she wouldn't get far, but she persisted.

"Anthony - I really think you should see a doctor. I'm worried about you. Shall I make an appointment?"

He looked at her for the first time. "What on earth for?"

"About your moods. Your depression." She saw him register the word. "Dr Stevens could help. There are treatments. I think we should look into it."

Anthony had picked up the mug but now plonked it down, splashing coffee. "I've no idea what you mean."

"You do know. Your moods. Your ups and downs – well, the downs. It's not right. You're not yourself."

"You think I'm mentally ill? Is that what you're saying?"

"I suppose depression is a mental illness. But it's not a stigma. It's a recognised condition. You don't need to go on suffering when there's medical help available."

Sitting down would make her posture less confrontational, but the spare chair was heaped with folders.

Anthony gave her a cold stare. "Drugs, you mean? You want me to dope myself up like a junkie?"

"I'm suggesting you should seek professional help. There's obviously something wrong. Something that could be put right."

"You assume. So you're an expert?"

"Of course not, but -"

"Look. I refuse to go whingeing to Dr Stevens, moaning that I get a bit fed up sometimes. Doesn't everyone? He'd tell me to get a grip and stop wasting his time."

"No, he wouldn't -"

"For God's sake! It's not as if you don't have your moods. I should know. Leave me alone. *You're* the one who needs help, getting hysterical over nothing."

"I'm not in the least hysterical." Bridget kept her voice exaggeratedly low and calm, hearing how irritating that must sound. "As I said, I'm concerned for you. You're not easy to live with. I – we – never know what to expect."

"Why can't you accept that this is how I am?"

"Because – you can't possibly be happy. And I can't, and neither can Suzanne – it's unfair to her. You've seen how it affects her." She paused. "Can't we talk about this properly, instead of arguing?"

"No, I'm busy. There's nothing to discuss – I'm perfectly fine. Please go away."

She left the study, closing the door firmly. In the hallway she let out a deep sigh. That had achieved nothing. A different kind of wife could raise the matter in bed, or while snuggled on the sofa. She and Anthony didn't do snuggling any more, let alone share a bed. How could she possibly approach him in a way he'd accept? All she'd achieved was to ensure that he'd react with hostility if she tried again. She replayed it, hearing the aloofness in his voice. And she'd been primly self-righteous. She'd only made things worse. As usual.

Her obstinacy hardened. She refused to let Anthony make her miserable. With so much to make him content - a lovely home, herself and Suzanne, more than adequate means, and health and strength – it was perverse to wallow in self-pity. From background reading she knew that depression was illogical, unreasoning, and that telling a sufferer to be grateful was insensitive and useless. But if Anthony rebuffed her, scorned every suggestion, what could she do?

The thought crossed her mind, as it had before, that he could be seeing someone else; that the strain of an affair was making him tense and uncommunicative. He had plenty of opportunity; she was vague about where he went for meetings and conferences. There could be a colleague, or – less acceptably – a student. Would he risk that?

I'd rather know, she thought, surprised to feel not outrage but weary acceptance. And then? If it were out in the open, she'd have adequate reason to leave. But if he really was suffering from clinical depression, would it be fair to walk out, no matter what he'd done?

Wearied by indecision, her mood veered between hopelessness and resignation.

She'd stay with him for Suzanne's sake.

She'd leave, taking Suzanne with her.

Which? When?

Easier, far easier, to do nothing.

As usual when perturbed, she pulled on boots and a coat and went out into fitful sunshine and a buffeting wind. There was bare earth in the beds, dug over and weeded, but the green spears of daffodils were showing, snowdrops and a few premature primroses already in flower. She felt a rush of love. The tangles of clematis looked bare but a closer glance showed the paired buds greening and swelling. Everything was poised for spring.

She thought: how could I leave this? It's part of me now: the best part.

Jane

DECEMBER

The box of decorations was in the spare bedroom. Jane's mother had loved dressing a large tree for Christmas; this last time, she'd buy a tree and do it herself. She unpacked, piece by piece, lining them up on the windowsill.

Many of the decorations were hand-crafted, bought over the years at art fairs; there were also silver-sprayed pine cones and items made by Jane as a child. She lingered over the angel she'd made in bedroom secrecy, aged nine or so; she recalled cutting the thin card, glueing arms, wings and halo, drawing the face in fine pen, eyes looking up as if to heaven, mouth open, singing; delicate touches to wings and halo, brush tipped with precious gold paint from the art shop. Then downstairs, holding her creation aloft: "Look what I've made!" and her mother's delight. "Oh, how *beautiful* – perfect! She must go on top of the tree."

The angel had been fastened to the tree's leading shoot every Christmas since, ready to fly – until the year of Bridget's death, when joyous flight would have been incongruous. That Christmas, the first without her mother, had been the strangest and worst of Jane's life, though this one might surpass it. She'd made a ceremony of opening the cards each day, reading messages to her father in an effort to cheer him, but there was no tree that year. Christmas Days since had been spent at Suzanne's. Bridget was so much the presiding spirit of Wildings that Christmas without her would be hollow.

December 21st had been the day for bringing the tree indoors. It was Mum's ritual on the winter solstice, a day of more significance, she said, than Christmas. "The turning of the year. Rebirth of the light. An ancient marker-point."

Jane remembered Mum saying that, the kitchen scented with cinnamon and cloves from cider warming on the stove. Dad had teased her, joking about her pagan tendencies, asking if she'd gone out at dawn to dance naked round a tree. He dipped a ladle into the cider and stirred it, releasing a waft of fragrant steam.

"I *was* outside at dawn," Mum said. "Of course, on this special day. But with plenty of clothes on. It was perishing cold."

It was a consolation to remember a time when they'd seemed happy together.

· · ·

Christmas at Suzanne's was a family occasion. With Ed's parents, his brother and sister-in-law and their young children, and Rhiannon's boyfriend, there were eleven people for Christmas Day lunch, and a vast amount of clearing-up afterwards.

"It's good to have the children," Suzanne said, as she and Jane confronted kitchen wreckage. "Stops us from getting morose. I can't face this yet - let's have another coffee. Have you thought what to do with the money Dad left you?"

"Not really. I could put it towards paying off my student loan, but that doesn't seem special enough, and wouldn't cover it, anyway. I wonder what Dad had in mind? Get myself an electric car? Or I could buy things for the cottage. It'd feel weird, moving in. I still think of it as Meg's."

"That's daft!" said Suzanne. "She moved out years ago and she's got her own place, didn't you say? Anyway, tell me more about your visit."

Jane told her about Meg's set-up, and her genuine surprise when the name Sean McBride was mentioned. "She knew about Dad and Marie, but she was certain Mum had never heard of Sean. And she was matter of fact about the house going up for sale. Said it'd be a very expensive white elephant, otherwise."

"True. I'm coming round to thinking the same."

"Maybe I'll go over again." This wasn't the time for questions about how close Meg and their mother had been; not now, with so many people around and so little time to talk.

"We could both go," Suzanne agreed. "I feel bad about letting things slip."

"She told me she asked Mum, once, why she didn't leave Dad. So she must've known things weren't easy."

"They weren't." In spite of what she'd said, Suzanne was making a start on the pans. "I remember awful rows. One in particular, when I got really upset, and gave them an ultimatum – I told them 'Stop this, or I'm leaving.' I was sixteen, O-Level time. And worse than rows, there were the silences. I hated that. At one time I was sure they'd split up. I even *wanted* them to, though I was frightened of it, as well. From selfish reasons, I guess, at that age."

Jane assimilated this. She couldn't remember her parents quarrelling; rather, it seemed that they'd reached a compromise of mutual tolerance. But then, after her mother died – no one could have thought Dad's grief insincere.

"But why *did* they stay together? There must have been something - Mum told Meg that they needed each other. Maybe you're right, they only stayed together for our sake? But what you said about me saving the marriage - I assumed I was a mistake. Mum said so."

"Did she?" Suzanne looked up from scrubbing a baking tray. "Oh, Janey, she shouldn't have. That's a tactless thing to tell a child."

"No, it wasn't like that. She made it sound special." Jane dried a saucepan, thinking of Mum cuddling her, saying, *You were a mistake. A precious one. It was as if you came from nowhere.* She'd pictured herself as an airy spirit, drifting in like a leaf through a window, a gift to the parents she'd chosen. Later, wondering more realistically how they could have conceived a child without intending to, she never doubted that she was loved and wanted.

"I remember being astonished when Mum told me she was pregnant," Suzanne said. "They'd had separate rooms for a while by then. I was typical teenager about that – you know, horrified at what must have been going on."

"Them having sex at such an advanced age?"

"Yes, late forties, fifty. Doesn't seem so incredibly old now, does it? Mum was only three years older than I am. The thought of having a baby in three years' time would be a bit much, but, well, my friend Jackie's trying IVF at forty-four. It's not unusual now, women having babies in their forties, but I was embarrassed at school, saying my mum was pregnant. It was exciting, too, though. When you came I was thrilled."

"I remember you looking after me. Playing games, reading stories. Bossing, sometimes."

"Yes, I loved all that."

"So – the awful rows you remember – could those have been about Dad having an affair, another one, before Marie? Which would make Sean McBride much older than me?"

"Possible, I suppose."

"Come on, you two!" Rhiannon was in the doorway. "Leave all that. We're ready for the quiz."

Bridget

1990, FEBRUARY

HER SEED PACKETS WERE her treasure. She exulted in looking through them, feeling the firmness of beans under her fingers, the fine trickle of spring onion seed, reading the packet's luxuriant promises. It was time for first sowings, in pots and trays in the barn: beetroot, leeks, spring onions, sweet peas. The hardier broad beans were in the cold-frame, parsnips and shallots already in the parterre beds. Seed potatoes were already sprouting their fleshy, purplish-green shoots. Next would come dwarf beans, carrots, courgettes. She pictured herself with trug and sun hat, unearthing potatoes, picking salads and fruit, creating wholesome meals for an appreciative family.

She recorded everything in two notebooks. In one she listed seed varieties, dates of sowing and first germination. In the other, liking the absorption of writing, she made observations of hoar frost, winds and skies and clouds, days of mild sunshine. She noted a blue tit investigating a nest-box, a woodpigeon strutting after a mate, a cock pheasant on the lawn, its plumage rich bronze against frosted grass. She recorded the budding of a clematis, the first unfurling of a scarlet camellia from its tight bud. The box and bay in the parterre had survived winter and now she made ready for runner beans and sweet peas, making wigwams from sturdy hazel poles.

She lost track of time, emerging only when she was hungry or realised that Suzanne would soon be home from school. Everything else took second place. With the income from workshop tenants, she now paid a cleaner to come twice weekly; she had no wish to spend her time on housework. The cooking was enough, and she found ways of making things last: casseroles to last two or three days, extra portions stored in the freezer. Often she came indoors giddy with tiredness; at night she dreamed of her garden, her attention turning to an overgrown bed, a planting opportunity not yet taken.

Work on Stables Cottage was progressing; the interior painting would be done, the garden tidied, and then it would be ready to let. Tempted to do the painting herself, she knew that it would take too long, with every room needing attention.

Walking out to the orchard with Adam to discuss the pruning of apple trees, she mentioned the need for a painter. "We used to know someone, but he's retired now."

"I could do that," Adam said promptly. "I used to work for a painter and decorator."

"Oh, *would* you?"

"Sure. I've got a few tree jobs lined up, but I can fit round those."

He'd been trimming the orchard hedges; properly, by hand. Bridget hated to see the carnage wrought by mechanical trimmers – twigs ripped out, raw ends hanging. He knew about trees, identifying wild service, Midland hawthorn and spindle; he'd learned from the friend of his dad's he worked with, he told her. The prunings were heaped at the end of the orchard, and he asked if he could burn them. "Not now - it's too damp. When the weather's a bit drier."

"Good idea. Only please move the whole heap before you light it. There might be hedgehogs in it."

She thought Adam might be scornful of that, but he agreed. Within days the weather turned sharp and frosty, and he lit the fire on Saturday afternoon. Bridget and Suzanne went to watch, Suzanne excited at the prospect of a bonfire, even at the age of sixteen. Adam had moved the heaped branches as requested, and now tucked kindling and paper all around.

It took a while, Adam and Suzanne darting around with matches and tapers. Flames flared briefly, catching, then a steadier, golden glow as fire spread through the kindling, touching twigs and branches, taking hold. Bridget stamped her feet, chilled in spite of layers of clothing, but at last the branches were properly blazing and she took off her gloves, holding out her hands to be warmed. The smoke was acrid-sweet, making Suzanne cough. Burning wood shifted and settled, and Adam threw stray branches farther in; flakes of paper and cinder floated in the air.

The day was ending with a calm pink sunset, the western sky seeming to reflect the glow of the flames. Bridget thought how primeval it felt to make fire, holding back the darkness; to stand mesmerised, the front of her body too hot and her back too cold, unwilling to leave this source of light and crackling energy. The new moon hung over the house, and a first star made a bright pinpoint, others emerging as she watched. It felt like an ancient ritual - herself, Suzanne and

Adam circling and surrounding the fire, held and bathed by its warmth. Smoke curled and billowed, blue-grey, holding the last of the light.

"We should have done this on Firework Night!" Suzanne called.

"Why don't we, this year?" Bridget told her. "Have a party for your friends."

"Cool! But we will be able to put it out, won't we?" Suzanne asked, turning to Adam.

"Yes, don't worry. I've got plenty of damp leaves and moss to throw over it when we're done."

"What's going on here?"

Abruptly the spell of fire and winter dusk was broken by Anthony's voice as he approached from the garden, walking fast.

"Dad," Suzanne said, in a tone of resignation.

"What the hell's this? I thought something was on fire."

"The fire's on fire," Suzanne told him, laughing. "It's all right, Dad!"

As Anthony came closer Bridget saw how pompous he looked, jutting his chin as if confronting a trespasser.

"You might have warned me," he said crossly. "Are you sure it's safe? Why wait till dark, for God's sake?"

"Because it's more fun." Suzanne stretched out both arms and let them flop. "*Honestly,* Dad."

Anthony hadn't acknowledged Adam, who was standing back. Awkwardly Bridget said, "You haven't met Adam, have you? Adam Mullen. I mentioned he's been doing the pruning - he's done a great job." She indicated the trees and hedges behind her.

Adam came forward, holding out a hand. "Hello, Mr Harper."

"Anthony," Bridget said.

The two men looked at each other for a moment before Anthony shook the proffered hand. For a second Bridget thought he'd say, "Pleased to meet you," though he obviously wasn't. Instead, he said, "You'll make sure the fire's safe before you leave, won't you? We don't want any accidents," and Adam answered "Of course." With a curt nod, Anthony headed back to the house.

Suzanne kicked a branch at the fire's edge. "Why does Dad always spoil things?"

"He hasn't, darling," Bridget soothed. "He was only checking up."

"Checking up on *us,* you mean. In case we were having fun. You know what? I'll never have a firework party, like you said -" Suzanne's voice rose to a shout. "Dad wouldn't let me. Even if he did, he'd show me up in front of my friends. I'm going in. It's too cold."

Adam had moved to a discreet distance; he fetched a rake from the hedge where he'd propped it and came over to Bridget. Watching Suzanne's retreating figure, she said, "Sorry about that. Anthony can be a bit -"

"Doesn't matter."

It did matter, but Bridget couldn't explain, caught between embarrassment and loyalty. She'd thought of inviting Adam in for tea and cake when they'd finished – she wanted to plant a specimen tree in the lawn, and thought he could help her decide - but not with Anthony in a strop.

"Let me help," she said instead.

"There's only one rake. You go on in - I'm in no hurry." He touched her arm. "Thanks, though. I'll see to this before I go."

His face was lit by the dwindling fire; she saw the shine of his eyes, the texture of skin. For a moment she was held by his gaze; then she stepped away.

"All right then. Thank you, Adam. See you in the week."

She went through the gate to the lawn, discomfited, trying to think of the welcome warmth of the kitchen, and the meal she would cook. But her feet slowed, and she looked back at Adam's shadowy shape as he moved back and forth with his rake, silhouetted against the glow. It called to mind a scene from her favourite Hardy novel, *The Return of the Native* – a scene in which Eustacia Vye, stirred by restlessness and longing, lit a fire to summon her lover across the dark heath.

Oh, stop it, she told herself, and went in, finding the kitchen empty: Anthony must be in his study. Defiant music pulsed through the floor from Suzanne's room above.

Later, when she went to bed, the sweet ashy smell of woodsmoke still clung to her hair and clothes.

Jane

NEW YEAR'S DAY 2019

"Here, sleepy."

Bleary-eyed, Jane stirred. She was in Tom's bed, and Tom, naked, was offering her a mug of tea.

"What's the time?"

"Early still. Happy New Year." He bent to kiss her. "Again."

How long had they slept? They'd been to a party at the east Oxford home of someone Tom knew; her throat was coarse from shouted conversations. At midnight they'd spilled out to the street to see everyone else's fireworks, then walked into the city centre with a group of Tom's friends, sidestepping drunks on the pavement and cars that hooted and swerved.

Tom opened the curtains and looked out at the street.

"Flasher!" Jane giggled. "D'you want to get arrested?"

His clothes were on the floor; she reached for his underpants and chucked them at him. Tom caught them but let them fall, got back into bed and snuggled close.

While they drank tea he asked, "What are you thinking? New Year resolutions? How about *spend more time with Tom?*"

"No resolutions. I don't trust New Year - it feels too risky. How about you?"

"You know what I'd really like? To move into your cottage."

"Are you serious? You want to give up this flat?"

He kissed her hair. "Why not? It's daft to run two places now we're back together."

She could think of several reasons why not, but said, "I ought to get up. There's lots to do at home."

He took the mug from her and placed it on the floor. "What's the hurry?"

...

At Suzanne's suggestion, the New Year's Day lunch was at Wildings. "Last chance for us all to be there, so we'll make it special. Tom, too?"

Jane had agreed, but was unsure about Tom. "We'll need to talk about house stuff and Will stuff, won't we? He'd feel a bit spare."

She had put it to him diffidently, expecting him to say no, but he said that he'd help get ready and find something else to do when the tactical discussion began. Before leaving for Oxford Jane had tidied the dining-room and put candles and festive napkins ready, and vases of holly, ivy and late rose-hips from the garden. She had bought nibbles, cheese and a dessert from the Summertown deli and had taken a chestnut roast out of the freezer; Suzanne would bring a main course for the meat-eating majority.

"Oh, your angel's on the tree!" Suzanne said, arriving at

Wildings with Ed. The day was still, mist settling around the house, sealing it in isolation.

"Yes. I'm glad we're doing this, Suze. It felt odd, decorating the tree just for myself."

"Hasn't Tom been staying?"

"A few times. I was at his, last night." Jane flushed, thinking of herself and Tom earlier, the duvet flung back from heated bodies, then their haste to get showered and presentable.

"Is that a new ring?"

"Yes. Tom's present." Jane held out her hand, showing the jet stone in a twisted silver setting. "Wasn't he clever, choosing something so lovely?"

"Gorgeous! Not on your left hand, though?"

Jane wasn't often irritated with Suzanne, but she was by this. "It's not like that!"

"Sorry. Only asking. I'd love to see you settled and happy. Tom's so sweet, and it's obvious he's devoted to you."

"Is it? But we're happy as we are, honestly, Suze. I'm not ready for more, and he certainly isn't."

Tom, the cottage, the ring – she could see that it all fitted together so neatly for Suzanne, but not for her. Neither she nor Tom was contemplating marriage or babies, she was certain. When she thought of a future with him she felt uneasily that it wouldn't be enough; but what she *did* want, she couldn't define. Although a year older than her he seemed too much of a boy, not ready to grow up. At present they could be together, at Wildings or at his flat, when they wanted, but just as frequently apart. Was she using him, then, as someone to go to when she felt lonely? But, if so, it appeared to suit him well enough.

Rob and Ingrid arrived, bringing wine and flowers, and there was an exchange of presents in the sitting-room, where

Tom had lit the fire. Rob and Ingrid's gift to Jane was a silk scarf, something she'd never wear; she simulated gratitude, already planning to give it to a charity shop. She had bought them a woven table-runner from India, and wondered as Ingrid exclaimed over it whether her appreciation was just as fake.

At the dining-table glasses were raised and clinked.

"Happy New Year."

"Happy New Year, everyone."

A year from now, Jane thought, where will we be? Not here. This should be a day of hope and expectation, but she saw only change, loss and uncertainty - a dangerous, unpredictable future for the whole planet, let alone for her family. In that context, what did their little lives matter?

"So," Ingrid said, while Suzanne passed plates, "when do you two move into the cottage?" She looked from Jane to Tom, who replied, "Soon, I guess."

Jane avoided his eye. "We, I, haven't actually made plans yet."

"It'd make sense," said Rob. "Get rid of whatsisname, the tenant, and move yourselves in. Then the house can be properly cleaned, ready for viewing. It'll add to the appeal if buyers can see it's vacant possession. You've given notice, I take it?"

"To Simon? No. I've hardly seen him."

"Oh, come on! Why delay?"

Ingrid gave Rob a reproving look. "Not now, sweetheart."

"You will, though?" Rob asked Jane. "Or – are you thinking of living in Tom's flat, keeping Simon on as your tenant? The income could be useful. I don't imagine you're earning much, working part-time."

"Could you please not make assumptions?" Jane said, more snappishly than she intended.

There was a brief silence. Rob gave a shrug, said, "Only trying to help," and turned to ask Ed how work was going. As if Ed wants to talk about work on New Year's Day, Jane thought. Suzanne passed gravy and offered more potatoes, and Ingrid asked Tom about his family.

"Did I tell you Rob's given me gym membership for my Christmas present?" Ingrid said, when Jane brought in the dessert. "I've already tried a few classes. Body pump and Pilates. They have yoga, but I need something more energetic to burn off the calories." She patted her slim middle and eyed the *tarte aux abricots*. "Ooh, wonderful - who made this?"

"No, it's a bought one. There's a deli near Tom's. Actually," Jane said, slicing and serving, "there are various kinds of yoga, and it can be *very* strenuous. People have the wrong idea if -"

"My next challenge is to get Rob to join some classes!" Ingrid gave her tinkling laugh. "It must be so boring, pumping away at weights."

"Keeps me fit, though. You only teach yoga, Jane, don't you? Have you thought of branching out, Pilates, or Body Sculpting? You'll never be short of work if you keep up to date."

"Rob!" Suzanne reproached. "Jane's a yoga specialist, not an all-round fitness instructor."

"And there's no limit to what you can learn," Jane said. "I've only just started."

"At a gym it'd pay to be more versatile," Rob went on. "You'd get work that way, standing in for people and so forth. They have any number of classes at Ingrid's gym – MetaFit, Body Combat, all sorts."

Jane saw Tom's deadpan expression and looked away to avoid laughing.

"Sweetheart!" Ingrid put a hand on Rob's arm. "If yoga's what Jane likes, you shouldn't try to push her into something different."

"These other things come and go," Jane said. "What I *like* about yoga is that it's five thousand years old. There are fashions in yoga too, but it's not going away."

"Besides, Jane gets lots of work now," Tom added, not entirely truthfully. "Covering classes as well as her regular ones."

"That's good to hear," said Ingrid. "Even if it's doesn't sound exactly secure. This tarte is delicious, Jane. I shouldn't, but just a *little* more, thank you. Undoing all my good work at the gym!"

Lunch over, Ed made coffee while Suzanne and Jane cleared the dishes; then Rob said, "Right. Family meeting time." Taking the hint, Tom moved into the sitting-room to watch a film, while the others re-settled themselves at the table.

Ingrid said, "Rob and I will be on hand, of course, when it's time to clear out the furniture. There are certain items -"

She cast a look at Rob, who picked up the cue.

"It'll all be part of the valuation, of course, but Ingrid and I would like to give a home to the Sheraton sideboard. That should stay in the family. And the William Morrell painting. I think those are the only items of real value."

Suzanne said smoothly, "I'm sure we'll sort it out amicably when the time comes," while Jane felt her blood pressure rising at their sheer cheek - pricing the furniture, plotting what they could get, not a hint of sentiment.

"We've had two valuations," said Rob, opening his folder. "Both around 1.4 million, as expected. Minus agents' fees and expenses, and then there's inheritance tax. Forty percent on everything above the threshold, so we'll get clobbered, as I thought. The 1.4 mill's for the house, land and outbuildings, excluding the cottage. So as soon as probate comes through, we instruct Bridges and Wade – sole agency at first, then joint with Strutt and Parker if they don't sell within a month. They'll conduct all viewings, so, Jane, you needn't be involved. They'll have their own keys."

He produced papers, lists of calculations, a draft brochure; he talked about agents' fees, a possible Open Day, adverts in property magazines.

Still feeling rebellious, Jane said, "Is it definite, then, that we're selling? There's no way we can afford to keep the house?"

"I did look into selling the orchard, with outline planning permission for six detached houses. We'd probably get around six hundred thousand for that – which might make it possible for Suzanne and me to buy out Sean McBride. But then what? We'd be stuck with the house and its upkeep, *and* have a building site next door for the foreseeable future. And there's not much to be gained by owning the house jointly – it'd lead to complications. We've both got houses of our own and neither of us could buy out the other, even if we wanted to. So I think that's a blind alley."

"I had another idea," Jane found herself saying.

Rob looked at her warily. "Oh? What?"

"Couldn't we take the chance to do some good? I mean, it's not as if any of us need the house for ourselves. You just said that. There are so many homeless people, refugees, people who've risked everything to travel from Syria. We've got *so much* – houses, Sheraton sideboards, far more than we need to be comfortable..." She plunged on, hearing as she spoke how insubstantial the dream was, a bubble blown by a child, rainbow coloured as it drifted away. It wasn't even a plan.

"I thought, maybe, you might see it as an investment," she finished. "A kind of loan. That way we'd still *have* the house, and it could be sold later if things didn't work out."

She saw startled faces around the table. Rob tapped his pen on the table. "Come on, Jane. This is a non-starter, you know that. Have you actually done any research? Looked into the costs, the implications?"

"Not really," Jane confessed. "I did look at some refugee organisations."

Rob puffed out his cheeks. "Look, I've put in a lot of work on this. I'm not wasting time on this sudden whim. Apart from anything else there's the obvious fact that Sean McBride is involved. It couldn't possibly work."

"I know you mean well, Janey," Suzanne put in. "But refugee centres tend to be in towns and cities, don't they? So that residents can make local connections, look for jobs. This isn't the right sort of location."

"Indeed," Rob said.

"The fact is, Jane," Ingrid said coolly, "that you'd be asking Rob and Suzanne to give up their inheritance for a venture you've barely thought through. I don't know about you two -" She glanced at Suzanne and then Ed - "but for Rob and me this inflow of cash will be tremendously useful. We've got two teenagers to see through uni and set up with homes of their own."

Jane already regretted having broached this. What had she expected?

"Ingrid's absolutely right," said Rob. "Suzanne?"

Suzanne shook her head. "Sorry, Jane. Same goes for Ed and me – university fees coming up for Rhiannon, *and* the likelihood of care home expenses for Ed's parents, not far off. That'll eat up money. Our share's a windfall we'll certainly make good use of. We're lucky, I know – incredibly privileged. I don't want to see the house sold any more than you do, but I don't see that we've got a choice."

"You're getting the cottage, Jane. It's a bit much to take your share but ask everyone else to give up theirs!" Ingrid's smile didn't conceal the barb.

"I know. Forget it. It was only a dream." Jane was furious with herself for showing Rob and Ingrid how poor a grasp she had on reality.

"Has there been any news of Sean McBride?" Ed asked. "Do we know any more?"

"Only that he agrees to the sale." Rob was sorting through his papers. "It's up to him whether he makes contact. I don't see why he would."

"Curiosity?" Suzanne said. "I would, if I were him."

Jane was silent, thinking of her email to the solicitor, which had so far produced no reply.

"He's in line for a big injection of cash, out of the blue," said Rob. "In his position I'd take the money and keep quiet."

"But," Jane said, "do we *know* it's out of the blue? Maybe he and Dad *were* in touch. Why would Dad give him such a large share, otherwise?"

"I asked my mother about this over Christmas," Rob said. "When I told her Dad had an illegitimate son, she – wasn't altogether surprised."

"She *knew?*"

"Not exactly. But she reminded me that she divorced Dad because she found out he was seeing an old girlfriend, someone he'd known before. He must have picked up with her soon after he and Mother were married. Finn, her name was."

"Unusual name for a girl," Ed remarked. "Finn McBride? Fionnuala, might that be?"

"Irish, yes. Mother couldn't remember the surname. She's not sure she ever knew it. This woman wasn't named as co-respondent in the divorce."

Suzanne frowned. "So – when Dad and your mother split up, Dad could have stayed with her, with Sean's mother? I wonder why he didn't, especially if she was pregnant?"

"We don't know that she *was* pregnant then," said Rob. "But - *if* she was - Sean McBride's older than we thought - around my age."

"So quite likely he'd have children too?" Ed ventured. "But if so, they're not mentioned in the Will."

Jane assimilated this, seeing that it fitted with what Marie had told her. "So – Dad *didn't* have another child while he was married to Mum! It was -"

"*My* mother he cheated on, not yours. Yes," Rob said drily. "And when he was much younger. It doesn't change anything, Jane."

"We shouldn't jump to conclusions," Ingrid said. "Cynical, I know, but if your father was unfaithful to his first wife -"

Why not his second as well? No one completed the thought, but there was a silence while it registered. Jane reflected that Ingrid didn't know the half of it. But then, most likely, none of them did.

Bridget

1990, MAY

AT A TIME WHEN she'd usually be up and dressed, Bridget was writing in bed, her new habit. At first her pen moved tentatively across the page, then gradually gathered momentum. Consulting the factual journal she kept as a record, she described the vegetable garden as she'd found it, rampant and half-wild, and her vision of transforming it into a plot both productive and decorative. She wrote about planning, designing, taking her inspiration from Victorian walled gardens and from Geoff Hamilton's developing garden at Barnsdale; she described the excitement of putting in the raised beds and arches, obelisks, geometric paths, and seeing her parterre take shape. She noted her early successes, her failures and disappointments (lettuces devoured by slugs or brassicas by caterpillars; seeds sown too early and failing to germinate), her plans for the coming year and beyond; she wrote of the pleasures of being in the garden at first light or at dusk, tasting the sweetness of a strawberry or twisting an apple to see if it fell into her hand.

She added, deleted, found better phrases. Not bad, she decided.

Someone was down in the kitchen, clattering dishes.

Reproach thumped into her. How had she forgotten? Suzanne was to sit the first of her O-Level exams today, and it was Maths, her least favourite subject. Bridget pulled on her dressing-gown; she heard voices as she went downstairs.

Anthony was frying eggs while Suzanne stood by the toaster, neat in school uniform, hair in a plait down her back. Radio news burbled in the background.

"You're late, Mum!" Suzanne said. "We thought you were outside."

"Morning!" Anthony was already dressed, unusual for him at this hour. "Shall I do you a couple of eggs? And I've made coffee."

She was relieved to be greeted so affably. She never knew what to expect, but on good days they could still be companionable.

"Lovely, thanks!" she told him; then gave Suzanne a kiss. "All right, darling? I'll drive you in today, shall I? Give you more time to get ready."

"It's OK, Mum. Dad's taking me."

"I've got a meeting in Milton Keynes," Anthony said.

"Oh? I didn't know."

"I did say. Examiners' briefing. Should be home mid-afternoon."

After waving them off, wishing Suzanne good luck, Bridget tidied the kitchen and went upstairs to shower and dress. There was plenty to do in the garden, but she would concentrate on her article today, typing it up on the word processor in Anthony's study. She would send the article, with accompanying photographs, to the county magazine.

Probably they commissioned their features and wouldn't be interested, but worth a try.

She should have asked Anthony about using his study, but went in anyway, surprised to see his desk bare and shelves relatively tidy, no clutter of papers, books and economics journals surrounding the computer and printer. Had he finished his book at last? Did that account for his cheerfulness?

Any discussion of his project had become impossible. The mildest enquiry about progress would be met with: "Fine. Why?" or, more belligerently, "For God's sake stop nagging." Any suggestion she made about regular hours or aiming for a daily word count was dismissed with, "Don't hector me, Bridget. You've no idea what's involved. Why must you interfere?"

On a new disk from the desk drawer she began typing her own piece. Able to touch-type, she was much faster than Anthony, who had to work laboriously, stabbing at the keys two-fingered. She'd offered to type while he dictated, but was spurned again. "No. I can't concentrate with someone else in the room."

When her document was saved and printed she put it aside to re-read later. She planned to make a special effort with this evening's dinner, regretting her lack of support for Suzanne on this important day. They'd have asparagus, new potatoes and salad from the parterre; there was still rhubarb, to make into a fool with ginger, honey and cream, Anthony's favourite. If she were lucky, his good temper would last.

• • •

Anthony wasn't home by seven, and had sent no message.

"We'll wait a bit." Bridget opened the oven to examine the asparagus tart.

Revising Geography at the table, Suzanne said, "Can't we have ours without Dad? I'm starving. It'll only get spoiled."

Bridget set places at the table on the terrace. "These long evenings are too lovely to spend indoors. Listen to the swifts! They're flying high – that means good weather."

They began their meal.

"Why hasn't he phoned?" Suzanne was restless, eating rapidly, with frequent glances back at the house. "What if something's wrong, something awful? He might've been in a car crash, or had a heart attack and dropped dead – how would we know?"

"Shh, shh! We'd hear if something like that happened. I expect his meeting ran on late, that's all."

"But it was this *morning!*"

"He'll have got involved in something else. A discussion with colleagues or a student crisis."

Rather than the flashing lights and ambulances Suzanne feared, Bridget dreaded a grumpy return that would turn the evening sour. She knew too well how his sullenness could infect all three of them. For Suzanne's sake she wanted at least superficial harmony.

When she heard tyres on gravel from the front of the house, relief was mixed with foreboding.

"He's here," Suzanne said. Bridget saw her wary expression, and felt a pang that she was so alert to good or bad signs, expert in divining every nuance of adult behaviour.

Determined to the point of belligerence, Bridget hurried into the kitchen. Anthony was taking off his jacket, looking tired but not irritable, she was thankful to see.

"It ran on a bit. Sorry," he said. "How was Suzy's Maths?"

"All right, I think. Come and ask her. We're eating outside. We did wait, but -" Anxious to avoid any hint of reproach, she said instead, "Glass of wine? There's Chenin blanc in the fridge."

"Thanks. Something smells good."

There had been a second impromptu meeting this afternoon, he explained outside, which had taken twice as long as necessary; afterwards he'd gone to the pub with Keith.

"You should have phoned," Suzanne accused. "We were worried, Mum and me. Wasn't there a phone??"

"Sorry, yes. I should have thought of that. You're quite right, Suzy."

Bridget noticed the sincerity of his apology, knowing that if she'd challenged him herself she would have received a curt answer. His regular tactic was to shift any blame to her.

. . .

A letter arrived from *Northamptonshire Life* two Saturdays later. Bridget's article had been accepted, and she was offered a fee.

"It will appear in our November issue, accompanied by one of the photographs you enclosed," the editor had written. "In addition, we'd like to send a photographer to take a few shots of you in your garden. Perhaps you could telephone our office to arrange a convenient time?"

She read it twice more, standing in the hall, before showing it to Anthony and Suzanne in the kitchen.

"Look! I'm going to be a published writer! How amazing?"

"Let me see!" Anthony reached for the letter.

"Cool!" Suzanne leaned over his shoulder. "*Both* my parents will be writers when Dad's book comes out. How many people can say that?"

"But mine's only a little local thing," Bridget said quickly.

"And Dad's already a writer. He's published lots of articles in journals."

"But that's boring stuff. Soon he'll have an actual *book*."

Anthony got up from his chair. "You'd find my book boring, too, Suzy, I assure you. Well, congratulations. I'd better get on."

"Well, *I* think it's jolly good, Mum," Suzanne said, when he'd closed the door behind him. "A photo, too! You'll be famous."

"Hardly! Why would I want to be, anyway?" But Bridget was elated by this validation of her work. Someone thought her writing worth publishing, and paying for.

Suzanne looked sceptical. "*Every*one wants to be famous."

Still light-headed, Bridget went to the yard to fetch trays of beans for planting out, looking in at Meg's workshop but finding no one there. Adam's van was in the yard, back doors open. He came most days to do the cottage's interior painting and a bit of replastering and filling – he was a useful person to have around, able to turn his hand to a range of tasks - and was now gloss-painting the doors and window-frames. New kitchen and bathroom fittings had been installed, and the cottage could soon be let.

Bridget went to say hello, stopping to look critically at the cottage's small garden. A paling fence surrounded the rectangle of unkempt grass and a strip along the front, with its own gate. The grass had been left to grow and flower, with ox-eye daisies and vetches among silky greens and silvers. It had its own beauty, but would have to be mown and tidied before prospective tenants came to view.

She heard laughter from inside. The front door was open, and she went through to find Adam on all fours in the kitchen, painting the skirting-board, and Meg leaning against the new worktop. The clean, spirity smell of gloss paint stung her eyes.

She hesitated, then Meg turned and saw her.

"Hello, Bridget! I came for a look round."

"Hi there," Adam said, turning his head from under a bent arm to look up at her.

Adam and Meg. Bridget sometimes wondered whether there was an attraction between them – why wouldn't there be? Two young people, single, both artistic, often spending time together. Adam: she thought of that moment by the bonfire, weeks ago, when – she acknowledged it now – she'd indulged herself afterwards in thoughts embarrassing to recall. For Meg, younger and unattached, such fancies wouldn't be out of place. Since, she'd been brisk and businesslike, seeking Adam out only to discuss paint charts and plaster.

"You haven't advertised for a tenant yet, have you?" Meg asked her. "It's looking good. It'd suit me perfectly, if I could afford it."

"Oh! You'd live here on your own?"

"Well, course," said Meg, laughing. "Who else is there? It'd save you the bother of advertising. I'd guarantee to look after it. What rent are you asking?"

"I'll talk to Anthony. I can't think of anything I'd like more, though," Bridget said, already deciding to reduce the rent, if necessary, to have Meg living here. "We were going to put some bits of furniture in – spare things from the house."

"Suits me. I haven't got any of my own. Not that I need much."

Adam had finished a stretch of skirting. He got to his feet, rubbing his free hand on paint-stained jeans, and smiled at Bridget. Aware of the three of them so close together in the small kitchen, she stepped back. She'd come to tell Meg her good news, but was reluctant to mention it with Adam present, not wanting to sound too pleased with herself.

"Will you be here all day?" she asked Meg. "I'll talk to Anthony at lunchtime and let you know."

Meg

1990, MAY

STILL, OFTEN, SHE FELT nostalgic for her days at the Kindersley workshop. A mixture of practicality and a yearning for independence had made her leave Cambridge; she couldn't afford to live there, and it was unfair to stay indefinitely with Uncle Terry and Aunty Eileen, even though they made her welcome. During her time with George she'd learned about running a business with the aim of setting up on her own, supporting herself.

Now, at Wildings, with the cottage soon to be available, she'd found her place. She would have everything she needed: ample workshop space, her lodging handy, enough commissions to keep going. Friendship with Bridget and even, possibly, with Adam were extras she hadn't looked for but found that she quite liked.

The rent Bridget asked was half as much again as she was paying for the Towcester bedsit, but she'd expected that. After going through her finances, she thought she could do it. Living on the spot would save on petrol; she still worked in the pub three evenings each week, but would give that up when she was sure of being solvent.

Arriving late next morning after delivering and installing a name plate, she headed up to the house. She went through to the parterre, then stopped as she saw Bridget there, posing for a photograph. She was by one of the raised beds, next to a hazel wigwam; a young man in denim fiddled with a tripod-held camera while an older man stood by, apparently directing. Meg could see that Bridget was ill-at-ease, her pose rigid, face fixed in an unconvincing smile. Seeing Meg she relaxed, and at once her smile became genuine.

"*That's* better." The camera clicked. "And again. Then we'll try a couple by the fruit trees."

Meg retreated, wondering what that was about. Adam wasn't here this morning. He'd finished decorating the cottage and was tree-pruning for two days this week in Buckinghamshire. He'd been working at intervals on a painting, a blodgy square in moody greys and purples, relieved with trickles and dribbles of fiery orange. Privately Meg thought she could achieve something similar any spare afternoon, given a big enough piece of board and some tins of paint. She was getting used to his ways, his unpredictable comings and goings and frequent unexplained absences. In his workshop he spent a lot of time standing and looking, his stillness a contrast to the regular *tink, tink* that came from hers. He'd sold a painting recently to someone with money to spend and expensive tastes. Meg was astonished when Adam told her how much he'd asked, and that the buyer had written a cheque there and then.

"If you don't put a high value on your work, why would anyone else?" he asked her.

"I do value mine. I know what it's worth. But that's different from plucking a figure out of the air. Why not add a couple more noughts while you're at it?"

"It's not quite like that. And I only sell two or three a year if I'm lucky. I haven't given up the day job, as you must have noticed. Actually I'm not sure I'd want to."

She missed his company, and their spiky conversations, after seeing him most days while he worked in the cottage. They'd fallen into the habit of sharing breaks in Meg's workshop, brewing coffee or tea. She told him about the qualities of the Portland stone which was her favourite to work on; it sent a shiver of awe through her, that it was made of the compressed shells and bones of creatures that had crawled the earth or swum in a warm sea a hundred and fifty million years ago. Fine dust flew as she worked, settling in her hair, on her clothes.

"So you're breathing dinosaur dust. It's in our tea, becoming part of us." Adam indicated the mug that stood beside her easel. "This is your speciality - Jurassic tea?"

"It's what we're made of. Minerals that have been around for ever. We're only a heap of atoms assembled in a particular way, temporarily. When we die it all goes round again."

Occasionally they walked to the Plough in Lower Stortford for lunch. Last time, in the pub's smoky lounge, Adam asked, "Do you have much to do with *him?*" and tilted his head in the direction of Wildings.

"Who?"

"Bridget's husband."

"Oh. Anthony. Not if I can help it."

"You don't like him?"

"Haven't exactly taken to him, no," she said. "And I think it's mutual."

"Same here. Does he actually like anyone?"

"Who knows." Meg shrugged, adding, "It's his second marriage. There's a son from his first, twenty-something - he visits now and then."

"Do he and Bridget seem OK to you?"

"Well. It's a bit of a mystery, how they get on. They don't seem to." Meg swigged her lager; it felt disloyal to talk about Bridget. She thought of something Bridget said yesterday, about Anthony being depressed. *Depressed?* Meg had wanted to retort. To her, *depressed* was Gillian, sunk deep inside herself where no one could reach. There's depressed, she could have said, and there's being a moody git. But what did she know, really? "So many marriages are a mystery," she added. "You have to wonder why people bother."

"You've never been tempted?"

"God, no. Another half?"

"I'll get it." Adam drained his glass.

"What about you? You're single, I take it? Girlfriend?"

"No one special. They come and go."

Meg took this to mean that he had a lot of sex; she imagined he'd have no trouble finding willing partners. Her thoughts veered dangerously in that direction, swiftly brought under control. While he waited at the bar she couldn't help appraising him, as she might look at a breedy horse or sleek cat; his physical presence was compelling, the way he stood, the long line of his back, the angle of his bent arm as he reached into a pocket. She wished she could capture that. She couldn't draw people, but all the same her fingers itched for a pencil.

Bridget

1990, MAY

"Right, I must get going." The photographer looked at his watch. "I'm due in Daventry at twelve."

He and Daniel, the editor, had arrived in separate cars. Daniel said to Bridget, "Have you got time to show me the rest of your garden? There's something I'd like to discuss."

He meant, Bridget assumed, that he wanted alterations – improvements – to her article. They went through to the main garden, where he admired the long border and listened to her plans for a wildflower meadow in the orchard and a streamside planting. He was less headmasterly than he'd sounded on the phone: around Anthony's age, with well-cut springy hair, a gentle manner and a way of looking intently at her as she spoke.

As they returned to the terrace, he said, "I wonder if you'd consider writing for us regularly? Four pieces a year? Your submission arrived at a good time – we've always had a gardening page, but along the lines of practical advice and seasonal tips. I was thinking of commissioning more literary pieces to publish alongside."

"Really? What do you mean by literary, though?"

"Well - what you do. I thought you could write about the seasons in your garden, and others you might visit, especially locally. All of us in the office like your way of capturing the garden moment by moment. Readers will enjoy it, too."

But I'm only an amateur gardener. I don't know enough. Bridget's thoughts raced while she said calmly, "I'd love to. Thank you!"

"Marvellous! We'll make it a regular feature, then." His smile transformed his otherwise serious face. "Have a think about the next piece – March, we'd publish it. Maybe send a brief idea, say by the end of this month?"

"Yes, I can do that."

She had the odd sense, rarely experienced on meeting a stranger, that she'd known him for years. She wondered if it was mutual, or simply his easy manner; in his job he must meet people all the time, and she was predisposed to like him for flattering her writing.

Hearing footsteps she turned to see Anthony coming out of the back door.

"Oh, Anthony! Come and meet Daniel – Daniel Burns, from *Northamptonshire Life*. I mentioned he was coming, with a photographer. My husband Anthony."

The two men shook hands.

"Bridget's been showing me around," Daniel said. "Such a lovely garden. Glorious, this time of year in particular."

"Yes, yes."

There was a pause which Bridget felt obliged to fill.

"Daniel's asked me to write more pieces for the magazine,

four a year. Isn't that wonderful?" She hated how gushy she sounded, how fake.

"Oh? That's good."

She looked at Anthony, willing him to say more, anything by way of small talk, but knew from his expression that he wouldn't.

"Would you like to come in for coffee?" she asked Daniel, who was looking puzzled, his smile hesitant.

"Er – no. Thank you. I won't take up any more of your time. It's been lovely to meet you, Bridget. Let's be in touch, soon. Bye, then, Anthony."

"Bye."

As she walked with Daniel to his car, Bridget felt she should apologise for Anthony, but words wouldn't come.

"Call in at the office next time you're in Northampton," he said. "Then you can meet the team." He touched her arm. "Thanks again."

Watching him drive away she felt slightly dazed, recalling everything he'd said. Could she do it, put words together in a way that would please him and engage readers? With her spirits so high, she resented Anthony's almost-rudeness. Why must he be difficult? She thought of marching in to challenge him, but was reluctant to deflate her sense of possibilities opening up.

Instead, she went up to her workroom and took out her notebooks, flicking through pages of writing and sketches. There was plenty of material handy to back up the more important research of simply going out and looking. *Yes,* she thought: I can do this.

Jane

JANUARY

Driving home from through a misted landscape, she contemplated yet more unwelcome change.

"I couldn't turn down such a great chance," Chitra had said; she'd been invited by two friends to set up a yoga studio in Leamington. "There could be something in it for you, too. Maybe you could take on some classes, as we expand."

"Sounds great!" Jane tried to hide her disappointment that she'd no longer see Chitra several times each week at the gym.

On her car radio, another report about melting icecaps and rising sea-levels. "We're sleepwalking into disaster," a commentator said. This was becoming the background to everything, yet weirdly not treated as an emergency, as if climate breakdown could be ignored while life went on as usual. When she'd tried talking about it to Tom, his response was that nothing could be done, so why worry?

It's like being in a sci-fi film, she thought. We're doping ourselves into acceptance, doublethink.

. . .

Tom arrived at Wildings later to stay for a couple of days.

"Can we go round to the cottage? I've never properly looked at it before."

"OK, only we can't go in."

Light filtered through the strange, cocooning mist in which time seemed suspended. Jane looked with a wrench of loss at the frosted lawn, the hedgerow trees receding to distant haze, the church tower barely visible across the valley. In the stableyard she thought of the days when these buildings had been busy with activity: Meg chipping stone, and two women friends, jewellers and silversmiths, in the middle studio. A succession of people – sign-painter, potter, weaver – had briefly occupied the third. The place echoed with their voices, yearning to be filled with purpose as it had once been. For Artweeks the yard was festive with pennants and banners, the tubs bright with flowers. In her last years, Bridget combined open studios with garden tours. A stand offered cards for sale, colour photographs taken by a professional. One year Suzanne and a friend served teas from the barn; then, as Bridget's reputation grew, she hired caterers. Jane handed out garden plans and plant lists, and directed questioners to her mother, who'd be in the parterre or down by the long border. "Oh, is Bridget Harper actually here? Can we *speak* to her?" Some of the visitors spoke in awed tones, as if Bridget's appearances on TV and in *Gardeners' World* magazine had elevated her above ordinary humanity. When Jane relayed this, Bridget was scathing. "You'd think I was Gertrude Jekyll, for goodness' sake!" She never dressed up for these occasions, appearing in her usual garb of jeans, shirt and waistcoat with capacious pockets for string and secateurs, her only concession to put on a newish straw hat instead of her battered old one.

So much endeavour, knowledge and love had gone into the creation of the garden.

"Why did we let it go?" Jane said aloud.

"What?" Tom was trying the door of Meg's old workshop, finding it locked.

Jane pushed her hands into the pockets of her mother's coat. "All this. And Mum's garden. We should have looked after it better. Rob's getting someone to come and tidy up. But it's not the same as having someone who *knows* the garden. At least the cottage has been well maintained. Dad had the bathroom refitted a couple of years ago, and the kitchen re-done."

She stood looking at the *STABLES COTTAGE* sign. As a child she'd loved to watch Meg drawing. Quick and adept with pencil or fine pen, Meg made sketches for her: cats, dogs and horses - she claimed to be useless at drawing people – or dragons with Celtic twists to their tails. One of these she later carved in stone for a garden Bridget made at the Malvern Show. Intrigued by Meg's independence and capability, Jane was shocked when Polly, a school friend visiting for tea, saw it differently.

"I bet she's a lesbian."

Not admitting that she didn't know what that meant, Jane asked her mother later, and was at first astonished by the explanation, then disbelieving. "Why d'you want to know?" Bridget asked.

"Polly says Meg's one. Because she lives on her own."

"That doesn't make much sense. And it's not something Polly, or you, should go round saying. Not that it's *bad* to be lesbian."

Jane was confused. "Polly made it sound bad."

Now, scarcely less puzzled, she thought of Meg saying that her parents' relationship was *unconventional*. Suzanne had said the same. What had Meg meant? If she and Bridget were lovers, could that explain Anthony looking elsewhere for sex? Throughout her childhood the two had been close, spending hours in the workshop, garden and cottage. But Meg came to the house only rarely, something which – in retrospect – struck her as odd. Because Dad didn't like seeing them together? Because they had something to hide? But they were colleagues of a sort, always planning designs and projects. Why read more into it?

"So," Tom said, his arm round her, "this can be ours, as you soon as you get shot of Simon. How does it feel, being a woman of property?"

She leaned into him. "Not sure. All this property talk – it makes me uneasy. And Rob and Ingrid bagging the best furniture! They've got so much already, and now they're getting more. People I saw in India have got literally nothing, but that's a world away from them, a different world. It makes me feel like giving everything up. Taking to the road with nothing but a begging bowl and a peacock feather, like the Jain Buddhists."

"The who?"

"They give up everything – friendships, attachments, eventually even food. They fast to death."

"That's just weird. And you wouldn't talk like that if you *really* had nothing. If you were on benefits or trying to get social housing."

"I know. I'm luckier than I deserve. Not lucky to have lost both parents, but you know what I mean. I've had all this cushioning."

"Don't beat yourself up," Tom said. "What's the point? Middle-class guilt is a luxury."

"Feeling bad, while intending to keep what Dad left me? You're right, I'm indulging myself. But Tom – would it really suit you, moving here?"

"Course! It's not as if I don't know the place. I've stayed often enough."

"Yes, but *living* here's different from staying now and then. You like Oxford – the pubs and cinemas handy, trains, friend to meet. You'd be on your own most weekdays and there'd be miles to drive to meet anyone. Wouldn't you find it boring here?"

He released her and drew apart. "You're saying you don't want me to?"

She was dismayed by his tone. "Just thinking aloud."

"Great. So you're happy enough to stay at mine whenever it suits, but the minute you get your own place you don't want to share? Thanks a bunch!"

"That's not what I -"

He'd already turned away. "Going in. Let me know when you've made up your mind."

Bridget

1990, MAY, JUNE

THE LAST WEEK OF May was half-term for Suzanne, after which she'd have daily exams. Bridget drove to Yorkshire to visit her mother, taking Suzanne. Anthony assured her that he'd be fine and was perfectly capable of feeding himself, but on her return she was perturbed to find stale food in the fridge, the bin full of beer cans and bottles.

"What have you been eating? Nothing but baked beans, by the look of it!"

"I went out a few times. Don't fuss."

"How's work going?"

"Fine."

As so often, he implied that the question was impertinent. He'd barely glanced at her, though he managed a hug and kiss for Suzanne, who pulled away.

"Great to see you too, Dad." She picked up her bag and clumped upstairs, and Anthony went back to his study.

Oh, God. Bridget sorted through the fridge, removing sour milk. She ought to try again to persuade him to see a doctor. For now her priority was to calm Suzanne, who was already fretting about her exams and not sleeping well. She'd spent the return journey hunched over her German textbook, resisting Bridget's urgings to relax and listen to the radio. "I can't remember all these stupid pronoun endings! German's my worst subject. I'll fail, I know I will."

"Even if you did, it wouldn't be the end of the world," Bridget had tried. "And I don't suppose you will."

"You don't understand! Everyone else will pass. I'll be the only one to fail and then I'll look stupid."

Bridget took a prepared meal out of the freezer to cook later. She felt helpless: Suzanne working herself into a spiral of agitation and Anthony shut away, both dismissing help and sympathy.

"I'm not hungry," Suzanne said, when Bridget went upstairs to tell her the meal was ready.

"You're not *still* revising? Come down and have something with Dad and me. You need a break."

"No thanks. I'll get a sandwich later if I feel like it."

Returning to the kitchen Bridget realised that she wanted Suzanne there to avoid having to face a moody Anthony across the table. What did that say about their marriage, that her husband was the last person she'd choose to be alone with?

· · ·

For her sixteenth birthday in April, Suzanne had asked for a bike. "I need to get around on my own. It's a pain asking for lifts all the time." Now in proud possession of a ten-speed Raleigh, she took herself off for rides, often to meet friends from school, sometimes alone. Her close friend for the last four years, Helen, had fallen out of favour, replaced by Lindsey, who lived on the other side of Haverton.

On the Sunday morning before her return to school Suzanne said that she was going to Lindsey's house to revise.

"Will you be back for lunch?"

"Don't know. Don't worry about it."

Bridget was irked by Suzanne's new habit of giving instructions not to worry about this or that, but she let it go. Nor did Suzanne appreciate the annoyance of preparing food for someone who might eat it as a favour if nothing better turned up. But the problem with Anthony was more pressing.

She was making coffee, intending to take it to his study and attempt conversation, when he entered the kitchen.

"My radio's packed up. Have we got spare batteries?"

"In the drawer." She indicated it. "Coffee's ready. Will you have yours here?"

"I'm busy," he said, but wavered, looking out at the sunlit lawn. "Oh well, a quick break won't hurt."

"We need to talk. Is this a good time?"

"What about?" Anthony pocketed the batteries.

"I wish you could tell me why you're so unhappy. I said before that -"

"Oh, for God's sake. *You're* happy, and that's all that matters, isn't it?"

"You know it's not. How can I be happy with you like this? I can't talk to you, can't make even the most harmless remark without you snapping my head off-" She stopped, remembering her vow to stay calm no matter how he responded. "What's bothering you – can't you tell me? Is it work, your book?"

Anthony gave a deep sigh and looked out of the window, arms folded. "Yes, it is the fucking book, if you must know. I'm giving up on it. I'm not enjoying it at all."

"Oh, Anthony -"

"Spare me your fake concern."

"It isn't fake! But – your contract – they've paid an advance, haven't they?"

"I don't give a toss about that. I'll pay it back. Peanuts, anyway."

"But -" Bridget sat down at the table. "I thought you *wanted* to do it, preferred it to tutoring. Couldn't you -"

"Be careful what you wish for, as they say. I did want it. But now it's like dragging a ball and chain around. They didn't like the first chapters I sent in. That prat of an editor – jumped-up little pansy, hardly old enough to shave - wanted hundreds of pointless alterations. I'm going to tell him where to stuff it."

"Isn't it worth sticking with it? When you got the deal you were talking about the opportunities it'd bring – conferences, journalism. You've done so much work, research – you can't throw it away!"

"You don't understand," he said plaintively.

"Anthony! You sound like Suzanne, getting into a state about her German exam," she said lightly, but he rounded on her.

"Well! Maybe we're both right. You really don't help. *It'll be all right if you keep slogging away.*" He put on a high, mimsy voice, and stood with one hip camply tilted.

Bridget gave him a scathing look. "Is there any chance of a sensible, adult conversation?"

"I doubt it."

"Would you at least consider going to the doctor? I think you should. If you're suffering from depression it's not surprising if it affects your work."

"Bloody hell, woman! I've told you, no! I'm not changing my mind -"

"Don't shout at me -"

"Isn't it fucking typical? If I don't agree with you on everything, stands to reason I'm mentally ill. That's your perverted logic. It's you that needs help, trying to control everyone's lives, so bloody superior -"

"That's not fair!"

"Who's talking about fucking fair? You're the big success now, aren't you? You're the writer in the family. At least you like to think so. Letting that man smarm all over you -"

She breathed in sharply. "For God's sake! Is that what you think? Is that why you were so rude?"

"I don't like to see my wife making a fool of -"

Anthony stopped abruptly, staring towards the lobby. Turning, Bridget froze too at the sight of Suzanne in the doorway, her face contorted, flushed.

"Darling, what are you – I thought -" Bridget half-rose from her chair.

Suzanne appeared to struggle for words; then they burst out. "Stop it! Stop it, both of you!" Her voice rose to a wail; she covered her face with both hands. "I can't stand this, I can't!"

While Anthony looked stricken, Bridget went to Suzanne, who stood taut with furious energy.

"Don't! Don't come near me! I hate you!" In an instant she was outside, running across the terrace.

"No, *wait,* Su -"

Pursuing, Bridget had no chance of catching up. Suzanne veered round the house; by the time Bridget stood panting by the gate, she was on her bike, speeding down the lane.

"Suzanne!" Bridget yelled.

She felt sick with reproach. Why had Suzanne come back – how much had she overheard? Helplessly she watched as

Suzanne reached the junction, turning in the direction of Haverton. Bridget thought of her arriving at her friend's house, distraught, tearful. She hurried indoors for her car keys, stopping at the sight of Anthony at the table, chin propped in hands, staring at nothing.

"Now look!" she fired at him. "She's gone. She can't bear to be near us, and who can blame her?"

"Gone where?" Anthony snapped from vacancy to alertness.

"To her friend's, I expect. In that state ... I'm going after her."

At the wheel, her thoughts raced. What could she tell Suzanne that could possibly make things better? She drove between verges lush with Queen Anne's lace and ox-eye daisies, through the archway of tree canopies, a tunnel of filtered green light that normally she'd slow to appreciate.

She'd never been to Lindsey's house but knew it was beyond the village, next to the farm shop. Pulling up there she saw a sign for Mulberry Place and, through the gate, a Georgian house, immaculate frontage of shrubs and planters, two estate cars parked on gravel.

Daunted, she glanced at herself in the mirror, dismayed by her taut face and messy hair. How would it help to knock at the door and create a scene in front of people she'd never met? Suzanne wouldn't forgive that. Better for her to spend time with Lindsey, confiding in her – though Bridget winced at the thought – then return later when everyone had calmed down.

She drove back slowly, unwilling to face Anthony, relieved that he wasn't in the kitchen. Mechanically she began tidying up. When the phone rang she went into the hall to answer, hearing the click that meant Anthony had picked up too, in his study.

"Is Suzy there?" A girl's voice.

"No – she's out. Who's this?"

"Lindsey," said the girl, her tone suggesting that Bridget should know.

"Isn't she with you?" A new fear clutched Bridget's chest.

"Obviously no. She was meant to come, but she hasn't shown up. I'm just checking why she's so late."

"I see. Could you ask her to phone home if she does arrive?"

Ringing off, Bridget tried to think rationally. So Suzanne wasn't safely at her friend's but out somewhere on her bike, distraught, possibly still raging and crying. Where would she go?

Anthony came out to the hall; she said sharply "You heard?"

"Yes."

"I'm going to look for her."

Her mind filled with lurid possibilities; what if Suzanne didn't return? What if they waited and waited until there was no choice but to call the police? But in all likelihood she'd simply ride around for a while and come home when she was tired or hungry, and at some point a difficult conversation would be necessary.

"Shall I come?" he said meekly.

"No, you stay here, in case she comes back."

She could hardly look at him. Maybe this would stir him into acknowledging that things must change, for Suzanne's sake if not for their own. She went to the yard instead of to the car; Meg was probably there, and Suzanne, if she returned, might prefer Meg's company to that of warring parents. Her steps quickened, but Meg's workshop was closed, and only Adam's van stood in the yard.

She let out a sigh of frustration, tearful again; she wanted Meg's calmness spread like balm over the morning's drama. But of course it wasn't unreasonable for Meg not to work on a Sunday.

"Bridget? Are you OK?"

Adam was at the open door of his studio, paintbrush in hand.

"I was looking for Meg."

"She'll be here this afternoon, she said. What's wrong?"

He put down his brush and came out to her. She turned away.

"Hey, what's up?"

"Nothing really."

"Come on. What is it?"

His voice was so kind that she blurted, "It's Suzanne – she's run off. We – there was a row, and she took off on her bike."

"She'll come back when she's ready."

"But I'm worried. She was meant to go to her friend's, but she's not there and I don't know where she -"

"D'you want to look for her?" Adam went inside, wiped his brush on a rag and picked up his keys. "She can't be far away. Come on, jump in the van."

In the passenger seat she said, "You're very kind. I'm stopping you from working."

"Doesn't matter. Where does this friend live? We'll head that way first in case Suzanne's shown up. I expect it's exams getting to her."

"It wasn't quite like that. It wasn't her fault."

Adam looked at her sidelong, pulling out into the lane.

"The row," she said. "It was Anthony and me. Yelling at each other. We didn't see her come in."

She saw his dubious look; he didn't respond, probably thinking it was none of his business. She shouldn't have revealed so much.

Arriving for the second time at Mulberry Place, Bridget went to the door while Adam waited in the van. The door was opened by a pretty, sulky-faced girl with hair in a sweep over one shoulder.

"Lindsey? I'm Suzanne's Mum."

"She's not here." The girl looked her up and down. "I *said*."

"D'you know where she might have gone?"

"How should I know?"

"Who else is she friendly with at school?"

Lindsey shrugged. "Loads of people. Mainly in town."

"You'll be sure to tell her to phone if she does come, won't you?"

"Yesss." Lindsey invested the word with a sigh, and a barely perceptible eye-roll; she was already closing the door as Bridget turned away.

She climbed back into the van. "No," she told Adam. "But Lindsey's manner – sounds as if they've fallen out, too. It's hard to keep up."

"So another reason why she's upset. And not all your fault. It's turbulent, being a teenager. Where next?"

They drove back to Lower Stortford, drawing another blank at Helen's house; then, at Adam's suggestion, drove around the lanes. Bridget strained her eyes for the slender figure on a bicycle, willing her to appear.

"She could easily have gone off-road. There are green lanes, and the ground's baked dry. Oh, this is hopeless. She could be *any*where. I'm sorry. I'm probably making a stupid fuss about nothing."

"You could phone home. More than likely she's already there," Adam said.

They stopped at the call box in the next village; Adam supplied coins.

Anthony answered quickly. "Where are you? Suzanne's had an accident – she's OK, but being taken by ambulance to Northampton General."

"*No.* Is she – how bad -" Bridget felt herself swaying. The red paint framing the phone-box windows, a smear of bird-shit and dog roses in the hedge beyond seemed to push themselves at her, insisting that life went on, indifferent.

"Broken arm, possible concussion. She fell off a horse."

"A *horse* -"

"I don't know the details. I'm leaving now for the hospital."

"I'll come too. See you there."

When she told Adam, he said at once, "Jeez. Let's go, then."

"I should've told Anthony to wait. But if you drop me at home I can be there in -"

"No, we'll go straight there. You shouldn't drive when you've had a shock."

It was reassuring to let him take charge. She was giddy with the thought that what had started as an ordinary morning had taken this dramatic turn.

"You OK?" he said, looking at her closely; she nodded.

Already the day seemed to have gone on for hours; she could have sagged with weariness, yet was on edge, jittery. Her mind repeated *This is our fault. It's all our fault.*

Meg

1990, JUNE

PULLING INTO THE YARD, Meg was piqued with annoyance that Adam's van wasn't there. He'd agreed to help move a boulder-stone - a heavy, irregular piece from the Great Tew quarry to be used freestanding for a house name - into her workshop from the corner of the yard. She couldn't manage alone.

She hesitated to ask Bridget, but went in search of her anyway, to say that she was leaving her bedsit at the end of the month and could move into the cottage then. With no sign of Bridget in the garden, she went to the back door of the house, finding it locked. Everyone was out, it appeared.

There was always something else to do. She put her trolley and rollers ready to move the stone if Adam did appear, and lined up her chisels to sharpen them on a diamond pad. She sprinkled water on the abrasive surface and carefully worked each blade against it in turn, testing for sharpness with her finger. They were a mark of her independence, these chisels; she looked at them with pride and affection.

It was more than an hour before Adam appeared, by which time she'd started a new drawing.

"Sorry I'm late. I've been at the hospital. Suzanne's had an accident, broken her arm."

"Shit - how?"

"She fell off a horse. Trying to impress a boyfriend, it seems - told him she could ride. Lucky it wasn't worse."

"So how were you involved?"

Adam explained: Bridget upset, a row, Suzanne taking off. "I left them in A and E. Suzanne had been X-rayed and was waiting to have her arm set. I don't think they'll keep her in."

"And she's got O-Levels. Brilliant timing." She saw that he'd liked being dependable in a crisis, relishing the chance to be helpful. To the family, or to Bridget in particular? She sensed, as often before, that he was keeping something from her.

Later she went to the house and found Suzanne and Bridget eating crumpets in the kitchen; Suzanne's left arm was in a sling, plastered up to the elbow.

"Adam told me what happened – well, some of it. Look at you, action girl! Whose was this man-eating horse, then?"

Suzanne flashed her a look that showed she was rather enjoying the attention.

"Monty, his name is. He belongs to Tim – that's Lindsey's boyfriend. At least Lin *thinks* Tim's her boyfriend -"

Following Suzanne's somewhat garbled account, Meg gathered that Tim was a boy two years older who lived on a farm near Cropredy. A week ago both girls had cycled over to see him show off his new horse, a thoroughbred and trained eventer. Wildly exaggerating the riding lessons she'd had at the age of eleven, Suzanne talked airily of her experience, prompting Tim to suggest that she came over another day to ride.

"I couldn't resist. He's *so* gorgeous."

"The horse? Or Tim?"

Suzanne smiled. "Actually both, but I meant Monty. Anyway, I thought me and Lin might go one day – she can't ride, so it'd make me look better. But she got all uppity and wouldn't – she wants to keep Tim to herself. So this morning, I -" She glanced at Bridget. "I was going to hers, but then I forgot something and came back, and after that – well. I went off on my own. Then I saw the signpost for Cropredy and went to Tim's farm. He was getting ready to ride – they've got their own stables and everything, and a paddock with jumps, and he offered me a go. I was scared, to be honest, when I saw those jumps, and I'd forgotten how *big* Monty is - massive, twice the size of the ponies I used to ride, but Tim rode round a few times and made it look easy, and I didn't want to look like a wimp so I let him give me a leg-up. Oh, it was so high up, and Monty's great long neck in front of me, but I tried to look cool with it. It was OK walking but then Tim told me to trot. With the ponies you had to give them a little kick, but Monty took off like he was in the Grand National - I hung on somehow and he was galloping, really galloping, and Tim was shouting and the reins were all over the place and I couldn't do anything, and we headed straight for this huge fence and I thought he'd jump, then he swerved and I crashed off and – next thing I was on the ground and my arm hurt like hell and I felt sick, and Tim was yelling for help." She closed her eyes, grimacing, then opened them and brushed at a tear. "It was stupid, I know."

"Stupid of Tim, it sounds to me," Meg said. "He should know better."

Suzanne managed a smile. "I know. He was mostly bothered about Monty at first, making sure he was all right.

Then when he saw I'd really hurt myself he was scared of getting into trouble."

"Anthony's gone there now," said Bridget. "To speak to Tim and the parents."

"Ah. Interesting."

"Yes. He was furious."

"I don't care." Suzanne waggled and stretched her fingers beyond the edge of the plaster. "I've gone off Tim. And snooty Lindsey - they're welcome to each other. Is there another crumpet, Mum?"

Meg left them discussing whether or not Suzanne could go to school tomorrow: Bridget thought she should spend a day at home, while Suzanne assured her that she was fine, and would only fret if she missed the exam. Whatever Adam had said earlier about a row, it appeared to Meg that the day's drama had brought the family together.

Jane

FEBRUARY 2019

On her way home from the supermarket she pulled up by the churchyard. Bringing flowers and foliage from the garden was a habit that persisted even though her mother would have told her not to bother. Since Dad, the experience was newly raw, like the disturbed earth of the grave. Another car was parked by the wall; not unusual, as people came to tend graves or walk dogs. But the churchyard was a haven, age-old ironstone yellow with lichen, jackdaws gathered chattily around the tower, the yew tree studded with berries.

It was a bright day, bitterly cold. She zipped her coat and got out of the car, carrying a bowl of crocuses she'd brought to replace the winter pansies that had stood on the grave since Christmas.

If a proper headstone was made - as she hoped - it would mean disturbing the snowdrops that had spread around the base. Wondering whether they'd survive transplanting, she walked through the lych gate and along the path, then came to an abrupt halt.

Someone was at the grave. A tall male figure stood there, head bent.

Someone who'd known them, or maybe just interested in gravestones, the way some people were? Whichever, she wanted him to go away.

She heard him sigh deeply; then he turned in her direction and stopped. He wore a grey duffel-coat, a pull-on hat and a striped scarf in shades of purple.

"Oh! Sorry. Didn't mean to make you jump," he said, although he looked just as startled.

"That's my parents' grave. Did you know them?"

His eyes widened behind wire-rimmed glasses; he seemed to take her in properly as she stood holding her bowl of bright crocuses like an offering.

"Jane!" It was part statement, part question.

She nodded, wondering if she should recognise him.

"You wrote to me," he said.

"Did I?"

She thought he meant with a funeral invitation, but he added, "Through the solicitors. I'm - Anthony's son."

"Oh -" Realisation thumped into her. "You're *Sean!*"

"Sorry if this is a shock." He stepped a little closer. "Well, obviously it is. I thought of coming to the house, but it wouldn't be fair to turn up without warning."

"The house is across there." She pointed to Wildings, visible above the bare trees that fringed the stream.

"I know. I just stopped off to see the grave. I'm on my way to Leicester."

She stared, thinking *This is him! My half-brother. Sean. Dad's son. A stranger.* All her speculation had solidified into an actual person, with a thin, expressive face, and grey eyes that surveyed her with keen interest. She wondered if they should shake hands or something, but she was holding the crocuses. She moved a little giddily towards the grave, and carefully placed the bowl. When she straightened, facing him, she did hold out a gloved hand.

"Well, hello. This is a bit weird, isn't it? To say the least."

"Yes, it is." Taking her hand in both his he clasped it with a warmth that surprised her. "But I'm so glad."

"But you didn't reply to my email?"

"I know. I would have. Wasn't sure when, or how. Wanted to leave time for it all to sink in."

"For yourself? Or for us?"

"For you, I meant. One shock after another. But it was a shock for me too. I never expected -" He broke off, shaking his head. "Any of this."

Her mind teemed with questions: *Where do you live? What do you do? What's brought you here?* But she couldn't rattle them out, one after another.

"You're going to Leicester? Now?"

"Yes, I've got a few days' work there. I thought of visiting you on my way back."

"Come now, if you like!" she said, on an impulse. "Easier to talk at home – it's brass monkeys out here."

"Thanks. I will, if you're not too busy."

"Too busy to spend time with my new brother? I don't think so. There's quite a lot to catch up on."

She felt unsteady, driving. In her mirror she saw the grey car following hers up the lane. *You invited him home?* she imagined Rob saying. *A complete stranger? With no idea if he was really who he said he was?* But she wanted to trust him. And of course he should see the house. He was in effect part-owner, with more right to it than she had.

He parked his car next to hers in the drive. Indoors he

pulled off his hat, revealing thick greying hair swept back from a high forehead. They looked at each other; it felt more intimate than in the churchyard, standing together in the hallway.

He was first to speak. "I know. I can't quite believe it either. So, Jane. I'm glad you contacted me – thank you. It was such a jolt, hearing that Anthony had died, and so suddenly."

"Were you in touch, then?"

"No. We had a sort of agreement to keep out of each other's way. Things were ... difficult. I haven't seen him for years."

"But then, the Will?"

"I know. That was a complete surprise. I don't know why he included me. I was – touched." His mouth twisted. "Astonished. Well. Are you the only one living here now? The solicitor thought so."

"Yes, till the house is sold. My boyfriend's here sometimes. Have you -"

While she hesitated, about to ask whether he'd been here before, he answered, "My mother used to live in this area. That's how she met Anthony, when they were both quite young."

"And your mother's name? We've been wondering who -"

"Fionnuala. Finn. She was a farm student, working nearby."

"Irish?" she asked, hearing no trace of an accent in his attractively deep voice.

"Yes, from Dublin. That's where I was born as well, but we left when I was two and I haven't lived there since."

"Did she bring you up on her own? Was it just the two of you?"

"No, no. She got married when I was small. I've got two sisters – well, half-sisters."

"And now us as well?"

"That's right."

She became self-conscious, firing questions, with so much more to ask. "Let's have tea. I've been wondering and wondering about you, and now we're standing here talking -"

"Great, thanks."

In the kitchen she put on the kettle and found sugar and biscuits. He took off his coat and slung it on a chair, keeping his scarf on over a black sweater. He was taller than her father – *their* father! - had been, and although he must be around Rob's age his slimmer build made him look youthful, only his greying hair and the beginnings of lines around his mouth and eyes showing his age. While she gave quick, surreptitious glances, curious for resemblances to her dad or to herself, he went to the window and looked at the sweep of lawn.

"Such a beautiful place," he said, turning to her. "The trees, the light on the church, the big sky. Anthony was a lucky man." He sounded wistful rather than bitter. "What a great shame it's got to be sold. But there's no way round it, I suppose."

"Not unless you're a millionaire and can buy out Rob and Suzanne."

He huffed a laugh. "No chance."

She brought the tea over and he sat opposite her, smiling, shaking his head. She had the sense that things would come out in time; first they must each adapt to the physical presence of a stranger who was also a close relative.

Sean spoke first. "I can't take this in, Jane. Here you are at last. And here am I."

At last?

"But I've been here all the time. We had no idea you existed," she said. "Did you know that? And how much did you know about *us?*"

"Oh – a bit."

"Why didn't you ever get in touch? Why didn't Dad *tell* us?"

"His first marriage ended because of me," Sean said, looking down. "I imagine he didn't want to put his second at risk, as well."

"But that was different! You didn't know my Mum. It, you, must have happened before he met her – I can't imagine she'd have been horrified that he had another son."

"But Anthony had no contact with me when I was young. My mother took me away – she wanted to be independent. That must have been difficult, painful. I never met him till much later, when things were too -"

The phone rang; Jane almost left it, remembered the estate agent, said "Sorry, I'd better get that," and picked up.

It was Rob, reminding her of a house-viewing that afternoon.

"Yes, I've kept things tidy," she told him. "Everything's ready."

"Good. I've spoken to Sam Wade and there'll probably be another two to fit in tomorrow, OK? Got to rush."

Ringing off, Jane said, "That was Rob. My – *our* – half-brother."

Their eyes met.

"You didn't tell him," Sean said.

"No."

"Why not?"

"I -" Jane hesitated, unable to explain that already she saw him as more of an ally than Rob ever was; it was irrational. "Rob likes to take charge. I don't want that, yet. You were saying about meeting Dad."

"Yes. Well – by then he'd kept me secret for all that time. It would've got difficult if he'd brought me out of the bag, as it were."

"Difficult for him?"

"For everyone, I should think."

"We will meet again, won't we?" Jane asked.

He looked at her steadily. "Do you want to?"

"Of course! Why not? There's so *much* – don't you?"

"Yes. Yes, I do."

"So what next? Should we arrange something with the whole family? I know Suzanne wants to meet you." She made no mention of Rob, suspecting he'd be chilly.

Sean looked towards the window, and in the turn of his head she saw a hint of her father – *their* father. Reassuring. Disconcerting.

"Yes," he said, "we should. We will. But maybe not yet. It seems a bit too formal."

. . .

With him gone the house felt newly empty. Unable to settle she roamed around, tweaking cushions and folding towels ready for this afternoon's viewing, then remembered her shopping in the car and fetched it, hardly noticing what she was doing.

Sean McBride, only a name till now, had walked into her life. She kept recalling how he looked, his voice, his every expression; she'd searched his face, finding shades of Dad in the line of his jaw, the bridge of his nose, his swept-back hair. At moments she'd glimpsed a resemblance to Rob, or to Suzanne; possibly even to herself. Mentally she replayed their conversation, and the way he'd more than once picked up a thought before she had spoken it.

She'd sent a message and he had come. Her half-brother, even if his age made him more like an uncle, and she had seen glimpses of sadness and regret that chimed with her. Almost she felt that she'd conjured him from nowhere, and that the meeting would fade like a dream.

Taking out her phone she looked at his number stored there. She hadn't made that up.

At his suggestion they'd agreed to meet for dinner in Oxford next week, and that she'd invite Tom. Already she longed to see him again, to talk and talk, to ask all the questions that milled about in her mind. She'd learned that he was divorced, had no children, lived in Newbury but travelled widely; he worked for an educational organisation that involved young people in environmental projects.

"That's topical. And so important," she'd said.

"Never more."

"I'm really glad. You could have been a banker or stockbroker or something dull like that."

"And you? Yoga?" he asked. "Tell me what drew you to that." And he'd listened, seeming to understand. Or to want to understand, which meant even more.

She sent a message: **Just checking you really exist. See you next Tuesday, if you do.**

He replied: **I think so, yes. Thank you for that. Looking forward to Tuesday.**

As if she were a teenager and he a new boyfriend, she kept taking out her phone to look at his words, hearing his voice saying them.

She began a message to Suzanne but deleted it, deciding to phone instead, later. She wanted to keep Sean to herself for a little longer.

Bridget

1990, JULY, AUGUST

SINCE THE ACCIDENT, BRIDGET was determined that Suzanne shouldn't be upset like that again. Anthony, too, was shaken, both of them regretting their conduct, treating each other with careful politeness.

At first no one referred to the bitter quarrel Suzanne had overheard. Days passed, dominated by Suzanne's exam timetable. With attention and sympathy at school for her broken arm, she quickly bounced back, and eventually it was Bridget who thought the cause of her distress shouldn't be glossed over.

"Dad and I – we say horrible things to each other sometimes. People do, when they row. We don't necessarily mean them."

"But mostly you do. Come on." Suzanne was blasé now. "It's OK. You don't need to make excuses."

"I wasn't. It's just -" That weasly *just* – "we annoy each other sometimes, the way people do when they know each other very well."

"Mum, *please*. I'm not five years old. I can see what it's like. You and Dad just about put up with each other. Don't worry. Helen says her mum and dad are the same."

Helen was back in favour now, after the brief interlude with uppity Lindsey.

Shocked by Suzanne's directness, Bridget blathered about love being changeable, about romantic love being misleading, even a kind of madness, and about a deeper, more permanent love that grew over time. She failed to convince either herself or Suzanne, who gave her a look of deep pity and told her, "I'll never get married unless I find someone I really love, and who loves me." She paused. "But how would you *know?*"

That was the question.

Once, Bridget had thought she did know. In the early days with Anthony she had felt herself to be desirable, interesting, capable; she thought, or wanted to think, that he saw qualities of which she was unaware, and brought out her potential – (but for what?) Perhaps the need to be loved overcame reality; anyone willing and reasonably presentable could be burnished in a misleading glow, the desire for love more important than its object.

I've tried, she told herself, knowing that she hadn't tried enough, and couldn't. Obstinacy drove her to find fulfilment without Anthony. And here it was at Wildings, in the changing canvas of the garden, the shifts of light, the cycles of growing and fruiting, seeding and dying. She loved her garden with a passion, in all its moods and weathers and seasons.

The end of exams came, and the summer holidays. They'd talked of spending a fortnight in Brittany, the three of them; Bridget ordered brochures and listed promising gîtes, but before she'd made a booking Suzanne was invited to Bournemouth with Helen's family. The Brittany idea was quietly dropped. "Maybe next year."

Anthony taught a week's summer school in August, staying away, and Bridget had the house to herself. She relished not having to bother about meals, instead making a salad or snacking on cereal and fruit. It was lazy, she knew, but in other respects she was far from lazy: she was outside from morning till dusk, between keeping her journal and working on her new article for *Northamptonshire Life*. How blissful, she thought, not to notice the time, or whether people needed food. She marked her freedom by not wearing her watch, eating when she was hungry, sleeping when she was tired.

The weather stayed mild and warm. On the Tuesday evening she took a glass of wine out to the terrace, watching the light change. More than a month had passed since the solstice and the season had already turned towards autumn, the trees well past early freshness, clad in the darker greens of maturity. She watched the pink-streaked sky slowly fade as a crescent moon rose high; her eyes adjusted, extending the dusk.

The beauty of the evening tingled through her. Loth to go indoors, she walked down to the stream, where the slow trickle after so many dry days caught the last light between banks lush with willowherb and meadowsweet. The shrieks of high-flying swifts gave way to night sounds: the sharp call of a little owl from the orchard, the bark of a fox, something scuttling through undergrowth close by. Her feet brushed long grass, her fingertips touching the soft sway of seed-heads.

But part of her was not content. She yearned for something more, with a longing that was almost painful. It was Daniel Burns who had unsettled her; she acknowledged that, though it had taken Anthony's goad to make her realise.

Letting that man smarm all over you, eating out of his hand - he'd been pettily jealous. His taunt was ridiculous, out of all proportion, yet she was gratified by Daniel's attentiveness and would welcome the chance to meet him again. *It's only a working relationship,* she told herself; *barely even that.* But a week ago, in Northampton for a dentist appointment, she'd followed his suggestion of calling in at the office.

She found him in a cluttered room shared with a female assistant, his desk piled with papers, files and photographs.

"Bridget! How lovely!"

On his feet at once, he introduced her to his colleague, Cheryl, who responded at once to her name and expressed delight at "having her on board". When he'd shown her around – which didn't take long, the magazine operating from two offices, with one more colleague – he took her to a nearby café. There he asked how the new article was going, seemed pleased with her response, then invited her to a private view at the Insch Gallery on the following Wednesday: "A group of local artists, some of them rather good. I think you'd enjoy it."

She hadn't committed herself, but when she realised that this was the Wednesday of Anthony's and Suzanne's absence she decided to go. She might make useful contacts for her open studios next year. Applications must be in before Christmas, not so far off. Meg's suggestion was to invite other artists or craftspeople to share the space, using the long barn. "A group exhibition. We're out of the way – we'll get more visitors if they can see a range of work, make it worth the effort of finding us."

Thus she justified it to herself, knowing that an evening out scarcely needed justification, and that she was excusing her wish to meet Daniel socially. He'd introduce her to others; he'd speak highly of her, boosting her confidence as Anthony once had. It's not as if I'm planning an *affair,* she told herself. But already she was planning what to wear, wanting Daniel to see her as interestingly arty. She could call herself a writer now, which she felt gave her a new status; she could talk about work in progress, research, deadlines.

Following the streamside path to the rough ground behind the stableyard, she was startled to see the outside light on. Meg, now installed in the cottage, was away this week, staying with her uncle and aunt in their caravan on the Dorset coast and visiting the Portland quarry to buy stone. Maybe she'd returned early. Or what if – Bridget stopped on the track that led up from the stream – what if an intruder was in the yard? Valuable things were kept here - Meg's stonework, her equipment and Leonard's, Adam's paintings. She and Anthony had talked of having an alarm and security light installed, but had done nothing. Aware that she was alone with no one to summon for help and had unwisely left the house unlocked, she walked on, keeping to the grass so that her feet made no sound.

Seeing Adam's van in the yard, she sagged with relief. It was unusual for him to be here so late, and he hadn't been around earlier. Leonard had been in his workshop and they'd exchanged their customary remarks about the weather; he was the only person she'd seen today.

Adam was locking up, his back to her. "You're late!" she called, and he turned in surprise. He saw her and moved towards the van, his elongated shadow thrown across the yard.

"Hi, Bridget. Came back to load some stuff. I've been with Dave, felling a tree, but I needed to collect something for tomorrow."

"Are you working with him again?"

"No, but I've got an exhibition in Northampton in the evening. I'm going over there first thing."

"Oh, the one at the Insch Gallery? The private view? I'm going to that." Bridget explained about Daniel inviting her.

"Why don't we go together, then?" Adam said. "I'll drive."

"If you don't mind. Thank you! That would be lovely."

Back indoors she went up to her room and stripped for a shower; the window was open, the air cool against her skin. Crossing on bare feet to her wardrobe she ran her fingers over various garments, rejecting them as too staid, then pulled out a kaftan with beading around the neck and cuffs. She held it against herself, feeling the silky caress. When had she last worn it? She recalled an outing with university friends of Anthony's, back in the days when they went to dinner-parties; she'd dressed carefully in the new kaftan and cream trousers, her hair swept up and pinned haphazardly. In the mirror her eyes were ravished by the rich colours – bronze, kingfisher, deep pine green. She thought she looked bohemian and artistic, but when she went downstairs Anthony only said, "Come on. We're late." When she pressed, asking "Do you like it?" he replied, "Yes, it's fine. Your hair's a bit of a mess, though." It was rare now for her to be presented as Anthony's wife, and she disliked it, unsure what was expected of her.

The weather next day continued dry and hot, so that even at nine in the morning the sun struck fiercely. Early, she watered her tomatoes, as she wouldn't be here for her evening routine; she sowed lettuce and rocket to keep the salad crops coming and put them in the barn's shade to germinate. It was too hot to work outside. She spent the afternoon on her article, dozed a little, then woke with a sense of anticipation. She liked the prospect of arriving at the gallery with Adam, one of the exhibiting artists and a more than personable young man. Mixing with artists and editors, going to a private view – it felt like her entrée to a new, exciting world.

The gallery, close to the Guildhall, was an austere space in a converted warehouse: industrial girders, bare brick walls, scrubbed wooden floor. Among the paintings on the walls Bridget's eyes went to the one Adam had been working on recently, the big square of greys and purples suggestive of a stormy sky, with runs and dribbles of fiery orange that leapt forward at the viewer, brilliant as lava flow against ash.

As they entered Adam was claimed by acquaintances. With a glass of wine in her hand Bridget drifted away to look at the paintings, absorbing the atmosphere. There was no sign of Daniel. Among the works displayed were some Modigliani-ish portraits that appealed to her, but she soon returned, compelled, to Adam's big square. Knowing that Meg was dismissive of his work, and because he rarely mentioned it himself, she'd taken little notice while the board was propped in the workshop amidst the clutter of tins, offcuts and crates, but here it commanded attention, the largest painting in the room with an end wall to itself. Lit from above, the colours vibrated against each other, pulling her in, her eyes swimming into purpling depths, then arrested again by orange fire. Would even Meg be impressed, seeing it in this context?

Two others were looking at it, two women of around her own age. "Yes, very much so," one said; then the other nudged her and they turned to look at the cluster of people near the entrance. "Oh, so *that's* him, the tall one with the stubble?" said the first one. "Mmmm, yes - I see what you mean."

Following their gaze Bridget saw Adam listening attentively to a small woman in a kimono, stooping to hear what she said. He turned his head and caught her eye, and as if something were understood between them he detached himself and moved towards her. She felt a frisson of interest from the two women as he approached.

"Sorry, Bridget," he said. "Didn't mean to abandon you."

"No, no! This is your show – you don't have to look after me."

"Let me introduce you to some people. That's Oliver, in the waistcoat – he's the gallery owner." His hand was on her elbow. "And here's Misha -"

Misha wore a tiny skirt, black leggings and biker boots and had purple hair and piercings; Adam pointed out her screen prints and they went over to look.

"Bridget! You made it - good," said a voice behind her. It was Daniel, with another, slightly younger man with hair sleeked back in a pony tail, introduced as "My partner, Hugh. Oh, you've met Adam – he's one of the artists I told you about."

She was sure he hadn't, but explained that Adam's studio was at Wildings and that they'd known each other for some months.

"Really?" Daniel raised his eyebrows. "You were telling me about Artweeks next year. So Adam's one of your protégés?"

"Hardly that. It's a useful working space for him, that's all."

"Stunning piece, Adam," said Hugh. "Exquisite. Have you had any offers?"

"Nearly."

Hugh gave a gusty sigh. "I wish we could – but we haven't got the space for it, have we, Dan?"

"Sadly not. If you should start doing miniatures, Adam, we'll definitely have one. Bridget, can I refill your glass?"

While Daniel signalled to one of the circulating waiters, two women came up, each greeted by Hugh with the double-cheek-peck that was the norm here. He introduced them to Bridget, who promptly forgot their names; they were talking rapidly, seeming to know everyone. The room was full, voices rising so that it was difficult to hear. Out of the conversation now, Bridget was amused at herself, recalling her silly, adolescent indulgence about Daniel. She hadn't guessed; should she have? He simply had the ease with women she'd noticed in other gay men; no doubt he was charming to everyone he met.

The man called Oliver summoned Adam to join the other artists, seven of them, for a press photograph; lightbulbs flashed. "Again. Look this way - yes, yes." It was the same photographer who'd come to Wildings.

"Are you writing this up for the magazine?" Bridget asked Daniel, who said, "We're covering it, but it's Felicity who does art events. Have you met Felicity?"

So many names, so many talented and busy people.

"Do you paint?" one of the women – Tash – asked, and she explained why she was here; Tash then told her at length about a disappointing art course in France which segued into a monologue about the difficulties of caring for elderly parents. Obliged to make sympathetic noises, Bridget was relieved when someone pulled at Tash's arm and said, "Darling, I must show you this, I've fallen in love with it," and led her away.

"OK?" said Adam's voice, close to Bridget's ear. "Tell me when you've had enough."

"I'm in no hurry."

"Adam, excuse me – have you got a moment?"

It was a man she'd seen earlier, studying Adam's painting. The two moved into a corner where they talked for several minutes, Bridget discerning that Adam was being flattered, his response to stare at the floor. Soon they were smiling and shaking hands, and Adam stood for a moment looking dazed; then he glanced at Bridget, and again she felt that odd, unexpected intimacy.

"Is he buying it?" she asked, when he came over.

"Yes. And commissioning another, a companion piece."

"Congratulations! A good evening, then." Bridget raised her almost-empty glass; Adam took it from her, and smiled.

"Shall we go? I never stay at parties to the end."

· · ·

When she woke, to early birdsong through the open window, Adam was in bed beside her, asleep, breathing gently. She rolled over, a hand to her forehead, her mind reeling.

What have I done? How could I?

But I did. And would, again. Oh yes...

It had felt inevitable: the exchanged glances throughout the evening, the little touches, his hand on the small of her back as they moved through chattering groups towards the door. The possibility had tingled through her then, and she did not resist.

"Thank you so much, Adam," she said, as the van pulled up; Wildings was in darkness, the windows blank. Her voice was prim in spite of the frankly lustful thoughts she'd let herself entertain on the drive home, stealing glances at the line of his throat, curve of eyebrow, lean length of thigh. "I enjoyed it. Enjoyed your company."

"Me, too."

Their eyes met.

"Well, goodnight." Losing courage, she turned and reached for the door handle.

"Bridget." He took her arm, leaned towards her; she yielded at first to the polite social peck, and then – she couldn't tell which of them initiated it - they were kissing, arms tightening, bodies close as their breathing quickened. She tasted wine on his breath, inhaled his warmth, laced with something astringent; felt the rasp of stubble against her cheek.

After a few moments, pulling back, she said, "You could come in. If you like." Even then she'd thought herself ridiculous to imagine that Adam, twenty years younger and surely not short of opportunities, could see anything desirable in her. Without a word he turned off the engine and they got out of the van, Bridget fumbling for keys. The sky was giddy with stars; a crescent moon hung bright as a lantern over the trees that bordered the lane.

"Are you sure?" Adam said, inside, and she nodded and pulled him to her. After all the months of abstinence she was astonished by the fierceness of her response, her breath fast and deep, hands roving, pulling at his shirt. It seemed for a few moments that they wouldn't get as far as the bedroom; then they broke off and laughed at themselves, and she took his hand and led him upstairs and into her room, leaving the lights off, opening the window wide, before turning to him and helping him pull the kaftan over her head, then to strip off his own clothes. Together they sank to the bed, and oh, the deliciousness of cool air on hot bodies, lips and hands moving over skin, his knee parting her legs; she had forgotten, but her body had not forgotten, opening to his touch, overcome by powerful animal instinct, sensation sharpening till it was almost unbearable.

Afterwards they lay beached by the intensity and release, still breathing fast. She felt detached from herself; thrilled, dismayed, astonished. A little tearful.

"What?" Adam said softly, and kissed away her tears, the sweep of his hair tickling her face.

"It was - " She struggled for words. "Like the tide, or the phases of the moon. Almost nothing to do with me or you. I'm talking rubbish."

"You and Anthony?" he said, moments later, or was it hours, while she was drifting in and out of sleep, and she murmured, "No. Not for a long while."

Fully awake now, she thought of Anthony in the hall of residence, his home for the week; he'd be getting up, thinking of the day ahead, possibly even thinking of her, and Wildings, wishing he were here to drink coffee on the terrace. *Anthony,* she thought, looking towards the open window. *I've been unfaithful. I am unfaithful.* But the word rang meaninglessly: so quaint it sounded, so irrelevant. What faith was there between them, living together but apart? Would he, in fact, be taking advantage of his single room, the ratio of male to female at summer school presenting ample opportunities for casual sex, if that was what he wanted? She'd wondered this before, with a coolness that surprised her. Now – it would be a relief, justifying her own conduct.

Casual sex? Was that all this had been? Yes, of course. But no – it felt momentous, vital, life-affirming.

Her clothes and Adam's were strewn on the floor, the rich colours of her kaftan against the pale linen of his shirt and jeans. Her mind filled with practicalities: it was Thursday, the day Maureen came to clean. Anthony would return on Saturday, Suzanne on Sunday ...

How could she face them? Act as if this hadn't happened? She slipped out of bed and went to the bathroom; cleaning her teeth she looked at her reflection as if at a stranger. This couldn't happen again, not without lying and cheating. After showering she pulled on her cotton wrap and went back to the bedroom, arrested by the sight of Adam still asleep: hair flung against the pillow, hand curled by his cheek, stubble shading his jaw, the long line of his back.

As if her gaze had woken him his eyes opened and focused, uncomprehending, then startled. She thought: he's wondering what the hell he's doing here, how to get away. Then his face softened and he reached out to her.

As she went to him his arms closed round her, the side of his face against her belly, and at once an ache of longing pushed aside any resolve.

"Adam, you've got to go," she said, but her fingers were in his hair, threading through to the nape of his neck, the warmth and smoothness of his skin.

"I know," he murmured. "But not yet."

• • •

Adam showered and left. At the door he touched her cheek, looked at her for a moment without speaking, then went out to his van. Neither he nor she referred to what they both knew: Anthony and Suzanne were away for another night.

No. I can't, she told herself as the day went on. Won't. It can't happen again.

But it could. She had Adam's phone number, on the agreement for the letting of the workshop. She thought of inviting him over for the evening, but was daunted by that. To cook a meal for him, to sit cosily over food and a bottle of wine, would seem somehow more adulterous than inviting him into her bed. It would feel furtive, a betrayal of Anthony; the same if she suggested going out somewhere.

She went about her chores in a haze of indecision. She chatted to Maureen, did her supermarket shop, changed the bedlinen and put out clean towels. Later she worked in the garden, with frequent glances towards the stableyard, wanting and not wanting him to appear. In the evening she tried to read her gardening magazine but couldn't concentrate; her eyes closed and pulse quickened as her thoughts swerved back to last night.

The shrilling of the phone made her jump.

"Bridget? It's me. Adam."

"Oh." Her heart was beating fast. "I'm on my own here. Do you want to - "

"Yes," he said. "I'm coming over."

Meg

1990, AUGUST

Approaching Wildings, her uncle at the wheel, Meg saw Adam's van by the house porch. Odd. Maybe he was delivering something for Bridget; it was barely seven-thirty, but Bridget was an early riser.

It was good to be back. Already she felt a tug of affection for Stables Cottage, her home now. She'd enjoyed the week by the coast, but after the cramped caravan she'd relish being alone again. This week she'd complete the *STABLES COTTAGE* sign; an irregular slab of Welsh slate was set aside, ready.

In the back of the van was a chunk of Portland stone, and some bookshelves bought in a second-hand shop in Bridport. Her aunt and uncle helped unload and she made tea and toast. Almost as soon as they drove away, well past nine, Adam pulled into the yard in his van, parking in his usual place by the barn.

"Hi, Adam," she called as he got out.

His head jerked round. "Oh – thought you weren't back till tomorrow?"

"Change of plan. Saw your van by the house." She looked at him quizzically. "You were here early?"

"Mmm – yes, I was just - " An awkwardness in his manner alerted her; his gaze shifted away. "Good holiday?" he said, jollily.

"Thanks, yes." Moving closer she saw that his hair was wet, sleeked down and dark, lightening at the ends as it dried; she smelled shower-freshness. "You were just what?" she asked. "At the house? You dropped in to use the shower?"

He didn't reply but gave a small *don't ask* shake of his head. It was answer enough.

"Adam!"

"'Scuse me - " He was jingling his keys in his hand, attempting briskness. She moved into his way, confronting him.

"Fuck's sake! What are you playing at?"

He looked at her directly for the first time. "I'm not playing."

"Seriously - what are you *doing?* Are you – you and *Bridget* – Christ! You're mad. *Both* mad. Or am I dreaming this?"

"Look, I - "

"Has this been going on the whole time Anthony's been away?" she demanded.

"No. Don't, Meg."

"He'll have your bollocks for dog's meat."

"Enchanting. Leave it, can't you?"

"Well! As long as you're happy." She turned away and strode to the cottage.

Her mind raced as she sorted her washing. She was deeply perturbed by the exchange, as if everything had shifted, her happiness here in jeopardy. Why *she* should feel that, she had no idea. She'd intended to find Bridget herself, to tell her she was back and ask if she'd share a cottage lunch, but now hesitated.

Adam and Bridget. Bridget and Adam. She dwelt on imagined details, feeling like a voyeur. It was a kind of envy, although who she envied, and why, she couldn't analyse. Either of them; both.

"Fuck's sake!" she muttered aloud. "Get on with something."

She started the washing machine and went to the workshop, by which time Adam's van had gone. Radio 1 (annoying!) pulsed from Leonard's open door, and Leonard was talking to Bridget in the yard.

Bridget saw her, excused herself and came over.

"Hello! Did you have a good time?"

"Lovely, thanks. You? How's it been, with the place to yourself?"

"Oh – quiet," Bridget said, with the same shiftiness Adam had displayed. "I've done a lot in the garden." She glanced towards Adam's workshop, then quickly away, and Meg saw the flush that rose from her neck. "But tell me about Dorset."

"I'll make coffee." Meg filled the kettle and washed mugs while she talked about the Jurassic coast, fossil-hunting on the beach, visiting Lyme Regis and the Cobb. "Aunty Eileen had a bad toothache yesterday, so we're back a day early. She got an appointment for this morning."

"Oh, that's a shame," said Bridget, distracted. She was looking at Meg's drawings on the cork board. "Did I tell you I was going to an exhibition in Northampton?"

She knows perfectly well she didn't, Meg thought. "The Insch Gallery? Adam said he was showing his painting there.

The mauve blodgy one, wasn't it? I'd have gone too if I'd been around."

And that would have spoiled your fun ...

"Yes," Bridget said, "but it was Daniel who invited me, you know, Daniel Burns from *Northamptonshire Life.*"

"You must have seen Adam there, though?"

"Yes, yes of course, and the painting," Bridget said quickly. "Actually, I know you don't rate his work, but it looked so different there, with the lighting. You couldn't help looking at it, the colours, the depth. It really stood out. It's - grown on me."

"I can see that." Meg poured milk.

"And he sold it, to the same man who bought his other one."

"The one with the big car and fat cheque-book?" Meg passed her a mug. "Most of what I say to Adam is to wind him up. It's grown on me, too. So you really think he's got something?" she added, to provoke.

"Mm," Bridget hedged. "Not that I'm an expert."

Meg waited to see if she'd offer more; Bridget didn't. But she was as transparent as a teenager, Meg thought - lit up, her mind elsewhere, hugging her secret but unable to resist talking about her lover. *Lover:* mentally Meg examined the word, so irrelevant to her own life.

They were both hopeless liars, Bridget and Adam. If Bridget went on like this she'd reveal herself to Anthony or Suzanne when they came back. Though perhaps it was a safe bet that Anthony would be too wrapped up in himself to notice.

Jane

FEBRUARY

Suzanne was excited and at first unbelieving when Jane phoned about Sean. "Did you find out – what did he say about – didn't you ask him -"

"No, not all at once," Jane told her. "I couldn't. It was enough to meet him. For him to turn up, a real person."

"Well, you obviously took to him in a big way. I can't wait to meet him too! We must arrange something."

"Yes, let's. Tom and I are meeting him in Oxford – I'll suggest it."

Suzanne offered to relay the news to Rob, for which Jane was grateful. Two days later, Suzanne reported that he'd been indignant. "He says Sean should have made an appointment through the solicitor, not just turned up. Not a good start, in his opinion." Only afterwards did Jane remember that she hadn't mentioned her email to Sean.

Chitra, over coffee with Jane after Tuesday's class, was also doubtful. "Well, *I* think he sounds a bit creepy."

"Creepy? How?"

"Lurking round the graveyard, not coming to the house. And you invited him *in?* He could've been *anyone!*"

"No, no," Jane protested. "It's not like that. If you met him you'd know. I – trust him."

"After one meeting?"

"Yes."

Chitra puffed out her breath. "What's he after?"

"Why should he be *after* anything? He just wants to meet the family. Wouldn't you? I'm meeting him in Oxford tonight for dinner."

"With Rob and Suzanne?"

"No – it's too soon for that."

Chitra gave her a sceptical look. "It sounds like a *date*. Look at you, all pink and excited. Be careful. You hear about brothers and sisters falling in love - you know, when they've been separated all their lives?"

"It's not like that," Jane protested, though heat rushed to her face. "I do like him ... a lot ... but he's *old*, fiftyish. And Tom's coming, so I'll be perfectly safe."

"Sounds to me," Chitra said, "like he wants you on his side. Before he meets the others."

Driving home, Jane passed a building site on the farther side of Haverton where one of the farms had sold land, two fields where cattle had grazed. Boards had gone up before Christmas, then the excavators moved in, turf was dug up, hedgerows torn out, the whole area flattened and staked. Excavators, hydraulic arms rising and dipping like mechanical flamingos, crawled around, brilliant orange against the mud expanse. Two Portakabins stood by the entrance next to a sign advertising *Haverton Meadows: exclusive rural development of quality 3- and 4-bedroom homes.*

"Nimby," Tom had teased, when she mourned. "You've got your cottage. Other people need homes too."

"I know. But not *here*."

This could happen to our orchard, she thought, waiting by temporary traffic lights. *Mum's* orchard, the trees with their prodigious crops of apples and plums. She thought of the purple bloom on plums, their perfumed flesh that brought wasps to feast. She hated to think of excavators tearing into the ground.

The viewing this afternoon was a return one. "I think it's likely they'll make an offer," Sam had said. "Would three-ish suit?"

Jane had agreed, but would be at home this time. She planned to spend the afternoon on her accounts before driving to Tom's for their meeting with Sean. The agent had by now brought several potential buyers, reporting back each time: "They loved it, but there aren't enough bathrooms ... Very interested, just looking at their finances ... Dependent on planning permission to extend ... Consulting their architect ... "

Mr and Mrs Pritchard, a thirtyish couple from London, were accompanied by a different agent, Gavin. Mrs Pritchard, "Deborah, please," did a lot of gushing. "*Such* a lovely house – must be a wrench to leave it. This is divine, a real country kitchen." Her husband paced and measured: "Space for an American fridge, darling - maybe a freestanding central unit."

At the kitchen table with folders and calculator, Jane tried to concentrate while footsteps moved up and down the stairs, but couldn't help hearing the hallway conversation. "Yes, we adore it, don't we, Oliver? ... Needs a complete bathroom refit of course, but there's scope to make that second bedroom ensuite..." She heard goodbyes and thank yous at the front

door, and Gavin came into the kitchen. They hadn't been into the garden at all.

"They're very keen. There's a bit of an issue about the stableyard. Ideally they'd like to have the cottage, for staff, but I said you're not selling. Might be possible to convert those workshops into living accommodation, though. That could swing it."

But they're not *right*, Jane wanted to say. They'd modernise the place and care nothing for the garden other than as a setting for drinks on summer evenings; she saw designer furniture, everything fashionably accessorised. Her misgivings grew when Gavin added, "There's the possibility of selling off the orchard to offset the cost of conversion."

Closing the door with relief after he'd gone, she went up to shower in the despised bathroom. When she checked her phone she found an email from Meg: **I'm in your area tomorrow afternoon delivering a birdbath. Are you at home? I'd like to see the place one more time before it's sold.**

Jane replied **Yes, great,** thinking that she could tell Meg about Sean. At the same moment a message pinged in from Tom.

Sorry cant make tonight ☹ ☹ ☹ urgent meeting with client See you at yours tomorrow 4ish Tx ♥

"Oh, *Tom!*" Jane chucked her phone on to the bed. Didn't he know how important this was? She sent no reply, phoning Suzanne instead.

"Would *you* come, if you're free? I'd like someone else there, and it'd be great for you to meet Sean before Rob gets involved."

"Oh, Jane! Sorry – really wish I could, but we've got a parents' evening, Rhiannon's last one. What a shame – I'd love to meet him. You go, and arrange something else in a week or so. Why don't you invite him to lunch here, on a Sunday, soonest we can all do?"

"That'd be good. But I suppose you'll have to invite Rob and Ingrid as well."

"Well, yes."

"It's only that Sean seems a bit – reserved. All of us together might be a bit much. Especially, you know. Rob."

"Mm. Well, see how it goes tonight, and ring me tomorrow."

As she chose clothes, Jane felt mounting annoyance with Tom. Couldn't he have put her first, met his client some other time? She had no misgivings about meeting Sean on her own; only that Tom's presence would have lightened things, made it seem less like – well, as Chitra said, a date.

You can't have a date with your half-brother, she told herself, putting on mascara, which she rarely bothered with, and clumsily smudging her eyelid.

In Oxford she parked in St Giles and walked along to Browns, a restaurant she liked the look of but had never visited. Large windows framed a welcoming interior: cream paintwork, dark wood, a great many potted palms, warm lighting. Sean was already seated by the window; he waved and smiled as she approached, then stood and kissed her cheek as she came to the table.

"You're cold! Have you walked far?"

"Only from the car." The wind was raw tonight, and she was well wrapped-up in coat, scarf and gloves.

"On your own, though?"

She apologised for Tom's absence. "Sorry, it was a bit late to let you know."

"Doesn't matter. Next time. I'm glad you could still make

it." Sean took her coat and hung it on a stand nearby. "What would you like to drink?"

He looked older than she remembered, soft light silvering his hair. She began to relax, feeling that it was like being out with a rather handsome uncle. He ordered drinks, lime and soda for Jane, white wine for himself; when the waitress brought them he raised his glass and said, "To Wildings. To us. To new-found family."

"Tell me about your other relations," she said. "About Fionnuala – lovely name! – and your stepfather, and Dad – well, everything."

"Life stories? All right, my turn first, then yours."

The waitress took their order; then Jane said, "Your mother was a farm student – you told me that. What did she do?"

"Dairying. She was a city girl from Dublin, but she came over here to study and then fancied farming. I think she had some hippy dream of wandering through meadows and milking cows in the dew, but it was more about slurry and culling and abbatoirs -" He broke off. "Sorry – you're vegetarian, aren't you? Not a good topic."

"Vegan. But how did you know?" She hadn't mentioned it while choosing from the menu.

"Oh – goes with yoga, doesn't it? And what you've just ordered."

"You've gone for vegetarian, too. Was that to spare my feelings, or -?"

He shook his head. "No - I gave up meat at New Year. Not sure I can do the whole vegan thing, but – well, it's more and more obvious that the planet can't support meat-eating, and I started to feel like a hypocrite, working with idealistic teenagers. Not that I don't crave a bacon sandwich sometimes – that's the cliché, isn't it?"

Jane stored this away: another reason to love him.

"Anyway," she said, "go on about your mum."

"So – she met Anthony when she was hitching a lift and he stopped for her. She was very pretty then, my mother, an Irish redhead – still is, pretty I mean, though her hair's white now. She thought it was her lucky day, and I suppose so did he. They started seeing each other. I think she was completely dazzled. She was only nineteen, he mid-twenties. His parents were ambitious for him, and didn't see her as marriage material, a farm girl with nothing to her name. They wanted him to make a successful marriage – successful in their terms, that is. Then he met his wife, his first wife -"

"Eliza," Jane prompted. "Rob's mother."

"– Eliza, yes, from a well-off family – old money, business, the lot - and that was that. All the same I'd like to think that he did love my mother. He broke off with her, but I gather the marriage wasn't happy, and when he got in touch again, a couple of years later, he -" He stopped, looking down at his hands, then up at Jane. "Sorry. This doesn't reflect well on Anthony. His side of the story would be different for sure, but this is what I know from my mother."

"Go on. It's kind of at a safe distance, before he met Mum. So, he...?"

"Made her believe the marriage was over, he'd leave Eliza for her. And soon she was pregnant, with me. She was delighted, thinking they'd set up home, start out properly together. But when she told him, it turned out he had no intention of leaving Eliza after all. He had too much to lose, especially as Eliza was pregnant too by then. He offered to pay for an abortion, but she wouldn't agree – she was set on having the baby – me – no matter what. So she told him to get stuffed, basically, and went home to Dublin. She knew her family would support her. This was in the sixties - it would have been deeply shocking to have an illegitimate baby by a married man, especially for an Irish Catholic girl. Her family put about the story that she was married, with a husband living in England."

"So – you told me you stayed in Dublin till you were two?"

"Yes. Then she met my stepfather, and they got married and moved to the Midlands, Chesterfield, for his work. That's where they are now, both in their seventies."

Jane was silent, taking all this in. Prominent in her mind was the thought that if her father had had his way, Sean wouldn't exist. Their food arrived and she began eating absently, hungry in spite of herself.

"But Dad's marriage ended anyway," she said. "From what Rob says, I don't think Eliza can have known about *you,* but she did find out he'd carried on seeing your mother after they were married – she told Rob that. He was only a baby when they split up – so you're the same age? He's, what, fifty-two now."

"I'm fifty-three, just."

"And you've still got a mother and a stepdad? You're better off for parents than I am."

He nodded slowly. "It doesn't seem fair, I know."

"My Dad – *our* Dad – was fifty-something when I was born. There's a lot I don't know about him – he'd had so much of his life before I was around. And it's a mystery how *that* happened – why he and Mum had me, so late. It seems unlikely that I'm here at all." She hesitated. "So - Dad *knew* about you, then, all along? Knew he had another son?"

"Yes. But my mother never claimed anything from him – his name isn't on my birth certificate, and later my stepdad adopted me. I didn't meet Anthony till I was much older."

"How did that happen?"

"I – well. I tracked him down. We only had a few meetings. It was awkward, you might say. So the Will was a shock."

"Yes - why would he do that? After keeping you secret for so long? I'm certain my Mum never knew about you. But then, after she died he changed his Will to include you, Rob said. So he must have – must have *cared,* mustn't he? Even if he never let you know."

He was silent, looking down at his plate; she wondered if she'd said something wrong. Glancing up, his face troubled, he began, "I -" A burst of laughter and exclamations came from the group at the next table; he shook his head. "That's enough about me. Tell me about yourself."

Still with much to ask, she told him about growing up at Wildings, about her mother's gardening success and modest fame; about her own career, such as it was; about the awfulness of her mother's illness and death, and how her father had never seemed to recover.

"I wouldn't want you to think he was all bad." She wasn't sure how to say this, or whether she should.

"No. I don't want to think that either."

"It was odd, him and Mum, how there was this distance between them, a kind of truce. He was so different with Suzanne and me. After Suzanne got married and I was the only one at home, he made me feel special. I was close to Mum too, but closer to Dad, in a way. With Mum there was a kind of coolness. Dad was often moody and he could be a pain to live with, but in the end it seemed to be him who suffered most. I had the sense that Mum would find a way to get what she wanted." She caught herself; she'd meant to paint her father in a flattering light, not criticise her mother.

Sean had listened intently, saying little. He said, "Tell

me something you remember from when you were small. At Wildings."

She thought for a moment, then said, "There was a poem Dad used to recite, one he specially liked. *Nicholas Nye*, about a donkey. *Thistle and darnel and dock grew there, and a bush, in the corner, of May* ... The old wall in the garden reminded him of it, this poem he'd learned as a boy and remembered. He could recite it by heart. I still can, too."

"That's lovely," Sean said. "You must always keep that."

The waitress cleared their plates; they both turned down dessert but ordered coffee. She asked about his marriage; he spoke of his twelve years with Jenny, ending in mutual disappointment and a sense of failure over their inability to have children; there had been IVF treatment, hopes and breakthroughs, followed each time by crushing loss. "I was thirty-five when we met, Jenny two years older. Our chances got lower, each year that passed. Eventually it was too much. The one thing we both wanted – Jenny especially - was the one thing we couldn't have. I'd adjusted to that, but for her it wasn't enough."

"I'm sorry," Jane said inadequately.

"She's remarried, but we see each other now and then. Anyway. Tell me about you and Tom. How long have you been together?"

"With quite a bit of on and off, about five years."

"On at the moment, though?"

"Yes, I think so," Jane said, and told him of her dilemma over the cottage: whether it would work, living there with Tom. "I don't want to live there on my own, not really. But I don't know if I can be with him all the time. Mum and Dad lived together but both had their own lives. They'd never have stayed together otherwise. At Wildings there was plenty of space for them to avoid each other. It sounds awful, put like that – their marriage only worked because they could keep out of each other's way. But that's how it seemed."

"Maybe not as unusual as you think," Sean said. "You and Tom could carry on as you are for a while longer, being apart when you want. Doesn't mean it's not a good relationship."

"I'd actually prefer that. How about you, now? A partner or anything?"

"Yes, for the last two years. Her name's Ness. We spend weekends together but we've got our own places and I can't see that changing. It works well - we both like our independence. And Suzanne? Is she happily married?"

"Oh, *yes*. She and Ed are rock-solid, if anyone is." Only now did she remember Suzanne's suggestion of a family lunch, and put it to him. "You would come, wouldn't you?"

"Would Rob be there? From the dealings with the solicitor, I haven't exactly taken to him. And I get the impression you're much closer to Suzanne."

"Yes, much," she agreed. "It'd be a lot nicer if it could be just her and Ed, at first – you'll like them, I promise. Shall I try for that? It's like a board meeting when Rob and Ingrid are there."

"In a couple of weeks? I'm going away again, for work."

The restaurant was quieter now; diners were leaving, staff clearing tables. Sean asked for the bill. Seeing Jane take out her wallet he said, "No, no, put that away! This is on me. When have I had the chance before?"

"Well – thank you. This has been lovely." It didn't seem adequate.

"Will you be OK, driving back? It's quite a way."

"I think I'll go to Tom's," she said, having thought of this earlier. Even if he wasn't back yet, she had a key. The evening had mellowed her to the point of being ready to forgive him and take an interest in whatever work meeting had been so crucial.

Sean walked with her to her car; his was in the underground car park farther on. They parted with a hug and a kiss, promising to speak very soon, and she drove to Summertown thinking how much there was still to discuss, all those missing years to account for. She'd talk to Suzanne and phone Sean tomorrow.

Unable to park in Tom's road she found a space in the next street. Lights were on in his first floor flat, so he was back; she let herself in and went up the side stairs.

"Hi!" She opened the door, ready to explain; and stopped dead.

Details rushed at her. Soft lighting, Amy Winehouse playing. Andrea on the sofa. Andrea, in Tom's dressing-gown, legs bare, feet in thick socks with a teddy-bear pattern, hair falling over one shoulder.

"For God's sake!" Andrea dropped her magazine. "Don't *do* that! I thought you were Tom -"

"What are you doing here?" Jane steadied herself against the wall, heart thumping.

"What does it look like? Waiting for Tom." Andrea unfolded her long legs and swung her feet to the floor. "I could ask you the same!"

Jane's voice came out clipped and tight. "Where is he?"

"Meeting someone at Jericho Tavern. I didn't know you still had a key."

"I imagine there are lots of things you don't know. Me too, it seems."

"Not expecting you, is he?" Andrea said off-handedly. "Hang on, if you like. I was about to go to bed."

The *cheek* of her! Jane was tempted to agree, to install herself on the sofa in Andrea's place, to see Tom's face when he entered. But she was too jittered, not sure she could control herself. "You do that. Don't let me keep you up. I'll talk to Tom tomorrow."

She hurried downstairs on shaking legs, followed by Amy Winehouse's plaintive voice. On the pavement she stood for a moment, mind whirring.

How could he be so – how could he -

Tom. *Tom.* There he was, in one of the residents' parking places, locking his car. She found new energy as she headed towards him. Maybe he didn't know Andrea was here. Did she have her own key too?

Summoning limited acting ability, she walked up and kissed him on the cheek. "Hi! How was your meeting?"

He was almost comically astonished, the streetlight illuminating his face. "Oh! You didn't -"

"Thought I'd surprise you. You don't mind?"

"No, yes, I mean -" He backed away, stumbling on the kerb edge. "Thing is, it's not a good time. I was going to tell you tomorrow."

"Tell me what?"

"Sorry," he said. "I really am. I didn't mean it to end like this."

...

She drove home too fast, dazed by shock and fury, eyes blurring.

How could he? Now? Like that?

It was no comfort to tell herself that she'd had her own doubts. Complacently, she'd assumed that she'd be the one to end the relationship when the time came. But this - moving Andrea in before he'd even made the break – was unforgivable! Or had Andrea been popping in and out for weeks, with Tom managing them both part-time? Among fragments of conversation that clamoured for attention she heard him say that he didn't like being alone.

Fuck you, Tom ...

The headlights swept verges and hedgerows as she took to the narrow lanes. A fox trotted across the beam of light, unhurried, eyes reflecting red before it slunk through a gap. She fought back tears of indignation and hurt pride. So many times she'd driven these lanes with Tom. His easy contentment had been good for her, soothing her worries.

But not content after all.

"You're so half-hearted," he'd said in the street. "I never knew where I was, with you."

She saw the truth of that, but fired back: "That's because I can't trust you! I was stupid to think I could, after last time. After everything you said! But oh, here's Andrea back. All cosy, ready for bed -"

Not much of an actor after all; anger had driven pretence out of her mind.

"You mean - you -" Tom blathered.

"Yes! I went in just now and there she was. How can you *do* that? - But maybe it doesn't *matter* who, as long as you've got one of us handy?"

"It's not like that!"

"Isn't it?" Her voice wavered. "How could you let me down again? With everything else – you *knew* I wanted you there tonight!"

"I've tried. You know I have. You didn't seem to want me around, half the time."

"I thought you'd understand – things are difficult right now. But no. It's all my fault?"

"I'm not saying it's anyone's *fault*. It's just not working out, is it?"

He wore the expression of boyish bewilderment that could be endearing, but now made her want to slap him.

"OK. Fine." She threw up her arms. "Well, this is a great way to end it, arguing in the street. Thanks a lot." She took the key out of her pocket and lobbed it at him. "Here. Bye."

Turning away she broke into a jog, already wishing she'd managed to keep some shred of dignity. She could hardly remember where she'd parked.

"Jane, wait!"

She thought at first she heard his footsteps following, but when she glanced back he was crouching under the street lamp, searching for the key in the gutter. When he'd found it he'd no doubt go in to be consoled by Andrea.

So that was that. Over. Finished.

The last stretch of lane from Lower Stortford was so remote that she might be the only person around for miles. Usually when she returned at night she scuttled in as fast as she could, but now she slumped in her seat, staring at nothing.

At last she made herself go in. The house received her emptily, her footsteps echoing as she walked through to the kitchen.

She felt like wailing or throwing things, and took deep breaths to calm the childish impulse to lash out. The only person she could hurt was herself. The words of *Back to Black* circled in her mind, underlining her self-pity.

Whatever she felt for Tom, she wasn't in love with him; knowing that, she'd stopped expecting more. Still, his deception, his shallowness, filled her with a physical ache.

Another absence. So soon. She thought of her father standing here brewing LemSip, after leaving her at Birmingham airport. As she went through to departures she'd turned to wave; he stood watching, waiting for the last moment before she passed out of sight. So recent, and such an age ago. Her eyes brimmed.

"Oh, Dad," she said aloud. "I wish you were here."

She longed for his sympathy; wanted to tell him, hear what he'd say. Nothing of startling insight, but he'd comfort and cuddle her as he did when she was a little girl, and assure her that everything would be all right. As if the end of a five-year relationship meant no more than falling over and grazing her knee.

Who could she talk to? It was past midnight, too late to phone Suzanne or Chitra for sympathy. Instead she texted Sean: **Thanks so much for tonight! Look forward to seeing you soon at Suzanne's. Jx** Then, on an impulse, she followed it with: **Told you it was on-off with Tom? All off now. Dumped.**

Bridget

1990, OCTOBER

When bridget realised she was pregnant she knew it meant the end of her marriage. How could it be otherwise?

At first she suspected imminent flu or a minor infection. A late period could be ascribed to approaching menopause – she was a little young, but it wasn't out of the question. Then, in the garden, almost overwhelmed by the scent of mown grass, the perfume of a ripe damson and the icing-sugar waft of sweet peas, she recalled her heightened sense of smell during pregnancy with Suzanne, and knew.

She felt not so much shock or dismay as a sense of inevitability. Her body had grasped its chance, in those fevered hours with Adam, to reproduce while it had time.

Adam mustn't know, she decided. It would complicate things intolerably.

But of course Anthony *must* know.

Instinct rebelled against the thought of abortion. No.

Although not opposed in principle, she couldn't think of jettisoning the new life that had been startled into being.

Arguments and objections ranged themselves like fingers ticking off points. A baby, in her late forties? How could it be done, if she had to leave Wildings, as surely she would – how would she support herself? And what about Suzanne? It would throw all their lives into turmoil. But while her mind churned with doubts and practicalities, she knew that she would have this baby.

The garden was in autumn maturity, low light bringing out the richness of colour, the green of dew-soaked grass. The swifts had gone and the swallows would soon follow. The orchard hedges were bright with hawthorn berries, blackberries and bryony; the seed-heads of grasses were golden against the bronze-reds of heleniums and the orange-peel flowers of *clematis tangutica*. The vegetable beds were at their most productive; she was picking courgettes, beans and tomatoes, and digging up carrots and onions, with winter vegetables to follow. Every time she walked through, she returned with a handful of cherry tomatoes or dwarf beans.

How could she uproot herself? Her life was here, all she cared about. That, viscerally, was how it would feel to leave, prising herself from the soil she nurtured and cultivated. Her writing, too, and the possibilities springing from that; without Wildings, she'd be nothing. And Suzanne – however the situation was resolved, it couldn't possibly be to her benefit. After the drama of August she'd settled into sixth-form routines, solid O-Level results behind her in spite of everything. Her arm had mended, she was best friends again with Helen, and excited about her first boyfriend, met at the swimming-pool. She mustn't be thrown into turmoil again.

For goodness' sake! How was that for wanting it all? Her life here unchanged: garden, comfortable home, husband, daughter, financial security. And another man's baby. She thought of suggesting it to Anthony as a kind of business arrangement – that they stay together, leading separate lives. Not so different from the way things were, except for a baby in the house. Anthony was past fifty now; when the child reached its late teens, he'd be seventy. Daunting enough if the baby were his own; unthinkable that he'd willingly disrupt his life for someone else's.

She was avoiding Adam. If his van were in the yard, she doubled back to the garden or house; if he arrived while she was in the barn or with Meg, she greeted him coolly. From years of practice with Anthony, her tactic was to pretend nothing had happened. She didn't flatter herself that Adam wanted a continuing relationship; why would he? But he came to her in the barn late one afternoon, where she was potting up seedlings.

"Bridget. Can we talk?"

"What about?"

"Just – I hardly see you. Everything's OK, isn't it?"

"What can you mean?" She couldn't look him directly.

He looked momentarily like a schoolboy in trouble. "For you, I mean."

"I think best to forget it, don't you? What -"

She didn't want to say *what happened,* acknowledging that something significant had, but he said it for her, his voice husky: "So it meant nothing to you, then, what happened?"

"You know it didn't," she said, in a softer tone.

"Well, then -"

He moved closer, as if to touch her; she held up her hands, shedding flakes and crumbs of potting compost.

"No, Adam. Don't. It's impossible."

Their eyes met; then he said, "Meg knows."

"You *told* her?"

"No. She worked it out. She's no fool. She saw my van outside the house that day she came back early."

Her attention was diverted by footsteps in the doorway, a shadow across the entrance.

"Cheerio, then, Mrs Harper -" Leonard insisted on calling her that, not Bridget. "I'm off home now."

The moment broken, she moved past Adam and out into the yard, brushing soil from her hands.

"OK, Leonard!" She produced a loud, cheery tone. "See you tomorrow."

• • •

She'd hardly needed to buy a pregnancy test. Positive: no surprise. She knew from the toughness of her nails and the absence of loose hairs on her brush that her body was making ready, holding on to everything, protecting new life inside.

Adam mustn't know. And that meant that one decision was inevitable.

Meg

1990, OCTOBER

ADAM HAD STARTED A new painting, commissioned as pair to the one he'd sold in August. Sometimes she saw him slapping on paint with big, broad strokes – though he always stopped if she came in - at other times staring at the huge board square in apparent despondency. It was as if he waited for some silent message from the accumulating colour and texture. He'd built up layers of deep indigo, the paint sometimes thick and glistening, elsewhere scumbled so that blue-grey wash could be seen beneath.

At her easel next door she worked industriously, the rhythm of chisel on stone a counterpoint to Adam's quietness. Eventually, neck and arms aching, she downed tools, leaned back and stretched; then looked in and found him sitting on an upturned crate, doing nothing.

"It'll be all right in the end. Have a break?" she asked, as if he were engaged in strenuous activity. "Jurassic tea?"

Today she had a favour to ask. She was to install a headstone on Thursday and couldn't manage alone; usually Uncle Terry helped, but he now had back problems.

"I can use his van, but could you come with me?" she asked, waiting for the kettle. "It's near Coventry, not far. Shouldn't take us more than an hour and a half to do the job. I'll treat you to a pub lunch, after."

Adam agreed, offering his own van to save the trouble of fetching her uncle's. When the tea was made he sat looking through one of her lettering books, while she picked up her tools again.

"You could stop now and then," he pointed out.

"Can't, with this waiting to be done." She resumed her valley-cutting; then winced and ducked, one eye clamped against searing pain. "*Ow!*"

"What?" Adam was on his feet.

"Bit of stone." She spoke through clenched teeth, blinking hard, eyes streaming, a hand to her face.

"No! Don't rub!" His hand on her shoulder, he turned her to face the light from the window. "Let me look."

Through a blur she saw his face close, his eyes gazing, intent: an oddly stirring moment of intimacy. She freed herself and shifted away. "I'm fine. Really."

"Sure?"

"Yes," she said, after more blinks. She looked at her lettering, saw it in focus again.

"Haven't you got safety goggles?"

"Course I've got bloody goggles." She had several pairs in a drawer. "I don't usually bother though. It doesn't happen often."

"Only got to happen *once*. Why risk it? A splinter in the eye could do serious damage."

"Yes, yes. All right. It was only a speck, gone now."

She didn't know why she was being curt. He was right about the goggles, though she rarely used them.

At that moment Bridget appeared in the doorway. "Meg, would you like -" She broke off, seeing Adam. "Oh. If either of you'd like apples or plums there's a basketful in the barn. Help yourselves."

She was gone before Meg could ask if she'd like to join them.

. . .

On Thursday Adam helped to load everything needed for the installation: the headstone, tools, cement mix, trolley. It had rained earlier – good, the ground wouldn't be too hard to dig - and the lanes shone purple-grey in dull light. The leaves of horse-chestnuts by the roadside were dry and crisped, ashes and oaks yet to begin turning.

Adam driving, Meg with the map, they found the small village, its sandstone church overlooking fields of sheep and a beech copse. They parked by the lych-gate and got out to almost resounding quietness, silence broken only by the crooning of woodpigeons.

Though Meg had no belief in eternal life; she liked churchyards: quiet places with ancient yews, space for contemplation, and the textures of weathered stone, the yellows, rusts and grey-greens of lichen. There was always interesting lettering to look at alongside the artless machine-cutting on most newer graves; she liked the thought of her own work being part of the place, reaching into the future. In rough grass behind the church, rows of tombstones formed irregular lines: some tilting, letters eroded by years of wind and rain, others more recent, in polished granite. Meg's diagram showed the plot for Mary Ann Ellwood, born

1919, died 1990, and there it was, marked by a plain wooden cross, earth mounded, a bunch of chrysanthemums tired and wilting.

"Better than plastic," Meg said, moving the flowers aside. Two nearby graves were adorned with false flowers stuck into urns or directly into the ground. "Why do people *do* that?"

She'd been commissioned by Mary Ellwood's son. Sometimes relatives came to see the headstone installed, but she preferred it when they didn't. Then it was simply a job, not a ceremony; her focus was on getting the stone in, properly aligned and stable. Any anonymous respect she felt for the dead person she'd already expended in the making, paying tribute with her skill and time.

They brought tools, Adam carrying the concrete shoe which would support the headstone below ground and keep it vertical. Meg pulled out the wooden cross before slicing off turves and putting them carefully aside; then she used a long ruler to establish the position for the stone, difficult because the gravestones either side were out of alignment.

"Now the digging." She marked the edges with swift cuts, then gave Adam her second spade. The soil was moist, marled with clay and threaded with roots; they threw spadefuls on to a plastic sheet laid on the grass. She measured, levelled the base and put down a layer of sand. Next the concrete slab went in, repositioned several times before she was satisfied, tilting it to put more sand underneath, checking her spirit-level.

"OK. Now the headstone."

This was the part she couldn't do alone. Protected by carpet, the headstone had to be carefully manoeuvred out of the van using wooden rollers, lowered to the trolley and wheeled to the site. There Meg explained that they'd walk it to the edge of the hole, align it with the slot in the concrete and slide it gently into place. This done, Adam supported it while she checked again with ruler and spirit-level, then mixed quick-drying cement in a bucket and trowelled it around the base. Soon the soil could be shovelled back and firmed, the turves replaced, verticality checked again, and the job was finished. She sluiced out her bucket with water from a butt, and together they carried the surplus earth on its plastic sheet to the heap in a corner.

"There you are, Mary Ann," Meg said, with the satisfaction of seeing work well done. "I hope you like it." She brought out her camera from her rucksack.

"It's beautiful. Really, Meg." Adam knelt to examine the detail: name and dates in italic lettering with sweeping flourishes, and on the back a design of oak leaves and acorns. "To see it here with the others - it's incredible, what you do." He smoothed a hand over the curved top and looked up as if seeing her properly for the first time.

She took photographs, front and back, and one with Adam in it. It was the biggest compliment he'd ever paid her; she would mark the moment.

"Thanks," she said briskly. "Right, I'm hungry, are you? Let's find the pub."

• • •

Adam was subdued. He said little over lunch, the conversation mainly provided by the landlord who was interested in their activity, having known Mary Ellwood. "Lived here all her life. Lovely lady. We had the wake in here, back in January. I'll stroll over to look when I've got a minute."

It was raining again when they left. In the van, retracing their route through lanes, Meg finally asked Adam, "What's up?"

"Nothing."

"Oh, come on. You've hardly said a word all day."

There was a pause, then: "I've got to leave Wildings. Bridget's chucking me out. She's given notice."

"Oh."

"You don't sound surprised. Did she tell you?"

"Not a word. But – she's been a bit odd, lately."

"Odd how?"

"Distracted. Dithery. A bit off-colour."

She thought of yesterday in the yard, talking to Bridget, aware that her attention had wandered; then Bridget visibly paled, muttered "'Scuse me," and rushed to the toilet. She spent so long in there that Meg gave up waiting and went back to her workshop. Reappearing more than ten minutes later Bridget was rueful and embarrassed, saying that she must have eaten something that disagreed with her. Now Meg felt the stir of a buried memory: herself, seventeen, running out of A-Level Art, reaching the girls' loos just in time to throw up, then lying to the teacher who hurried after her that something had upset her stomach, when she knew full well that –

Fuck.

"She's pregnant!"

She shouldn't have said it aloud.

Adam's head jerked round; his eyes met hers. Instinctively she grabbed the steering wheel as they swerved towards the ditch: a tree loomed, a gateway, tyres skidded on wet road. Then he regained control and they lurched to a halt.

"Don't kill us both," she said mildly.

"Sorry. But *shit.* D'you really think -"

"Only guessing. She was throwing up yesterday."

"Doesn't necessarily mean -"

"No. But then telling you to leave? Wouldn't she have kicked you out back in August, if it's only because she can't stand the sight of you?"

Adam was silent, clutching the wheel, looking at his hands.

"Maybe, if she is, it's Anthony's," she said. "Seems unlikely, but what do I know?"

Adam shook his head. "I can't believe that."

"But surely you - did the possibility never cross your mind? You're not stupid. Did you really not think?"

"Only after," Adam said. "I suppose I thought she'd be on the pill or something."

"So you *didn't* think. Except with your dick." She looked at him in exasperation. "Christ - and she was just as bloody stupid, obviously, to take the risk."

Slowly Adam exhaled. "What now? I clear off and leave her to it? That's what she wants?"

"Your part in this is over and done with. Can't see how staying around would help. Some women in her position," Meg said carefully, "might engineer a situation where the husband would think the baby was his."

He gave her a scathing look. "You think Bridget would do that?"

"What's the alternative? *Anthony dear, I shagged Adam while you were away and now I'm pregnant. You don't mind, do you?* Maybe she wants you out of the way for your own safety. In your place I wouldn't want to be around when Anthony finds out."

"You don't have to sound as if you're enjoying this."

"I'm not," she said, more seriously. "It's a mess, and now a baby no one wants. If there *is* a baby, if she goes ahead. She might not."

Adam slumped forward, hands to his forehead. Looking

at his hunched shoulders and the tanned nape of his neck, she resisted the urge to comfort him for what was blatantly his own fault. A car rounded the bend and braked, the driver glaring at the van slewed half across the road.

"Look," she said. "We're way ahead of ourselves. I shouldn't have blurted it out. We don't *know*, not yet. You OK, or shall I drive?"

Bridget

1990, OCTOBER

THE ONLY WAY WAS to maintain a cool distance, as if watching another person. She'd managed it through the interview with Adam, only afterwards reproaching herself, feeling the wrench of his departure.

"Why?" he said.

"You know why."

"I won't make things difficult. Won't you reconsider?"

Things could hardly be more difficult, if only he knew.

"I'm sorry," was all she said. "It's best this way."

Now the much harder prospect of telling Anthony. She owed it to him not to dissemble, not to try cheap tactics of softening him up with wine or his favourite food. She briefed herself to stay calm, even businesslike.

Her words dropped into the quiet of his study, cold as marbles.

He didn't shout or fly into a fury. He said nothing at all, at first. After one straight, appalled look at her he sat fixed in stillness, seemingly as numb as she felt.

"We must decide what to do," she said, "when you've had time to think about it."

"I see," he said. "The father, I assume, is that magazine editor you've been fawning over?"

"*Daniel?* No, no."

"Then who?"

"Someone I met. It's - over now."

"And that's all you're prepared to tell me?"

"Best to leave it at that. Dinner at six-thirty."

She went out, closing the door. With a sense of unreality she prepared the meal, warmed plates, set the table; she felt curiously at peace, as if watching herself from a height. She'd done something irrevocable but here she was as usual, stirring gravy and starting a shopping list.

Suzanne came down, asking what was for dinner; Anthony joined them, ate, made spasmodic conversation and mentioned a TV documentary he wanted to watch later. If Suzanne noticed the stilted atmosphere she made no comment; awkwardness between her parents was nothing new.

There was no further discussion that night. Bridge and Anthony moved carefully around each other, stepping aside if they met in the hallway or on the stairs.

In the morning, with Suzanne at school, Anthony came into the workroom, where Bridget was reading through yesterday's garden notes. Since she'd made this room her own, he rarely entered; now he looked with disapproval or envy at the comfortable furnishings, the sofa with patchwork cushions, writing desk, shelf of gardening books: such a contrast to the cluttered austerity of his own study.

"I've given careful thought to what we discussed," he said,

without preamble. "I assume you intend to terminate? If so, we'll carry on as we are."

"Thank you. That's kind of you," she said; his formal tone was infectious. "But I've no intention of doing that."

"Ah. In that case we'll need to think again."

"You want me to leave?"

He stood by the window, hands in pockets, looking down at the terrace. "I didn't say that. No, I don't, but you're not giving me much choice."

"And Suzanne?" she asked.

"Suzanne is precisely the reason I'd prefer you not to leave. I'd like to keep some semblance of normality."

She almost said *Keep up an act, you mean?* But what had their marriage become, other than a pretence?

"If we separate," she said, "Suzanne must decide which of us to live with. She's old enough to know her own mind."

"Yes - more than can be said for her mother. Have you told her yet? That you've behaved like a bitch on heat, and this is the result? A fine example to a teenage girl."

"Anthony, I refuse to discuss it that way," she told him. "If you want me to leave, I will, and if Suzanne decides to come with me you'll have to accept that."

"Why would she? Leave her home, everything she knows, to live with you and a squalling baby? And where will you set up home, exactly, and support yourself?"

"I don't know."

"Oh, you don't know," he mocked. "Time to do some hard thinking, then. I've explained my position. A termination is the obvious answer, and I think I'm being more than generous. Why must you be obstinate?" He looked at her directly for the first time; she glimpsed sadness beneath his air of martyrdom. "Create all manner of difficulties for yourself?"

"I'll think about it," she said, aloof.

"You'd better. I'll be out for the rest of the day," he told her; and minutes later she heard the front door closing.

It seemed that in that conversation the position had subtly changed. If she stayed, it would be on his terms. But he didn't want her to leave, and that gave her a bargaining position.

She felt that she was reciting lines she didn't know she'd learned, running ahead of her capacity to absorb what was happening.

. . .

Retreating to the garden, she occupied herself with digging. At the lower end, where she planned a streamside planting, there was much to be cleared: tough reeds and grasses, creeping periwinkle that threaded fine roots through the soil. She filled a barrow, trundled it away, returned; sliced into heavy soil, prised, freed her spade from a rooty tangle. Dark and fertile, the soil was humus-rich, its smell mingled with scents of wet mud and grasses from the stream. Nearby a blackbird was busy in fallen leaves, scuffing and turning them over, unalarmed by her presence.

A snatch of poetry came to mind: *Today I think only with scents – scents dead leaves yield, and bracken...* Edward Thomas, a poet who'd grown on her while she worked so closely with the soil. Often, remembering a line, she'd think Ah, yes, that's what he saw, or smelled, or touched – the poet's thoughts like a spark leaping the gap of years.

Here she planned to grow yellow flag irises, marsh marigold and purple-leaved bergenia alongside the meadowsweet, willowherb and reedmace that fringed the bank in summer. She'd ordered a bare-rooted sapling willow, and pictured it in maturity, graceful, its fronds casting shade over the bank, light flickering between leaf and water; she imagined herself on the grass, reading, soothed by the stream's murmur.

In reality she rarely did sit reading in the garden. She was too easily distracted by dead-heading or the collecting of seeds, or fetching tools to rescue a plant being smothered by a rampant neighbour. By the time her willow-tree reached maturity she might be long gone. What was the use of planning? But the vision was sharp in her mind, clearer and – for the moment – more important than anything else, as if her imagined plants would anchor her to the soil.

Intent on digging, she didn't see Adam approach. His voice startled her as he spoke her name.

She straightened, shaking clods from her spade, as he walked closer and stopped. Something about the way he placed his feet, the way he stood, gave her a twist of regret. The laces of one of his work-boots trailed in damp grass.

"I'm packing up," he said. "I'll be gone by tomorrow. But I had to talk to you first." His eyes searched hers: serious, anxious.

"What about?"

"Meg thinks you're pregnant.".

"Oh." She pushed a loose strand of hair behind her ear.

"So you are? Does Anthony know?"

"Yes, I've told him. It's all right. I didn't mention you."

A moment's pause. "That's not why I was asking."

"He knows it's not his. That – would be impossible."

"What, then?"

"He's willing for me to stay here if I terminate the pregnancy."

A beat, then: "No. You won't – will you? Can't we -"

As he moved closer, she stepped back, boots sinking into dug soil; she almost overbalanced. He put a hand on her arm to steady her, and did not let go.

"Come with me," he said quietly. "Come away with me. We'll find a place together."

"You don't mean that!"

"I do. Would I say it if I didn't?"

She couldn't look at him.

"Adam, please!" She detached herself and looked towards the house, to the dipping line of the roof, green-grey with lichens on weathered slates; the back door was open, the table and chairs on the terrace not yet put away for winter. Wildings was so solid, part of the land; indifferent to human trauma, the muddles people made of their lives. "It's – it's sweet of you," she said, "but you can't have thought about it. Lumber yourself with me and a baby? I'm twenty years older than you!"

"That doesn't matter. Nothing matters. I love you."

In that moment, seeing his expression, she was dismayed by what she'd done.

"No, Adam, you don't. Don't say that. You'd regret it, I promise you."

"I'm not a child you need to protect," he said, with a flash of anger. "I can make up my own mind."

"But you can't make up mine. I've decided. The truth is - I can't leave Anthony."

"Can't leave Anthony?" He took a step back to the grass. "You'd rather stay with a man who – who doesn't love you, and gives you an ultimatum like that? You'll have an abortion because he says so?"

"I didn't say that. But I won't leave him."

He gazed at her in hurt bewilderment; she heard what she'd said, unsure whether to believe it. The words fell into a silence.

Adam looked down, saw the trailing bootlace and knelt to tie it. When he stood up she saw the shine of tears in his eyes.

"I thought better of you than that," he said quietly. "I thought you had more courage."

"I -" she began, but he'd already turned away.

She watched as he walked quickly up the lawn and through the archway out of sight. Unconsciously she had placed a hand on her belly; realising, she closed her eyes, sensing the precious life there, so fragile, so tenacious.

Meg

1990, OCTOBER

"This is such a bugger," she said. "I wish you weren't going."

Adam was sweeping the floor of his empty workshop. His equipment was stowed in the back of the van, his paintings already gone.

"Where will you go?" she asked, and he shook his head.

"Dunno. I'll operate from the back of the van till I find somewhere."

"It won't be the same without you around," she said, meaning it. "I've got used to you coming and going, slapping paint."

"Thanks. I know." He a twisted smile. "I'll miss your Jurassic tea. You, too."

"One more before you go?"

"Thanks. In a little while?"

"Why, what have you got left to do?"

"I need to go up to the house with my keys."

"Bridget's not there - she's gone to Milton Keynes with

Suzanne. You can leave them with me." She guessed that Bridget had contrived to be absent.

"I know," Adam said. "Just a last look round. The garden. The orchard."

"Well, don't bump into Anthony."

He locked up, and she went back to cutting letters on sandstone for a house-name. When Adam returned he was brisker, less wistful. She made tea, and he looked at her work as if everything were normal. They talked about keeping in touch, finally parting with a hug and a kiss. Meg hated kissing, being touched, but made an exception.

She stood in the yard as the engine sound faded. Though used to spending time alone, she felt bereft. Odd now to recall her resentment when he first appeared, all hair and saunter, as she'd thought, too pleased with himself. Since, she'd come to see more in him: complexity, need, self-doubt. She would miss their companionship, and the mutual respect that had grown between them, in spite of her taunts about paint-splodging.

Everyone she cared about disappeared from her life: her mother, Gillian, her stepfather. Carrie. She had limited faith in friendship, and would never trust anything that might call itself love. Uncle Terry and Aunty Eileen were her only constants, and they wouldn't always be there. She'd trained herself in solitude.

Now she scorned herself for feeling let down. She blamed sex: it spoiled everything. Why did otherwise sane people let themselves be consumed by lust, blinkered to the consequences? She could believe it of Adam, but *Bridget* – it was as if she'd set out with the intention of getting pregnant, seizing on the nearest available provider of quality sperm ...

Adam had told her, with some bitterness, that Bridget was determined to stay with Anthony. So: baby or no baby?

If Bridget *did* go ahead, it would be Adam's child that grew up here, and she herself would be his only link – if they did indeed stay in touch. Would he bother? Wasn't he likely to put this behind him, even move out of the area? He had no local ties, and his tree-pruning work was easily transferrable.

Maybe, yet, he'd make his name as a painter. He had something; she conceded that now, even if she'd been slow to appreciate. If he did stay around she'd probably hear of him through the network of local artists and exhibitions.

The *t-tink* of her chisel echoed around the yard. It sounded so different when there were others around: workmanlike, companionable, productive – but now the sound bounced off the walls, emphasising her isolation. This was how it would be all winter, unless Bridget found another tenant. Leonard hardly counted; his visits were intermittent, his conversation sparse and predictable.

And things couldn't be the same with Bridget: Meg felt keenly hurt. She'd let herself think they were friends, a safe friendship based on a business arrangement, neither with much at stake beyond enjoyment of each other's company. Now Bridget had withdrawn: avoiding her, not even mentioning that she'd told Adam to leave, high-handed as a feudal landlord.

Why must everything change? She worked on, thinking of times she'd wandered over to the barn to see what Bridget was doing, or when Adam had watched her tracing letters, or all three gathered by the wood-burner for coffee on chill winter days. No more. Simple, everyday happiness: unacknowledged, too quickly sliding into the past.

She was surprised to hear footsteps, having thought no one was around. Anthony was in the yard, hands thrust into coat pockets.

"Ah," he said, in her doorway. "So no one's here."

"I'm here," she said, pointedly.

"Yes. Fine. Won't disturb you, then."

Meg rarely saw Anthony, only occasionally in the garden. He looked older than she remembered, greyer, drawn, collar turned up although it was mild today.

"Have you come for Adam's keys?" she said. "He's packed up and gone."

Anthony had turned away, but now looked at her blankly.

"No," he said. "I was looking for Bridget. Doesn't matter."

Surely he knew that Bridget was out with Suzanne? Meg watched him walk out of sight, then returned to work, turning on her radio. Bridget's relationship with Anthony was unfathomable, and none of her business.

Bridget

1990, OCTOBER

Returning with Suzanne, Bridget saw that Anthony's car wasn't in the drive. Neither of them commented, but in the kitchen Suzanne picked up a key ring from the table. "Whose is this?"

"Oh – Adam's." Merely saying his name brought a flush to her cheeks.

"Why did he have to go?" Suzanne fingered the key-tab. "I *like* Adam. He's cool."

"I know you do."

"You could get him back for that Artweeks thing you talk about. That'd be good."

"Maybe." Bridget filled the kettle, regretting the lies she'd already told and those she'd have to tell in future. Whatever the future would be. So far she'd mentioned only that Adam needed to find another studio – which was, in a way, true. Perhaps it'd be less complicated, and fairer, to tell the truth; but how could she?

Anthony hadn't mentioned going out. She cooked a meal, but he hadn't appeared by the time she was ready to serve.

"Shall we go ahead without him?" Suzanne was opening the fridge door. "I'm starving."

"We'll wait a few more minutes. Don't start nibbling things."

An hour and a half later they had finished eating and cleared up, and still Anthony wasn't home. Suzanne went to the hall to phone Edward, her boyfriend, and Bridget tried to read; later they watched television together.

"Looks like he's staying out all night. Is he having an *affair?*" Suzanne said, yawning, flippant.

"Don't suppose so. You look ready for bed. Me, too."

In the morning Bridget found Anthony's bedroom door open – he always closed it at night – and his bed untidily made, unslept in.

Suzanne was slow to appear on weekend mornings. When she did, Bridget didn't at first refer to Anthony's overnight absence, remembering the evening when Suzanne feared some dreadful accident. But now Suzanne was dismissive. "He's staying with one of his friends, I suppose. He could have *phoned.* Imagine if I did that!" She gave Bridget a sharp, suspicious glance. "Have you had another row?"

"Mm, sort of."

"Oh, for God's sake," Suzanne said through a mouthful of cereal. "You and Dad. I don't know how you put up with each other."

Bridget almost said *How would you feel if we didn't? If we split up?* – but stopped. The situation was too delicate, too undecided. She couldn't have an honest conversation about love or marriage; better avoid it, or postpone. At some point – soon – she'd have to tell Suzanne that she was pregnant. She foresaw incredulity, even disgust.

"OK if I go to Ed's for the day?" Suzanne said now. "He'll come for me."

"Yes, fine."

It was only two weeks since Edward passed his driving test, giving Bridget a fresh anxiety: "He does drive carefully, doesn't he?" she asked, and Suzanne gave a theatrical sigh. "Mu-um! This is *Ed* you're talking about. He does *everything* carefully. How d'you think he passed his test first go?" And both Bridget and Anthony did like Edward: studious, rather shy, clearly devoted to Suzanne. For her first boyfriend, Suzanne could hardly have found anyone less likely to get her into trouble.

When Suzanne left, Bridget drafted an advertisement for the vacant workshop and put it ready to post. She felt awkward about Meg, having avoided her for days, but that couldn't go on indefinitely. She put on her coat and went down to the yard. It was a grey, blowy day, leaves swirling, collecting in heaps in the corners.

Meg's workshop was locked; all three were, the yard looking sadly deserted. But lights were on in the cottage and her car parked outside. Suddenly nervous, Bridget knocked at the door.

Meg opened it and looked at her, unsmiling.

"Are you busy?"

"Yes," Meg said, but stepped aside. "You'd better come in."

Papers were spread over the table; Bridget saw a calculator, pencil case, columns of figures. "I'm interrupting."

"Boring admin," Meg said. "Invoices, quotations, accounts. I don't mind taking a break. Coffee?"

"Thanks." Bridget stood awkwardly. "You're so organised, Meg. I never see you wasting time."

Meg gestured to her to sit. "I waste plenty, believe me."

Sinking into the only armchair, Bridget saw as Meg went into the kitchen that she didn't intend to make this easy. A tap gushed, a cupboard door slammed; minutes passed. Meg returned with a cafetière and two mugs.

"So," Bridget said, "how's things?"

"Quiet." Meg gave her a look of reproach. "Without Adam here."

"You're annoyed with me. I don't blame you."

Meg plunged the cafetière and poured coffee.

"I'm sorry," Bridget went on, into the pointed silence. "I should have explained. I've messed everything up, haven't I?" Alarmingly, a sob rose in her chest and her eyes brimmed; she groped in her pocket for a tissue. "I don't know where to start. What will you think of me?"

"Why does that matter? And I may have worked out quite a lot, if that helps."

"Have you?" Bridget recalled what Adam had said; then, with no point hedging, "I'm pregnant."

"Yep. Got that. The throwing up. And look at you now."

Bridget dabbed at her face. "Sorry. Hormones. I was like this last time. Have you got any tissues?" The remnant in her hand was already soggy.

Meg went into the kitchen and returned with a kitchen roll.

"Anthony isn't the father." Bridget snatched off a piece, looking at Meg for a reaction.

"Got that as well. Put two and two together when I saw Adam's van by the house, that morning I came back. Why else would you kick him out?"

"You didn't say."

"Why would I?" Meg gave a shrug. "Not my business. And you haven't been around much, have you?"

Bridget dabbed at her eyes before venturing, "Are you shocked?"

"Yes. No. Yes. Fuck, I don't know. I've seen enough of people and how they mess up. But yes - shocked that you were careless enough to get pregnant. Unless you wanted that."

"Of course not! But now that I am – I wouldn't change it," she said, finding it true. "Is that mad?"

"Barking," Meg said drily. "Raging hormones. So. What about Anthony? Does he know?"

"Yes. He wants me to have a termination."

"Well, there are worse things. People do that and get over it. I should know."

"You've had -" Bridget broke off, hearing her own astonishment, unsure what she was asking or implying; but Meg shook her head.

"Ancient history. Not something I want to remember. But why not, if it saves your marriage? Assuming you think it's worth saving?"

"No." Bridget shook her head. "I can't."

"And Adam? He's got a right to know, hasn't he? And he *does* know. It was me who told him, if you want someone to blame."

Aware of Meg's simmering resentment, Bridget said, "I'm sorry. I know you were friends. *Are* friends."

Meg nodded. "I didn't take to him at first but now - yes, he's a friend. It feels like you've hi-jacked him, and now got rid of him to suit yourself. What does friendship matter, once sex gets in the way? Madness, how it takes over. Turns people into idiots."

Bridget looked at her, startled by the sudden vehemence, wondering what had shaped such a view.

"Perhaps you'd like me to move out, too?" Meg was apparently on a tide of indignation.

"Course not. Why would I?" Bridget said, her own voice rising; then, more quietly, "Friendship does matter. *Your* friendship, Meg. Please - don't let's quarrel. I'm sorry, really I am. But I don't know what I can do."

Meg gazed out of the window, silent.

"Will you stay in touch with Adam?" Bridget asked.

"You think I can be your go-between?" Meg huffed a laugh. "When you've had his baby?"

"That's not what I mean!"

"Hmm, maybe not. More convenient if he disappears, I suppose."

"Oh, Meg." Bridget sagged with hopelessness. "I don't know what to do for the best."

"Bit late for that," Meg said. "Look, don't ask me to help. Even if I knew how. It's your mess."

Bridget gulped coffee. "I'd better go," she said, getting up; but Meg put out a restraining hand.

"No, don't. Please - excuse my rant. I'm glad you came round. I don't want to quarrel, either. It's all this personal stuff I can't handle. My own life's sorted out, but there's no stopping what other people get up to. Even people I think I know quite well, it seems. *Especially* people I think I know."

Her tone had lightened; Bridget risked a tearful smile. How little I know about her, really, she thought.

"Look. I can't help," Meg went on, "but I'll be here, OK? Best I can do."

. . .

Dr Wilcox spoke of the risks associated with pregnancy at Bridget's age: in this context, forty-seven was considered elderly. He talked about Down's Syndrome and pre-eclampsia, diabetes and high blood-pressure. "I know all this sounds alarming. But there's every chance that you and your baby will be completely healthy." He recommended gentle exercise and plenty of rest, and said that in three weeks she could have an ultrasound scan. These hadn't been available when she was expecting Suzanne, but a friend had told her how astonishing it was to see the baby in a kind of sound-shadow, its profile, its hands and limbs, and to understand that it was alive, beginning to function.

The baby was more than a concept now. It was a person who would come into the world with needs and demands for which she'd be responsible, probably on her own.

In two weeks the clocks would go back for winter. Drawn outside, her senses heightened by the self-awareness of pregnancy, she thought that she loved each season in turn but that surely October must be the most beautiful month. Low sunlight brought out the velvety texture of the lawn, vibrantly green. The light was shifting and strange, presaging rain; the church tower was warm ochre against its trees, the ridge beyond the village lit green-gold. She felt the first heavy drops on her face and hair as clouds obscured the sun.

Two more nights passed and still Anthony did not return. She tried to justify it by saying that he needed a break, in the face of Suzanne's increasing scepticism. She felt irrationally angry: he should have phoned, left a note, for Suzanne's sake if not for hers. But what if he'd done something drastic? No, she'd have heard. Yet she began to dread a knock at the door or the ringing of the phone, imagining scenes in which a kindly police officer sat her down before speaking awful, irrevocable words, telling her that she'd driven him to suicide or recklessness. Her mind reeled in panic.

No, no: not Anthony. He was too solid. Stolid, maybe. So she'd thought. But there was his depression - what if this had pushed him too far?

She occupied herself with washing and ironing his shirts, preparing freezer meals, tidying his bedroom. She discovered that the larger of a pair of matching suitcases was not in its place on top of the wardrobe; so he'd packed, not left on impulse.

She sat on the bed, staring at nothing.

Surely he'd come back? He would never part with Wildings; it was his family home, his for life. Unthinkable that he'd be the one to leave, and like this.

• • •

On Thursday, soon after Suzanne left for school, she heard a key turn in the front door lock. From the landing she saw Anthony bringing in his suitcase; he glanced up, saying nothing.

"Anthony!" She ran down, stopping short of kissing or hugging him. "I've been so worried – where've you been?"

"Away."

"But where?"

He gave a humourless laugh. "Surely you understand that I feel no obligation to tell you where I go or who I see." He hung up his coat, not looking at her. "But, over the last few days, I've reached a decision."

He'd retreated into loftiness and pomposity; she must allow him that. She waited for his verdict.

"I'm going upstairs first. Then we'll talk."

She heard his case thump on the bed, the creak of his wardrobe door. When he came down they sat at the kitchen table, facing each other. All important conversations seem to take place here, she thought, dabbing at spilled salt, tracing a knotty pattern in the wood. This oak table had been here since his parents' day, probably his grandparents'. What arguments and crises and reconciliations had it seen?

"I propose this," Anthony said. "Against my better judgement, but nevertheless. If you want to stay here - I assume you do - I'm willing to bring up the child as my own. On condition that no one knows otherwise. Not even Suzanne. Nor the child, when he or she is old enough to understand."

Her thoughts whirled. "You'd do that? But why? And – it'd be no way for a child to grow up, in an atmosphere of hostility and – mistrust."

"I don't think I need to hear from you about *mistrust*, Bridget." He smiled, not unkindly. "Wasn't I clear? I'll treat the child as my own. Be a – a father to him or her."

She saw that he relished his magnanimity. He liked seeing himself as deeply wronged, but able to accept – to forgive would be too much - and do his best for her and the child, and Suzanne.

"But why would you do that?" she asked, mystified. "Before you went away you were talking about abortion. You gave me an ultimatum. Now this. What's happened? Where did you go, who did you see?"

"I've told you – I've no need to tell you about my movements. Not any more."

She swallowed the urge to reply, "As if you ever did?" and looked at him silently. His glance slid away; then he said, "I always expected to have another child. It – never happened, and I know there are reasons. Now here's a chance. We've got money, this house, we can give a child a comfortable, secure life. It's the best solution."

He *wants* this, she realised. If she refused, insisted on leaving, or even on termination after all, he'd be thrown all over again.

"I don't know what to say."

He gave a tight smile. "I don't want to live here alone. Don't want disruption and upset for Suzanne. This is the best way. My only other stipulation is that you won't communicate with the child's biological father. You must promise that."

She nodded, but it wasn't enough; he looked at her sternly and said, "Do I have your promise?"

"Yes."

"Then that's what we'll do."

"Thank you," she said. "It's more than I deserve."

"It's not for your benefit, Bridget." He turned his head in a gesture of impatience, as if she'd failed to understand. "It's for the child. And for myself."

Jane

FEBRUARY 2019

WAKING TO DAWN GREYNESS, she hunched herself against the renewed shock of last night: Andrea, Tom, the quarrel in the street. Her eyes stung as she turned on her lamp, dried tears tightening her face.

Tom. Bastard.

What an idiot she'd been.

Everything was going, gone. Leaving her adrift and alone.

She thought of Tom in his borrowed suit on the day of the funeral, standing in the hall, saying that he loved her. She hadn't believed him, and doubted that he believed himself. It was too easy to say – like putting a stamp on a relationship, claiming someone for your own. But what did it mean, beyond the fact that your attention was focused on that person at that precise moment? How could your feelings not shift and change? Having told herself often that she wasn't truly in love with Tom, she could think only of the times he'd supported and comforted her, how kind and funny he could be.

Had been. No doubt he was kind and funny and supportive with Andrea now.

Sean hadn't replied to her texts. She checked again: nothing. It felt like another desertion, though she reasoned that he might simply have been asleep – it was gone midnight when she sent them. Or maybe he thought she was making a drama out of nothing; she'd described her relationship with Tom as on-off.

Off, now, definitely. No longer a question of whether she thought Tom was right for her, as if hers were the only opinion.

Rain battered her window, and parting the curtains she saw hedgerow trees receding into mist below a sullen sky. Lethargy dulled her senses. What if everything fell apart, everything she'd thought she could count on? The loss of both parents was bad enough, but what if she lost all purpose? She'd seen depression often enough in her father to know how deadening it could be. In her mother's lifetime he'd strenuously denied that it *was* depression. In recent years he began to acknowledge it, though Jane could never persuade him to seek advice. Mum, she realised, had been the wrong person to help him, her air of martyred impatience only hardening his resolve.

Suzanne had often said that Jane resembled her mother both physically and in her largely optimistic temperament, but there were times when she feared the dark declines she'd seen in her father. Heredity, she knew from online searches, could be a factor.

For God's sake, she told herself. You've just been dumped by someone you thought was on your side – how do you expect to feel? But the fear remained. Perhaps she'd never really understood her father, too quick to say Oh, it's just one of his moods.

In the end only three things matter: how well you have loved, how gently you have lived, and how gracefully you give up the things not meant for you. It was a saying attributed to Buddha and one she liked, sometimes using it to question herself. She thought: I haven't loved well enough, I know that. Not yet. But *how gracefully you give up the things not meant for you?* What more could she be required to part with? Mum, Dad, Wildings; now Tom. The first three were beyond her control; Tom was the only one she could try to keep. *Could* have tried. Hadn't, not really, because she didn't truly love him. It had been dishonest to pretend.

But *gracefully?* No. That was too much.

There was time for an hour's yoga before getting ready to teach at the gym, but when she unrolled her mat she couldn't summon the will. Without joy, yoga was simply a series of moves; it needed dynamism and mental engagement to mean anything. Her limbs were heavy, her mind clogged.

Instead she pulled on a sweater and sat on the bed to text Chitra: **Meet later? Lunchtime or this afternoon?**

Chitra's reply pinged back: **Sorry! Out with Rich. You're covering for me at 11, remember? See you tomorrow maybe.**

She had a new boyfriend now, someone she'd met on a meditation course. Last time Jane had seen her, she was buoyant and even smug, basking in male appreciation. At the moment she wasn't the person to go to for sympathy.

Setting off, Jane felt almost relieved to feel the cramp of period pain. Two days early, but at least there was a reason – a partial one - for the sense of things plummeting out of control. She had tampons in her bag and was at the gym in good time to sort herself out.

She assumed an air of calmness as she settled into the class, leading, demonstrating, moving round the room to adjust postures. "Lengthen your spine, eyes to your toes, hinge forward into *passchimottanasana* ..." Her words sounded hollow, a sulky girl playing at being a yoga guru.

My little life, she thought. What does it matter, really? She was watching herself being inadequate.

When she went out to her car she felt a wave of dizziness, her hand shaking as she fumbled with the ignition. It was as if her body had sustained a shock her mind hadn't fully registered. This was more than menstrual sluggishness; more like the start of flu.

The drizzle had cleared, giving way to fitful sunshine. At home, not wanting lunch, she wondered how to spend the rest of the day, resisting the urge to lie down and sleep. A new worry was beginning to nag, now that she faced the prospect of living alone: she barely earned enough to support herself. Her part-time work at the gym, supplemented by yoga classes and intermittent cover, brought in enough to run her car and buy food, but soon she'd be paying her own bills, council tax and insurance. For all this time she'd been buffered, Dad paying for housekeeping, boiler servicing and things she'd never thought about. How will I manage, she wondered? And how pathetic *is* that, when I'm getting the cottage and won't even have to pay rent?

Perhaps Rob was right when he said she'd been foolish to resign from her marketing job. The thought of a full-time salary arriving in her bank account was enough to make her salivate, but was that worth sacrificing her freedom, and what – in brighter moments – she saw as her vocation? But what sort of vocation was it, really? She could hear Rob all too clearly: "Teaching people downward dog or upturned newt or whatever? How to get their foot behind their ear? Mm, yeah - *really* useful." Once the house was sold, she'd maybe find volunteer work, though that would hardly help financially. Or a pregnancy yoga course, to extend her teaching. She needed more.

Looking at her phone she brightened, seeing that she'd missed a call from Sean. He'd also sent a text: **Are you at home? Can I come and see you this afternoon? Something I need to tell you.** Mystified, she returned: **Yes, I'm here. Jx**

What could that mean? While she speculated, the house phone rang: the estate agent wanted to arrange two viewings. The Pritchards, she said, were likely to make an offer in the next day or two. Jane had been trying but failing to keep everything tidy, especially in her own room. She went up to check for remnants of Tom, and had already found two CDs and a sweatshirt when she heard a car pull up outside.

Sean. She felt a rush of relief.

He was wearing his duffel coat and scarf, no hat today; he stepped inside and hugged her, and again Chitra's warning flashed into her mind, about falling in love.

I do love him. Already. I can't help it. It was as if her feeling for Tom had been diverted to Sean, tenfold: a physical warmth coursed through her: uplifting, unsettling, as she gazed at him with the sense that all would yet be well, that he'd somehow make everything right. He'd known she needed him, and had come.

"Got your text," he said. "Are you OK?"

"Oh, gosh. Sorry for being a drama queen." She gave an embarrassed laugh. "Aren't you going away, for work?"

"I am. On my way now, to Wolverhampton. But I had to see you first." He followed her into the kitchen, taking off his coat.

"You shouldn't have come out of your way," she said. "It's lovely of you, but I'll - get over it."

"Are you sure things can't be mended?"

"No. I mean yes, I am sure. It's really finished this time and I'll have to get used to it. Awful timing, though - you know, now, with everything else up in the air – house-viewers coming, these awful people who might buy it – they'll probably make an offer. You'll hear about that from the solicitor. I keep forgetting you need to agree, as well as Rob and Suzanne." She looked at him, seeing awkwardness in his manner. "But - you said there was something?"

"Yes. I wanted to tell you last night. Nearly did, but it wasn't the right moment."

"What?"

He gestured to the table. "Let's sit down."

She pulled back a chair, wondering what it could be that sounded so ominous. He sat opposite, clasped his hands and gazed at them; opened his mouth, closed it, took a deep breath, began again.

"Jane - I've let you believe I'm your half-brother." He looked at her. "I'm not."

"Not -? But – then who –"

Her thoughts raced: what was he saying? He was an imposter, a stranger who'd lied his way here, tricked her? But then - how could he know all the things he knew?

"I'm your father," he said.

"My -" She gazed at him. "What? How can you be? Dad's my father."

"I'm your father," he repeated, "and Anthony is – was – your grandfather."

The silence that followed buzzed in her ears. His words echoed meaninglessly. He watched her; they both spoke at once.

"No. That doesn't make sense."

"Your mother didn't know -"

"But what do you -" She slumped back. "I don't understand."

"Bridget and I, we had a brief – I can't call it an affair. It was less than that. And much more. She became pregnant, and Anthony agreed to bring you up as his own."

"Wait – wait. You and my *Mum?*"

Sean nodded slowly.

"No. No. I can't believe it - Mum wouldn't do that! And you're saying I wasn't Dad's, but he pretended I was?"

"Yes."

"But -" She threw up both hands. "Why would he? Why would *she?*"

"Anthony knew. I told him. He knew you were his grandchild. But I don't think your mother ever did know."

Her eyes blurred. "I can't get my head round this," she said slowly. "How it happened. Who knew what. How did you even know my mum?"

"I'm sorry. It's a lot to take in, I know," he said gently. "I told you I tracked Anthony down. I didn't say how."

"Tell me then."

"It was almost by chance. I'd heard about Wildings from my mother. She worked near here, as I said – used to meet Anthony here, at the cottage. It was empty at that time."

"And you came here to find him? When?"

"I was in my mid-twenties, looking for a workshop to rent. I had a small flat in Northampton. When I saw an advert and the name Wildings, and Harper, I was curious, and took the chance to come for a look. That was all I intended, but – well, Bridget showed me round and I liked her, and she said that Anthony wasn't much involved. I should have resisted, but I didn't. Being nearby, seeing him occasionally, seeing how he lived. There was no chance he'd recognise me – he'd never seen me even as a baby. So I rented the studio for a year and a half."

"Studio for what? Mum rented the workshops to artists and crafts people - jewellers and potters. And there was Meg, a stone-carver. She lived here for years."

"Yes, I know Meg. She's my good friend. Has been since then."

Jane caught her breath. "*Meg's* involved in this? She's your friend? But - I visited her – I *asked* her. She's never heard of you."

Concluding that he must be lying, she was thrown by his answer:

"I know. She told me. It's true that she'd never heard of Sean McBride, not then. She knows me by a different name."

Words flitted past while she snatched at meaning. "You used a false name? You were hiding who you were?"

With every moment he was becoming a different person. A fraud. Seducer. Deceiver. She was ashamed now of her rush of feeling, how easily he'd taken her in.

"No, no, Jane. It wasn't false. Sean McBride is how Anthony knew me, so that's what's in the Will. But it's not the name I go by." He was trying to hold her gaze..

"How can I believe anything?" Her voice was croaky. "If you're not who you said? Not Sean McBride after all?"

"This is the truth, Jane. No more secrets. I promise." He reached for her hand; she snatched it back, suspicious now, remembering Chitra's doubt. *Well, I think he sounds creepy. What does he want?*

"What *is* your name, then?"

"Adam. Adam Mullen. I was christened Sean McBride. McBride was my mother's name – Fionnuala McBride. So that's the name Anthony knew."

Jane had stalled at the name Adam, remembering things Suzanne used to say. "You're *Adam?* The Adam who used to be here? The artist?"

"Yes. No one knows me as Sean apart from your – apart from Anthony. Not since my mother married my stepdad. He's Sean too, Sean Mullen, so they started calling me Adam, my middle name. I've been Adam Mullen ever since."

"Suzanne used to talk about you. Mum never did." It didn't feel reassuring. "You knew Suzanne. You knew – you know Meg! And my Mum. You hid all that when you were here last week," she said, her voice thickening. "You let me think you'd never been here before. If what you say is true, you tricked my mother – you *must* have done! - and now you've tricked me."

"Jane, please believe me. I'm not trying to trick anyone. *Especially* not you. That's why I need to tell you everything."

She pushed her chair back from the table. "I don't like this. You could've told the solicitors your real name as soon as they got in touch about the Will. Why didn't you?"

She saw alarm flare in his eyes. Fear of losing the trust she'd so foolishly given? Fear that she'd seen through him?

"Because I didn't want to barge straight in when you'd lost Anthony," he said, "and -"

A loud rapping on the back door startled both of them.

Through the back lobby window Jane saw Meg outside: red scarf, curly windblown hair, navy raincoat. She'd forgotten that Meg was coming today; it was a relief to see her, even if – she adjusted her thoughts – Meg had connived to deceive her. Or a new suspicion - had they arranged to turn up at the same time? No coincidence at all?

Seeing her, Meg waved and pushed the door open. *I really ought to keep it locked,* Jane thought, on edge now; anyone could walk in.

"Sorry if I made you jump. Couldn't resist nosing round the yard as I was early -" Meg kicked her shoes off on the mat, then stopped, looking through to the kitchen.

"Come in," Jane said, although Meg already was.

Meg and Sean stared at each other, Sean half out of his seat, Meg frozen as if in a game of grandmother's footsteps.

Sean said, "Meg? What are you -" and moved towards her. Meg said nothing, her eyes questioning him.

Jane had stood up too fast; her head reeled and she put a hand on the worktop to steady herself as she confronted Meg.

"What's this about? I suppose you're here because *he's* here - Sean, or Adam, or whoever? Why didn't you *tell* me you know each other?"

"Look, I'm sorry." Meg stepped back. "I had no idea -"

"Neither did I. Obviously. Excuse me." Jane brushed past, grabbed her mother's coat from the lobby and stepped outside, slamming the door.

The air soothed, cool and moist. She walked out to the grass and down the lawn. A chill wind blew from the east but birds sang in expectation of spring: the jaunty see-sawing call of great tits, croon of woodpigeons, cawing of rooks from the tree-tops. Where a path curved between trees towards the lower garden, the earth was brightened by snowdrops, the kingcup-yellow of aconites and fresh green of hellebores. Usually she saw all this as her mother's work but now her mind teemed with thoughts of Dad. She had to hold on to him now that this Sean, this Adam, had made his astonishing announcement.

Dad had been taken away for a second time. Once by sudden death; now by the revelation that he wasn't her father after all. If she could believe that ...

Except, of course, that in every important way he *had* been her father. There were twenty-seven years' worth of fathering, set against three brief meetings with this other one, this stranger.

The feelings she'd been nurturing for Sean, for Adam, were confused and disturbing no matter who he was. But Dad - *my Dad*. Never, ever had she been in doubt that he loved and wanted her.

Her mind was a muddle of fragments, puzzles, memories. *So - I'm not quite who I thought I was. There's all this, opening up.*

Or a false floor dropping away ...

If it made sense. How could it? She felt the same mental baulking she'd experienced when Dad died: this couldn't be real. She'd wake up and everything would be normal. Dad would still be Dad, no one pushing him aside. Her mind-fuzz was compounded by the dizziness she could no longer pretend was shock. In addition to the drag of her period her knees ached, her legs felt shaky and she wanted nothing more than to lie on her bed with her churning thoughts. She wanted hot Lemsip from the packet Dad had left. But to get to bed she'd have to go in through the kitchen.

Meg was coming down the lawn in her purposeful way. Jane felt the trickle of a tear down her cheek, found a crumpled tissue in Mum's coat pocket and faced her.

"Look, this was awful timing," Meg said. "I'd no idea Adam was coming. Best if I go – you've got a lot to talk about. Unless you'd rather I stayed."

"So - you knew? You've always known?"

"That Adam's your father? Yes. Bridget made me promise – before you were born - never to tell anyone. Not even you. So I never have."

"It's true, then?"

Meg's manner - consoling, like a kindly aunt - made Jane feel small, in need of protection. She felt herself resisting.

"Yes, it is," Meg said. "As for him being Anthony's son – *that,* I didn't know till much later, after your Mum died. And she certainly didn't. He kept that to himself all those years."

"Why?"

"You'll have to ask him."

"Didn't you mind? If you're friends?"

"I did mind. I was furious when he finally told me. But – well, things were complicated by then."

"Thing are complicated *now,* wouldn't you say? So you've been in touch with him since I came to see you? Why didn't he – or you - contact us as soon as he heard about the Will?"

"We talked about it. A lot. Especially after you wrote to him. He wanted to answer, badly wanted to meet you, but we agreed he'd better wait, not give you one shock on top of another."

We? It made them sound like allies.

"Well, he's certainly done that," Jane said flatly.

"I know. Let's go in - you look pale." Meg rubbed her arm, in the manner of someone not much used to physical contact. "Come on. You shouldn't be out in the cold."

Too weary to protest, Jane began walking slowly back to the house, Meg beside her.

"Is he still here?" She didn't even know what to call him now.

"Course!" Meg looked at her. "Look, you need time to take this in. All I can tell you is I've known him for years. Since before you were born. You can trust him, Jane. Really. You might not think that now, but – give him a chance. Please. I know how much he wants it."

"Wants what?" Jane said, thinking of the Will, the house, the money.

"You. To be his daughter."

Jane gave a mirthless laugh. "It sounds like I'm lost property waiting to be claimed. Why wait twenty-seven years?"

"I'll let him explain," Meg said.

"No. No more. Not yet."

He had been looking out of the kitchen window. As they entered he turned to her, his face full of concern.

"Oh, Jane. Come here."

But instead he came to her and folded her in a hug. For a moment, startled, she let herself lean against him, yielding to the desire to be held and comforted. Then she said, "No. Don't," and stepped back.

"You shouldn't be alone tonight," Meg said briskly. "You don't look at all well."

"I'll be fine." She sank into a chair. "I'm used to being on my own."

Adam and Meg looked at each other; he spoke first. "Could someone come and stay with you? Your yoga friend, or Suzanne?"

"Or I could stay the night," Meg offered.

"Suzanne -" Jane said slowly. Everyone's place in her life had altered; they'd shuffled around, some retreating, others taking the lead. Suzanne had become – what, her aunt as well as her sister? while her father stepped back a generation. And *he* - Sean McBride, unheard of till November except as Adam Mullen, someone Suzanne had spoken of - was her closest relative.

"I'll phone her now," she said, and went into Anthony's study, closing the door. She picked up the phone and listened to the dialling tone, at a loss for what to say, how even to start. Besides, Suzanne would be at work; she couldn't dump this on her without warning. After a few minutes she replaced the handset and returned to the kitchen.

"It's OK. Suzanne's coming, leaving right away. You can both go now."

Bridget

1991, MAY

SHE'D FORGOTTEN WHAT A wondrous thing a baby was, a presence from the moment of birth: helpless but self-contained, frail as a paper dart launched at the future, strong as the millennia of evolutionary forces that had shaped it. This new person, this baby girl, hadn't existed and now emphatically did. For those few days in hospital the world was stilled and awed, shrunk to the dimensions of the cot beside her bed, tuned to the rhythms of sleeping, waking, feeding. Visitors appeared from another life of busyness and trivia, talking of traffic and parking. She was relieved when they went, leaving her in slow baby time.

She had feared that Anthony would look at the infant with indifference, in spite of his intention of bringing her up as his own. There'd been no question of his attending the birth, but afterwards, while Bridget lay exhausted, he was as captivated as he'd been by Suzanne as a baby. Having suspected that he hoped for a boy, Bridget saw that she needn't have worried.

She knew that he had wanted another child. She hadn't known how much, but could hardly have produced one when he'd shown no sexual interest in her for years. How odd people are, she thought, looking at the smile that softened his face. She wondered if this child would prove, in spite of everything, to be a blessing.

At Anthony's suggestion they named her Jane; his mother had been Catherine Jane. It was a name Bridget liked, and she was relieved that he wanted this continuity, as if the irregularity of conception could be overlooked.

As she rested in the sunlit ward she wondered where Adam was, and whether instinct would alert him to the birth of his daughter: living, breathing, crying. She allowed herself this indulgence, knowing that from now on she must curb such thoughts. Jane was to be Anthony's daughter. Adam would have no role in her life.

Sunlight flickered over her closed eyelids. Outside was the most perfect of May mornings; it was auspicious that the child had arrived on such a day. Mentally she took herself to the garden: the scream of swifts, the hawthorns at the field-edge almost weighed down with blossom, ash trees unfurling their leaves, the blessing of spring that astonished her each year. I'm far luckier, she thought, than I can possibly deserve.

Meg

1990 – 91, OCTOBER - MAY

THE PHOTOGRAPH OF ADAM by Mary Ellwood's gravestone was pinned to her noticeboard. More than once she'd seen Bridget looking at it, but neither commented. To Meg it was a rare, touching moment: Adam, kneeling, with one hand resting on the headstone, looking up at her with frank admiration. She could still hear his exact words and how he said them.

He had left the address of his Northampton flat, saying he'd be in touch. After weeks of silence she sent a postcard suggesting they meet, but received no reply. She felt rebuffed, but – more pointedly – concerned.

On a spare afternoon she drove into Northampton to find where he lived, an unprepossessing place above a newsagent's in a road leading to the town centre. She was startled when the door was opened by a young woman, toddler in arms, who looked at her blankly. "Adam? No. The guy who was here before? I've only been here a month."

Meg asked for the landlord's phone number and called to ask if he had a forwarding address, but without result. "No idea, love. He settled up and left. Five, six weeks ago, that was."

His parents lived in Derbyshire, she knew; perhaps he'd gone there, but with only the name Mullen to go on she had little hope of finding them. Thinking that the Insch Gallery might help she tried phoning, but was given the Wildings address. Reluctantly she asked Bridget for an address, but Bridget had only the Northampton one.

He didn't want her to find him.

She was annoyed, hurt, frustrated – by herself as much as by him. She'd broken her own rule, trusting in friendship. But her grudge was spiked with anxiety. Several times she'd known Adam withdrawn and uncommunicative, sitting on a crate in his workshop, doing nothing but stare into space. He passed it off flippantly as muse-seeking, while she teased him for being idle, but what if it was sheer hopelessness that drove him into himself – then, and those times he'd disappeared for days on end? She knew how that could take hold, and he'd certainly been downcast when he left. What should she read into his silence - indifference, a wish for a fresh start? Or something more alarming?

She thought of Gillian. And herself, in the hot street, walking home from school with a yoghurt pot she'd papier-machéd and painted. The pot was clumsily painted with red and yellow flowers and splodgy leaves; her pride in it was the last thing she recalled before the awfulness indoors. She was going to give it to Gillian as a present. The curtains were closed but the door was on the latch. Inside, Radio 1 pulsed into the room where Gillian lay on the sofa, hair strewn over her face. Meg shook and shook her, at first puzzled, then frightened. In the end she ran to a neighbour, who summoned an ambulance. When her stepfather came home from work she remembered him crying hopelessly. It was the first time she'd seen a grown-up man cry; she hadn't known it was possible. He and Gillian had planned to marry. "I never fixed the day," he kept saying, dazed, while the neighbour tried to comfort him. "I was going to. I was going to." Meg sat on the floor staring and staring at a worn patch of carpet. Later they found the empty pill-bottle under a chair.

Adam had once told her that he'd had bouts of depression as an art student. "Nothing felt worth doing, even getting out of bed. I just couldn't see any point in living."

"So how did you get through?" she asked.

"Trees," he said. "And painting."

"Trees? How?"

"That had started as a holiday job, helping out a friend of my stepdad. Pruning and stuff. A lot of it was garden work but often we were out in orchards and woods. It was like ... I don't know ... trees were just there. Breathing. Keeping me sane."

"So why don't you paint trees, if you like them so much?"

He shrugged. "I used to. But when I was really down I couldn't give a shit about trees or anything else. Then once when I was completely sick of myself I tried painting what it felt like. It was a way out, mindless if I wanted, or it could take my whole concentration. Soon I was looking forward to picking up my brushes, thinking about it all the time."

"So painting saved you," she said lightly. "It's your one true thing. The thing that makes you you. Everyone needs that."

"Yes. It is." He smiled. "And here's yours." With a fingertip he stroked the descending curve of a y. She was warmed by his confiding in her, and their shared understanding.

"It's what makes us happy," she said, though happiness

was not quite what she meant. It was more than happiness: purpose, dedication, love.

He'd never since been as low, he told her when she asked. Now he was gone, not wanting her to know where. She felt a pang of hurt.

Wherever he'd gone, she hoped it was for good reason. And that he was painting.

Then, in January, a postcard arrived from Cork, saying that he was working with his cousin, a builder. To her exasperation he gave no address, no way of replying. In March, a card showing the Liffey Bridge in Dublin. Since, nothing.

While Bridget was preoccupied with giving birth, Meg took over Artweeks. Two potters had moved into Adam's studio, as she would always think of it, and installed a kiln. She'd invited an acquaintance who made silver jewellery to exhibit alongside her own work, Leonard's signwriting and the ceramic jugs, vases and platters made by Katy and Tamsin. For the last week in May an Artweeks banner hung outside, with arrowed signs from the village and crossroads. The trickle of visitors over nine days brought several enquiries leading to commissions, and Leonard reported the same, while the pottery and jewellery sold well.

Although this had been Bridget's project she did little more than appear sometimes with the baby in her arms. Adam's baby, Meg thought, gazing at the screwed-up face of infant Jane. He must know, of course, that it was time.

On the final Saturday another postcard arrived, with an address in Brighton as its only message.

Jane

FEBRUARY 2019

She locked up and retreated to bed, but lay awake, restless, hot and cold by turns. Her head reeled even when she lay still; she turned on the radio but the background noise interfered with the fast spin of her thoughts.

Dad...

She must hold on tight or lose him for ever. Through the filter of her new knowledge, nothing made sense, and everything did.

When she was small he used to carry her on his shoulders, holding her legs and pretending to be a horse; he made little cantering steps as she clutched his hair and squealed with delight.

"Go on, Dad – say the poem! The donkey poem!"

Nicholas Nye was lean and grey, lame of leg and old; more than a score of donkey's years he had seen since he was foaled ...

At primary school, other children said *But your dad's so old! Old as my Grandad!* And often she thought that unfair, wishing she had a younger and fitter dad like those who ran races at sports day or made scenery for plays.

There was a photograph Mum had taken and specially liked: toddler Jane with Dad, their backs to the camera, intent on her walking. Dad was holding her hand, stooping, his other hand on her back. Fat-bottomed and chubby-legged, hair frizzed out like a halo, she had one foot planted while the other took a wavering step, confident in his support. His head leaned towards her and the camera caught the affection in his glance, in the corner of his smile.

Fatherly pride. Grandfatherly pride. She was his first grandchild, not his afterthought of a daughter.

Her family tree must be redrawn, everything reassessed, as if thrown into doubt by false memory syndrome.

And Sean, or Adam? She didn't even want him in her thoughts.

Everyone's let me down, she thought. Everyone. Tom. Sean/Adam. Mum. Meg. Even Chitra, with her new friends and new boyfriend. The only person who hadn't failed her was Suzanne, but she couldn't face telling her yet.

Dad?

He'd loved her, for sure, but he hadn't told the truth. No one had, all her life.

What if I'm ill, really ill, she thought, like Dad was with galloping sepsis, and no one knows? Eventually she slept, waking groggily to full daylight. She had a raging thirst; rousing herself to drink from the glass by her bedside she glanced at her watch and saw that it was past midday.

Had she slept for more than twelve hours? When she turned on her phone it buzzed with a series of messages and missed calls. The first she saw was a text message from Beryl, about the village hall yoga class:

Are you OK, Jane? We waited 20 mins then gave up. Hope nothing's wrong.

Oh, God. What day was it? Her head was spinning; she lay back, squinting at the too-bright screen of her phone.

Thursday. It was Thursday, and she'd let down her village hall people, both groups. Beryl sounded kind, but she could imagine the others being less well-disposed: "This is a bit much! Not bothering to let us know? Wasting our time..."

And she was due at Reception for the late shift, four till ten. She called in sick, knowing she'd barely left time for the manager to find a replacement. Weakly she got herself to the bathroom, had a pee and sluiced her face. The phone rang downstairs, but she'd forgotten to bring a handset upstairs and was already exhausted.

Let it ring. Whoever it was, she didn't care.

• • •

Someone was in the house. Waking from fitful sleep, she registered sounds below.

Dad, was her first thought. He's back.

Then a tread on the stairs, and Suzanne calling from the first landing: "Janey?"

"Up here," she croaked, and Suzanne came up, still in her coat.

Raising her head she felt sick, and quickly lay down. "What's happened? What time is it? Why are you here?"

"Oh, Jane! Why didn't you phone? Why didn't you answer my calls?" Suzanne sat on the bed. "Janey – I've talked to Adam. Sean. Adam. He told me. But first – you look awful. What can I get you? Have you drunk plenty of water?"

"You did what? How?"

Through her mental fog, Suzanne's explanation was barely

even surprising. Adam had tried calling, first Jane's mobile and then the house phone; worried to get no answer, suspecting she hadn't been truthful about Suzanne coming over, he'd got Suzanne's number from the solicitors.

"You've talked to him? He told you everything?"

Suzanne nodded. "I don't suppose everything, but – well, a lot."

"He - says he's my father?"

"Yes. I know. I mean I *didn't* know, of course not – oh Janey, what a shock for you. For me, too. I could hardly believe it ... it's been going round and round in my head ... but it does start to add up. You need looking after. We'll talk more, but first I'm taking your temperature. Is the First Aid box in its usual place?"

"Seriously? It's nothing major. I just need sleep."

But Suzanne insisted, and the thermometer gave a reading of ninety-nine.

"Thought so. You're coming home with me. Let's get your bag packed." She ignored Jane's protests that she was fine, that it wasn't fair to risk infecting the family, and that more house viewings were scheduled. "All the better, then, if you're not here. The last thing you want is strangers gawping at you in bed. And don't tell me you're planning to teach yoga when you can hardly stand."

・・・

At Suzanne's there was plenty of time to talk: for questions and reinterpretations; fragments combining, slowly beginning to make a kind of sense.

"Delayed shock, I expect," Suzanne told her. "Not just this latest. From Dad dying so suddenly. It all takes a while to register."

"It's like everything's turned upside-down."

"I know," said Suzanne. "How did I not see, back then?"

"But why would you? Generally people are who they say they are. And *Mum* - can you believe she'd do that?"

"No. Yes. It ought to be unthinkable, but, well, the way they were, Mum and Dad..." Suzanne said. "I keep remembering bits and pieces. I knew Dad didn't like Adam. Once we had a bonfire in the orchard, and Dad stomped over in one of his moods. I thought he was jealous because Adam was young and good-looking and Dad got miffed when he started doing jobs for Mum. I said that to her, once. She laughed, but I know she thought the same. I thought Dad was being ridiculous, but perhaps – I don't know."

"Poor old Dad -" Jane stopped, hearing what she'd said, knowing she couldn't think of him as *Grandad*.

"To be honest I had a secret crush on Adam myself," Suzanne said, with a little laugh. "I used to dream that he'd notice me, when I was older. Now he turns out to be my *brother*. And he knew that all the time."

"Mm. That's what I can't get over. He was the only person who knew everything - it was an unfair advantage. Can you forgive him for that?"

"You need to go to bed. We'll talk more tomorrow."

Checking messages Jane found an email from Meg: **Are you all right? I'd like to come over again when you've recovered.**

She replied that she was at Suzanne's and would email when she was back at Wildings. From Adam there was a message that followed several he'd sent yesterday: **Hope you're OK. Will write. Adam x**

She didn't reply, but when she thought back over their conversations she realised that he'd never once called himself

Sean. *I'm Anthony's son* was how he'd introduced himself, which was of course true.

For several days she loafed around at Suzanne's, reading, listening to the radio, sleeping for more hours than she thought possible, with the luxury of being looked after. Her various losses, blurring and combining, dulled into background ache.

"If it's real flu you won't get over it in a hurry," Suzanne said. No one else had succumbed, so Jane didn't have to feel guilty on that score, and Chitra arranged cover for her classes.

Rob phoned on Saturday to say that the Pritchards had made an offer, considerably lower than the asking price. "He says we won't accept," Suzanne told Jane. "There are others interested."

"Good. I don't want them to have it." It was a reprieve.

"We'll have to tell him about Adam. God knows how. I'd prefer to meet Adam myself before we involve Rob."

"And give us time to adjust. I keep thinking I've dreamed it."

"I know. But I keep remembering things I must have half-noticed at the time. Mum and Adam at the hospital after my accident. The way Mum was so funny about Adam leaving, never properly explaining. And when she told me she was pregnant – so matter of fact. I knew she didn't want to talk about it but I put that down to embarrassment."

"So after all our speculating about Dad, *Mum* had an illegitimate child, as well. And it's me! People don't think that way now, but it's what Rob said about Sean. Adam."

"But Jane - you mustn't be in any doubt that Dad loved you."

"I'm not," Jane said, meaning it. "The Will, though. It sort of makes sense. Dad including Adam. Putting me in a different category from you, Rob and Adam, his three children."

"Yes," Suzanne said. "I've been thinking about that. It has to mean that after he was gone, he wanted Adam to come forward and identify himself. He must have wanted you to have that ... consolation. Not to be left on your own. You've got a father after all."

"But do I want him? A liar and a cheat? And I do feel cheated – I *liked* him ... a lot. Until now. How can this not change everything?"

"That might be a bit harsh," Suzanne said carefully. "I mean, Mum must have met him halfway."

"Did she, though? We don't know how it happened, but he hid the one thing that would make it out of the question. If she'd *known* who he was ... Which makes it grossly unfair. One-sided."

"You'd better talk to Meg," Suzanne said. "She was there the whole time, good friends with both of them."

Jane did, by phone on Monday when Suzanne was at work and she had the house to herself.

"I need to ask you about Adam."

"Yes, I know," said Meg. "And I need to tell you."

'How can I forgive him for the awful thing he did? Deceiving my Mum. Lying, or at least not telling the truth. Even though I'm only here because of it."

"Ye–es," Meg said slowly. "There's no getting away from that. But I don't think he exactly planned it, if that's what you're thinking."

"I honestly don't know what to think."

After a pause, Meg said, "Your mother didn't love Adam. It was just a quick fling. But he was in love with her."

The surprise of this, the reversal of what she'd imagined, silenced Jane for a moment.

"Did he tell you that?"

"Didn't need to. I saw it. And think how things worked out," Meg went on. "Your mum was happy enough. Anthony, too, with his first grandchild – *and* taking the moral high ground, though he had no right. Adam was the one who tore himself to pieces, having a child he could never know. And look at it from his point of view. When he met Anthony he was meeting the father who didn't want him, who never made the slightest effort to find him. How must that have felt? And the bargain they made – that Anthony would bring you up, would be your father, as long as Adam never tried to contact you? You've been an absence in his life since you were born."

Jane was silent.

"You won't know this," Meg continued, "but he suffers badly from depression, has done since his teens. I've picked him up off the floor more than once."

"Like Dad?"

"Like Anthony, yes. It's hereditary, isn't it? I can't see many ways they're alike, but that's one."

Jane absorbed this: the weirdness that in all her weighing of who did what and who was most to blame, the key piece of evidence was her own self. To wish things otherwise was to wish herself out of existence.

"Give him a chance," Meg said. "Please. And come over again. Soon."

Meg

1991, JUNE

ADAM'S POSTCARD WAS ON the table. After the initial leap of anticipation and hope on recognising his handwriting, she'd looked at it every time she went indoors.

A Brighton address. No phone number: he hadn't even signed his name. She studied the writing, so much *him*, though he usually used black ink; this was fainter, in pencil. He'd occasionally left her a note or written down the name of an artist he wanted her to look up, and she teased him that her letterer's eye saw more artistry in his writing than in his paintings.

Was this a diffident call for help? A test he was inviting her to fail?

She didn't fail.

As soon as Artweeks was over she investigated trains to Brighton and set off, without telling Bridget. She could do it there and back in a day. Arriving, she asked for directions and found her way to a side-street of Victorian terraces not far from the station. Adam's van was in front of a house with a scruffy front garden, weeds between paving slabs, the door in need of painting. There were two doorbells; she rang both, and waited.

After an interval, feet clomped down stairs. Adam opened the door and stared at her without surprise or interest.

"Hello," she said, when he didn't speak. "Can I come in?"

"Yeah," he said, offhandedly, and led her up to the first floor. He wore shabby jeans and a none-too-clean shirt with half the buttons undone; his feet were bare, his hair lank and uncombed. This main room had kitchen units along one wall, the window looking towards the backs of similar houses. The room was furnished with a television, a sofa with sagging cushions and an armchair with a plaid blanket thrown over it. Through a doorway she saw an unmade bed and half-drawn curtains. As tidy in the cottage as she was in her workshop, Meg recoiled at the smell from a waste-bin and unwashed dishes piled in the sink. She couldn't be sure that Adam himself wasn't contributing to the musty, unwashed aroma that pervaded.

"Are you renting this?"

"No. A friend from art school lives here. He's gone travelling. I'm looking after his cat."

Even the way he spoke lacked energy, as if it were too much trouble to articulate.

She saw a saucer of meaty remnants on the floor, flies buzzing.

"Cat? You don't seem to be looking after yourself very well."

He shrugged. She wondered what he'd been doing when she rang the bell. There was no sign of activity – no book, newspaper or art materials. A radio played something irritatingly jingly. She couldn't tell if he'd fully registered her presence, and that she'd travelled for hours to see him.

"Adam, are you on something?"

"No," he said dully. "I don't do drugs. Not since art school."

She wasn't sure she believed him, but persevered: had he got work here? No. Friends? Not really. Was he doing any painting? Not since Wildings. Everything met the same blank indifference. She knew better than to try to jolly him out of it. Practicalities were the only answer.

She cleaned and tidied, emptied the bin, cleared stale food out of the fridge, washed up and scoured the sink. Her activity threw his lethargy into contrast and after a while, at her suggestion, he roused himself to strip the bed. Glancing in, she saw that he'd tugged the sheets and duvet cover off but stood gazing at the heap on the floor as if unsure what to do next. She went in and bundled them into a bin-bag she'd found under the sink.

"Is there a launderette nearby? If you changed and showered we could take your clothes as well."

She thought he might resist being bossed, but he said, "I suppose I could."

In fresh clothes, damp hair in a pony tail, he looked more presentable, but she saw the dullness in his eyes and thought *I'm not going home tonight. Can't leave him like this.*

The launderette was three streets away. While the washing was in progress she made him walk with her to the seafront; she bought fish and chips and they sat on a low wall to eat them. It was a mild, cloudless evening, the beach and promenade felt festive, strung with lights in the dusk. Two young women walked past hand-in-hand, stopping to kiss and embrace. Meg heard one of them giggle. Brighton: such a place to be young and exuberant and in love. Completely the wrong place if you were on a downer, all the art and brightness and freedom counterpointing your own malaise. But it was soothing to sit quietly and watch the sea: the mesmeric rise and fall of waves, the soft sigh as they pulled at the shingle, advance and retreat, on and on, like the planet's breathing. It said that nothing mattered much and at the same time that all would be well.

After a while Adam rolled up chip papers and said, "There's something about the sea. I ought to come down here every day."

She took that as a good sign. He stood up, looking for a bin.

"OK if I stay?" she asked. "I've left it too late to get back tonight. I can sleep on the sofa."

She sensed his relief. On the way back with the washing, they stopped at a supermarket where she bought a toothbrush, milk and bread and coffee.

"You can have the bed," Adam told her, and took the plaid blanket to the sofa for himself; though looking at the saggy two-seater and the length of his limbs she doubted he could sleep there in comfort.

She got into the double bed in her T-shirt, thinking that she hadn't yet mentioned Bridget or the baby. He hadn't asked, though surely he'd worked out the dates. She couldn't leave without telling him, but when would be a good moment? Wide awake, she heard him move about in the bathroom then settle on the sofa. After a while she heard the radio playing softly, got out of bed and went to him where he sat hunched.

"Come on. It's not fair to turf you out of your bed. There's room for two."

She felt sure he wouldn't take it as an invitation to sex, and he didn't; just lay down with a sigh and appeared to fall asleep immediately, while she rested next to him, not touching. She liked having him near and safe, listening to the steady sound of his breath. Her fear for him and what he might do, left alone, was assuaged by the simple fact that he was here and quietly sleeping.

Never before had she shared a bed with a man.

As a teenager she'd had sex with boys but only in snatched encounters in parks or bedrooms, leading to the disaster of her pregnancy and hushed-up abortion. It had been somehow combative, the boy left exultant, herself shamed and sometimes bruised and sore: an ordeal she chose to put herself through, she couldn't now think why. Only later did she acknowledge that she preferred women, and that had led to love and loss, complications she'd trained herself not to seek again.

But this was Adam. She trusted him, even loved him. This was now, not a prelude to some muddled, recriminatory future. Wanting for once to hold and be held she shuffled against his turned back and slipped an arm around him; he murmured and clasped her hand and moved so that she was hugging him more closely, and she smelled his skin and felt his warmth, the jut of a shoulder-blade and the tickle of hair against her face, and felt blessed with completeness. It was an intimacy she needed as much as he did, neither wanting more.

By morning the tabby cat had joined them, lying behind the crook of her knees, purring loudly as she stirred. Adam stretched and smiled, looking at her as if this was quite normal, and she got up to make coffee.

• • •

She stayed another night. On the second morning she woke to find Adam up and dressed, sitting on the bed facing her, notebook on bent knee. She smiled blearily before registering with surprise that he was drawing.

"Can I see?"

With a show of reluctance he handed her the small notebook. He'd drawn her in pencil, sleeping, eyes softly closed, face squidged against the pillow. She was astonished: embarrassed that he'd been studying her while she was oblivious. But touched, too, by the tenderness of the little portrait.

"I didn't know you could draw like that!"

"Why so surprised? You know I went to art school."

"Doesn't necessarily follow these days. Thought you just chucked paint about."

He smiled. "That as well."

"Anyway, you're good." She looked at the sketch again. "Can I have it?"

"No." He reached for the notebook. "I'll do another one some time if you like."

She was vastly relieved: he'd come through. She would go home later, feeling that she could safely leave him. They went out for breakfast in a busy cafe in The Lanes, where he said that it felt like a sick headache clearing, his head filling with clean air instead of sludge. Afterwards they went to an art shop where Meg encouraged him to buy a sketchpad, 2B pencils and a soft eraser, and they spent the rest of the morning on the sea-front, both drawing in companionable silence.

"You will keep in touch, won't you?" she asked. "Promise? Please don't disappear again."

"I will." He paused, looking at the ground. "You can tell me now, Meg. About the baby."

"A girl. Jane. Born on the fourteenth, just over a week ago. She and Bridget are both fine."

He nodded slowly, compressing his lips.

"Anthony?" he asked, after a moment.

"You won't believe it, but tickled pink. Look, if you need company again, if you'd like me to come - phone. Don't wait. Phone." She handed him a piece of folded paper. "Here's the number for the cottage."

He walked with her to the station.

"I don't know what to say, Meg. Thank you. You don't know what a difference you've made, being here."

But maybe she did.

From the carriage, looking out at the passing landscape, she caught herself wondering if she might find a workshop and somewhere to live down here, on the South Downs. Ditchling, perhaps, where Eric Gill had set up his workshop; she could continue the stone-carving tradition he'd established.

But that was stupid. She had all she needed at Wildings; besides, Adam wouldn't necessarily stay in Brighton. "What will you do?" she had asked, and he said that he'd look for a place to rent, either there or back in Ireland. He could easily get maintenance work, tree-pruning or painting and decorating, and maybe he'd find an art group to hook up with.

Not Ireland, she hoped; she'd never see him.

The countryside was patterned in soft greens with the occasional glare of oilseed rape. Hedges and trees, lanes and gentle hills, passing in a blur. She had a book but was too unsettled to read.

Her thoughts returned to the two girls on the sea front in the dusk, kissing, laughing. She rarely let herself think of Carrie, but now memories seared her. Carrie's sudden radiant smile, her shy glance; the dark hair that kept falling across one eye, pushed back with a slender hand. The two of them in a group of friends, laughter and inconsequential chat made piquant by the looks that flashed between them. The deliciousness of wondering but not being sure: *is she ... does she ... might she ...* They'd found ways to be alone: an evening walk by the river, a gallery visit. Meg had the sense of something unfurling inside her, warm and pervasive: a feeling that transformed everything she saw, like a sunrise.

Love, she had to call it. She'd never thought it would happen. It felt clichéd. It felt miraculous.

It wasn't her first experience of sex with another woman but for Carrie it was a revelation. Meg loved to shock and delight her with the intense pleasure she could give. And receive in turn, when Carrie learned to reciprocate. Two female bodies, each knowing the other's potential, mirroring sensations, intensifying them to the point where self seemed lost. "I love you," Carrie would whisper, her face tear-streaked. "Oh Meg, I love you!"

No one had ever told her that. She said it back. Heard herself saying it. Wondered how such declarations came easily to other people, and why she couldn't make it sound as if she meant it, even when she did.

Carrie lived with her boyfriend, Phil; both worked at a nearby comprehensive school where Carrie taught English, Phil Geography. Meg was still at her aunt and uncle's in Fulbourne, driving daily to George's workshop, twelve miles west of Cambridge. To spend nights together she and Carrie had to find B&Bs or cheap hotels. Once, when Phil was on an A-Level field trip, they slept together in the bed Carrie usually shared with him, but she was jittery with guilt, and Meg left after one night of the planned three, unable to calm her. It was their first row: "When are you going to tell him, for fuck's sake? How long can you keep up this charade?"

"I can't tell him – how can I? It's different for you. No

one minds. You don't work in a school – everyone would talk about me if they found out. And the parents ... You don't know what it's like."

"I wasn't suggesting you announce it in a staff meeting. I meant when will you come clean with Phil?"

But the decision Carrie eventually made was not that. Recently qualified, she was anxious for her career. A new local government act, Section 28, had been brought in by the Thatcher government, making it illegal for schools to promote homosexuality or present it as acceptable. Carrie fretted that if her sexuality were known or suspected – by colleagues, let alone by pupils or parents - she'd be considered a risk to the teenage girls she taught.

Meg was outraged. "That's pathetic! Why would you be? How's that any different from straight male teachers and young girls? For God's sake don't let yourself be brainwashed!"

And much more.

"It's wrong, Meg. It's – perverted. I don't know how I got into this but it's finished now. Has to be. I can cure myself." Then the final, wounding words: "It's your fault. You've made me feel dirty. Used."

Used! Meg was left speechless. Had Carrie needed coercion? Had her enthusiasm and openness when they made love been nothing but pretence?

No. No. The pretence was now.

Within a month Carrie was engaged to Phil, wearing a diamond ring. Meg nursed the bitterness of rejection for a while then dismissed it as folly; she'd let herself be taken over by temporary madness. Never again. Never would she let someone into her life to hurt and betray. Perhaps it had been an illusion; a different person had imagined herself in love with Carrie, not her at all.

She began looking for somewhere to live and work, well away from Cambridge. From Carrie.

• • •

Back at Wildings, after pocketing the parking ticket from her windscreen and noting the hefty fine for leaving her car at the station for two nights, she didn't seek out Bridget. Next morning Bridget came into the workshop, curious about where she'd been, and why she hadn't mentioned going away.

"Went to see a friend."

"Oh?"

When Meg made no further response, Bridget went on, "I really appreciate all you did for Artweeks. It went well, didn't it? But I feel bad, lumbering you. All I did was hang round admiring things."

"No prob. You'd set it all up."

Bridget held the baby in her arms, rocking it gently. Meg - not in the least baby-minded, seeing them only as noisy, demanding encumbrances - looked at it. At *her*. She ought to start thinking of it as a person. Jane. Adam's child. Fully aware that this was what had sunk him, she looked at Bridget's face, softly complacent in new motherhood, and thought: She's got no idea. Probably hasn't given him a thought.

Bridget

1991 - 1996

BUOYED BY THE MODEST success of Artweeks, she was already planning to apply again. Next year she'd be fully involved, selling plants, providing teas, even offering garden tours. Paintings could be displayed in the barn, she thought, envisaging neat framed landscapes.

It was the little artistic community she'd wanted, but how different from her dream: herself with only a background role, a new mother, her marriage salvaged against all odds.

A month later she had a commission of her own. Her first *Northamptonshire Life* articles had appeared, with a third scheduled; someone made contact through the magazine, asking her to design a vegetable garden similar to hers, and oversee its construction.

She was amused by that, bringing the letter to show Meg.

"Imagine! They must have more money than sense."

Meg studied the letter. "Will you do it?"

"Course not! I'm not a professional garden designer."

"But why not? They want you. They'll pay. You could easily fit it around looking after Jane."

Meg's persuasiveness worked. Bridget took on the task and enjoyed it, drawing, consulting books, making plant lists, while the baby dozed in her carry-cot. For site visits she left Jane with Suzanne, who loved the novelty of having an infant sister and enjoyed taking care of her.

"Make a portfolio." Meg was ever practical. "Before, during and after. Good for publicity."

"I don't want publicity!"

But she was getting it, wanted or not. Those first clients held a party to celebrate their new potager, with Bridget as guest; several people there asked for her business card. Meg told her to get one printed: *Bridget Harper, Garden Designer.*

"I can't put that!"

"Stop being modest! Just do it. If you're bothered you can do a course or something. You can pick and choose what you take on. You can say no."

Feeling that she'd be caught out if she didn't acquire qualifications, Bridget took a correspondence course. She engaged Maurice, a retired gardener from Haverton Hall, to take care of maintenance at Wildings.

Anthony was often away. He'd published a series of articles and was invited to speak at conferences and university open days. He was vague about his comings and goings, and she suspected an affair, but didn't ask. He was unfailingly good with Jane - ever patient, willing to crawl around the floor or pretend to be an elephant. Her main concern was that Jane should grow up unaffected by her parents' strange relationship; somehow, it seemed to be working.

In Jane's third summer, Anthony informed Bridget that he was going to Nice for a fortnight. "With Marie, who I've been seeing on and off. A colleague."

"Sleeping with, you mean?"

"Of course."

Of course. It rankled that Marie came into the category of desirable woman, from which she'd been excluded for some while.

"How long has this been going on?"

"Nearly a year. I'm only telling you this so that you know," he said. "I'm not making any changes."

She confided in Meg, who was unsurprised.

"You'd have grounds for divorce, if you wanted."

"So would he! But it's best for Jane and Suzanne if we're together. And in an odd way I think we need each other."

She was surprised to hear herself saying this.

Meg wasn't convinced. "What about you? If he can find someone else, you could, too."

"Oh, come on! When would I have time?"

Occasionally she let herself think of Adam. From this distance he'd slipped into mythology, a golden youth who'd briefly bestowed himself on her, leaving the precious gift of Jane. Occasionally, awkwardness constricting her throat, she asked Meg about him. Meg said only that he'd settled in Brighton, but whenever Meg disappeared for a few days without explanation Bridget suspected that she'd gone to see him. It made her uneasy, but apparently he took no interest in Jane; or if he did, Meg didn't relay it.

It was fortunate, she told herself, that he'd moved so far away.

. . .

Anthony's fortnight in France set a pattern for separate holidays. Sometimes he took Jane to visit Rob, who now worked in Manchester; Bridget visited her mother, or went on cultural trips to Paris or Prague, and once spent a Bank Holiday with Meg and Jane in Uncle Terry's Dorset caravan. When necessary she and Anthony could present themselves as a couple. At Suzanne's wedding to Edward, where Jane was bridesmaid, they posed for photographs and played their roles admirably, only later casting off mutual devotion along with their formal clothes.

For much of the time they could get along amicably, sharing meals, discussing their respective days. Sometimes he invited colleagues for Sunday lunch, which Bridget cooked and served; not confident as a cook she could at least show loyalty and support. Only once did she invite Meg to supper with Anthony and herself. He showed himself at his worst, barely speaking, taking no part in the conversation other than giving curt replies when addressed. When Bridget challenged him afterwards he said he was tired, and wasn't interested in small talk.

"Meg doesn't *do* small talk. You know that."

Bridget couldn't understand why he disliked Meg, eventually concluding that he resented their friendship. This she found ridiculous – or was it evidence that he still, in his odd way, felt something for her? But after that she took care to keep Anthony and Meg apart, inviting Meg to the house only when Anthony was away for the night, with Marie or at a conference. More often she and Meg shared lunch at the cottage: simple meals of bread and ham and salad, or – when Meg felt like cooking - vegetables from the garden.

She had more than enough to occupy her. At first her design commissions were undemanding: a vegetable plot; a planting plan to refresh a tired border; pots and planters for a courtyard. Then she was offered the more enticing task of making a sundial garden for a client who'd seen Meg's work during Artweeks and wanted to engage both of them in a joint project.

The site, a walled square within the grounds of a Victorian house, was a formal rose garden the owner wanted to replace. Visiting, she was daunted by swathes of immaculate lawn, pleached limes, a walk leading to a lake and boathouse; she confided to Meg on the way home that she felt out of her depth. Meg was brisk: "Come on, Bridget. It's a gift. Clean slate, money no object? We should bite his hand off."

By next evening Meg had made drawings for her sundial, and Bridget got to work on the rest. A hexagonal bed surrounding the Bath stone sundial; brick paths; deep borders, with white Lutyens benches facing east and west. White roses on the walls, alpine clematis twining through; silver-leaved weeping pear, and the rest of the planting in blues and purples: lavender, salvias, tall verbascums and verbena, softened by the seedheads of flowering grasses and the green of alchemilla mollis.

The owner was well-connected. The following summer, with the plants established, his garden was photographed for a *Telegraph* feature. Other offers followed, more than she and Meg could keep up with: separate commission and joint projects. Often Bridget was stupid with tiredness by evening, dozing over her sketchbook or notes, waking when her pencil clattered to the floor. But her head was full of planting plans, new combinations to try, ways of adapting to clients' preferences while still developing her own style. Her plantings were rampant, dense with subtle colours and contrasts. Influenced by the new approach coming from

Piet Oudolf in the Netherlands as well as by Vita Sackville-West and other great gardeners of the past, she favoured a naturalistic appearance with plants scrambling into each other and spilling out of their beds, rather than anything neat and controlled.

It was more than she could have dreamed. By luck and circumstance she'd fallen into a new career – yes, she could call it a career - that absorbed her. People paid her to do what she loved. She could look with pride at gardens and plantings that hadn't existed until she made them; at trees and shrubs that would grow and mature long after she left them behind.

One doubt she voiced to Meg. "It's so *elitist,* though. We're working for people who can have what they want, pay whatever it costs, then employ someone else to look after it. Some want their garden as a showpiece, rather than a space to live in. You can't really love a garden without getting your hands in the soil. It feels like I'm abandoning my working-class origins."

Meg made a sound between laugh and snort. "Working-class origins? You've left those a long way behind, living where you do. You can't have it all ways. You do what you love. It's how you make your mark. Ideas filter down – the planting you do for a country mansion gives ideas to people with small town gardens. Your vegetable plots inspire people to have a go. Anyone can grow something, even a window-box or some pots. Same for me, really, what I do. It costs money to have a hand-carved gravestone – far more than a machine-cut one from a funeral director. But wouldn't it be a loss if no one did the real thing, from socialist principles or whatever? If the old skills died out? Art has always needed patrons. You should look on your wealthy mansion-owners as patrons of gardening art."

"Even if it's only for themselves?"

"We all do things for ourselves when it comes down to it. We do what makes us feel good. Along the way we influence others, without even knowing. Bring pleasure and beauty into their lives. That's worth doing."

Bridget's thoughts turned to the garden at Wildings. Wasn't that only for her own satisfaction? Anthony liked the garden but was no connoisseur; to Jane it was a playground, to Suzanne and Ed a pleasant place to sit out on summer visits, chatting and drinking wine. None of them needed a place on this scale. Could she share it with others? During Artweeks she offered tours and sold plants, but she could do more: run workshops on design or propagation, or on making a vegetable garden. If she opened more regularly, for the National Gardens Scheme, charities would benefit, and the garden would make some small contribution to society.

Soon a new opportunity arrived. She was approached by a special school for children with illnesses and disabilities, to work on a sensory garden. An architect had been engaged and Bridget was to consult with him about materials, textures and design..

"There you go," Meg said. "Perfect. A salve to your social conscience. And different from anything you've done before."

With Chris, the architect, Bridget visited the school to meet children, teachers and carers, to assess the possibilities. She came away with notes and sketches and a head full of ideas: wheelchair ramps, raised beds, shady seating areas for craft activities or storytelling in summer. Wind-chimes and trickling water would add sound, and a range of textures would invite touching: flaky bark, woolly leaves of lamb's ear, silky grasses, and varied materials for paths and screens. There would be bird feeders, edible plants, scents; a practical area with a lean-to greenhouse where children could grow and tend vegetables.

She threw herself into this, constantly scribbling ideas in her notebook or waking in the night with a new thought. When the garden was complete, there was a Family Day to celebrate, and for the first time she saw children exploring the paths and arbours, reaching out to touch the windchimes, exclaiming over the mosaic wall made from broken china. It was the most satisfying thing she'd done. Jane, who accompanied her, immediately wanted a wheelchair and ramp, and asked Bridget to build a garden like that at Wildings. "Can't we have it in the orchard? There's nothing there, only trees."

Photographs in local papers led to an invitation to create a show garden for *Gardeners' World Live* at the NEC in Birmingham. She worked with Chris again, which made her feel uneasily disloyal to Meg. However, Meg was unconcerned, saying there'd be other chances.

Her meetings with Chris took her to his stylish Birmingham flat, where on several occasions they ended up in bed. It was easy, uncomplicated, neither expecting commitment. Chris was divorced, with teenage children and his main home in France, conveniently distant. Bridget knew that when they finished working together their affair would end too, without regret on either side. Chris was a satisfying if predictable lover, and as the lustre of novelty wore off she found herself tiring of him.

Sometimes, in Chris's bed, she thought wistfully of Adam. She wondered why she still harboured such thoughts; their encounter had been too brief even to be called an affair. When he said he loved her, with his ludicrous idea that they should run away together, she'd thought him a foolish boy.

How soon would he have regretted that? How would he feel now, saddled with a woman well into her fifties?

She could see him clearly, standing on the lawn with his bootlace trailing; the set of his shoulders as he walked away, that last time. His final words still burned: *I thought you had more courage than that.*

She considered herself more cautious than courageous, but honesty demanded that she tell Anthony about Chris. When she did, his main concern was that Jane shouldn't know or be affected. She assured him that she'd be as discreet as he was about Marie; *more* discreet.

That seemed settled, an unimportant practical matter. About to leave the kitchen, he turned and said, "I've been meaning to ask. That young man who used to rent a workshop here – the artist. Are you still in touch?"

Bridget stopped just short of replying, "Of course not. I promised." Afraid her face would give her away, she began sorting through the pile of newspapers and magazines that mounted up on the table. Did he know? What had made his thoughts jump from Chris to Adam, and why else would he ask?

She made her voice sound casual. "Meg sees him sometimes. He lives in Brighton now. Why d'you want to know?"

"Just wondered if he'd got anywhere as a painter. I saw something on a website recently, an exhibition, and thought it might be him."

"Could have been." She gave an indifferent shrug. "Meg would know," and Anthony nodded and closed the door behind him. Her heart was racing: did he suspect? She didn't believe the chance online sighting. When had Anthony ever been interested in art?

About Chris, he'd been less disapproving than Meg, who – to Bridget's surprise – was shocked. Bridget wondered, as she often did, whether opportunities ever came Meg's way; she certainly didn't seem to look for them.

"No," was all Meg would say, when Bridget ventured to ask. "Why would I bother?"

"But has there ever been anyone? Surely -"

For some time she'd suspected that Meg's preference was for women, but Meg wouldn't be drawn.

"Yes, a while back," she answered, in a way that discouraged further questions. "I've made stupid mistakes. Enough to put me off making more."

Jane

FEBRUARY 2019

"You needn't go back to Wildings," Suzanne said. "Why not stay here till the sale's completed?"

"Thanks, but I need to be there. Otherwise everything'll feel half-finished."

Adam had emailed: **I'm glad you're at Suzanne's, being looked after. Hope you're feeling better and that I can come and see you very soon.**

He'd said in a text message that he was writing to her. A proper letter? But no one wrote letters these days, and the suggestion made her think of solicitors, as if he had an announcement to make, a formal claim. Nothing arrived by post, so if there was a letter it must have gone to Wildings. Although Suzanne, who'd spoken to him twice more, was all too ready to forgive, Jane wasn't sure, and didn't reply. Surfacing from hours of sleep she fancied that she could simply forget him, pretend he hadn't barged in between Dad and herself with his absurd suggestion.

"I've told Rob," Suzanne said. "About Adam. I didn't think it was fair to keep it from him."

"Oh. What did he say?"

Suzanne huffed a laugh. "He was Robbishly uptight. Said Adam sounds despicable. I'm sure he'll tell you so himself."

Rob did, phoning that evening.

"Suzanne's told me about Adam, or Sean, or whatever he calls himself. Another shock for you."

"Yes, it -"

"He needn't think he's got any kind of hold over you. After showing no interest for twenty-seven years. He clearly can't be trusted. So deceitful, sneaking into Wildings with a false identity – then wheedling to you first, instead of approaching through the solicitor, which any decent person would do."

"It wasn't like -"

"He probably hopes that through you he gets the major share of the estate. The cottage, to add to his third of the sale proceeds. I'll bet that's it."

"But why would -"

"Don't worry. You needn't see him again if it bothers you. After all, Dad was your dad when all's said and done. Leave it to me – Malcolm can handle it. Once the sale goes through we'll have no more to do with him. He may be my half-brother but I've no inclination to welcome him into the family. And you don't want to bother with this while you're ill. Can you pass me back to Suzanne?"

. . .

At last, the second weekend approaching, she was ready to return. Suzanne and Ed drove her home on Saturday morning, stopping at the supermarket, and left only after repeated assurances from Jane that she was fine, really, and would phone regularly.

There was a heap of post: catalogues, three letters for Anthony, and one for her.

It's him, she thought, looking at the bold black handwriting. Adam. Her hands shook as she fumbled the envelope and unfolded the sheet inside.

Dear Jane,

I know you're angry and confused. I don't blame you. On top of all the other changes you're facing, I've given you this massive shock. But I hope you'll read this, and afterwards – soon! - let me explain more.

You think I've lied to you, and deceived you. Perhaps not as much as you think, though, and with the aim of explaining as soon as I could. It wouldn't have been fair to contact you while Anthony was alive – to you, him, or your mother. In fact I promised not to. Before you were born, I promised him to stay out of your life. I agreed, believing it was best for you to grow up loved and well cared-for by two parents, as you thought. But now that both Anthony and your mother have gone, there's no need for secrecy. I always intended to make myself known to you when he died, and because he included me in his Will, I think that must be what he wanted too, so that you're not left parentless. Of course he might have lived for another ten or twenty years, in which case I wouldn't have this chance now. So I can't in all honesty say that I'm sorry he's died.

I'm not proud of my behaviour back then. It was wrong of me to come to Wildings so furtively, and not come clean when things got complicated. I won't make excuses. But I don't and never will regret my liaison with your mother - not least because you're the result. How can I truly say I'm sorry, when the worst thing I ever did – the most stupid and irresponsible – has turned out to be the best?

As you know, I have no other children. But I don't want to suggest that you're only filling a gap. Now that I've met you, and see so much to admire, respect and learn to understand, I dearly want to bring you into my life, and to be part of yours. I want to love you, and begin to make up for the missed years. Jane, I've never wished for anything as deeply as this. With all my heart, I hope you'll be able to forgive me, and be my daughter.

With love, and far later than I would have wished,

Your father,
Adam

She sat reading and re-reading: studying the broad pen-strokes, the swooping tails of gs and ys, the flourish of the capital A as he signed his name. The date at the top was the day of his visit. The day when everything changed.

One of the days when everything changed.

He'd written to her that same evening.

Your father, Adam. The words blurred into nonsense.

My father.

Her thoughts chased and contradicted each other. Was she being too easily persuaded? Was Rob right to say that Adam was untrustworthy?

She wanted to warm to him as she'd done at first. But during her stay at Suzanne's, in hours of wakeful brooding, she'd made one decision: she needed to know more about his motives when he came to Wildings. What had he wanted? What did he think he was doing?

"Whatever," Suzanne had said during one of their conversations, "I have to say it doesn't reflect well on Dad. Does it? He *knew* you were his granddaughter and obviously loved you to bits. But all those years he must have let Mum think he was doing her an enormous favour."

Jane struggled to sort through the muddle. "I can't tell who was the biggest deceiver. How can we know?"

As yet she hadn't replied to any of Adam's email or texts since his visit ten days ago. She owed him that, at least.

She sent: **Home. Got your letter. Thank you.**

Almost instantly her phone rang.

"Jane." She heard relief in his voice. "How are you? Suzanne said you've had flu, the real thing."

"Yes, I've been right out of it. Better now, though."

"It's wonderful to hear your voice. I wanted to come and see you, but Suzanne thought best not, yet."

"It was me, really. I – needed time to think."

"And now?"

"I need to talk to you again," she said.

"Yes, of course. When? Tomorrow? I could come over."

She hesitated, not wanting to replay their previous encounter. "I'd prefer somewhere else. Oxford again?"

"Wherever you say, if you're well enough."

"How about the modern art gallery?"

They agreed to meet there at twelve; she hesitated, then added, "Thank you. For the letter."

"I was afraid you'd ignore it," he said gruffly. "Or tear it up."

Bridget

2000, SEPTEMBER

ROB AND INGRID'S WEDDING was swankier than any Bridget had ever attended.

"Do you really want me to come?" she had asked Anthony, who replied: "Obviously. It'd look most odd if you didn't."

Although many things about their marriage were odd, wedding formalities must be observed. She'd met Ingrid only twice and couldn't see that any degree of closeness would be likely, or expected. Ingrid was smoothly good-looking in a way that seemed to expect admiration but hold it at a distance. Predictably, to Bridget, Rob was marrying money: Ingrid's father was a London property developer for whom Rob now worked.

At the wedding she was caught up in the kind of social situation she despised. Wealth and privilege flaunting itself, everyone required to dress up and play roles she considered frankly demeaning to women: the bride, in virginal white, given away by her father in a show of transferring property from male to male; bridesmaids scrambling for the thrown bouquet as if subjugation to the married state was to be yearned for, achieved at all cost. Such a fuss people made about weddings, fretting over the tiniest details. Suzanne's wedding to Ed had been more elaborate than Bridget had expected, but this was a whole other level of ostentation.

She'd bought a two-piece outfit for which she saw future use, but felt under-dressed when she saw Rob's mother Eliza, resplendent in an ice-blue brocade coat and dress with matching plumed hat. They hadn't met since Rob's M.A. graduation, where Bridget had carried Jane, still a small baby. Now, at the church chosen for its photogenic properties, Eliza greeted her with pouty air-kisses. "Aren't we blessed? *Such* perfect weather. Oh, here's Jane – *goodness,* how you've grown!"

Jane, in a green velvet pinafore, looked at her with solemn wariness; then saw Suzanne coming through the lych-gate with Ed, and ran to her. Suzanne was visibly pregnant, prompting Eliza to remark, "So you'll soon be grandparents – congratulations!"

Bridget thanked her, and said, "Yes, we're delighted. And Jane's excited about being an aunt."

"Oh, sweet," said Eliza. "She's *so* like her father, isn't she?"

Wrong-footed, Bridget hoped she wasn't flushing. For a dizzy moment, avoiding Eliza's gaze, she thought *She must know, somehow.* She made her voice calm. "Do you think so? Most people say she takes after me."

"Yes, I do see that – her hair, her colouring, but she's got Anthony's eyes and his way of looking. Who'd have thought it, a father again at his age? He's so good with her! It's quite touching."

Throughout the service Bridget was distracted by this, recalling Eliza's arch expression. Maybe she'd only imagined provocation behind the remark. It was hardly surprising if Jane had picked up some of Anthony's mannerisms. Seated between her and Anthony, Jane was anxious because she didn't know the hymns. "Don't worry, darling," Bridget whispered. "Just listen, or hum a bit." Unsure of her own voice she joined in quietly and self-consciously, holding Jane's hand. Anthony sang in a confident baritone heard only at weddings and funerals, surprising her every time.

At the reception, at a five-star country hotel, Jane stared at her plate. "I don't like eating animals," she said, her voice loud and plaintive. "Why do we?"

"Come on, eat up," Bridget cajoled. "This is a special dinner for Rob and Ingrid. It'd be rude not to eat it. And you like lamb."

"I like *lambs*. I wouldn't eat the lambs in the fields. How can it be right?"

Bridget almost said, *Don't think about that.* But what sort of advice was that for a child – for anyone? Not to think, make connections? Instead, she said, "We'll talk about it at home," and her eyes met Anthony's over Jane's head; he gave her a look of wry amusement, reaching over to cut up the offending flesh. "Be a good girl, Jane. It's delicious, and good for you."

Jane wouldn't be swayed. Pointedly she ate all the vegetables on her plate, spearing peas on her fork, leaving the meat untouched; eventually Anthony shared it between himself and Bridget, saying that it shouldn't be wasted. When Jane was obstinate like this, Bridget could see her own younger self, all too clearly.

"They go through these phases, don't they?" said the woman opposite. "My youngest was like that for a while, till the smell of bacon was too tempting. I expect she'll soon forget all about it."

Meg

2001, JANUARY

SHE WAS WORKING ON a design that didn't much appeal to her: large letters in relief, background cut away and textured, blocky letters standing out. The client wanted a lettering style he'd seen on a Bauhaus poster of the 1920s and – unusually – had provided a detailed drawing. Meg disliked working from other people's drawings and had subtly altered the spacing, but accepted the task for the challenge it offered.

Having been away for the weekend she must make good progress today and was at work early, lighting her stove against January chill. Mid-morning, Bridget came in with designs for a joint project: a memorial garden at a school for a child who'd died. After they'd chatted, and Meg had roughed out ideas, Bridget asked about her trip.

"Brighton again?"

Meg answered the unspoken question. "Yes, to see Adam. He got married two weeks ago."

"Oh? To who?" Bridget said, with studied nonchalance.

"To Jenny."

"So you've met her?"

"Yes, a few times now. She's nice." The phrase fell limply into silence and she saw from the lift of Bridget's head that she'd registered lack of enthusiasm, but in fact Meg had liked Jenny at once: she was warm, rather lovely in an unshowy way, very eager to be friends. Meg found it touching that both she and Adam seemed astonished by their good fortune in finding each other; the relationship was still new. Jenny came from Taunton, and as a gift Meg had carved their initials on a piece of Somerset Blue Lias she'd kept for something special: A and J, swoop-tailed and joyous, overlapping on the blue-grey stone. Jenny was almost too grateful, thanking her again and again, while Adam in his quieter way turned the stone in his hands and gave her a look that was better than words.

She feared now that her friendship with Adam wouldn't be the same. They'd been meeting three or four times yearly, at a London gallery or on her visits to Brighton. The longish intervals in between hadn't mattered much, but now she wondered if she'd only see Adam with Jenny. As ever, she resented change.

"You weren't at the wedding, then?" Bridget asked.

"No, that was just the two of them and a couple of friends. They didn't tell anyone till afterwards."

"What does she do, his wife?"

The word sounded odd, awkward.

"She's head of Art at a comprehensive school. That's how they met – Adam teaches there part-time."

"Teaching – really? I'd never have imagined him doing that. Is he qualified?"

"Yes - did a PGCE at Chichester a few years ago. He likes it. And he teaches evening classes at an FE college."

She thought Bridget might ask more, but all she said was, "Good. I hope they'll be happy," and took another sheet from her folder. "Bee-friendly plants, they said. Here's the list I've started."

It would surely occur to her that there might be children of this marriage, who'd be half-brothers or sisters to Jane. And to wonder, as Meg did, whether Adam's Jenny knew that he was already a father.

. . .

Later, going up to the house to check something with Bridget, she saw Anthony and Jane in the garden, both in coats and scarves. The stillness of their pose caught her attention; she stopped, and saw that they were watching a squirrel on the bird table Bridget had bought to encourage Jane's interest. Sitting upright, the squirrel nibbled at a peanut held in both front paws, its tail a fluffed-out S behind it. Jane saw Meg and waved, and the squirrel ran fluidly along the wall, the peanut in its mouth.

"Oh, now I've frightened it!" Jane called, and her breath made a cloud in the air. "It was really close. Did you see? It's so pretty."

"Yes, I did. I expect it'll come back."

Anthony gave her a cool nod - the most she ever expected – then tweaked the bobble on Jane's hat. "Come on, Janey. Let's see if the ducks are there."

"We've got bread," Jane told Meg, waving a plastic bag. "D'you want to come?"

"No, I'll see you later."

They walked down towards the stream, Jane talking happily to the man who'd wanted to end her life before it began but now appeared to dote on her.

One thing Meg was sure of was that she would never understand Anthony. She watched them for a few moments, then walked on up to the house.

Jane

FEBRUARY 2019

Turning into the tunnelled gallery entrance she saw him inside, through glass doors, looking at the shop's book display. She felt an odd stab of familiarity, as if instinct knew him as her father even if her brain hadn't yet caught up. Their greeting was charged with this knowledge: he looked at her differently, expectantly.

"Shall I come too?" Suzanne had offered, but Jane preferred to meet him on her own: Suzanne saw only the best in people, too ready to forgive and accept.

The café was a cavernous space with bare brick walls, strip lighting and industrial girders. Adam bought coffee; they sat facing each other. High windows looked out to the street behind. It was an unusually warm day for February; glancing out, Jane remarked, "It feels more like April. I'm always glad to reach the end of February, though. It's not a month to be trusted." When Adam gave her a quizzical look, she added: "Mum died in February."

"I know."

"How? Oh, from Meg, of course."

He nodded. "I was at the funeral."

"You were there?" She gave him a sharp look. "Without us knowing?"

And somehow they had plunged straight in.

"I wasn't invited, of course not. I didn't speak to anyone except Meg, and didn't let Anthony see me. But I had to come."

"So – you saw me, too?"

He nodded again, slowly. She was silenced by the thought that he'd been so close, and she hadn't known. He'd seen her, must have noticed how she struggled to hold herself together, reading the Hardy poem, and had gone away without speaking.

"I wanted to tell you then," he said. "Desperately. But I couldn't, it would have been terrible timing. Meg made me see that."

"Look, Adam -" She stopped, hearing herself call him by name for the first time. "I need to know. When you came to Wildings, when you and Mum got together, however that happened – was it deliberate, to get back at Dad?"

He paused before answering, looking out towards the street. "Honestly I'm not sure. Maybe. I resented him, but mainly I was curious – I liked having the advantage, him not knowing. So, yes, you could say I was spying. Stalking, even."

"It *was* stalking." Her voice hardened. "It was dishonest. Unfair. You must have known that."

"I did. I do. I'm not making excuses. But - he wasn't around much, I hardly saw him, and with Bridget I felt this odd connection, I think we both did. And it began to seem inevitable. I knew what was happening but couldn't stop, or didn't want to."

"But if *she'd* known -"

He nodded slowly. "Yes. I was deceitful. Yes, in a way I'm still ashamed. But I can't wish it hadn't happened. How can I?"

She couldn't answer his naked plea; she sipped her coffee, not sure where this left her, or what to do.

"What was it about her?" she asked.

"Her spirit, her determination, a kind of defiance. Her marriage wasn't happy – as I saw it, anyway – though perhaps that changed after you were born. The way she got so caught up her projects, her ideas."

"But she was so much older than you. Didn't that make a difference?"

"It didn't at all." He gave her a quick, quizzical look. "Love is where it happens. There are no rules."

"But there should have been, about that."

"Yes." He was silent for a moment, then: "If you can't forgive me, Jane, I don't know what more to say. I don't even blame you. All I can tell you is the truth. When I found out she was pregnant – and she wouldn't have told me, it was Meg who did – I asked her to leave, come away with me. I wanted us to be together."

"But she wouldn't?"

He gave a small shake of his head. "She wouldn't leave Anthony. Or Wildings. She thought I was talking nonsense, that I'd soon regret it if she'd agreed."

"But you meant it?"

"Yes. Of course."

"And if Dad had known …? But he *did* know! You said you told him."

"Yes. Because when Bridget told him she was pregnant, he said she could only stay at Wildings if she had an abortion. He was angry. Unsurprisingly."

Jane looked down at the table, taking that in.

"Abortion? We've got that in common then, you and me. He didn't want either of us to be born."

"So," Adam said quietly, "the only thing I could do was tell him. The child he wanted to abort was his own grandchild. You. And of course that put an end to the idea."

"Would Mum have, otherwise?"

"I don't think so. But she'd have had an awful choice to make."

"But - when Dad realised you were his son? What then?"

Adam grimaced. "He was furious. Accused me of manipulating him, even blackmailing. Which I wasn't, but – well, we both said awful things. Unforgivable. Then we made a deal. I'd clear off, and never interfere, and Bridget mustn't know who I was. He'd bring you up as his own child. And as it turned out, he was happy with that."

"And you?"

"I – honestly, Jane, I thought it was best. For you, for Bridget, even for him. For myself – well, I was young enough to think I'd put it behind me." He shook his head. "But as the years passed I couldn't bear the thought that I'd done exactly what he did. Even though he chose it and I didn't, I had a child who was no part of my life. A child growing up who didn't know me, wouldn't recognise me if we passed in the street. I told you before how I resented him for making a life I was no part of. How can I blame you for feeling the same about me?"

"But it's not the same at all," she said, after a pause. "Is it? And I don't. So did you see Dad again? Were you in touch?"

"He said he'd never see me again. So the only other time I saw him was at Bridget's funeral."

"You didn't come to his?"

"No. I was away, didn't know about it till Meg texted me afterwards. I think she wanted to keep me away, because of ... well, because of you. Too risky. But I'd have gone. I wrote to him after Bridget died – after I saw him at her funeral, so bowed down and frail - but he never replied. Maybe, after losing Bridget, he was afraid of losing you, too. I'll never know."

She looked at his hand cradling the coffee cup, at his long fingers and flat nails; then spread out the fingers of her own right hand, to compare. She imagined a scene in which Adam went to her dad, saying, "I'm your son"- a scene in which Anthony, shocked, delighted, decided not to be secretive or ashamed, but welcomed him, wanting to make up for the lost years.

If it hadn't been for me ... then, maybe ... But she could only clear up the mess by erasing herself from existence. Adam's fault. Mum's fault. Dad's. *Everyone's* fault. Her mother would have left Adam unaware of his own child; Dad had made out he was doing her a great favour, while getting what he secretly wanted.

The stark fact remained that Dad had exiled his son, his first son, from his life: once, then again.

"Such a waste. Such an awful waste." She shook her head slowly. "I'll never understand why people behave as they do. Cut themselves off from their own happiness, through obstinacy, or pride, or shame, or whatever. That's how it seems."

"I know." He looked at her. "That's why I'd hate it to happen to you and me, Jane."

She knew then that she could love him.

"It won't." Her eyes prickled with tears. "I mean it. Your letter - I wouldn't have torn it up! I haven't answered yet, what you asked."

"And -?"

"Yes. Yes, please."

He reached for her hand across the table and clasped it, and she saw that he was unable to speak.

Bridget

2010 - 2011

"You won't believe this," Meg said, at the back door.

Bridget looked up from the new potatoes she was washing, while Anthony sat at the table with coffee and the *Guardian*.

"What?"

"Morning, Anthony." Meg came inside, waving a printed page at Bridget. "Look at this - we're offered the chance of a garden at Chelsea, no less!"

"You're joking!"

"I'm not. Here." Meg handed over the letter, and Bridget scanned it, too eagerly at first to make sense of the words. The letter was from Natural Stone, in Dorchester; it complimented Meg on her work for the sundial garden and other projects, then explained that the company wanted to sponsor a small garden for the Chelsea Flower Show and would like Meg and Bridget to create it.

"Chelsea?" she said, dazed. "Could we?"

"Course. Why not?"

"Look, Anthony!" She handed him the letter; he adjusted his glasses, read it, said, "Well, well," and gave it back. "Very good. I'll leave you to make plans."

Meg took his seat; Bridget gazed at her in awe and disbelief.

"Chelsea! Us!"

"It's me who should be dumbstruck. You've done the Birmingham show a couple of times, and Malvern. I've never done anything like this."

"But it's you they've contacted." Bridget looked again at the letter. *"The Stonemason's Garden.* Artisan's garden. Perfect! I like those smaller ones at Chelsea. They're manageable, not like the huge show gardens. You've never been, have you?"

"Only seen it on TV. We'd better start researching."

This year's Chelsea Flower Show had taken place two weeks earlier. Bridget went most years; by now she knew several exhibitors and designers from her involvement with other shows. Usually she went alone but this time Suzanne had taken a day off work. On Main Avenue, as they filed past magnificent show gardens groomed and styled to perfection, Suzanne said, "You ought to do one, Mum!"

"Oh, right!" she said, laughing. "If a millionaire sponsor should think of asking me, rather than one of the big names. Why would they?"

Camera-crews threaded through the mass of people to interview a designer, filming against a backdrop of burnished steel or cascading water, while the crowds looked on, caught by the mystique of celebrity, recognising a *Gardeners' World* presenter or a medal-winner seen on the daily TV coverage. Both she and Suzanne especially liked the smaller plots in the adjoining Ranelagh Gardens, set along a curving path through trees. The big show gardens often looked too opulent, though she made copious notes on plantings and materials; these small gardens were more realistic, more achievable. "*That's* what I'd like to do," she told Suzanne. "Something on this scale."

"Why shouldn't you?" Suzanne was ever loyal. "These are gorgeous, but yours would be just as good."

Now, because of Meg and her specific skill, it could happen. Not for the first time she thanked whatever fate had brought Meg into her life. How astonishing, she thought, that at an age when most people had retired she'd been given such a marvellous opportunity – daunting, exhilarating.

Anthony, now in his seventies, *had* retired, and appeared bemused by her flurries of activity, taking only passing interest. He wrote occasional articles, attended to household finances and kept in touch with former colleagues; he'd joined a bridge club and played weekly with a group, sometimes going away for weekends. Marie had joined too and their relationship continued, though in lower gear, as far as Bridget could tell. His seventieth birthday was marked by a celebration lunch at a country hotel, Marie invited along with Anthony's other friends. Most of those present – apart from her own children - knew that Marie was Anthony's lover. She'd met Marie several times by then, and after overcoming initial resentment had decided that it would be pointless and even petty to dislike her.

Since her own affair with Chris had petered out, she hadn't sought other male company, apart from Daniel, for whom she still wrote articles, and Hugh, his partner, both now good friends. Her closest confidante was Meg. It was Meg she went to with doubts, problems and triumphs, or sometimes to share a bottle of wine. If she saw a great-spotted woodpecker in the garden, deer in the fields or the brilliant flash of a kingfisher by the stream, it was Meg she told.

She couldn't imagine life without her. At first she'd worried that Meg would move on, find bigger premises and leave the cottage; without grudging her that possibility, Bridget wanted their friendship to continue unchanged. But Meg seemed content, self-sufficient. She was alone now, without family since her aunt and uncle had died within a year of each other.

"I'm OK." Meg always shrugged off Bridget's concern. "I've got my work."

"And friends. You've got me."

"Yes. I'm lucky, I know."

"We both are," Bridget said lightly. "You're good for me."

Meg rarely talked of anything personal, but her look, and slow smile, acknowledged all that was left unsaid.

"I'm never getting married," Jane had said recently. "I don't see the point," and Bridget felt a pang of regret: marriage as Jane had seen it, growing up, was such a cool arrangement, operating only at a practical level. Thankfully Suzanne set a better example, as if in choosing Ed, unfailingly kind and considerate, she'd resolved that her marriage would be nothing like her parents'. Jane, studying English now at Southampton without much idea what to do afterwards, had had two or three boyfriends, though Bridget was unsure whether they were friends or lovers. One, she suspected, was gay, but when she mentioned this Jane was dismissive. "Maybe. Maybe not. Doesn't matter. You don't have to put people in boxes, Mum." Rebuffed, Bridget protested that she didn't and hadn't. Maybe Jane was finding out that feelings of love and desire could be fluid, capricious.

Anthony appeared to have moved into an older generation. He moved stiffly, sighing when he heaved himself out of an armchair; his hair, faded to iron-grey, was still thick, but his face was lined and often set in a querulous expression. For herself, she was determined to resist ageing. She'd lost weight rather than gaining it, and her reflection showed that her eyes retained their brightness, her hair its springiness. She was always active, busy in the garden or with commissions, giving way to backache and tiredness only in the evenings, then reading in bed until she found herself dozing over her book or gardening magazine. Whenever a new project excited her, she found reserves of energy and enthusiasm she hoped would never desert her.

She'd certainly need them now. She set to, studying Chelsea show gardens on line, sketching the first rough beginnings.

Jane

FEBRUARY 2019

Surya namaskar, sun salutations. Indian music, sky slowly lightening, seen through full-length studio windows that faced east.

It had been a while; she hadn't practised during her illness beyond a few stretches. Now she reached into the familiar moves, strength returning. Early practice with Chitra and Karen was worth the early alarm, the scraping of windscreen ice and the drive through darkness to the gym. "Rule one," as Chitra said, "no one regrets getting up early for yoga. *Ever.*"

Though not deliberately watching the other two she saw their reflections and her own in mirrored walls; the beauty of the asanas, graceful as ballet even when punctuated by thumps from the gym next door where people heaved weights and worked treadmills. Stretch into *utthita trikonasana* – turn feet, reach forward, hand planted on mat, rotate into *parivritta trikonasana* ... She often did the same practice at home, but sharing it gave an extra dimension: communion, ritual, a homage to something. To *what,* she'd found herself unable to explain, when Adam had asked. Only that it felt like reaching out to something beyond self.

It was impossible to put aside busy thoughts and concentrate on breathing. She could think of nothing but yesterday.

I'm not the same person as last time I was here. I'm Adam's daughter. I've got a father to love. A father who wants to love me.

Alarming. Exciting.

The practice ended in stillness, all three seated in lotus, attempts at meditation foiled by the need to watch the clock, as the studio would soon be in use for a class. There had been an overnight frost; the sky was streaked in sugared-almond pinks and mauves before the sun rose, flooding the studio with light. Gazing out at the end of practice she often had the sense of floating outside time while still aware of it, as if looking down at her body seated on the mat.

In the art gallery cafe – how long had they sat there, talking? - Adam had told her about trying mindfulness years ago when at a low point. "It didn't help at all. Trying to think of nothing lets bad thoughts float up. Does it work for you?" She said that the closest thing to the blissful state she'd read about was at the end of a practice when she simply sat listening to music, or lay in *savasana,* corpse position. "I *feel* the music then in a way I don't at any other time. It seems to vibrate through my whole body. It's as if there's a great spring of happiness inside me, and the yoga and the music have released it. Does that sound silly?"

He said no, it sounded wonderful. "Maybe I should try a class. Or am I too old to start?"

"No! You're only too old for yoga once rigor mortis has set in - that's what my teacher in India said. You should definitely try. So many people, once they start, can't get enough," she told him, and he said in that case he'd give it a go.

Namaste. The reluctant last moment of calm and inwardness. It was time to turn off the music and let the body pumpers take over; for Karen to leave for her office and Jane to change for reception duty.

"Time for a quick coffee?" Chitra asked, as they rolled mats and pulled on sweaters. "I need a double shot of caffeine."

"Not very yogic!"

"It's my only vice - I'm not giving it up. Anyway, for someone recovering from flu you're looking very pleased with yourself. What's happened? You're not back with Tom, are you?"

"No." Jane shook her head vigorously. "Like that could happen!"

"Whoa! Sorry I asked. You can't have met someone else already?"

"You think I can only be happy because of some new man?" She stopped, realising. "Actually, yes – only not like you mean. Tell you downstairs."

. . .

She and Adam had wandered through the galleries looking at installations and sculptures. She felt floaty – from the after-effects of flu, or the strangeness of this - and exhibits loomed at her, swimming in and out of focus. She wondered if she could take his arm, knowing he'd like that; tentatively she did so and he looked down at her and smiled, and pressed his arm against his side, her fingers with it.

"I don't understand most of this," she said. "Don't know what I'm meant to see in it. Can you tell me?"

"A lot of it's beyond me too, but I'll try. I'm so looking forward to showing you my favourite artists and finding out what you like. Making up for the missed years."

"I know. It's a bit overwhelming." They had so much to catch up with: opinions, places travelled to, tastes and preferences. "Anyone looking at us can't tell we're only getting to know each other. They see a father and daughter," she said, caught by the novelty of this; when he didn't reply she saw that again he was moved beyond words. This meant so much to him; too much. It made her uncomfortable, invested with a power she hadn't earned. All she'd done was to exist.

"Tell me about your own painting," she said, Suzanne had told her about the big abstracts he'd done at Wildings. "*Do you still paint?*"

He told her that he'd stopped a few years ago but had recently made a fresh start. On his phone he showed examples: an impression of a mountainside, tumbled rocks, greenness below and a thread of river catching the light; a stand of hillside trees, dawn sky behind; closer textures of flaking tree bark and gnarled woody roots.

"I'd love to see more," she said, and he replied that of course she could.

"But you don't have to like them. I won't mind."

"I do! Far more than some of the stuff here."

"These grew out of the work I'm doing with teenagers. I started to paint in a different way – a sort of free representation of landscapes and setting and light. At first it was for them – it worked better than abstraction. Then I began to like it for myself."

"Working with teenagers must be a challenge. Chitra does yoga in schools but she prefers younger children. She says teenagers can be so hard to reach, so conscious of themselves."

"It *is* a challenge, but worthwhile. It's about getting them to engage with the natural world – mainly they're from inner-city schools. Some have never been in a forest or walked across moorland or climbed rocks. For some it's a lark, just another thing they're expected to do. But for others, it could open up a whole world of experience. It might not happen now, they might not even realise, but it gives new possibilities. And some of their paintings have been astonishing. It's the most rewarding work I've ever done."

"So you're teaching them a kind of mindfulness," she said. "Giving something their whole attention."

"I'd like to think that. It's something we've all become bad at, with the distractions we make for ourselves. Focusing on painting – yes, I suppose it is mindfulness. Or is it mind*less*ness? Letting go, letting things happen."

"That's meditative too," she said. "Watching the many things. *Vipanassa*."

"And now, with the climate crisis so urgent - that's got a few of them fired up. This amazing girl from Sweden who's galvanising young people – have you seen her?"

"Greta Thunberg! Yes."

"And this. There were campaigners in Cornmarket – look." He took a flier from his pocket and handed it to her: a green and black design, an hourglass inside a circle, TELL THE TRUTH.

"Extinction Rebellion!" Jane remembered the protestors on London bridges last autumn, the arrests, and how she'd thought *Yes! We need this!*

"I'm going to sign up," Adam said. "Brexit stupidity has pushed climate breakdown into the background, but it needs to be top priority."

"I know. This gorgeous warm day - it's lovely, but it's not right. It's *February*."

"George Monbiot's giving a talk here in Oxford," Adam said. "Shall we go?"

. . .

Driving home from the gym, she thought of what Adam had mentioned about things falling apart – although he hadn't said so, she inferred that his lowest point had come after her mother's funeral. When she asked, he said he'd had bouts of depression since his student days. "Adolescent angst, back then. I found a way to put it into my painting. I don't mean that I saw myself as a tortured genius. But the painting was *mine*. Even if it was rubbish it was where I was truly myself. So when I couldn't even do that, it was like my one true thing had deserted me."

"Your one true thing?" Jane repeated. "Meg used to say that!"

"Yes, I got it from her. She says everyone needs it to be sane and happy. The place where you find yourself, or lose yourself, both at once."

Jane thought about this, wondering whether she'd yet found her own.

"I'm not sure Dad ever had one. He suffered from depression too," she told him, "though it took years before he'd admit it."

Adam showed no surprise; she guessed he knew as much from her mother or Meg. "It's easier now to be open about mental health. But still it's typical male behaviour to make out there's nothing wrong, like Anthony did. I was like that till Meg made me get help. I wouldn't have, otherwise. I got through, with support and good luck. I hope you'll never have it, Jane. You know it's at least partly hereditary."

"Yes, that's crossed my mind. I have fits of the glooms – everyone does, I suppose. How can you not, with politics gone mad and the world heating up? But never as bad as yours, or the way I saw it in Dad."

"And your one true thing? Yoga?"

"I'm not sure." She paused, gazing at a scratchy mural that looked to her like railway graffiti. "I thought so, but now I'm not sure. I feel like a fake, teaching middle-class people – which they mostly are – to do a few moves. And the *yoga* feels fake, which is worse. I don't know how to show people what I get from it myself. I need to connect the two, make it mean more. That's what yoga means – yoking body and soul. Not just exercises in stretchy Lycra."

"Nerves? Inexperience? You feel you're putting on a performance?"

"Yes, exactly. I'm not a natural, like Chitra. She says I need a guru. I should go back to India." Her tone was light, but he listened gravely.

Afterwards she thought that when talking to him she sounded calmer and more settled than she felt. She sounded like the person she wished she could be.

"There's a Buddhist text I like," she told him. "*Your work is to discover your world, and give yourself to it with your whole heart.*"

. . .

"As well as a new father," she'd told Chitra, "I've got a grandmother, aunts and cousins, step-grandfather, second cousins in Ireland ..." So many people yet to meet, a bewildering proliferation of family, adding to her sense of being a new person.

"Sounds like an awful lot of birthdays to add to your list," Chitra said.

And Rob, since the family adjustments, was her uncle rather than brother, though that made little difference to his place in her life. He phoned later that morning.

"We've had a good offer. From the Howards, the couple who came for a second viewing. They're very keen on the garden in particular. I've told Suzanne, and the solicitor's going to phone Sean McBride later on" – he persisted in using that name. "So we can get things moving."

So that's it, she thought, ringing off. Done, or almost. She felt a new stab of regret that they hadn't managed to keep the house, impossible though she knew it was.

She wandered through the silent rooms. Already this place, her home, felt like someone else's property. Diamond-pattern of sun through windowpanes, curve of banister as the stairs reached ground level, the quality of light on carpet, all seemed to etch themselves on her mind. Her instincts rebelled at the idea of strangers moving in, making it their own.

In the end only three things matter: how well you have loved, how gently you have lived, and how gracefully you give up the things not meant for you.

Since her illness and her meeting with Adam, she no longer felt bitter towards Tom. Having acknowledged her own doubts, she should be – almost – grateful to him for ending the relationship. It had been good, and now it was over.

But this ...

Could she gracefully give up her home? No choice about the main house; but there was the cottage. She could stay - live close to the memories of her childhood.

Or she could give that up too. Find her own way, search for what had so far eluded her; not settle for what she'd been given.

Bridget

2010 - 11

PLANS FOR CHELSEA WERE under way. Setting a budget, the sponsors left the details of design and planting to Bridget. After the initial application, a detailed plan must be submitted for the judges to use in assessing how well the finished garden met its stated aims.

The following months were dominated by experiment and consultation, and, for Bridget, making endless lists, sourcing plants and materials. Over the winter she fretted that some plants would be held back by late frosts or others might flower too soon; she had back-up plans and lists of substitutes, and paid obsessive attention to weather forecasts. Her world revolved around a little piece of ground and a few days in May.

In dreams, her plot flooded in a freak storm which oddly left every other garden untouched; or she received a vanload of parched, withered plants, dead from neglect. In one recurring dream she arrived on opening day to find a bare patch of grass, bemused judges and irate sponsors.

"No chance of that," Meg said. "You've made it fifty times in your imagination."

The Stonemason's Garden was to be framed by a dry-stone wall and one side of a stone building, indicating a workshop. A flagged, curving path would run alongside trickling water, suggestive of a hillside stream. Towards the front, a working area where Meg's easel and tools would be placed. *The Stonemason's Garden* cut in slate would be fixed to the building; planting behind the wall would indicate a wild-flower meadow lush with cornflowers, buttercups and grasses.

They were allocated their plot in Ranelagh Gardens, and in May the build began. Even with her experience of designing for lesser shows, Bridget felt daunted to be making one within these hallowed grounds. "Wow, Mum! It's like the Olympics of gardening," Jane had said, and that first day, standing in her marked-out area, Bridget felt sure that her design was inadequate, too loose an interpretation of the *artisan* brief; the judges would sneer.

But there was no time for anything but work. The area swarmed with people in hard hats and high-vis tabards; lorries and vans, cranes and forklift trucks, pipes and cables, sackloads of soil and sand and ballast. She and Meg stayed at a hotel booked by the sponsors, returning there only to sleep; early at the showground each day, they lived on takeaways and sandwiches. Occasionally, taking a break, they walked past the big show gardens on Main Avenue and the Rock Bank, where full-size trees were being craned into position and entire buildings constructed. The urgent activity in every corner of the showground sent Bridget scurrying back to her own plot, conscious of how much remained to be done.

She was dismayed by her lack of stamina, which had never troubled her before. I really am getting too old for this, she caught herself thinking. She slept poorly at the hotel, not used to traffic and sirens; a persistent backache kept her awake, even when she'd been almost too tired to undress and shower before flopping into bed. She put it down to stress; she could rest as much as she wanted when this was over. But she lay awake, unable to lie comfortably, often giving in and reaching for her notebook. Maybe she'd see a doctor when all this was over.

Oh, come on, she told herself. It's only a bit of stiffness, hardly surprising. If only I could *sleep* ...

At last, late on the final Sunday, *The Stonemason's Garden* was complete. After all her worry about whether the Francis E Lester rose would bloom in time, there it was against the wall, buds pointed and pink-tinged, uncurling into flowers as simply beautiful as hedgerow dog roses; the birches were in leaf, the grey-shaded white of their bark echoing whites and creams in the foreground planting. She'd chosen a restricted colour palette dominated by green, and by the silvery grasses which had become her signature. Beside the path she'd planted white astrantias, with taller cream foxgloves and sweet rocket at the rear; the only other colours were the lilac-shaded geranium 'Mrs Kendall Clarke', the purple-red thistly flowers of *cirsium rivulare* and the darker foliage of 'Ravenswing' cow parsley. By the time she'd tucked and repositioned for the hundredth time, the plants might have seeded themselves there in happy juxtaposition, the grasses and taller stems stirring to the breath of wind, light shimmering on silky seed-heads.

After the flurry of preparation and anxiety over the judges' decision, the days of the show itself were a blur of congratulations, discussions with journalists and members of the public. The garden was awarded Silver Gilt, better than she'd dared hope. She and Meg were interviewed on live television, with close-ups of Meg cutting letters and talking about the beauty of stone, and Bridget explaining her plant choices. The *Telegraph* report gave them a whole sentence: "The Stonemason's Garden is as masterly a piece of restrained planting as any I have seen at Chelsea." Bridget had the phrase by heart, to carry with her for ever.

On Wednesday the sponsors took Bridget and Meg for a champagne lunch in the Rock Bank restaurant. Afterwards Meg said she'd like to meet a friend for an hour or so; would Bridget mind?

"Fine," Bridget told her. "I'll be there."

The garden had to be staffed for all the hours the show was open, either by themselves or by a company representative; usually either Meg or Bridget was present, more often both, to hand out leaflets and answer questions.

There was a hesitation, then Meg said, "I should have said – Adam's here, on one of the trade stands in the pavilion."

"Oh?" Bridget felt herself prickling with insecurity the way she still did when Adam was mentioned. She was light-headed from champagne but still it seemed incongruous for him to be at Chelsea.

"In the Education area," Meg explained. "He works for an environmental organisation now. Greenways."

"So it's him you're going to meet?" she asked, and Meg nodded.

She was on edge all afternoon, wondering if Meg would bring Adam to the garden: surely Meg wouldn't, but nevertheless she was curious to see how he looked, how the years had changed him. She found Greenways in the show guide, locating the stand's position. Like all the pavilion stands it had only a brief description: *Environmental projects for schools*.

"Excuse me – is the geranium Johnson's Blue?"

"No, it's Mrs Kendall Clarke. Everything's listed here." Bridget handed out leaflets, smiled, accepted compliments. "That purple thistly thing's popular this year," someone else was saying *"Is* it a thistle?"

She was almost disappointed when Meg returned alone, saying nothing. Obstinacy prevented Bridget from asking about Adam; but that night in her hotel room she thought of yesterday, when Jane had missed a lecture and seminar to come by train from Southampton, joining Suzanne and Ed. She was unsure whether to be huffy with Meg or grateful that she hadn't mentioned Adam sooner. Had she known, she'd have been anxious all day, fearing a chance encounter, unlikely as it was that Adam or Suzanne would recognise each other after so long.

It's too much, she thought: the excitement, all the *talking*, being bright and sociable all the time. Now this, the fear always shadowing her. Although winning a Chelsea medal was the pinnacle of her achievement she longed to be in her own bed at Wildings, waking to the swell of birdsong. In London she felt exposed, and at the same time hemmed in by buildings and traffic. Her little showground plot was a sanctuary, especially in the early morning before the crowds arrived.

Next day, in a break from garden duty, she was irresistibly drawn to the Great Pavilion. She'd already spent several hours there admiring the displays and making notes of specialist nurseries and plants, but now she was looking for stand G21, having told herself not to. Moving along congested pathways between exhibits in the heady, almost overwhelming scents of lilies and roses and bark mulch, she approached the quieter corner allocated to colleges, research units and gardening schools. Her intention was only to look, walk slowly past; all she wanted was a glimpse.

Unsure whether she'd feel relief or deflation if he wasn't there, she saw him at once: tall and slim in a dark-green sweatshirt, talking earnestly to a woman of about her own age, his head bent to catch what she said in reply. He was clean-shaven now and wore glasses; his hair was greying and swept back, but from the way he stood and his gestures she knew that this was indeed Adam.

How foolish could she be, that the sight of him was enough to make her catch her breath? Someone collided with her from behind and apologised. A pretty wild-haired young woman with Adam at the stand stepped forward with a leaflet. "Would you like to know what we do?"

"Thank you." Bridget intended to take it and move away; but in that instant Adam glanced straight at her, and she saw his shock of recognition. Finishing his conversation he came to her.

"Bridget," he said, and smiled; of course he knew she was at the show. "Congratulations on your medal. It's beautiful, your garden. Brilliant."

She remembered his voice so well.

"Thank you," she said, in a bright, neutral tone. "You've seen it?"

"Yes, with Meg."

There was an awkward pause, as if Meg, the missing point of the triangle, couldn't easily be spoken of.

"Could you spare half an hour?" Adam said. "Shall we go to one of the cafés?"

She nodded, and he spoke to his pretty colleague; then they moved through the crowded aisle into cooler air outside. Years fell away; they might have been back at the art gallery, with him attentive and alert, catching her eye across the room. He waited while a chattering group took up the whole width of the path. "I didn't know I was coming till last week," he explained. "A colleague was taken ill."

"Your first time?" she asked, and he said that it was.

In the exhibitors' restaurant they found a corner table with their tea. She thought: *This is too risky. For Jane. Possibly for all of us.*

"How are you, Bridget?" he said.

He was the Adam she'd known and at the same time a stranger; less eye-catching than in youth, more guarded, but still undoubtedly an attractive man; she saw a woman at the next table cast sidelong glances. He'd be in his late forties now, same as Meg.

"Oh, I'm fine, thanks. Tired. This is all pretty full-on, as -" She caught herself; she'd almost said *as Jane would say.*

"I'm sure it must be."

They chatted for a few minutes about her show garden and its making; then he asked, "And Jane? How is Jane?" and she knew this was what he really wanted to talk about.

She couldn't meet his eye. "She's well. Studying English at Southampton, finishing her second year. But you're in touch with Meg, so presumably you know that."

He nodded. "Is she happy?"

"Seems to be enjoying it. She was here yesterday."

"Jane, here?" he said, and she wished she hadn't mentioned it.

"Yes, with Suzanne and her husband Ed."

"And Anthony? How's Anthony?"

"He didn't come - it's not his thing. Crowds, fuss. London. He's retired now, slowing down, but OK. How about you?"

She hadn't asked about him for some time, since hearing of his marriage; she'd been annoyed for feeling disturbed by the news, and had instructed herself to be glad that Adam was happily settled. "I know from Meg that you're married. A few years now, isn't it?"

"Yes, to Jenny. Ten years." A pause, then: "No children," as if he anticipated the next question. "Only -" He shook his head and looked down, and she knew he meant *only Jane*.

"Happily married?"

"Yes," he said, though on a questioning note which she decided not to pursue.

"Still painting?"

"Not so much." He looked wistful. "I've had a few ups and downs."

"I suppose we all have those?" she said, for the sake of saying something.

"True. You, though!" he said, brightening. "Your career's taken off amazingly. It's a wonderful achievement, a Chelsea medal."

"Well, I've had a lot of luck. Meg's been a big part of that. It's through her we had the invitation to do this. But tell me about your work," she said, and he explained a little about the Greenways organisation and his role as project director for secondary schools.

"Sounds interesting."

"Yes, it is." Lightly he touched her sleeve, the beading around the cuff. "This is very Bridget," he said. "Your tastes haven't changed." She was wearing a kaftan from East bought specially, in shades of indigo and hyacinth blue to harmonise with her plants, and she felt herself flushing as she thought of his clothes and hers dropped on the bedroom carpet, that other kaftan he'd said he liked. So long ago – more than Jane's whole lifetime – but memories crowded her mind, treacherous, compelling. It would be ridiculous to imagine that he wanted to revive that madness, as she thought of it; not at her age. They would have no relevance to each other's lives if not for Jane.

"Could we keep in touch?" he asked. "Even if only an email now and then?"

"I'm not sure it's a good idea. Not fair to Jane, or to you. Nor to -" She left the thought unfinished: *nor to Anthony*. "No. Sorry. I don't think so."

Their eyes met; he was about to say more when someone exclaimed, "Bridget!" and clapped her shoulder, making her jump. She looked round to see a gardening journalist she knew slightly.

"James," she said flatly.

"How splendid to see you. Congratulations on your *wonderful* garden!" He stooped to give extravagant air-kisses, left-right. "Let me introduce you to Mary Gulliver – you must have seen her stunning orchids -"

"Yes, hello, how lovely." She stood, shook hands. "And this is – oh -"

Adam had got up too. He gave a nod of acknowledgement to the newcomers but said, "I'll leave you to it. Ought to get back." He looked at Bridget, unsmiling, and turned away.

On the point of hurrying after him she instead sat down limply. For interminable minutes she made small talk to James and his companion; at last she excused herself and left. At the marquee entrance she scanned the crowds. She thought of a moment that had stayed with her: Adam by the stream, kneeling to tie his bootlace then standing up with tears in his eyes.

She had never realised it could mean so much. She'd been careless, taking what she wanted, then discarding him.

Of course he could have asserted his right to Jane at

any time over the past twenty years, if that was his wish; she wondered why he hadn't. If he wanted to prove himself Jane's father he could take a DNA test. As far as she knew, he'd never tried to contact Jane; he could have come to Wildings or sought her out at Southampton, though she hoped not. Jane, she was certain, had no idea of his existence. It was possible too that his wife was unaware he was a father. Married people often hid secrets from each other, as she knew too well.

A time would come when both she and Anthony were gone, and there'd be nothing to stop him from claiming Jane as his daughter. Dispassionately she told herself that his marriage was faltering along with his art, he had no children, and now he was interested in Jane, having forgotten her for twenty years. Or was that over-cynical?

Although she could easily find him again, she knew she wouldn't. Aside from her fear that he'd contact Jane, there was her own promise to Anthony, a pledge she'd kept until now. She wouldn't risk another meeting.

For the rest of the day she was offhand with Meg, and left the showground early, saying that she needed an early night. For a long time she lay wakeful, her back aching, her mind in turmoil. When at last she slept, she dreamed that she was searching and searching for Jane, helped by someone who started as Adam but then grew older, turning into Anthony. "There is no Jane," a voice was saying. "Never has been." In desperation she called Jane's name over and over until the cry snagged in her throat and woke her. With relief she found herself lying in her hotel bed, hot and trembling.

Five a.m. She sent Jane a text message: **Are you OK?**

There was no reply until she was ready to go down for early

breakfast, about to knock on Meg's door and try to smooth over yesterday's curtness. Her phone rang.

"Hi, Mum." Jane's voice was cheerful, reassuring. "Yes, I'm fine – why wouldn't I be? How's it all going?"

Jane

MARCH 2019

With the bedroom heater on and her favourite sitar music playing, she sat in lotus position attending to the wave-like flow of her breath. She thought of the meditation sessions in Kerala, in the shala at tree-canopy height, following chants led by the teacher. Bird calls from surrounding banana and palm trees – unidentifiable whoops and chatterings that could never be mistaken for the birdsong of home – were magnified, full of energy. It had filled her with pure joy, elusive, fragile.

She returned to this *now* – pale sunlight patched on the wall, a robin singing from the ash tree close to the window. Soon, when she moved out, it would be this she was nostalgic for, the simple everydayness of her room: bookshelves, curtains faded by sunlight, the wide windowsill where as a child she sat stargazing long after she was meant to be asleep.

The sale was agreed: searches and surveys done, contracts exchanged, completion due in April. Furniture had been cleared, and the part of the house she occupied had shrunk to bedroom, kitchen, bathroom and her mother's old study. She avoided the empty rooms; they made her feel that she was already gone, in transit. The sitting-room especially made her think wistfully of winter evenings, curtains drawn, fire glowing, and of all the Christmases. It was her childhood she had packed up. And revisited, its relationships swapped about.

"So," Adam said, on the phone, "you've met the buyers, Suzanne says?"

"Yes, the Durhams. They asked if I could be there when they came back to do some measuring. I liked them!"

"You sound astonished. What did you expect?"

"Well, you know. Rich, loud people like those Pritchards, wanting to change everything. These two don't."

The Durhams, moving out of London, were in their fifties. Anna Durham, scruffily stylish in layered clothing, with hair caught up in a comb, told Jane, "You're so like your mother! We spoke to her at Chelsea – her garden there was wonderful. We were so sad when we heard she'd passed away. So when we saw this for sale, *her* house, *her* garden, we could hardly believe it. I can't tell you what an honour it'll be, taking over, trying to do it justice!" It had been love at first sight, they both said. "So important. You can't just like a house, you must *love* it. And we do."

Jane felt wrenched all over again at the thought of strangers moving in, but relieved that the house and garden would be properly appreciated.

"And," she told Adam, "they recognised the liquidambar!"

"Bonus points, then."

Jane hadn't yet told him – couldn't, on the phone – of her new plan.

"I need some kind of marker," she told Suzanne later, in

the garden. "Something big. I'm ending one phase of my life, starting a new one."

"Yes, I can see that."

"I'm going back to India. It felt unfinished last time, because of being called back for Dad. There are volunteer schemes. I'd have done something like that after uni, only Mum was ill. I can go for a year."

Suzanne looked at her in dismay. "That long? Have you told Adam?"

"Not yet. I've only just decided. But I will soon."

"He'll be devastated!"

"He'll understand, though," Jane said, hoping she was right.

They walked down the lawn, their feet trailing through rain-wet grass. The trees were bare, the meadows opposite still winter-pale, dotted with sheep, but in the borders were the fresh green flowers of hellebores, and primroses delicate against bare earth. Their mother had loved this quiet pause, this time to notice each emerging plant before the great rush of April and May. Today there was warmth in the sun, making her think of long evenings, meals outside and the smell of mown grass. How could you not be filled with hope and optimism, with the year poised to surge into spring?

Looking towards the stream she pictured her mother working there, crouched among reeds in her straw hat. Hours and hours she spent doing that, forgetting the time. Once, when she was small, Jane had asked, "When will it be finished, Mummy?" and her mother laughed. "It'll never be finished, Janey. I don't want it to be. Digging and planting and planning is the whole point."

Now, thinking of the Durhams, she said aloud, "It's going to be all right, Mum."

Suzanne smiled at her and linked arms. "Yes, it is. I was thinking of one of the poems Dad liked. Do you remember? The one that goes *I did with a stranger talk -*"

"And his name was Dream," they recited in unison.

"He was so good at remembering," Suzanne said. "And I'm rubbish. But I'll never forget those favourite bits of Dad's."

Meg

2012 - 13

A CAT HAD ADOPTED her. It appeared in the yard, thin, dishevelled: a black tom with green eyes and a dirty white front. She bought food for him, contacted vets and put a notice in the pub, and when no one came forward she decided he could stay. She named him Eric, after Erics Gill and Ravilious, and took him to the vet for neutering, microchipping, worm and flea treatment. Soon thoroughly at home, Eric had one basket in the cottage and another in the workshop; he roamed the yard and gardens, caught mice and shrews, and ate ravenously. He became sleek and glossy, with the smug air of accepting all this as his due.

"I'm turning into a dotty old woman who dotes on her cat," she told Bridget, who laughed and said, "Old? For goodness' sake, you're not fifty yet."

Meg's appearance at Chelsea had led to a great many enquiries: requests, commissions, people wanting to visit her workshop. Although she took no credit for the Silver-

Gilt Medal – that was for Bridget's garden design – she'd certainly benefited from the association. She now accepted only those projects that interested her. She thought seriously about taking on an apprentice, a way of passing on her skills to a new generation, keeping the line unbroken from Eric Gill, through David Kindersley and now herself. There would be employment implications: tax, National Insurance contributions and other things she must investigate. Already a good deal of her time was spent on admin, and maintaining her website.

Last year, with Bridget and herself caught up in Chelsea preparations, it hadn't been possible to host Artweeks, but this May the studios were open again, the event organised by Celia, a screen-printer who'd moved into Leonard's workshop when he retired. Bridget, able to take her pick of designing offers, concentrated on her own garden, opening for Artweeks as well as for the National Gardens Scheme. She employed a gardener, leaving her free to work on individual plantings and on a spectacular array of potted succulents at the house front.

The Natural Stone Company had a stand at Chelsea this year, with Meg on hand to give demonstrations. She expected Bridget to attend the RHS Members' Day, but Bridget told her that she wouldn't make it after all.

"Something's come up. Sorry. A hospital appointment. You'd better give my ticket to someone else."

"Can't you change it?"

"Not really," Bridget said, but deflected further enquiries.

With limited appearances on the stand, Meg had plenty of time to wander around the show. Adam had gone quiet lately, but she sought out Greenways in the Grand Pavilion in case he was there, though surely he'd have said. He appeared in some of the photographs and in the brochure, but wasn't there in person. The display was staffed by earnest young women in green T-shirts, including the wild-haired one Meg recognised from last year.

"Adam? No ... he's on leave."

Meg sent a text, getting no reply. She feared he might be on one of his downers; she hoped not, but soon a new worry took hold.

The stone company's stand featured pictures of last year's show garden. Studying them, Meg realised how Bridget had changed since – how had she not noticed? Small-boned and slight, Bridget had never been plump, but in the photographs she was round-faced and smiling compared to her present appearance; she'd lost weight since, weight she couldn't afford to lose.

It sometimes struck Meg that being single and childless she took little notice of her own age, expecting to go on as she did now, with the same strength and capability. It was mainly through Bridget and her family that she registered the passing of years: a seventieth birthday celebration for Anthony, the growing-up of grandchildren, Jane about to graduate. Only occasionally did she remember the twenty-year age gap; Bridget would be sixty-nine this year. Meg had never been ill, other than the odd cold or sore throat, and had a healthy person's lack of interest in medical matters and the ailments of others; Bridget, never one to fuss, had said nothing about a problem.

She sent a text: **Hope it goes well today,** and Bridget replied almost immediately: **Thx. Would much prefer to be with you at Chelsea. Enjoy!**

That was reassuringly ordinary, and the show's busyness eclipsed Meg's anxiety. When she returned to Wildings Bridget was keen to discuss the gardens and exhibits she'd seen on television, and only afterwards did Meg ask, "How did it go at the hospital?"

"Oh, it was only tests. I'm going back in a few days."

"Tests for what?"

There was a long silence, then Bridget said, "Possible cancer. Of the pancreas."

"Bridget!"

"Don't tell anyone. I haven't, not even Anthony. I should, I suppose."

They were in the long barn, where Bridget was calmly sowing beans. She carried on lining them up methodically: a scoop of compost in each pot, shaken level then pressed firm; she poked an indentation, dropped in a mottled bean and sprinkled soil over. She didn't look at Meg. Meg was the one who felt the ground tilt, the shiver of foreboding.

"Of course you must tell him! Now. Today. You shouldn't face this on your own!"

"All right," Bridget said. "But I don't want to worry Suzanne or Jane. It might be a false alarm."

"Shall I come with you next time?"

"Oh, there's no need. But thanks. I didn't mean to tell you yet. I was going to wait till I know for sure."

In the cottage Meg Googled *pancreatic cancer,* finding nothing to reassure her. *Difficult to diagnose,* she read. *Difficult to treat...rarely causes any symptoms in the early stages, so often not diagnosed until the cancer is fairly advanced ... surgery only suitable for 15–20% of patients ... chemotherapy ... radiotherapy ... overall, pancreatic cancer has a poor prognosis ...*

"Fuck," she whispered. She turned off the laptop and sat with fists pressed into her eyes.

Over the years she and Bridget had talked of all manner of things, and often enjoyed the deep companionship of being together without talking much at all, but Meg recognised that some topics were off-limits. Anthony was one, Adam another, and she had one or two of her own. Now this, apparently.

What would it be like to face such a possibility? Meg saw her own body as a tool, a piece of equipment; when it creaked or complained, she took little notice. She imagined the sense of betrayal if it turned against her to work stealthily towards its own destruction.

She got up and stood in the front doorway, gazing out into the May evening. Everything was going on in defiance: swifts screamed high, a late bee wavered over the honeysuckle. Bridget loved the swifts, awaiting their return. "There!" she would say, squinting at the sky. "Look! *Now* summer's here." The sun was setting, lighting the barn's stonework to golden ochre. Meg watched while the light dimmed and a chill crept into the air. She could already see the first evening star – no, must be a planet, as bright as that: Venus? – over the trees.

She couldn't imagine this place without Bridget. She never cried, but now felt the warm wetness of tears as they brimmed over. Angrily she wiped them on her sleeve.

And in between ... it wouldn't be as simple as Bridget being here, then gone. There would be deterioration, pain, hospital, treatments ...

For God's sake! She was assuming the worst. Perhaps it wasn't so bad. Perhaps there was time for surgery. But she kept hearing Bridget's words: *yet,* and *till I know for sure,* as if she already did know.

Typical, bloody typical, she raged. I'm thinking of myself. But if I lose Bridget, and all this ... I'll be lost. She had the sense of slipping and sliding, unable to hold on. She was nine again, finding Gillian in the darkened room, afterwards sobbing alone upstairs, blaming herself because Gillian had said "I wish I was dead," and she'd told no one, frightened, but not believing it was seriously meant. Death, back then, was something that happened in stories, melodramatic and thrilling. Not sneakily, in her own home.

So she had thought.

At Christmas Bridget had given her a special card, an art card bought at Chelsea, with the inscription: *To dearest Meg, with my love. Thank you for blessing me with friendship, and for all you bring to my life. Bridget xxx.* There had been a separate and more traditional card, signed *with best wishes from Bridget and Anthony.*

Too undemonstrative for any similar declaration, Meg was too embarrassed to give more than muttered thanks, but was touched. In Bridget she'd found what she'd given up expecting. It didn't involve sex, or possession, or jealousy, or any kind of recognition from others beyond their working partnership, but it was the nearest thing to love. When she threw out her other cards she kept Bridget's special one in a drawer, together with some postcards and drawings Adam had sent.

Adam ... but he had Jenny now, their home together, his new career. He didn't need her as he once had. Would she end up alone, without her two closest allies?

She heard a plaintive miaow, and a black shape detached itself from the shadows by the long barn. Eric trotted across, wanting food; when he twined himself around her legs she picked him up and buried her nose in the fragrance of his fur.

...

A week later Bridget returned to the hospital, and this time Anthony went with her. Meg was edgy all morning, getting up from work only to walk about and sit down again; her chisel slipped on a hard piece of fossil and took out more stone than she intended, and only later did she notice that she'd caught her thumb, making it bleed. When she washed the graze under running water the blood flared and thinned on the porcelain before swirling away; the small wound would heal, her body knowing how to mend itself. But the human body could be treacherous and unknowable, concealing secrets.

She waited for Bridget to return, to come down to the yard. What if she didn't? It would be like her, in the mood of nonchalance that was her main defence, to tease with silence. At last she heard footsteps. Bridget appeared in the doorway, with such a beatific smile that Meg's heart leaped.

"Oh! What did they say?" she blurted, putting down her tools.

"Well." Bridget made a wry face. "It's not good, Meg. I might have a year, maybe. If I'm -" A pause, then: "- lucky. Probably not that long."

"Oh." Meg clapped a hand to her mouth. "You can't mean that," she said, stupidly. "Is there nothing -"

"Too late. It's spread too far – metastasised. See, I'm already talking the talk." Bridget was doing what she usually did in the workshop; she looked at sketches, touched slabs of stone prepared for house-names, stroked Eric, who sat blinking on a blanket. "I should have gone to the doctor sooner, instead of putting it off. But it's no great matter, really, is it, in the scheme of things? You could make me a beautiful headstone. I'd like that."

・・・

"Mum's going to die," Jane said. "You know, I suppose?"

"Yes," Meg said carefully. Jane was back from Southampton; Meg guessed that Bridget had waited till now to give her the news. "Well, I'm here all the time. She had to tell someone."

"Maybe you knew even before Dad," Jane said. "I wouldn't be surprised." She was watching Meg work, the way she used to as a little girl. She was twenty-one now and a new graduate, but Meg saw blank fright in her eyes, as if shock had jolted her back to childlike helplessness. She'd returned from university slimmed-down and with a new and flattering short hairstyle; Meg saw in her both the obvious resemblance to Bridget and the occasional shade of Adam. The two people Meg cared about most: one already gone, the other not here for much longer.

"What would you do, if you knew you were going to die?" Jane asked.

Meg continued shaping a serif, considering. "Don't know. Much the same as I do now, I imagine."

"That's what Mum seems to want. Just carry on gardening. Planting things. Digging. People talk about bucket lists - for Mum it's *actual* buckets, and barrows and trowels and secateurs."

Meg looked at her. "What would you do?"

"Travel. Have lots of sex. Not bother about work. Do a sky-dive. Go to Thailand and India." She attempted a smile, but was close to tears. "Actually, though, I think I'd have to kill myself. Before it got me."

"You might not," Meg said, "if it came to it."

"I probably wouldn't be brave enough. But you'd need to be brave either way, wouldn't you?"

There was a silence while Jane gazed out into the yard and Meg stood back to assess her work, wondering whether to say, "I don't know about bravery. It's a cliché people come out with about cancer – bravery, fighting. Either you die or you don't. It's luck and physiology, not courage." She didn't say it, but Jane went on, tearful now, "I'd want to know that my life had made a difference. That there was some point having lived. Mum can say that, with all the gardens she's made."

"Inspired people to have a go," Meg said. "Given a lot of pleasure. Made those gardens for special schools. Sparked people off. Things like that, you don't necessarily know about."

"Yes," Jane said, adding wistfully, "I don't know how I'll *ever* make a difference."

"Most of us only manage that in a small way." As often before, Meg was uncomfortable in the wise-woman role Jane wanted her to play. Fuck, she thought, I'm the last person to ask for advice. "But small things are important when it comes down to it. You're at an in-between stage, just graduating – must feel a bit peculiar. But there'll be all sorts of possibilities! You'll find something that feels right."

Jane gave a hefty sigh. "I can't imagine what. English Literature – we used to call it the Sex and Death course, there was no getting away from either of them. What use is a degree in Sex and Death? It's no help when you come up against actual death. Real life death."

"No," Meg agreed. "Nothing can help you out there."

"It's Dad I'm worried about." Jane gave her a pleading look. "How's he going to get through this?"

Bridget

2013, FEBRUARY

SHE'D BEEN MOVED TO a hospice. She knew that, though often when she woke she couldn't remember where she was. It was brighter and lighter than the hospital, with flowers and paintings and an air of calm. People moved about and spoke in quiet voices, but also she heard laughter.

Days and nights blurred, sometimes interminable, sometimes sliding together. People came: Suzanne and Ed. Jane. Meg. Anthony, every day. She wondered why they kept coming. Once, when Jane came alone, she whispered, "You'll look after him, won't you?" and Jane's voice quavered as she answered, "Oh, Mum, of course I will."

When I get home, she thought, I'll bring the *iris reticulata* to the front of the house, in time to flower. And all the vegetables will need sowing. So much to do, this time of year. Why am I wasting time here?

Time. She kept thinking about the tricks it played.

Her mind repeated and repeated a stupid song she'd liked as a teenager. She couldn't make it go away.

Her skin wasn't hers any more. It had thinned and browned like parchment, and every smallest touch hurt. Perhaps she could shed it and find new skin underneath, fresh and smooth. She thought she was getting smaller, shrinking in the bed, sometimes floating above it. So this is where it all ends, she thought. Where I end. And she was no longer sure what it was, this *I* that had been so important, with its wants and demands. Had she ever known, really? Where was her self? She was the eyes that gazed, the ears that strained to hear but often gave up the effort. The useless body.

She dreamed of her streamside planting, of the rich, moist smell of earth. She heard the thud as she tossed a clump of weed into her barrow, the ripple of water, the robin's thin, wintry song from the alder. Simple, fulfilling work: she longed to do it again, down on her knees, trowel in hand. Where I belong. When I get out of here that's what I'll do. She saw him standing there with tears in his eyes but couldn't recall who he was or why he'd come.

How long, how long? She felt impatient. But patience was all she had left. Nothing to do but wait, try to hold the thoughts that skittered away.

Anthony was with her again and she struggled to find words for the things she had to tell him, the things that came into her mind at night.

"Jane. You will look after her?"

"Of course, of course I will, my love."

She wondered what he meant by *my love*. That was his endearment for Jane.

"Don't tell her," she whispered. "Promise you'll never tell her?"

"But - wouldn't it be best if I did?" he said. But already she'd forgotten what she'd meant, and it exhausted her to speak. She knew there was something, and tried: "Promise? Please!" He made a muffled sound, part sob, and she became aware that he was holding her hand as he said, "I promise." Her arm was a dead weight; she couldn't move it, or squeeze his fingers to show that she knew.

Thank you, she said silently. She could trust him.

She saw him holding Jane's hand in the garden, reciting their favourite poem: *Thistle and darnel and dock grew there, and a bush, in the corner, of May ...* Phrases floated back: *More than a score of donkey's years he'd seen since he was foaled...*

He was the one that mattered. Such a good father.

"What are you smiling at?" said the nurse's voice.

At times the pain made her gasp, and she thought she might as well let it take her. Then the nurses gave her the sweet relief of fading and sinking into a still place where light played and danced and she had nothing to do but lie and watch.

The voices came from far away. She heard Jane crying and wondered why. *What's the matter?* She'd have said, if she could speak. *This is dying, that's all. It's what happens. Not important.* Her eyes flickered open and she saw, on the wall outside her window, shadows cast by a tree out of sight. What kind of tree? She should have asked. When her eyes closed again she thought she'd take them with her, those beautiful tree shadows. Light, bare tree, shadows, the promise of winter ending. The great surge of energy that astonished her every year.

Meg

2013 - 2016

MEG'S BLACK COAT, BOUGHT for Aunty Eileen's funeral three years ago, had been worn again for Uncle Terry. She had felt bereft then, but at least her aunt and uncle were well into their eighties.

This was far worse.

For all Meg's work in graveyards and her devotion to creating headstones, funerals never felt right. Too churchy, too formal, as if the person had been taken away twice: once by death, next by the rituals which assumed mourners, family and everyone involved to be devoutly Christian. Meg wasn't and neither was Bridget. The solemn setting and timeworn phrases must comfort some of the grieving relatives, but she wouldn't want that for herself. She hadn't made a Will, but perhaps she should, stipulating jazz, anecdotes and laughter. Who'd take care of such things, she had no idea. Most likely no one: she was alone now. But this was no time for self-pity.

She wanted to remember Bridget squinting up at the first

swallows or admiring the flowers of a rose she'd planted, not fading and confused in the hospice. Entering the church, not sure she could keep her composure, she chose a pew at the back so that she could leave if necessary. She would take her own farewell of Bridget, less publicly, by making her headstone and installing it. When the coffin was carried in, she nearly did give way to a howl of grief and rage that swelled painfully inside. Then, seeing Jane, she felt ashamed. So young to lose her mother, Jane entered the church arm in arm with Ed; Suzanne, in dark glasses, supported Anthony, who was visibly weeping. Jane held her head high, her face set and pale.

Although she'd had days – no, months – to get used to the idea of Bridget being dead, sorrow thumped Meg in the guts as her eyes went to the coffin. Bright spring flowers were laid on top: dwarf daffodils and irises, yellow tulips and sprays of broom, offset by laurel. Better than funereal lilies, and more suited to Bridget.

The family had done their best. The funeral programme was fronted by a photograph of Bridget sitting in the arbour in an old shirt and straw hat, smiling into the sun. There were hymns (another assumption – that everyone could *sing*) and some of Bridget's favourite music, the Vaughan Williams *Fantasia on a theme of Thomas Tallis* and Erik Satie's *Gnossiennes;* a tribute by the vicar (had he even known her?) and two poetry readings. The first of these was a Gillian Clarke poem Meg didn't know, read by Ed; the second, Thomas Hardy's *The Darkling Thrush,* she did.

It was Anthony who stood to read this. Suzanne helped him to the lectern; he looks so *old,* Meg thought, and somehow smaller. The book's pages fluttered in his hands. He lowered his glasses to look at his audience and spoke so quietly that she could hear only by straining. "Bridget always liked this," he said, and began to read. *"I leant upon a coppice gate / When frost was spectre gray / And Winter's dregs made desolate ..."* Then his voice wavered alarmingly, and he put a hand to his eyes.

The next moments seemed freeze-framed. No one knew what to do: wait for Anthony to collect himself or guide him back to his seat. The vicar made a move towards the lectern but Jane was there first; she took Anthony's arm and guided him to the front pew. Ed got up quickly and helped him to sit between himself and Suzanne, leaving Jane with the book open in her hand. She glanced at it, then stepped up to the lectern, standing alone: a slim straight figure in her black dress and jacket, disarmingly like a young Bridget. Her eyes flickered over the congregation in dismay; then she lifted the book in both hands and began quietly to read. She stumbled once, corrected herself and carried on; her voice gained strength, clear in the church's stone-walled acoustic.

"So little cause for carolings / Of such ecstatic sound / Was written on terrestrial things / Afar or nigh around / That I could think there trembled through his happy good-night air / Some blessed Hope, of which he knew / And I was unaware."

Finishing, she stood for a moment then quickly returned to her place; Meg saw Suzanne hug her and Anthony place a hand on her shoulder, his head bowed.

The small drama, Jane's brave effort and the words of the poem had lifted the mood. The final piece of music was the joyful *Anitra's Dance* from Peer Gynt. As everyone filed out into chilly sunshine there were tears and sniffles but also smiles.

The grave had been prepared on the farthest edge of the churchyard, nearest to Wildings. Meg couldn't watch Bridget being put into the ground; it was too stark and literal. Her aunt and uncle had chosen cremation, which was at least accomplished quickly, out of sight. Not wanting to intrude on the family she held back, nodding to those people she recognised, exchanging a few remarks. The wake afterwards was to be at Wildings. She had walked down to the church earlier and would walk back, giving herself a bit of space. If she waited for the cars to leave first, she wouldn't be overtaken by them, or offered a lift she didn't want. On the way she'd seen yellow aconites under a belt of trees by the roadside and knew that Bridget would have noticed those. It felt wrong that the aconites were here when Bridget was not, but she wanted to walk back alone and see them again.

"Meg," said a quiet voice in her ear.

She turned, did a double take.

Adam.

He looked unfamiliar in dark overcoat, white shirt and tie. She'd never seen him formally dressed.

"Were you in the church? You can't have been invited ..."

"Yes. No. I only knew about this from you."

"You OK?" she asked.

His face gaunt, he didn't answer, but his gaze went to the mound of earth and the dark-clad group gathered round the grave.

"Come on." She took his arm, urgently needing to get him away. *Jane*, she thought. Jane wouldn't recognise him, but Suzanne might. "Let's go."

He took a long look back but let her steer him through the gate. Abandoning her plan to walk to Wildings she turned in the opposite direction towards the Plough, their old haunt. Some funeral guests were walking back to their cars, the hamlet taken over by black-clothed solemnity. Clouds fitfully obscured the sun and the wind gusted cold from the east; it could have been a day for a brisk walk, but Meg was too dressed-up in her long coat and rarely worn shoes that pinched her toes.

They walked in silence until Adam said, "Oh, Meg. *Jane.* So brave. So lovely..." His voice broke; he held a hand to his face, took off his glasses and brushed his eyes with his sleeve.

"You must have known she'd be here."

"Yes. But I had to come."

"You shouldn't have," Meg told him. "Too big a risk."

"I came in late, at the back. I wouldn't have let them see me."

She said, "Too big a risk for you, I meant."

He shook his head slowly. "She's my daughter."

"Yes, Adam. I'm well aware of that. I've kept it to myself for more than twenty years."

"I've got to tell her," he said. "I can't bear this."

"No," she said firmly. *"No.* She's just lost her mother, for God's sake! This is the worst possible time. And Anthony -" She'd never have expected to find herself standing up for Anthony. "You saw him. He's devastated. You can't do that to him, not now."

"What, then?"

"Do nothing. What *can* you do?"

He said, as if he'd already decided, "Write to him."

"To say what? You've never so much as seen Jane till today – you haven't claimed to be part of her life. Why now?" She gave him a sharp, suspicious look. "There's more, isn't there?"

A pause; then he nodded.

"I'll buy you a drink," she said. "You can tell me about it." I'm not cut out to be an agony aunt, she thought, but here I am again. Her thoughts raced; had she been wrong to pass on bits of information? He'd been circumspect, asking about Jane and Bridget only occasionally, rarely pushing for more, as if he feared taking too keen an interest.

The Plough had barely changed since the days when they walked down from Wildings for sandwiches and beer; under different management now, it had no pretension to stylish dining or rural chic. Horse-brasses caught the light, a log smouldered in the hearth and an elderly Labrador lay close to the warmth; a group of elderly men sat at the bar but there were no other customers, to Meg's relief. The room smelled of woodsmoke, not cigarette ash, the way it used to.

The men nodded at her and Adam as they entered, deferential to their funeral garb. "Lady from Wildings, weren't it?" one said. "Famous gardener, she were. Saw her on telly once." In that case he must have seen Meg too, but didn't recognise her.

They went into the snug with their drinks and sat at a corner table, Adam facing the fire, Meg with her back to it, the heat pleasantly warming her legs and feet. "So," she said brightly, but Adam looked down, shaking his head.

"Will you let me know how she is?" he asked, after a pause.

"I won't be around much longer. I'm looking for a new place."

"You're leaving Wildings?"

"No point staying on without Bridget. Wouldn't be the same. And I could use more space now I'm planning to take on an apprentice. I'm looking for a bigger workshop."

"You're doing so well," he said. "You deserve it." But his tone was flat, his words addressed to the table; they both knew that when she left Wildings his link to Jane would be gone.

"How's the painting?" she tried. "You haven't been very communicative lately."

"Haven't picked up a brush for a year or more."

"Why? Don't you want to?"

"Sometimes wish I could want to. But I can't."

She digested this. "So what else is happening?"

"Nothing really."

"And Jenny? How's she?"

"That's all finished. Should've told you. That's why I went silent on you. We've split up. Divorce under way."

"Oh, Adam! I'm so sorry."

"Thanks. Me too," he said, with a shrug, as if it were irrelevant.

She knew the signs well enough.

"When did that happen? Why?"

"You don't want to know."

"But I do. I wish you'd told me sooner. What went wrong?"

"Everything."

She thought that was all she'd get, but after a few moments he went on, "We assumed we'd have children, but it didn't happen. Not for lack of trying, but you can imagine how that starts to feel. For Jenny, especially, it was heartbreaking, failure after failure, time going by. Inevitably there were tests, and – in the end I couldn't go on pretending. I told her I'd already fathered a child."

"Ah," Meg said slowly.

He went on, in the same flat monotone: "Should have told her years ago, I know that. She couldn't forgive me - for not being honest from the start. I don't blame her."

"Oh ... Is it too late?"

"About twelve years too late."

"How about work? Is that OK?" she asked, recalling that when he first told her about Greenways, two or three years ago, he'd been full of ideas and enthusiasm.

"Yeah. Keeps me going, just about."

"So where are you living?"

"Brighton, still. The flat's up for sale. Jenny's gone back to Taunton."

"You're living alone?"

He nodded. "Course."

This was beginning to feel like an interrogation, but she felt that if she stopped talking he'd sit silent and morose, staring into the embers. She knew well enough that when he went dull and listless it could take days to get through it. Even allowing for the fact that they'd come from Bridget's funeral, it alarmed her, stirring memories of Gillian. "Get a grip, for fuck's sake," she heard her stepdad shouting. "If you can't pull yourself out of it, no one else can. Why don't you get a bloody job? Give yourself something to do, stop drooping around like a wet week?" Neither threats nor cajoling made any difference. Gillian couldn't see the point of looking for a job, or the point of going out, getting dressed, seeing anyone.

"How long have you been like this?"

Adam looked directly at her for the first time since they'd sat down. "Dunno. It's like something's turned off and I can't find the on switch."

"Worse than usual, then?"

He nodded slowly. "Please don't tell me to snap out of it."

"You know I won't." She touched his arm. "Adam! You shouldn't face this on your own. You need professional help."

"See a shrink?" He gave a humourless laugh.

"Not a shrink. That's silly prejudice. A doctor. Therapist."

He shrugged, as if he didn't care enough to bother. But he made the effort to come today, she thought. And that's made things worse.

She sat back, took a deep breath.

"Two things. Listen. One - you mustn't approach Jane, not when you're like this. Not yet, and not without thinking about it very, very carefully. You just can't. And, two - I'm serious about getting help. Go to your doctor. It's not something to be ashamed of. Please, Adam. Will you promise?"

It took many minutes of cajoling before he grudgingly agreed; then he stirred, seeming to come to a decision. "There *is* more. You were right. Something I should have told you years ago."

• • •

She left him there. Walked out in a daze, past the men at the bar and out to the garden at the back where she stood staring at the ragged grass and forlorn benches.

"Fuck, Adam!" Her reaction had been quick and fierce. "I don't believe this. I thought I could trust you, thought we were good friends - why didn't you *tell* me?" She'd tried not to raise her voice, and he replied miserably, "I wanted to. But how could I, with you so close to Bridget? It wouldn't have been fair."

"Fair? What's fairness got to do with it?"

Anthony's son. He was *Anthony's son*, and that meant ...

"Wait. I need to get my head round this." She stood, grabbing her coat, and he made no response as she walked out. In those few moments, sympathy had turned to anger and hurt – and resentment, because in all the times she'd gone to him when he needed her, *all* the times she'd dropped everything and set off, he'd never trusted her enough to tell her this basic, simple fact. The fact that explained why he'd come to Wildings in the first place, in search of Anthony.

No wonder he's screwed up, she thought. Serves him bloody right.

Except that clearly it had done him no good, placing himself in such proximity to the father who'd abandoned him. Then falling in love with his father's wife – what would a Freudian psychologist make of that?

Anthony. Adam. Bridget. A triangle of secrecy and resentment that had trapped all three. Herself the observer, thinking she knew it all, when it turned out she knew practically nothing.

But in spite of her outrage she couldn't abandon him.

It was different this time, with the loss of Bridget so raw and painful. She needed *him* now, to get through this. But as she headed back inside, she had no idea what to say.

The snug bar where they'd been sitting was empty.

Oh, *fuck*. Now what?

Where would he go? To Wildings? Somewhere else? She turned her anger on herself: what had she been thinking, walking out on him at such a low point? He shouldn't be on his own, shouldn't even be driving. She tried ringing his mobile but got Voicemail.

"Adam, I'm sorry," she said. "I mean it, truly. Call me. Please! I'm here."

. . .

By the end of March she was packing to leave Wildings.

Filling bags and boxes she instructed herself to be ruthless about decluttering. *No point looking back,* she'd taught herself. But how could she not?

She kept thinking about Anthony, and how Bridget had seen him as so forgiving and selfless, treating Jane as his own. How often had he played that to his advantage? And now Jane was staying on at Wildings to look after him. If anyone was being treated unfairly, it was Jane.

Jane should know the truth. But when, and how? At her last meeting with Adam, he'd spoken again about writing to

Anthony. Maybe he'd thought better of it, or maybe he *had* written, in which case it might bring about a reconciliation. More likely not. Whatever: it was out of her hands.

As Anthony never came down to the yard, she'd had to find him to give notice on the cottage and workshop. She checked that his car was in the drive, then rang at the front door instead of going round to the back as had been her habit. When, after a while, Anthony answered, he looked at her unrecognisingly for a moment.

"Can I come in?" she had to ask, when he said nothing.

He led the way to the kitchen. She looked around, sensing the absence of Bridget so strongly that it was almost a presence. Everything was tidy, too tidy. When Bridget was here there'd be a posy of flowers or leaves in a jar on the windowsill, whatever the season, and gardening magazines and books on the table. Now there was only the Sunday paper, folded and apparently unread. There was no sign of Jane.

"How are you?" she said, for the sake of saying something, and he shrugged.

Now that she knew he was Adam's father, Jane's grandfather, she wanted to stare and stare at him for traces of both in the shape of his nose and cheekbones and in his glances. He was Bridget's husband but in spite of living in close proximity for more than twenty years Meg knew him mainly through what Bridget told her. And often through what Bridget didn't say. So much concealment, on both sides! There was the depression, too, which she knew from Bridget that Anthony had always denied, apparently inherited by Adam. She hoped Jane hadn't been handed that particular poisoned chalice along with her genes.

Anthony didn't invite her to sit, but said, "What can I do for you?"

His curtness made it easy to be brisk.

"I'm planning to move out of the cottage and workshop. I've found a new place in Stroud. So I've come to give a month's notice. That's what we agreed when I moved in."

"Oh." He was taken aback. "You're leaving the cottage? Bridget wanted you to stay."

"That was kind of her. But it won't be the same without her and I've made other plans."

For a moment his face changed; glimpsing desolation, even panic, she recalled how he'd looked at the funeral, almost a different man. Fleetingly she wondered what would happen if she ventured to touch his arm and express sympathy, if they sat down and talked about Bridget, even wept together.

Then he regained his composure, and looked at her with indifference.

"As you wish," he said.

· · ·

A van and driver took her heavy equipment and chunks of stone; the rest went with her by car, including Eric the cat. Irate at being confined in his basket he yowled and grappled all the way.

She had already said goodbye to Jane, who'd left early for Oxford. After several months of temping, not sure what to do with her degree, Jane worked in marketing, but had moved back to Wildings when Bridget went into the hospice, and still spent several nights each week there to be with Anthony. Owing it to Bridget and possibly to Adam to keep in touch, Meg felt bad about leaving; but Jane had Suzanne and Ed, as well as her new boyfriend, for support.

The final meeting with Anthony was perfunctory.

"I'm off, then," she told him. "Here are my keys. I've turned off the water."

"Thank you," he said. "Hope it goes smoothly."

"Thanks. Let me know when you're ready to talk about the headstone."

She drove out of the yard without looking back.

. . .

She resolved to keep in contact with Adam now that he was alone again. She texted frequently to ask how he was and to update him about the move, receiving brief but prompt replies and a request for her new address. Two weeks later the post brought a card to her workshop, addressed by hand.

In these days of instant messaging and emails she hadn't seen his handwriting for some while, but recognised it at once. She held the envelope reverently before opening it, oddly touched.

Inside was an art card with good wishes for her move, and a folded page. He said that he'd taken her advice about seeking help, been referred to a therapist and was beginning to feel more like himself. The Brighton flat was now sold, and he'd moved to a flat in Newbury for which he gave the address.

She pinned his card on the noticeboard next to the one Jane had sent and looked at the two of them side by side. Then she went to her desk and took out the drawing she'd made for Bridget's headstone, ready to send to Anthony.

She thought: well, it's none of my business.

But that meant there was little to lose.

She could do nothing. Or she could write a letter to enclose with her drawing.

She would have a go, at least. She could always tear it up and not send it.

. . .

"No more secrets," Adam told her, four years later when Ness came into his life. "I've had enough of secrets."

She took this to mean that Ness knew about Jane.

"Good." Meg nodded approval, thinking about the secret she'd kept from him, her letter to Anthony: *You should know that Adam has kept his promise, but at great cost to himself. Possibly to Jane and even to you. Isn't it time to put an end to this?*

Anthony never replied. When she heard from Jane that he'd made alternative and – as she saw it – deliberately insulting arrangements for the headstone, she had his answer.

Well, let him stew. But Meg felt the awkwardness of her relationship with Jane, owing it to Bridget to keep in touch, while not wanting Adam to yearn for more than it was fair to ask or tell.

Eventually, she supposed, the truth would come out. Meanwhile she was glad that Adam had found Ness: clever, serious, quietly humorous, seeming to understand him and accept his hang-ups. They'd met while Adam was having therapy; she was a medical journalist with a special interest in mental health, perfectly placed to listen and steer. Adam was eager to introduce her to Meg, pleased when they quickly took to each other, and Meg in turn was glad that Ness seemed to acknowledge the importance of her own friendship with Adam.

So she was surprised and dismayed when he turned up at The Old Fleece with someone else. He was in Stroud for a weekend stone-carving workshop she'd organised, staying in a B&B nearby; they'd arranged to eat at the pub this evening and she expected to have him to herself.

"Meg, I want you to meet Robin. I've been telling her about you."

"Hi, Meg. I hope you don't mind me gate-crashing."

Meg shook her head, though she *did* mind. She took in bright brown eyes in an animated face, glinting earrings, thick brown hair: small, slim body dressed in jeans and a green Indian-printed top.

Robin. The name suited her.

"I've just come for a quick drink," Robin added, "then I'm meeting someone."

"We met at the B&B," Adam explained. "Robin's a photographer. Anyway, what will you have?"

He went to the bar, leaving the two women at the table. Meg threw a reproachful look at him, thinking: what's he doing? Chatting over breakfast is one thing; bringing her along tonight is something else. If he's drawn to her, it's because she's like a younger Bridget. Does he realise that?

"Photographer?" she said, turning to Robin.

"Yes. Freelance. Adam showed me your website – it looks brilliant, what you do. I'd love to visit your workshop some time. Take pictures."

Meg had been thinking of updating her website, and said so; Robin produced a card. "Yes, Adam said. I specialise in black and white – that'd work well for letters in stone."

"So what's brought you to Stroud?"

"I've got an assignment for a local magazine. But I'm looking for somewhere to live locally, too. I've been in Bristol six years but it's time for a change."

"Why here, then?"

"I like the town, the arty vibe, the countryside. I need a break from city life."

Adam returned with the drinks and Robin smiled her thanks. As the conversation continued Meg was aware of the triangle they formed, seated around a small table, and the glances from Adam to Robin to herself, and from Robin to Adam but also frequently in her direction. Her own eyes were drawn irresistibly; there was something appealing in Robin's frank gaze, her bright eyes and the smile that showed wolfish eye teeth, her face warm in lamplight. She thought: who's attracted to who, here? The air sparked with possibility.

Stirring. Disturbing. Best not go there.

"Well, I split up with my girlfriend," Robin was saying, in answer to a question from Adam, and her glance quickly went to Meg. "No bad feelings on either side, but it was the right thing to do. So actually I can't afford Bristol on my own."

There was a question in that look, Meg thought. Or was she imagining it?

"Anyway, I must go." Robin drained her half-pint and gathered up bag and scarf. "Thanks, Adam. You've got my card if you want to get in touch," she said to Meg.

"I have," Meg said, and put it in her jeans pocket. "I will."

Jane

APRIL 2019

"Didn't dad leave her ten thousand? Now you want to give her another two grand on top?"

Rob was at Wildings for - Jane hoped - a final meeting, and she and Suzanne had revived the idea of Meg making a headstone. To pre-empt argument, Jane had already asked for a quotation: two thousand pounds for headstone, installation and diocesan fees.

"It's not *giving*, Rob," Jane said. "It's paying the proper rate for highly skilled work. It'd usually be two thousand five. Meg's taking off five hundred as her own contribution."

"And if that was what Dad meant," Suzanne pointed out, "he'd have said so in the Will. He didn't. I think the ten thousand was a gift from Mum to Meg."

"Wouldn't he have made that clear?"

"We're not asking Meg to work for nothing," Jane said. "It's not that much, is it? Five hundred each, against everything we've been left?"

"Your choice, not mine. Anyway, how do you get five hundred? It's a bit over six and a half, by my reckoning."

"No. Two thousand shared by four of us."

"*Four* - oh, you're including Sean McBride. Adam. He's willing to fork out, is he?"

"Yes, course," Jane told him. "He's already agreed."

Rob gave an exaggerated sigh. "I see – a *fait accompli*. Well, all right, but it would be far simpler to add new lettering to the headstone Dad chose. If we were starting from scratch then fair enough, but why haul out something that's already in the ground?"

"Because it matters," Jane said heatedly. "Because we know what real letter-cutting looks like. It might not matter to you, but it does to me and Suzanne and Adam. And especially to Meg."

"Have it your own way. It strikes me, Jane, that all your yoga and meditation doesn't make you very calm."

"It strikes me," she retorted, "that all your money doesn't make you *generous*."

Suzanne suppressed a smile. Rob threw Jane a haughty look; he ran through final instructions, collected his papers and got up to leave.

At the door he turned back. "Ingrid was saying we'd better have Adam over for dinner, as it seems he's one of the family. I'll get back to you to find a date to suit us all."

"Well," Jane said, deadpan, when he'd gone. "That's something to look forward to. We'd better warn Adam."

"At least he's making an effort, or Ingrid is," Suzanne said. "It's a start. Let's not think about it now. Are you going to show me the website for your India trip?"

"Mm, OK."

"You're not having second thoughts?"

"No, I do want to go. It's just that there's so much to keep me here, now. There's this big climate change protest planned, in London. Adam's going but I'll have left by then."

After attending two Extinction Rebellion meetings she thought she'd found her spiritual home. There was sorrow and anger about climate breakdown and mass extinction, but also there was strategy, inventiveness, boundless determination. The clear-sighted focus gave her hope; she could *do* something instead of silently despairing. She could be part of a crusade that brought to mind the suffragettes, or the civil rights movement in America: a tide of protest that was surely irresistible.

And no sooner had she found this new and absorbing purpose than she'd committed herself to leaving for a year. The hardest part had been telling Adam.

"I don't think I can bear to part with you!" His dismay was so transparent that she almost wavered. But she had to go. She assured him that she'd text, Skype and email, and that they could be in touch every day. He was already planning to join her for a week or two in the autumn. "I know. Flying. A habit we all need to break. But if it's that or not seeing you for a whole year ..."

She was using the money Anthony had left her to fund a year's volunteering at a project near Kochi, helping to build a communal farm. Chitra knew of a yoga ashram there, too, for her free time. She could live cheaply in India, especially with accommodation provided. Her flights were booked, visa applied for, and she'd given notice at the gym. Her next task was to sort through and reduce her possessions and store them in Suzanne and Ed's attic.

On the phone that evening she reminded Adam that she was visiting Meg next day.

"Give her my love. Maybe you'll meet Robin, too."

"Hope so! It's weird, thinking of Meg with a partner after all these years."

"Janey, I know you think fifty-something's well past it, but when you get to Meg's and my age, you'll see things differently, I assure you."

"Not because she's fifty-something. I mean because she's *Meg*."

. . .

Propped on the bench in Meg's workshop was a piece of slate with italic lettering painted in light grey:

> *Words –*
> *Let me sometimes dance*
> *With you,*
> *Or climb*
> *Or stand perchance*
> *In ecstasy,*
> *Fixed and free*
> *In a rhyme*
> *As poets do.*
>
> *Edward Thomas*

"I've seen that before," Jane said.

Meg glanced up. "Not this, though. This is new. The first one was sold in Artweeks a few years back. Bridget gave me the words. It's part of a longer poem."

"Fixed and free," Jane read aloud. "Clever. The words are set in stone, but their meaning floats free." The lettering suited the idea, ascenders and down-strokes curling away like wind-blown streamers.

"That's what Bridget said, more or less. I'm making this one for myself. Anyway, here's what I've got to show you." Meg removed a plastic sheet from a slab of stone propped against the wall, cut and shaped. "I'd planned to use Hornton. But then I got some of this - Yorkshire sandstone from the Woodkirk quarry, near Leeds. It's a bit special, with these swirls. What do you think?"

Reverently Jane touched the surface. The stone was the colour of wet sand, a lighter tone rippling across in an effect like marble.

"It's beautiful." She pictured it in the graveyard, facing Wildings across the valley. The sand tones would echo the ironstone of the church; she pictured snowdrops and dwarf daffodils planted around its base.

"Thought you'd like it," Meg said. "It's grey when they cut it out of the ground, but weathers to this lovely buff brown. I'll email you a photo, and you can show Suzanne and the others. I won't start till I know everyone's happy. And you've all agreed on the wording?"

"Yes. Thank you." Jane moved to the board to examine the sketch she'd seen before.

"It'll take about six weeks." Meg replaced the protective sheet. "So you'll be away when I install it, unless you'd rather I waited."

"No, I think go ahead. We weren't planning to make a ceremony of it. It'll be lovely to see it when I get back."

"So, how's things?" Meg asked, while Jane looked at the other drawings and photographs on the noticeboard. "You've got buyers for Wildings, I hear? And it's going well with Adam?"

"Great, thanks. He's met Suzanne and Ed now, twice, and we're both in Extinction Rebellion." She indicated the XR symbol sewn to her backpack.

"Adam said! He's all fired up."

"Me too – it was so great, being with people set on *doing* something, not just waiting while the climate crisis spins out of control. I'm gutted to miss the big protest next month. There's a slogan I liked: *If not me, who? If not now, when?*"

"That's good," Meg said. "I could carve it in slate."

"Next week I'll meet Ness. You know her, don't you?"

"Yes – I like her a lot. And she's good for him."

"That's what Adam said about you and Robin."

Meg smiled. "Did he? It was thanks to him I met her – did you know?"

"No, but he said it was because of you he met Ness. After you made him have therapy."

"All I did was shove him in the right direction. He did need shoving." Meg pulled on her coat, winding a scarf round her neck. "Did he tell you he had a go at letter-cutting?"

"No?"

"I've been doing workshops for beginners, couple of times a year - four or five people each time. Most do relief carving but he wanted to try lettering. Made quite a good start." Meg glanced out of the window. "Oh, here's Robin. We're treating you to lunch."

The door opened in a flurry of colour and flying scarf as a small woman entered.

"Hello *Jane!* I've heard so much about you. Great to meet you at last."

She gave Meg a quick kiss in passing and came to Jane, taking her hand in both hers. Jane saw brown eyes in a small face beneath a green pull-on hat and henna-coloured fringe; silver earrings, purple scarf under a green-printed cotton jacket; a ready smile that showed pointed eye-teeth.

"I know you're vegan. Me too. The pub we're going to has great choices."

Ready to be charmed, Jane already was.

Later, driving home in the falling dusk, she thought how different Meg seemed with Robin: content, at ease. Noticing their quick exchanges and frequent smiles, she felt reassured. At low points she still felt bereft and hopeless about Tom, as if there'd never be anyone else; but here was Meg, and there was Adam, both twice her age, with satisfying new relationships. She was touched and intrigued by the complicated ways things worked out.

• • •

Friday was the day of completion. By midday she'd leave Wildings for the last time, and it would belong to the Durhams. Her possessions, apart from the case, rucksack and yoga mat in her car, were in Suzanne's and Ed's attic.

Although there had been weeks to prepare, she still had the feeling of unreality. Since November her life had been dismantled and put together differently; there was a sense of things progressing too fast, as if Dad might yet turn his key in the door and demand to know why his house had been stripped. Leaving home was another kind of bereavement; the shock of parting needed time to be fully felt.

Both Suzanne and Adam had offered to be with her today, but she wanted to do this alone. As she wandered through bare rooms she heard voices: her own, Suzanne's, Dad's and her mother's; she recalled Christmases, birthdays, summer days with the doors and windows open; rows and reconciliations, failures and successes, visitors, countless meals, Suzanne's wedding on a day of ceaseless rain that had somehow added to the sense of celebration. Her earliest memories were here, and her most recent: her whole life, on fast-forward, led to this still point.

She was putting off the final exit. On her way to Suzanne's she would hand over the keys at the estate agent's office, and would then have no means of re-entry, and no right.

The voices faded; she was alone. They weren't here, her parents; they had gone, truly *passed away*, with the slow removal of their belongings, their treasures, their clutter. This was no longer their habitat, or hers. Whatever she had to keep of them must be independent of this house, these rooms. She stood in the sitting-room looking at indentations in the carpet where furniture had stood for years, and rectangles of wallpaper brighter than the rest where pictures and mirrors had hung. It was a shell. Already, the home that Wildings had been existed only in her memory.

In the hall she whispered goodbye to a part of herself, then stepped outside and closed the door.

. . .

"It's on time." She looked at the departures board, wanting to put off the moment of parting. "Quick coffee before I go through?"

It felt surreal to return to Birmingham International, with Adam, to this portal between worlds, shiny and anonymous. She thought of the last parting: Dad, with his cold, seeing her off before buying his Lemsip, the last few moments she'd ever spend with him. That was vivid in her mind, and she knew that Adam knew, and that it was his father, not hers, who drove home alone that night.

They sat with their coffee while minutes ticked away fast, too fast; she thought wildly of saying *I've changed my mind. I'm not going.*

"I'll think of you next week, in London," she said. "Don't get arrested."

He smiled. "If I do, it's an honourable tradition, after all."

"I'm so sorry I can't go!"

"I'll tell you all about it. Climate protests won't have finished by the time you come back, that's for sure. Meanwhile - " He reached into a pocket and handed her a small package wrapped in saffron-coloured paper. "Wait till you're on the plane before you open it."

Their pace slowed as they reached the sign for *Passengers Only* and the wide corridor to Departures. Time for final goodbyes. He folded her in a bear-hug, which she returned, holding him tightly. A sob rose in her throat.

"Take care of yourself, my precious Jane," he said, his voice husky.

"I will. You, too."

"Text me as soon as you can."

"Yes."

"I'll come and see you. And be here to meet you when you get back."

"Promise?" she said, tearful.

"Of course. I'll be here. I promise."

At the turn of the corridor she turned to look back. He was there, watching her, standing in the way of people coming through. She gave a final wave, and he blew a kiss and smiled, and still did not move away. She had to be the first to turn, moving towards security, her eyes blurring.

I'll be here. I promise.

On the other side of the conveyers and scanners she walked through duty-free, past garish displays of perfumes and watches, designer clothes and gadgets, and she kept hearing his words, like a mantra.

...

The airfield lights dropped away. She gazed down, gripping her seat-arms as she always did on take-off. The woman next to her had been inclined to chat at first, but Jane felt too stirred up for small talk: a blend of excitement and anxiety, regret and certainty clutched at her heart.

She was holding the small package, waiting for the aircraft to reach cruising height. Unwrapping it she found a tiny marble figure: a Buddha, in graceful lotus position, smiling. Folded around it was a piece of textured paper, and, in the distinctive handwriting she loved: *For your passage to more than India. A xxx*

She held the cool weight in her palm. A talisman, small enough to go with her everywhere.

Thank you, she whispered.

"Sweet!" said the chatty woman, watching. "A present?"

"Yes. My father gave it to me."

Father. Such an ordinary word, so charged with promise and meaning.

...

She returned first to the Kerala coast for a few days of yoga and meditation before travelling to Kochi for her volunteering. On the final night of her stay she and the rest of the group went down to the beach.

She had come here each evening after practice, with others or more often alone, wanting to imprint the scene on her mind: the rise and fall of waves, moon-path on the sea, lights of fishing-boats far out. Farther along, beyond a small promontory, was the sacred beach below a temple where Hindu mourners committed ashes to the sea. In the other direction, towards the yoga centre, lights were strung along the low cliff path; she heard music and voices, inhaled the spicy drift from several cafés. She'd swum a few times, wary of the strong currents that alarmed her at first, careful now yet revelling in the experience of swimming in the Arabian sea, under the stars.

The group of twelve felt relaxed in each other's presence after three days of yoga and visits to local temples and shrines. Tonight Venkatesh, who led daily meditation sessions, said it was time for the ritual of letting go.

Self-conscious about entering into this so publicly, Jane succumbed to the spell of a never-to-be-repeated experience. Venky scooped a hollow in the sand, and made a small fire of twig, dried leaves and something scented; he sat his group in a circle around it and asked them to focus on yogic breathing. Gradually they were asked to bring their thoughts, silently, to something that was holding them back: a regret, a fear, a feeling of anger or resentment. Then he gave each person a leathery leaf, and a felt pen.

"Write on the leaf. A word, maybe a phrase. Don't show anyone. Say the word, or words, silently to yourself. Hold it in your mind: your doubt, or your grief, or your resentment. Then bury the leaf in the sand."

A mood of solemnity had settled over the group. They'd been chatting and giggling as they came to the beach, but now only Venky spoke, everyone listening intently. Some people paused to think; others wrote immediately. Jane, aware that she was being too self-conscious, too buttoned-up, too *English* about this, thought for a few moments, then wrote *Loss. Change.* She added silently: *Dad. Mum. Tom. Home.* An unbearable catalogue of absence.

Yet – was anything really lost, after all? She had lost Dad, but gained a grandfather, a grandfather who'd loved and wanted her. She'd lost the man she thought was her father but found the man who really was: a father she already loved and was learning to know and understand. She had lost a boyfriend, a lover, but he had never been hers; she could give him up gracefully, and wish him well. And her mother's presence was everywhere in the Wildings garden, known so intimately to Jane that she could picture each change of season even here in the heat and humidity of India. The garden would thrive, with others there to wander and admire. And yes, the world might be doomed, but now, *now*, it was full of beauty and wonder and intensity.

The rhythm of her breath echoed the rise and fall of waves.

There was nothing to fear, nothing really to regret. Everything to feel thankful for. Everything was possible.

Venky waited, his eyes shining in the light of the flames. When he judged that everyone had finished writing, he began to chant: *Om Namah Shivaya*.

Om Namah Shivaya

Om Namah Shivaya

Gradually the others joined in, soft voices carrying into the darkness beyond their circle. After countless repetitions, Venky rang a clear note on a bell to hush the chant, and said, "Now you'll take your leaf out of the sand and let it go in whichever way you choose. You can tear it into pieces and scatter them on the sand. You can burn it in the candle-flame. You can bury it again, more deeply. Or you can give it to the sea."

Unfolding, Jane stood, brushing sand from her clothes, then went to the tide's edge and waded in, knee-deep. Her eyes, closed throughout the meditation, were dazzled now by the moon and the stars. Holding the leaf in both hands as if launching a toy boat, she released it to be carried out on the next wave, and watched until it was gone in the darkness and immensity of the sea. Slowly she straightened, looking at the far-off lights of fishing boats. There had been something spellbinding about the communion - the setting, the words, the serious faces lit by firelight – and now in the silence afterwards, broken only by the fall of waves, the tinkling of bells and distant voices from the cafes. She stood silently, not wanting it to end.

Behind her she heard quiet sobbing. She didn't turn back until she sensed movement from the others, and heard Venky murmuring to the woman who was crying, crouching beside her. A man and a woman, the only couple in the group, were embracing, comforting each other. For each, the ritual had meant something different, something deeply felt. For herself she was aware only of warmth that tingled through her, flooding her with energy and joy. She felt like running, dancing, doing handstands. Maybe she would, when the others had drifted away.

I am here. In this place. Living with all my senses. This is me, now.

Meg

MAY 2019

LATE ON A STILL afternoon, with swifts flying and the last trees coming into leaf, Meg met Adam at the churchyard.

Their first task was to remove the old headstone. This was easily done: the concrete slab at its base simply rested on the ground, with a steel post driven through a hole to secure it.

"There. I'll keep it." They dragged the headstone to one side. "The family don't want it. It'll be useful to have a piece of machine-carving, to show the difference between that and the real thing."

They took turns digging, in hard ground threaded with strong roots and with chunks of stone embedded. When Meg had spread a layer of sand, put in the concrete shoe and checked with ruler and spirit level to her satisfaction, they went to the van for the new headstone.

"There's another bit of carving to do before we move it. If you agree."

He looked at her in surprise. "Whatever you say."

She rolled back the protective carpet to show a line marked in pencil on the sandstone where ground-level would be. Below that, on the part of the stone that would be buried, she had carved her initials, *MG,* and had pencilled his, *AM.*

"No one will see, but we'll know. I thought you could carve your own."

It was a while since his attempts at lettering, and she saw his hesitation as she passed him the chisel and dummy.

"Remember? Angled like this." She demonstrated, then handed back the tools.

"It'll be so clumsy, next to yours."

"It's not the look that matters! But we'll know it's there. More definite – that's it."

Mixing concrete, she watched him work. They lowered the headstone to the trolley, wheeled it across the grass and manoeuvred it into position. Adam held it upright while Meg scrutinised it from all angles then cemented it into place. Finally the shovelling-in of earth, concealing their initials, and the firming and treading. When they'd stowed tools and equipment in the van, she removed the fleece wrap and stood aside for Adam to see.

The lighter swirl rippled across the sand-coloured York stone like a wave through the lettering:

Bridget Harper, 1943 - 2013
gardener and maker
and her husband
Anthony Harper, 1936 - 2018
writer and academic
lovingly remembered
by their children and grandchildren

On the back, in the half-round of the top, a thrush perched on hawthorn, above the inscription:

> *The thrushes sing as the sun is going*
> *... as if all Time were theirs*

It was beautiful, she knew: one of the best she'd done. She felt a surge of pride, and of contentment, because it was here at last in its proper place, for Bridget.

Adam was silent, smoothing a hand over the letters. "It's wonderful, Meg." He turned to her. "Perfect. Oh, come here."

She submitted to being hugged.

"There's something I haven't told you," she said. "Saved it for now. After I'd left Wildings, when Anthony and I had our disagreement about the headstone, I wrote to him about you."

He looked at her sidelong, startled.

"I probably shouldn't have," she went on. "It was interfering, and I'm as subtle as a hippo. But he was sunk in misery, and so were you, and I thought I'd give him a shove. See if he'd think differently, with Bridget gone."

"What happened?" Adam's voice was hoarse.

"Nothing. He didn't answer. I didn't expect him to. But – you know he sent for me, the day he died, and I went to the hospital? Too late to find out what he wanted. I assumed, and so did Jane and Suzanne, he'd changed his mind about the headstone. But later I wondered if what he really wanted was to contact *you*, through me. I was the link."

She looked at Adam for a reaction; he made only an incoherent sound.

"Sorry for barging in," she said. "None of my business. Might have messed things up even more."

He gave a wavering smile. "I don't think he or I needed

much help, fucking things up. But -" He gazed at the inscription, then looked at her. "We'll never know, will we, what he wanted. Maybe, right at the end, he -" He broke off, then said gruffly, "Thank you, Meg. For that possibility."

"I'm going to pick some flowers," she said. "I'll give you a few minutes on your own."

Buttercups, Queen Anne's lace, forget-me-nots and ox-eye daisies grew in profusion in the wild part of the churchyard. She filled a jar with water and arranged them in it: the simplest flowers in the simplest container, like the posies Bridget used to put on the kitchen windowsill.

She waited by the wall while Adam stood by the grave. When at last he turned away, she placed the jar of flowers by the headstone. It would be for Suzanne and, later, Jane, to choose more permanent plants or bulbs, and tend them.

At the gate they hesitated, loth to part.

"Pub?"

"Yeah."

They took their drinks to a bench table in the garden. The unmown areas of lawn were thick with buttercups; Meg watched swallows looping under the eaves of the building, and the swifts' high flight. There were fewer swifts than there used to be, but – by some miracle of instinct – they were still here.

"A May evening in the English countryside," she said, tilting back. "What could beat it?"

Adam sighed. "I know. Maybe it's all doomed, and us along with it, but all the same ... it's perfection while it lasts. I can't help but feel happy – happier than ever before."

"I can see that."

"It's because of Jane, of course – even if she's not here. But it's XR, too, being part of all that energy and fierce determination. Does that sound crazy?"

"Not at all."

She was thinking how much had changed since their visit here after the funeral. She saw traces of the old confident Adam, mellowed by loss and love and regret. "Your new life as a rebel seems to suit you," she told him. "I'll be ready to bail you out if you're thinking of getting arrested again."

"Well, it was certainly an experience. They can't arrest a whole movement. And what's to lose? The future of the planet, if we do nothing."

"People talk about saving the future for their children or grandchildren," she said, "but that sort of implies those of us without children don't have any reason to care."

"And that's not true. I know that. I've got Jane now, but I won't have grandchildren, she's made that clear. That doesn't limit my concern for the planet and everything that lives. Why should it?"

She nodded. "I know. I sometimes think I'd like to drop back in, a hundred years from now, or two hundred, so see what's left. Whether future generations can make a better job of looking after the world."

"And how they look back at us. What did we think we were doing?" Adam said, adding, "It's Jane's birthday tomorrow."

"Oh! - I forgot, but I'll send an e-card. Have you spoken?"

"Yes, we Skyped this morning."

"Give her my love. Is she enjoying the volunteering?"

"Loves it! She's planting veg, cooking, looking after children, building huts and toilets – a bit of everything."

"Good for her." She raised her glass. "What'll you do with your share from the house sale?"

"I'll sell the flat and look for a new place. Jane thinks she'll settle in Leamington or Warwick when she's back, to be with Chitra and her yoga friends. I want to be near her and closer to Ness, too, so I thought north Oxford, if I can find something affordable."

"Affordable? North Oxford? Good luck with that."

"Well, it's a windfall I never expected. Thanks to Anthony."

In the lane he unlocked his car and reached inside.

"Nearly forgot!" He handed her a card with the familiar Artweeks logo. "Private view. At a small gallery in Summertown."

Artweeks. It brought back memories: guest artists with their pottery, jewellery and mosaics, signs pointing to the garden, Bridget showing people round.

Happy days. Adam had never been part of that; the first open studios week at Wildings had taken place after he left.

"It's on Saturday evening," he said. "Great if you could come."

The card showed three images: ceramic pots, a woodcut, and a pastel drawing, showing what she recognised as Waterloo Bridge during the protests: banners, the XR symbol, and various figures and faces, some sharp, others blurred in movement; light and dark, festivity and anger. A carnival of outrage.

"This is you?" She looked at him in surprise. "You've gone a bit Banksy."

"I know. I did a lot of drawing, on the road as well as in a sketchpad. Later I worked some of them into a series. A record of an amazing few days."

"You've found it again. Your one true thing."

"Yes," he said, and smiled. "More than one."

"I'm so glad, Adam. I'll definitely come, with Robin if she's free."

"Ness is coming, too. We could eat afterwards at the restaurant opposite."

"Great. Let's."

He was first to drive away, raising a hand in farewell. About to start her engine Meg sat looking at Wildings, across the valley. Dusk was starting to fall; the hedgerows were pale with hawthorn blossom, haze settling over the fields and the trees. In the Wildings garden the climbing rose would soon flower, Bridget's special climbing rose whose name Meg had forgotten. She pictured Bridget standing by the wall in her straw hat, showing her the small pointed buds, so like hedgerow dog roses. "Listen!" she would say, gazing up. "Swifts! *Now* summer's here." Bridget used to say that she loved every month, every season, but especially May – the tide of green, the heady rush of growth. "You can smell it, see it, almost hear it. Every year it's astonishing all over again."

And now it was touched with a kind of grief, because everything, *everything,* was under threat; but there was joy in that too, because this evening was now, here, poignant in its fragility.

She got out of the car to stand on the verge. She thought of a new design, swifts in exultant flight, cutting through lines of text – if she could find the right words. Already she pictured it, saw the light, elongated letters with flourishes like swept-back wings; felt her hands on the tools, shaping her vision. Her eyes and ears followed the swifts' arrowed shapes as they hurled themselves through fading sky.

Acknowledgements

With grateful thanks to all the people who have given their support to the writing, revising and production of this novel.

To Bernard Johnson, stonemason, for his inspirational and accomplished work, for teaching me the rudiments of carving and letter-cutting and for letting me help with two headstone installations.

To my writer friends, for encouragement, advice and friendship: Jon Appleton, Yvonne Coppard, Graeme Fife, Adèle Geras, Julia Jarman, Cindy Jefferies, Celia Rees, Jane Rogers and Linda Sargent.

To Nina Sperinck, for all the yoga. Namaste.

To Lida Kindersley at the Cardozo Kindersley workshop for a memorable visit and much useful information.

To Trevor Arrowsmith, for many kinds of support.

To Owen Gent for his striking cover design and to Victoria Heath Silk for the beautiful interior layout and motifs.

About the Author

Linda Newbery is best known for her fiction for young readers, with titles including *Set in Stone* (winner, Costa Children's Book Prize), *The Shell House* and *Sisterland* (both shortlisted for the Carnegie Medal), *Lob, The Sandfather, The Key to Flambards*. Her first novel for adults, *Quarter Past Two on a Wednesday Afternoon* (published in paperback as *Missing Rose*) was a Radio 2 Book Club choice. She is an active campaigner on animal and environmental issues and has published a guide to compassionate living, *This Book is Cruelty Free – Animals and Us*. She lives in Oxfordshire.

Writers Review Publishing is an author-led publishing collaborative linked to the literary blog **Writers Review**, which is hosted by Adèle Geras, Linda Newbery and Celia Rees. Since its launch in 2016, the blog has featured recommendations, round-ups and interviews with authors. All reviews are by authors or independent booksellers, with guests including Tracy Chevalier, Patrick Gale, Joanne Harris, Anthony Horowitz, Val McDermid, Diane Setterfield and Jane Rogers. **www.reviewsbywriters.blogspot.com**

Also from Writers Review Publishing:

The Poet's Wife by Judith Allnatt

David by Mary Hoffman

Death Stitch by Sally Prue